THE
CUTTING EDGE

PART·ONE·A·HANDFUL·OF·MEN

BY DAVE DUNCAN
PUBLISHED BY BALLANTINE BOOKS

A Rose-Red City

West of January

Shadow

Strings

Hero!

The Reaver Road

THE SEVENTH SWORD
The Reluctant Swordsman
The Coming of Wisdom
The Destiny of the Sword

A MAN OF HIS WORD
Magic Casement
Faery Lands Forelorn
Perilous Seas
Emperor and Clown

A HANDFUL OF MEN
The Cutting Edge
Upland Outlaws★
The Stricken Field★
The Living God★

★*Forthcoming*

THE
CUTTING EDGE

PART·ONE·A·HANDFUL·OF·MEN

DAVE DUNCAN

A DEL REY BOOK
BALLANTINE BOOKS • NEW YORK

A Del Rey Book
Published by Ballantine Books

Copyright © 1992 by D. J. Duncan
Map by Steve Palmer

All rights reserved under International and Pan-American Copyright
Conventions. Published in the United States by Ballantine Books, a
division of Random House, Inc., New York, and simultaneously
in Canada by Random House of Canada Limited, Toronto.

Grateful acknowledgment is
made to The Society of Authors, as the
literary representative of the Estate of John Masefield, for
permission to reprint excerpts from
"Tomorrow" by John Masefield.

Library of Congress Cataloging-in-Publication Data

Duncan, Dave, 1933–
The cutting edge / Dave Duncan. — 1st ed.
p.   cm. — (A Handful of men ; bk. 1)
"A Del Rey book."
ISBN 0-345-37896-2
I. Title.   II. Series: Duncan, Dave, 1933–   Handful of men ; bk. 1.
PR9199.3.D847C88   1992
813'.54—dc20   92-53220
CIP

MANUFACTURED IN THE UNITED STATES OF AMERICA

First Edition: September 1992

10 9 8 7 6 5 4 3 2

Oh yesterday the cutting edge drank thirstily and deep,
The upland outlaws ringed us in and herded us as sheep,
They drove us from the stricken field and bayed us into keep;
  But tomorrow
By the living God, we'll try the game again!

—MASEFIELD, TOMORROW

CONTENTS

A NOTE ON TIMING

THIS BOOK, THE FIRST OF FOUR COMPRISING THE STORY "A Handful of Men," follows as a sequel to *Emperor and Clown,* which was itself the fourth and final part of "A Man of His Word." It is not necessary to have read the earlier series in order to appreciate this one (although of course I hope you will read and enjoy both).

No dates were recorded in "A Man of His Word," because history had little interest for the humble folk of Krasnegar. When required to make reference to a particular year, they normally counted from the accession of their current monarch, a system that would have no meaning for outsiders. As far as the Impire was concerned, the events reported ran from the late spring of 2979 to the fall of 2981. Detailed narrative begins in this volume with the Battle of Karthin, early in 2997, a little more than fifteen years later.

Such Imperial dates were counted from Emine's founding of the Protocol, the system that for almost three millennia had controlled the political use of sorcery. Without the Protocol, the world would have collapsed into the sort of chaos it had known during the War of the Five Warlocks, or the Dragon Wars, or even the Dark Times . . .

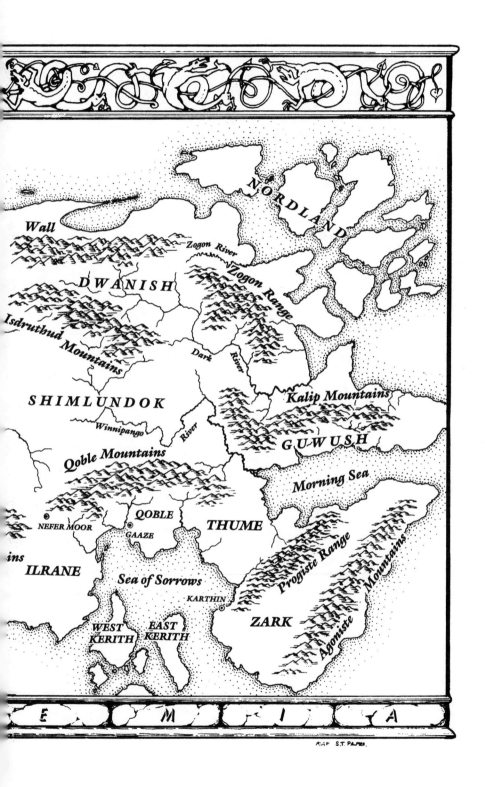

T H E
CUTTING EDGE

PART·ONE·A·HANDFUL·OF·MEN

PROLOGUE

IN THE SUMMER OF 2977 THE YLLIPOS GATHERED AT YEWDARK
House to pay their respects to the Sisters, as they had done
every year for more than a century. On that occasion well
over four hundred men, women, and children arrived from
all over the Impire, including six former consuls, four senators, and numerous praetors, lictors, and legates.

The annual family convocation was mainly a social event,
although much political scheming was conducted as well.
The Sisters themselves were merely an excuse. They were
twins and no one could tell one from the other, which was
unimportant as no one remembered their names either. They
had become part of the Yllipo clan when one of them had
married some obscure younger son, a man long dead.

The Sisters claimed to have occult powers and would

prophesy upon request. The prophecies were sometimes fulfilled, sometimes not fulfilled, and never taken seriously, usually being passed off with a laughing remark that all families had a few odd characters.

Nevertheless, the annual meeting invariably included one peculiar ritual. Everyone professed to regard this as just a foolish superstition, yet it was never spoken of to outsiders. The senior males would accompany the Sisters to the Statue and would present to it the new Yllipos, those born during the past twelve months. The Sisters would then foretell each child's fortune, depending on whether the Statue smiled or frowned.

The Statue stood in a gloomy clearing not far from the house. It was so weathered that no one except the Sisters could make out much of its features at all, let alone detect any expression on them. Tradition said that it represented Arave the Strong, an imperor of the XIIth Dynasty who had raised the first Yllipo to the nobility. The stone slab before it was believed to mark Arave's grave.

In 2977, four proud fathers brought their new offspring to this ceremony, and the last to step forward was Lictor Ylopingo, bearing his eight-month-old third son, Ylo. The day was unusually stormy for midsummer. At the exact moment the youngster was laid on the monument, a stray gust caught the Statue and toppled it. It impacted the slab close to the child, shattering into fragments.

Incredibly, the boy escaped injury. The lictor was cut and bruised by flying gravel. The Sisters went into convulsions. The family gathering broke up in confusion and everyone went home.

The significance of the omen was much discussed. Some of the boy's more credulous—and distant—relatives suggested he be put to death because of it. Interpretation was not helped by the diverging views of the Sisters, for no one could ever recall them disagreeing before.

One said that the portent signified the destruction of the Yllipo family, the other that it was the Impire itself that was to be overthrown. Neither would explain what part Baby Ylo might play in such an unthinkable catastrophe, and they could not even agree whether he would survive it.

Both Sisters died within the year, and thereafter the midsummer convocations were held elsewhere. In time the two sinister prophecies were forgotten.

And in time they were both fulfilled.

CHAPTER ONE

BLOW, BUGLE!

1

THE ELVES HAD A PROVERB, *MINNOWS MOURN WHEN bridges fall.* Unlike most elvish sayings, it even made a sort of sense—especially to minnows.

The Marquis of Harkthil was arrested on a bright and sunny afternoon in the spring of 2995. By sunset the Impire was in the throes of the sensation that became known as the Yllipo Conspiracy. Day by day the scandal spread and the toll mounted. The marquis' relatives followed him into the dungeons, one after another.

Even at the first, there was considerable doubt that the treason was as widespread as Emshandar maintained. More than likely, the gossipmongers said, the imperor was merely seizing a Gods-given chance to subdue a family that had grown too powerful and troublesome for the good of the realm. Whatever the truth, the old man's vengeance was savage. By the time the affair was over, eight senators had bared their necks for the ax, and no one counted the lesser victims.

One of those lesser victims seemed likely to be Recruit Ylo of the Praetorian Guard, youngest son of the disgraced Consul Ylopingo. His fellow Guardsmen were doing the arresting, so Ylo was not surprised to find himself confined to quarters. From there he watched the tide of blood creep ever closer to his toes, until he was the only member of his family outside the imperor's prisons. His friends had disappeared, also, and who could blame them? Public confessions, private executions, rumors of torture . . . When the inevitable summons came, it was almost a relief.

Ylo had enlisted three months earlier, on his eighteenth birthday, feeling he was doing the Guard something of a favor. Apart from being a consul's son, he was related in various ways to at least a dozen senators, and his grandfather had become a national hero by dying dramatically during the Dark River War. All the hereditary titles would go to his eldest brother, so Ylo's ordained future was obviously a career in politics. In the Impire, political careers began in the army.

In Ylo's considered opinion, the regular legions engaged in far too much unpleasant marching around. They were also prone to violent activities involving goblins, dwarves, djinns, and other inferior races, and those could be positively dangerous. The Praetorian Guard, however, spent its time posturing around the Opal Palace in Hub. Few things were as effective with girls as a Praetorian uniform.

So the decision had been easy. A five-year stint in the Guard, followed by a little traditional impish nepotism, would guarantee him a profitable posting as lictor in some congenial city not too far away from the capital. Thereafter, he would see.

Ten days after being confined to quarters, Recruit Ylo was summoned to the guardroom. Any lingering hopes died when he saw that the man behind the table was Centurion Hithi. The Yllipos and the Hathinos had been mortal enemies for more generations than Ylo had teeth.

Like all of the Praetorian barracks, the guardroom was lofty and ancient. The mosaic floor illustrated dramatic scenes of legionaries battling dragons, but there was one spot where thousands of military sandals had worn the colors right away, and that bare white patch was directly before the officer's table. Ylo marched forward, placed his feet on the marker, and saluted. He was surprised—and very gratified—to realize that his knees were not knocking, or his teeth chattering. True, his palms were sweaty and there was an unpleasant tightness in his lower abdomen, but those effects did not show. He waited to hear his fate with proper military impassivity.

In the Guard, even centurions were gentlemen. Hithi seemed genuinely regretful as he explained how a reassessment had revealed that Ylo fell just short of the Guard's height requirement.

He laid down one paper and lifted another. "Seems there is an opening in the XXth. A transfer might be arranged."

It could be worse, much worse. Blisters and calluses were better than thumbscrews and the rack. A barracks was better than an unmarked grave. The XXth Legion was not one of the scum outfits—and no alternative was being offered.

Ylo said, "Thank you, sir!"

"There's a tesserary from the XXth here at the moment, as it happens. He and his men could escort you."

"Sir!" Ylo said.

The centurion smiled.

The smile very nearly broke Ylo's self-control. He wanted to weep, for it was a brutal reminder that there was no one to appeal to; the feud between the Hathinos and the Yllipos was now over.

Thus was Guardsman Ylo toppled from the giddy peaks of the aristocracy to the rat-eat-rat world of the common foot soldier. From all-night dancing to all-day marching. From fine wine to sour beer, and silk sheets to bedbugs. From sweet-skinned debutantes in rose gardens to toothless harridans who took all his money and kept telling him to hurry up.

With thanks to the Gods for each new dawn, he accepted his fall from grace and set to work to survive the brutish, penniless, mind-crippling life of a legionary.

The standard tour of duty was twenty-five years.

Always at Winterfest the Imperial Archivist named the year just ending. No one was very surprised when he proclaimed 2995 to have been the Year of his Majesty's Ninetieth Birthday. By then the Yllipos were all dead and forgotten.

And 2996 turned out to be the Year of the Great-grandchild.

The superstitious and those who knew some history were already starting to worry about the coming millennium, but 2997 was destined to be known as the Year of Seven Victories.

The troubles began in Zark. A few days after Winterfest, the emir of Garpoon received an ultimatum from the caliph and appealed to the imperor for help.

The emir had very little choice in the matter, as the Imperial ambassador was holding a sword under his chin at the time, but such fine points of diplomacy were of no concern to a common foot soldier. Five thousand strong, the XXth Legion marched south to Malfin and embarked. Ylo learned then that he was just as prone to seasickness as any other imp and that there were worse experiences than a forced march in winter.

After four weeks at sea, he disembarked at a large city, which might possibly be Ullacarn. It was very hot and had palm trees. The mountains to the north were perhaps the Progiste Range. The XXth formed up and marched away along the coast, maybe heading for somewhere called Garpoon.

The hot, arid country was hostile and unfamiliar. The rocky hills were full of cryptic wadis that could be full of djinns.

Ylo had no illusions about heroism or glory. He knew the odds against a tyro surviving his first battle. He knew that even those odds were vastly better than the chances of a simple legionary ever winning as much as one word of praise from his centurion, let alone recognition from the officers. He admitted to himself that he was terrified, and would be perfectly satisfied if he could just conceal that terror from his companions.

The best he had to look forward to was another twenty-three years of this.

He survived the first day's march. And the second. On the third day he found himself in the Battle of Karthin.

Karthin eventually ranked as the first of the year's seven victories, but it was a very narrow win. Proconsul Iggipolo held to the standard belief that Zark was one huge waterless expanse of sand; he knew that djinns were red-eyed barbarians who fought on camels in the brightest sunlight they could find. He therefore marched three road-weary legions into a swamp, an evening thunderstorm, and the caliph's trap.

Bogged down in mud by their armor, the imps soon learned that djinns fought very well on foot and could conceal ten men behind every clump of reeds. Sunset failed to halt the slaughter, and dawn revealed Ylo's maniple isolated, surrounded, and hopelessly outnumbered.

Honor, politics, and even discipline had vanished in the night. Hunger, terror, and exhaustion were unimportant. Survival was all that mattered. The morning was a foggy blur of noise and blood, sword strokes and the screams of the dying. The maniple shrank steadily. The centurions and the optios fell; the standard disappeared. A tesserary shouted commands until he took an arrow in the throat, and after that it was every man for himself, and no one seemed to know which way was home.

Whether he had tripped or been stunned or had merely fainted, Ylo never knew. He lay facedown in a bloody ooze for a long time, keeping company with the dead. That was not cowardice, and he was far from alone in his collapse. Imps rarely made great fighters. They were never berserkers, as the jotnar often were, nor fanatics like the djinns. They did not covet martyrdom, as elves did in their darker moods. They lacked the suicidal stubbornness of fauns or the stony stamina of dwarves. Imps were just very good organizers, with a driving urge to organize everyone else as well as they had organized themselves.

Eventually Ylo realized that he could still hear the beating of his heart. Then another beat, as well. And a bugle! He was very tired of the swamp. He rose from the field of dead, lifted a sword from a nearby corpse to replace the one he had lost, and decided fuzzily that he was too weak to carry a shield. He trudged off through the mud, heading for the drums and those twenty-three more years.

He had lost one sandal; bare skin on arms and legs was blistered raw by the sun. His sodden tunic was rubbing holes in his skin, something heavy had dented his helmet so that it no longer fitted properly, yet none of the swords, arrows, and javelins that had been directed at him had penetrated his hide.

The sky was blue; the fog had faded to patchy ghosts haunting the vegetation. The first Ylo saw of his salvation was the top of an Imperial standard advancing toward him, the four-pointed star shining in sunlight. Then out of the mist and the bulrushes below it came a wall of legionaries, driving a ragtag mob of exhausted djinns before them.

Ylo was on the wrong side of that mob. Either courage or blind panic spurred him into life. Yelling like a maniac, he struck down a couple from behind, plunging into the free-for-all, clawing his way toward the impish standard. He would certainly not have made it, except that a murdering, screaming horde of djinns appeared out of nowhere at his back like a tidal wave and swept him up.

The shield wall collapsed before the onslaught. Ylo was borne forward, all the way to his objective, the standard. He arrived as a javelin felled its bearer. Two years of training stamped certain lessons on a man's bones, and the first of those was that standards were sacred. Without conscious thought, Ylo dropped his sword, caught the falling staff with both hands, and raised it erect.

And thereby became a hero.

2

EVEN AS A TERRIFIED YOUNG MAN CLUNG GRIMLY TO A POLE amid the raging clamor of the Battle of Karthin, a woman lay quietly dying a hundred leagues or so to the north, beyond the Progiste Mountains.

She knew that she was dying, but she didn't mind any more. It was time. She had been rather surprised to see the dawn and would be even more surprised to see another. Meanwhile she was in very little pain. Slow-moving shafts of sunlight in her cottage kept her company. The busy sounds of the forest outside were like familiar friends coming to visit, pausing to chat among themselves before they bowed under the lintel—breezes moving through the branches, the chattering of the stream over the rocks, buzzing insects, the impudent call of parrots.

Her name was Phain of the Keez Place. She was very old. She could not recall how old, and it didn't matter. She had even outlived her cottage, for the roof had a serious sag to it, and the walls had more windows now than they'd had when Keez had built them, many, many years ago.

Keez was long gone, so long that she could hardly recall what he had looked like with his silver hair and his stooped back. She could remember him in his youth, though, strong and graceful as a young horse, bringing her here to show her the place he had found, with its stream and its giant cottonwoods soaring to the sky. She could recall the eager, anxious look on his big, smooth face as he waited for her decision; the relief and joy when she said yes, this place would do well. Very clearly she could remember how right it had felt, and how she had decided to be kind and not make him suffer more, for his longing was so great—and hers no less. *Now!* she had said, sitting down and pulling him down beside her. *Yes, now!*

She remembered how his strength had delighted her—that first time under the sky especially, and uncounted later times under the roof, too. But there had never been another time quite like the time when they'd first lain together in the sunshine, right here, making this their Place.

It had been a good Place. Here they had loved; here she had brought forth sons and daughters—four she'd borne and four she'd reared, not many women could say as much. Here Keez had died, but easily, without pain. Here she was dying. The forest could have it back now, and thank you; she was done with it.

A shadow moved. Phain opened her eyes. The sunlight was angling steeper, so she must have slept. Yes, the walls were a network, holes held together by wicker. Time to go.

"Do you need anything?" asked a small and tremulous voice.

Phain shook her head on the pillow and tried to smile, to put the child at ease. It was a hard time for a youngster. Death Watch was never easy.

She couldn't remember the girl's name. Terrible how the old forgot! She could remember Keez clear enough. She could recall every ax stroke and every knot as the two of them had built the cottage together, over their special Place. But for the life of her she could not remember which poor child had been sent to keep her Death Watch. She could not even remember all the family coming to say good-bye to her, but she knew they must have. How long had she been lingering and making this poor girl wait? She licked her lips.

"Drink?" the child asked. "You want a drink? I'll get you one." Eager to please, eager to feel that she was doing something useful . . .

Phain recalled her own turn at Death Watch. A nasty, stringy old man named . . . couldn't remember, never mind. He'd taken a week to die, given her no thanks, thrown up everything she fed him . . . He had smelled quite horrible, as she doubtless did to this youngster now helping her hold her head up to sip from a half gourd. The water was cool, so it must have come fresh from the stream.

"Name, child? Forgotten your name."

"Thaïle of the Gaib Place."

Gaib? Didn't mean anything. Phain tried to speak again.

"Yes?" the child cried in sudden panic. "What? I can't hear!" And she sprawled over Phain on the bedding, pressing an ear close to her lips.

Poor thing was terrified, of course. Frightened of death, frightened of suffering, frightened of messing it all up.

"Not yet!" the woman gasped, almost wanting to laugh.

"Oh!" The child—Thaïle—scrambled back. "Oh, I'm sorry. I didn't mean . . . I thought . . . I mean, I'm sorry."

Phain dug down in her lungs, finding just enough air at the bottom there to make a chuckle, and a few words. "Just wanted to ask who your mother was, Thaïle."

"Oh! Frial of the Gaib Place."

Ah, yes! Frial was her oldest granddaughter, so this leggy filly must be one of her great-granddaughters. Fancy that! Not many lived long enough to pass on their word to a great-grandchild. Gaib was the quiet, solid one with the pointy ears. Pointier than most, she meant.

"Food?" Thaïle asked. "Can I get you something to eat, Grammy?"

Phain shook her head and closed her eyes to nap a little. She hoped she wouldn't linger much longer. She was too weary to speak more now. Only one word left to say, and she knew she would find breath enough for that.

Maig! Maig was the name of that smelly, stringy old man she'd done Death Watch for. Maig had taken a week to go. She hoped she didn't take a week. Or hadn't already taken a week. Hard on a child. Maig hadn't been able to speak most of the time, but he'd found enough breath at the end to pass on his word.

And no good had it ever done her, Phain thought. Perhaps she'd never had any special talent, or the word had been too weak, or she'd just not had the Faculty.

No, there'd never been any magic in her life, just a lot of hard work.

And love. Much love. But no magic.

The wind sighed through the little ruin. She thought she would nap now, and maybe eat something later . . .

3

THE STANDARD WAS A PIG OF A THING, ALMOST TOO HEAVY for Ylo's spent muscles to manage, but it was life. As long as he clung to that pole, the whole Imperial Army was going to fight to the death to defend *him*. He clung.

Battle screamed around him and he ignored it, concentrating on holding the standard vertical and avoiding being knocked down by his own countrymen in the scrimmage.

He had saved a standard. He might be going to survive this.

This wasn't the XXth Legion, though. He glanced up and registered that he had just transferred to the XIIth.

The XIIth! One of the crack outfits!

A man who saved a standard won the right to bear it till his dying day—assuming that day was not this day. No more filthy ditch-digging . . . no more mind-destroying weapons drill.

He was a signifer, a standard-bearer.

Attaboy, Ylo!

Signifers wore wolfskin capes over their armor, with a hood made from the wolf's head. Barbaric? Romantic! He could guess how girls would react to that. Women would be free again.

Signifers had the nearest thing to a soft job the army ever offered. Even those twenty-three years might not seem too bad as a signifer—not much danger, and lots of respect. Perks!

Yea, Ylo!

Then he took another look. This was no mean run-of-the-mill standard he'd rescued, emblem of maniple or cohort. At its top was the Imperial star and below that the lion symbol of the XIIth. Red bunting floated from the crosspiece, and the rest of the shaft was laden with battle honors in silver and bronze. This was the legionary standard itself.

Signifer for the XIIth Legion?

Hey, Ylo!

You are going to eat meat again, Ylo!

The war had gone away. Order was being restored. Bugles were sounding in the distance.

Suddenly officers were beckoning, and he led where they pointed. They followed him to the crest of a small hillock, the only high ground in sight. A voice beside him barked, "Pitch camp!" and his shredded wits were just operational enough to realize that it was addressing him. He swung the standard in the proper signal, barely registering protests from his battered muscles. Distant bugles picked up the call.

Signifer!

And of course the speaker had been the legate himself, with a green-crested helmet and gold-inlaid breastplate. Of course. Where else would the legate be but beside the standard? Legates were not supposed to have blood on their swords, but this one did. He was dirty and sweaty, and his dark eyes blazed below the brim of his helmet as he appraised Ylo. He held a canteen in his left hand.

"Well done, soldier! I saw."

Ylo muttered, "Sir!" but his mind was on that canteen.

With the bottle almost at his lips, the legate paused, and his mouth showed that he was frowning. "What outfit?"

Ylo had lost his shield; his mail shirt was totally coated in mud and blood, although none of that seemed to be his. He was anonymous. "The XXth, sir."

"God of Battles!" the legate said. "All night? Here, you need this more than I do." And he handed over the canteen.

That was Ylo's first inkling.

The Impire had held the field. The fighting was ending as the surviving djinns surrendered or were cut down. More standards were arriving, and more officers.

One of those was the commander, Proconsul Iggipolo himself, and the way he returned the legate's salute was another inkling.

Ylo glanced up again at that potent pole he held. How could he have missed it? Above the battle honors and even above the crossbar shone a wreath of oak leaves, cast in gold.

Only one man in the entire army could put his personal signet on a legionary standard.

Ylo's mind reeled. He forgot honor and comfort and doe-eyed girls. He thought *Revenge!* He thought *hatred.* He thought of his father and brothers, his cousins, his uncles. He thought of his mother, dying disgraced, in exile. He thought *that man killed my family.*

Trust. Confidence. Being close in dark places.

He thought *knife between the ribs.*

And then he was limping painfully along, bearing the standard high, heading for the tents that had sprouted like a field of orderly mushrooms at the edge of the swamp. Behind him came the legate.

And all the way battle-weary soldiers were scrambling to their feet to laud the leader of the XIIth, the hero, the man who had saved the day. Their cheers rang sour in Ylo's ears and the sound was bitter. He thought *most popular man in the army.*

"Shandie!" they shouted. "Shandie!"

Emshandar. The prince imperial. The imperor's grandson. Heir apparent. The most popular man in the army.

4

NEVER BEFORE HAD YLO ENTERED A COMMANDER'S COM-pound, but now he marched straight in and was saluted as he did so. He set the pole in the base prepared for it and spun around to face the procession he had been leading—or tried to, but his legs failed him, and he almost fell. The imperor's grandson saluted the standard, ignoring the stagger. He gave Ylo a nod that was a personal summons and headed for his tent, followed by a gaggle of shiny-helmeted officers, few of whom had likely bloodied their swords this day.

Ylo tagged on the end. Halfway there, his way was blocked by an oak tree garbed in the uniform of a centurion. Eyes like two knotholes peered out of a face of bark.

"Who're you, soldier?"

Ylo was too exhausted to be humble. "The signifer!"

The man's wooden eyes narrowed. He glanced back at the standard. "Dead or wounded?"

"Dead."

The centurion again blocked Ylo as he tried to move. "Do you know who he was?" His voice creaked like falling timber.

Ylo shook his head dumbly.

"His cousin. Prince Ralpnie. Fourth in line to the throne."

Ylo stared at the arboreal face for a long moment as his beaten brain wrestled meaning from the words. Eventually he decided they were a caution. And help. He had forgotten such things, in two years of being a nonperson, a number.

He dragged up the proper response from some deep-buried memory. "Thanks!"

The man nodded. Then he sank down on one knee. By the time Ylo had realized that the centurion was unlacing one of his own sandals, the man had removed it and placed it in front of Ylo's bare foot. Ylo stepped into it. The big ox even fastened it for him—no matter how muddy and bloody he might be, a signifer must not go into a legate's presence barefoot if there was a spare shoe around.

Ylo said, "Thanks," again as the centurion rose.

Without as much as a nod, the tree shifted his roots and eased out of Ylo's way.

Ylo dragged himself as far as the tent and then into its scented dimness. The walls were made of purple silk. He had not seen silk in two years. Carpets. Furniture. A smell of soap.

There were at least a dozen men there, most in uniform, some not. As he entered, the muttered greetings were ending, the condolences and congratulations. He sensed the roiling dark mood—victory, but oh, the price! Triumph and loss. Heartbreak and joy. Relief and sorrow. The legate's cousin was but one of many not destined to share the victory.

Carpets. Iron-banded chests. There was one chair, and as Ylo arrived, the legate sat down wearily, glanced in his direction, and raised a foot.

This time the reaction came faster, fortunately. Ylo limped forward and removed the prince imperial's boots.

Then he stepped back, and the tent fell silent. He felt the eyes on him. The stranger. The newcomer. The usurper.

His cousin!

These were the prince's battle companions. Some might have been with him since Creslee, and most would have been with him at Highscarp and on the bloody field of Fain. Now one of their number had fallen and here was the replacement.

Not a cousin. Not an aristocrat. A common legionary— or so they would assume.

And Ylo was staring at those hateful imperial features. The prince had removed his helmet. His face was a motley of mud and clean patches, his hair a sweaty tangle. Physically he was nothing special, but his eyes burned like black fire. Twenty-six years old, and the man the army worshipped.

On his lap was a folded wolfskin. His cousin's cape.

So? One cousin. This man murdered my whole family.

"Your name?"

"Ylo, sir. Third cohort, XXth Legion."

"You have done well. Imperial Star, Second Class."

"Thank you, sir."

"And signifer, of course?"

Pause. Would the upstart dare?

"Thank you, sir."

The onlookers rustled, like dry grass when something prowls.

The prince nodded sadly. His hand lay strangely still on the wolfskin. "By tradition, the honor is yours." He glanced at the others. "The XIIth has a new signifer, gentlemen."

Revenge! Close. Dark night. Knife in the ribs . . .

Then those imperial eyes—imperious eyes—slashed back at Ylo. The legate seemed vaguely puzzled, as if seeing or hearing something not quite right.

"Service?"

"Two years, sir."

More hesitation. "Mmm . . . Can you ride?"

"Yes, sir."

Surprise.

"Read and write?"

"Yes, sir."

Astonishment. Puzzled glances.

Then a voice in the background said, "Ylo? Ylopingo . . . ?"

There had never been much chance of keeping it secret.

"Consul Ylopingo was my father, sir."

The legate stiffened. "An Yllipo?"

Stunned silence.

Then the prince said softly, "Thank you, gentlemen," and everyone else melted away. Remarkable. Empty tent.

Just the two of them.

Prince Emshandar nodded toward an oaken chest. The new signifer tottered gratefully across to it and sat down, thinking that he would have fallen over had he been left on his feet much longer. His bones burned.

"Tell me."

Ylo told his story. It did not take long.

The legate stared hard at him all the time, fingers still motionless upon the wolfskin. Then he gestured at a table in a corner. "Wine. And take one for yourself."

Ylo rose. He snapped open the sealed flask with an expertise he had forgotten he had, but his hand trembled as he filled the goblets. He had just realized that he must be a problem for the prince, and men who embarrassed princes had a very short life expectancy. His hand shook even harder as he passed over the drink, because he was thinking *poison*. That was another possible means of assassination, safer for the assassin. Revenge would be sweeter if he could himself survive to enjoy it. Oh Gods! His mind was a rats' nest. He didn't know what he was thinking. Kill the heir to the throne? What madness was that?

He went back to the chest.

They drank, and the legate's gaze never left him. Good wine . . . brought back memories.

"Signifer," the prince said softly.

Not certain he was being addressed, Ylo said, "Sir?"

"Your predecessor was a close confidant of mine. Did you know that?"

"Yes, sir. Your cousin."

That display of knowledge won a nod of surprise, and approval. "Yes. He was my signifer. He was also my personal secretary, my closest and most trusted aide, and chief of my personal staff." Emshandar sipped at the wine without taking his eyes off Ylo. "I assumed you were just a common legionary. I assumed you would become the legion's signifer—but not mine. You understand? You understand the distinction?"

"Yes, sir."

"There's a world of difference between a man who waves a pole about and one who ciphers letters to the imperor."

"I understand, sir."

The prince laid his goblet down on a table beside him and rubbed his eyes with the knuckles of both hands. Then he fixed that dark, burning gaze on Ylo again.

Had he been capable of feeling anything, Ylo might have felt relief then—or even amusement at the thought of him, Ylo, attempting to function as aide-de-camp to the prince imperial. Being signifer to the legion was enough—it would be heaven after being a common sword banger. And there would be opportunities for revenge if that was what he wanted after he had considered the pros and cons.

Then the prince said, *"Could* you serve me?"

God of Madness! Ylo had thought the matter was settled. Serve this murderer?

The imperor was ancient. Any day now the Gods were

going to call in his black soul and weigh it—good luck to Them if They found one grain of good in it! This man would mount the Opal Throne as Emshandar V.

His close friends and aides would roll to the top of the heap at once. His personal signifer would be in line for heady promotions, even a consulship, perhaps. That long-lost political career was back on the table again. In fact it was shining brighter than it had ever done.

Sudden caution warned Ylo that politics had turned out to be more dangerous for his family than soldiering ever had. What he wanted now was a little security in his life. Yet . . .

Revenge? To serve this man would be a betrayal of his ancestors, his parents, his brothers . . .

Or would it be a sweeter revenge? And the opportunities for murder would be unlimited, day and night.

Confused, he muttered, "You couldn't trust me!"

The prince had probably read every thought in that hesitation.

"You have the legion's standard; you have earned it, and no one can question your loyalty to the Impire. For the rest, I will accept your word."

Ylo stuttered and then blurted out, "Why?"—which was almost a capital offense in the army.

The legate frowned. "I was in Guwush when it happened, Signifer. I disapproved. It was a bloody, inexcusable massacre! I tried to stop it. Can you accept my word on that?"

Such words would be treason on any other lips. And he had no need to lie. He did not *seem* to be lying.

To Ylo's astonishment his own voice said, "Yes, sir. I believe you."

"And I would like to make what small recompense I can. Can you believe that?"

Ylo must have nodded, because the legate rose, and Ylo reeled to his feet, also. He laid down his goblet and lurched forward to accept the cape being offered. Surely the Gods had gone crazy?

"I appoint you my signifer, Ylo of the Yllipos!" the legate said solemnly. He pulled a face. "My grandfather will have a litter of piglets!"

There was no safe reply to that remark. Ylo was incapable of saying anything anyway. What had he fallen into? And how?

A curious gleam shone in the prince's eye. "I hate being devious. You must be the senior surviving male in your family? If you want to claim the name and style yourself Yllipo, then now is the time to do it!"

That would be a direct slap at the imperor's face. That would be a spit in his eye. It might even be illegal, or treasonous. That was much too dangerous!

Fortunately Ylo had a good excuse to hand. He found his voice. "I may have an aged uncle still alive somewhere, sir, I think." An outlaw, of course, attaindered and penniless.

"He is not likely to dispute your claim, though?"

"No, sir . . . but I would hate him to hear of it."

The prince nodded gravely. "The sentiment does you honor! Ylo it is then. Your duty is always to the imperor, then to me, then to the legion, in that order. But you will never find those loyalties in conflict."

He was very sure of his own motives, Ylo thought. He himself was not. In fact he was a lot less sure of them than he'd been ten minutes ago. Why had he accepted? And Yllipo? Why should the prince imperial suggest a bravado like that?

What had Ylo won this day? A consulship, or revenge? If he played his hand right . . .

For a moment longer the legate studied his new aide—was he having doubts? But then he held out a hand to shake. Unable to believe this was happening, Ylo took it.

"I mourn my cousin deeply," the prince said, "but I welcome you in his stead. I think it was not only the God of Battle Who was with us out there today, Signifer. I think the God of Justice was busy, also."

Tears sprang suddenly into Ylo's eyes.

He wondered if he had just given away his soul.

5

THE TERRIBLE DAY WAS NOT OVER—INDEED, IT HAD BARELY started.

Ylo staggered out of the legate's tent into blinding heat, although the hour was shy of noon. The army did not consider a major battle any reason to slacken discipline. The camp lay spread out around him, rows of tents straight as javelins in all directions. On the outskirts, exhausted legionary grunts were digging the encircling vallation. The centurions' screamed threats drifted in faintly. Well, there was the first blessing . . .

"You have your own duties to attend to." Shandie had dismissed him with those words, but what in the Name of Evil did they mean?

The massive centurion accosted Ylo again and saluted. He had replaced the missing sandal.

Bewildered, Ylo returned the salute and only then realized that he was holding the slain signifer's cape. That had been what this leather-faced thug had been saluting.

"Hardgraa," the monolith growled. "Chief of his bodyguard."

"Ylo," Ylo said. "Personal signifer."

That felt curiously satisfying.

Not believable, just satisfying.

"Thought you might need these," Hardgraa remarked. He held out a wad of rags and a rolled red cloth.

Of course a signifer's first duty would be to tend his standard—clean it, replace the bunting. That was what the legate had meant. Ylo took the offering with shaky hands. "Thanks." He forced his aching feet to move.

The centurion paced beside him until they reached the

standard. The easiest way to dispose of the cape was to put it on. It did keep the sun off, and the hood was certainly more comfortable than the massive, dented helmet. As Ylo was about to start work, the centurion muttered, "A moment, Signifer," and straightened the hood for him. Bug-eyed perfectionist!

Ylo began polishing the lowest of the emblems. He would need a stool to reach the star, for he must never lay the pole on the ground. He tried to ignore the watching Hardgraa.

"See that civilian over there, the one who looks like a retired priest?"

Ylo forced his eyes to focus and grunted.

"Sir Acopulo—his chief political advisor. And the butter-ball just going into the tent? Lord Umpily, chief of protocol. And me. Anything you need to know, any help you want . . . just ask. Ask any of us, but one of those three especially."

Ylo grunted again, squinting against the incandescent desert sun reflecting in his eyes. "Thanks more."

"Anything concerning security or his safety—anything at all, no matter how trivial—tell me with your next breath."

Ylo nodded and decided not to mention his own ambitions for a sharp blade between the royal ribs. He went back to work.

The centurion rubbed the bark on his chin. "You did say *personal* signifer, Signifer?"

"Yes."

"Curious. An Yllipo? He must be making some sort of political statement."

Ylo clenched his teeth and went on polishing.

"Important job. Sure to screw it up, of course. Maybe that's it."

Still Ylo held his temper. His skin was streaming sweat under his chain mail and felt rubbed raw in places, as if the links had worn right through his tunic. Every joint ached, every muscle trembled with fatigue.

Hardgraa scratched his cheek. "And I've never known Shandie to go for a pretty face before. Tribune of the

Vth Cohort, now—he's a rogue. Vets all the young recruits . . .
but not Shandie."

Ylo spun around, staggered, steadied himself with a hand
on the accursed pole. He scowled at the crude, weatherbeat-
en veteran. A rock-eater, this one. He'd met some tough
centurions in his time, but this looked like the original, the
prototype. "I understood that his personal signifer was his
chief of staff, Centurion?"

"Correct."

"Then . . . I . . . you . . ." He was too muddled to find the
right words.

"You don't give me orders, Signifer. You pass on his orders. If he hasn't given any, you tell me what you think his
orders would be. I obey those orders."

Oh, Gods—responsibility!

"We're a team!" The older man chuckled dryly. "You
think we'll try to pull you down? You're expecting a rat
pack, maybe?"

Dumbly Ylo nodded. He was an outsider. He had been
thrown into this close-knit coterie with his fur still wet and
his fangs not grown. His loyalties were as questionable as
his abilities, and they must all know that.

The centurion shook his head. "If Shandie wants you,
then he gets you. Trust us! You're *in*, understand? One of
us. And the sooner you can be useful to him, the happier
we'll all be. You can't do my job, and I can't do yours,
because I'm not gentle born. We each sing our own songs,
understand? A team. And if you ever let him down, in any
way at all, I shall personally rearrange that pretty face until
you look like a retired gladiator with a bad case of—"

"What're you telling me, Centurion?"

"The council of war's in half an hour."

Ylo threw down the rag.

"Why the Evil didn't you say so? I want two of the maniple signifers here soonest. If any other legion's standard
outshines the XIIth's at the council, I will personally roast

their balls on a stick. I need a shave, a wash, and clean kit—
right now!"

Hardgraa grinned, showing a ragged assortment of amber
teeth. *"Yessir!"* he said, and took off at the double.

An hour later Ylo found himself still awake, attending the
council of war. At least, he thought he was still awake. Who
would ever suggest that a man wear a wolfskin cape—with
a hood, yet—over full armor in a tropical desert? But to
attend a council of war, standing on shaking legs in back of
the prince imperial, facing a proconsul . . . No, he had to be
awake; no dream could ever be this unlikely. If the Gods
weren't insane then he was.

Under the furnace glare of the sun, the circle of legates
huddled within the circle of their signifers. Ylo was not close
enough to hear what was said, but he had already heard
Shandie tell his advisors what he expected to be said, and
what ought to be said, and the conversation would not veer
much from that path.

Technically Shandie was Iggipolo's subordinate, but everyone knew that state of affairs might terminate at any
minute with a courier on a steaming horse bringing word
of the imperor's death. Furthermore, it had been Shandie
who had brought up the XIIth in time to turn Karthin from
utter disaster to slim victory. Thus the proconsul would be
very considerate of that particular legate's opinion. Shandie's opinion was that the caliph had been taught a lesson,
but the Impire would need to field more resources before it
could apply any further education. There had been no formal declaration of war, there would be no formal treaty.
The status quo had been restored and the issues must wait
for another day.

No one was very happy about that. There were too many
dead imps being dug out of the mud. Even a battle-shattered
tyro like Ylo could yearn for the caliph's head on a pole at

short notice—preferably after someone else had collected it—
but to argue with reality was crazy. The Impire had held the
field and could do nothing with it, a useless victory.

When everyone agreed to that, the council dispersed, and
the army turned to its own affairs: tending the wounded,
burying the dead, thanking the Gods . . . prisoners and fodder and victuals and transport and sanitation and replace-
ments and all the concerns of a mobile city. The cowards
were strung up and flogged before the assembled legion—
four died, and the rest were crippled. Shandie had confirmed
the sentences; he watched impassively as they were carried
out. His signifer stood at his back and watched also and
remembered the hours he had lain in the swamp, playing
dead.

Rumor said that the VIIth Cohort of the XXXth had run
from the field and was going to be formally decimated.

In the Imperial Army, a tribune might command a cohort
or a troop of cavalry or an administrative department or
even the legion itself at times—or nothing at all. The dis-
tinctions were subtle and deathly important. The legate of
the XIIth had about a score of assorted tribunes at his call.
Being a prince as well as commander of the crack XIIth, he
also maintained a civilian staff, a court in waiting, and it
comprised a dozen or so advisors and flunkies. Ylo was now
expected to coordinate all these people and oversee every
matter, military or civil, large or small.

Lists and reports, dozens of reports—reports above all.
Every one of them involved the legate and his signifer. Signifers had duties of their own, also. Standards did not, without assistance, signal commands or carry themselves at
parades or honor the Gods. The legionary signifer had command of all the lesser signifers; Shandie's signifer had charge
of the coding sticks and all his secret correspondence.

Ylo should have gone stark raving crazy during the next
few hours, but he just did not have the time. What had he
gotten himself into? Looking beautiful while holding up a
stupid pole was a job he thought he could handle. He had

not wanted all this. The aftermath of battle was no time to be breaking in a new man, but obviously Shandie was going to do it anyway. Ylo wondered more than once if he was just being worked to death to get rid of him. In one moment of particular despair, he even suggested that to Hardgraa.

"Not Shandie," the monolith growled. "His grandfather would, certainly. Not a scruple in his head, that one. But not Shandie. It's always like this around him."

Out of uniform, the prince imperial was nothing much to look at. Even in his bathtub he went on working, listening to reports, so Ylo knew exactly what he looked like, and he wasn't a patch on Ylo himself for looks. Like any imp, he was dark-haired and swarthy; his complexion was poor. He was slighter and bonier than most, with hardly a hint of his grandfather's aquiline arrogance. His eyes, though . . . his eyes gave him away.

He was eerily impassive, never wasting a move, and yet he had more energy than a hurricane. Oh, he was quiet. He was patient. He would explain in detail—but Ylo dared not give him cause to explain twice.

He dictated to four pairs of secretaries at the same time— a burst of short sentences to each, then on to the next, and by the time they had written down his words he would be around with another burst. He rarely needed to ask for a read-back.

Ylo was supposed to organize all that, making sure both versions of each letter were the same, coding those that were especially secret. It went on without respite until dark was falling and insects batted and fizzed around the lamps. He could not remember when he had last slept, and his head was stuffed with rocks.

Accepting a bundle of letters to be sealed, he swayed on his feet. Shandie reached out and steadied him. Ylo peered blearily at that now-familiar black stare. He began to mutter an apology and was cut off.

"Can you last another twenty minutes?"

"I think so, sir." Liar!

"Good. Now, who else wants to see me tonight?"

Ylo turned to the door, struggling to remember names and faces.

Perhaps it was only twenty minutes. It felt like an hour before taps was sounded and Shandie suddenly called a halt. The secretaries clutched up their writing cases and hurried away.

Ylo stepped outside and ordered a military escort to see them back to the auxiliaries' quarters. The moon was up. Distant peaks in the Progistes glimmered like pearls. He shivered—he had never known a place to cool off as fast as this one, and he had never known a man could be so weary and still live. He returned to the tent that seemed to have become his prison. He removed the benches the secretaries had used. He straightened up the chests and rugs; he tidied up odds and ends.

Shandie was sitting on the chair, studying a sheet of vellum in the wavering light of an oil lamp above him. He seemed unconscious of the flies and moths wheeling around him.

He was nothing much to look at, but he could twist a man like a string. Ylo hated him, didn't he? Hated him for the way his grandfather had slaughtered the clan? Hated him for the torment of overwork? Hated him just for being Shandie? Didn't he?

Maybe he was just too tired to hate, and his hatred would come back in the morning. Maybe he wasn't the hating type.

Ylo tucked a few stray blades of grass back under the edge of a rug. The prince's bedding must be in one of the chests, but he did not know which. It would be his job to find it and set it up. He did not know where he himself was supposed to sleep, but any flint quarry would do nicely, thank you.

Shandie was watching him.

"Bedding, sir?"

"It's in that one, I think. But we shan't need it, I hope. Pass me my helmet."

No more, no more! Gods let it end!

Ylo fetched the helmet. He knew the drill now—they stood face to face; he inspected the prince, adjusting his plume, rubbing smears off his cuirass. At the same time, Shandie inspected him, straightening the wolfskin hood so the ears stood up evenly, checking his chain mail and even making sure he had no inkstains on his fingers.

Shandie must be just as exhausted as Ylo, but he didn't look it. He had as much reason to be exhausted. He had marched all the previous night at the head of his legion—Shandie never rode into battle, which was one reason the men all loved him so. He had fought as hard as Ylo, certainly, and driven himself as hard ever since. Yet the bastard wasn't showing it.

Those imperial eyes were on his face . . .

"You're doing very well, Signifer."

Gulp. "Thank you, sir."

"Extremely well. I appreciate what this is costing you. Now, we're probably going to have another visitor." The prince lowered his voice. "I can't guarantee it, but he does like to watch battles. Close the door."

Ylo went. The night air outside was perfumed with some plant he didn't know, and sweet as wine, now that it was cooling off. The camp was dark. The inside of the tent stank of oil. The flaps fell, shutting out the desert night, shutting in the two men and the dance of lamplight.

Shandie was standing at one side, waiting like a boulder.

Maybe the man was crazy. Ylo limped over and stood behind him, the two of them facing the entrance. The single chair sat in the center, empty. The water clock dripped monotonously. Superstitious tinglings stroked Ylo's scalp. This was madness.

Then the flap on one side flicked up momentarily, and a man entered—except that Ylo had the curious delusion that he'd seen the darkness of the opening uninterrupted until the flap was falling again, and in that case . . .

Man?

He was very big. His armor shone in gold, with jewels on his breastplate and greaves. His helmet lacked cheek pieces or noseguard, so that the handsome young face could be clearly seen.

Shandie saluted. Ylo froze, but fortunately that was what he was supposed to do. Then his knees began shaking.

A God? But people who had seen Gods didn't describe Them as looking like that. The crest on the helmet was gold. There was no rank in the army that merited a *gold* crest, not even the imperor himself. This was the largest imp Ylo had ever seen, as big as a jotunn, or a troll . . .

God of Terror! A sorcerer! The warlock of the east, of course.

The giant returned the salute, muscular forearm across chest. "You nearly screwed up!" he said, his voice deep as thunder, thrilling as a bugle call. Ylo wondered how women would react to this marvel. Of course all that would matter would be how he wanted them to react—a warlock got whatever he fancied.

"You could have helped!" Shandie snapped.

Ylo almost moaned aloud. How dare the prince lip a warlock?

Then he remembered that the Protocol forbade anyone to employ sorcery on the imperor or his family, and Shandie was certainly family. So he was safe. But that didn't mean that *Ylo* wasn't in danger. The wardens were laws unto themselves. Sweat streamed down his ribs, his legs shook wildly. He had reached the limits of his endurance.

The sorcerer scowled. "I chose not to help."

Shandie shrugged his armored shoulders. "Your Omnipotence, may I present—"

"An Yllipo? The old bugger will disown you!" the giant

said, striding across to the chair. "You trying to kill him with an apoplexy?"

"Of course not!"

Protocol or not, how could Shandie dare use such a tone to a warlock? Or such a giant? Of course a sorcerer was not necessarily what he seemed, and Warlock Olybino was mentioned in the stories Ylo's family told of his grandfather and the Dark River War, and that had been forty years ago.

He could not possibly be as young as he looked.

"He'll breathe fire! An Yllipo?" The hostility seemed to be mutual. The warlock's black eyes locked onto Ylo. "So you want me to tell you whether the traitor's spawn is going to be loyal, or whether he's planning to stick—"

"*No!*" Shandie barked. "That is not what I want. I told him I'd trust him, and I will trust him. That is *not* what I want."

"What then? Why's he here?"

"Part of his education. *Was* his father a traitor?"

"No. One of his brothers was being stupid, but nothing serious."

Shandie said, "Ah!" sadly, but he did not turn to look at Ylo. "Besides, even if he planned to cut my throat in the next hour, you couldn't warn me, could you?"

East scowled. He leaned back and crossed one massive thigh over the other. "Don't say '*Couldn't*' around me, sonny. '*Shouldn't,*' maybe. That's not quite the same. 'Sides, there are precedents for handing out warnings. That's not direct use of magic."

"My apologies." Still Shandie did not turn. "Signifer, this is Warlock Olybino, warden of the east."

Ylo saluted. If military etiquette required anything more than an ordinary salute for a warlock, the details lay beyond Ylo's ken. He was far more concerned by the realization that the Protocol, while it forbade the use of magic against the Imperial Army, made exception in the case of East. *The Imperial Army was the prerogative of the warden of the east.* So Warlock Olybino could use sorcery on Signifer Ylo any way he liked, although no one else could, not even the other three wardens. He could pry into Ylo's mind and discover whether he was truly loyal or was planning revenge. Ylo would like to know that himself.

But the warlock was now ignoring him. "So—you want me to report your great victory to the Old Man?"

"I'd be grateful if you would," Shandie said respectfully. "And that I'm well. He worries."

"He should. Want me to tell him how that second javelin almost made a two-month baby heir apparent?"

"Better not, your Omnipotence. I did wonder if you'd bent that one a little?"

The golden horsehair waved as the warlock shook his head. "No."

"Or organized our young friend's feat with the standard?"

"No. I stayed out totally."

Now why would the warlock of the east have refrained from influencing the Battle of Karthin? Why let the XXth Legion be demolished, and three others badly savaged, and all for no real gain?

Shandie did not ask, and Ylo certainly wasn't about to.

But Ylo had grown up in a very political family. Politics, his father had told him once, was a matter of layers. If you could see it, it probably didn't matter, and vice versa. The bottom layer was always the wardens. Their schemes were the real schemes, he had said. The Four got what they wanted, and they ruled by majority.

Olybino had been bought off, or scared off, but no one but the wardens themselves would ever know which, or why, or how.

"Fine," Olybino rumbled. "I'll tell him. It will ease the news about Guwush."

"What about Guwush?" Shandie snapped.

The warlock bared his teeth. "Oshpoo has taken Abnila-grad. Razed it. Yesterday."

The prince groaned.

"Everything you won has gone," Olybino said meanly.

Shandie muttered a curse and walked over to one of the chests. He sat down and glared at his boots. Ylo stayed where he was, wishing he was not now so exposed to the warlock.

"If I could just get the XIIth up there!" the prince muttered.

"No way," Olybino said. "It would take a month or more to sail around Zark. I doubt that the caliph would give you safe conduct to march through."

Shandie looked up. "We could go across Thume?"

Ylo gulped, and even the warlock seemed startled. He glowered.

"Not if you're in your right mind, you can't! The Protocol doesn't apply in Thume, you know that! I can't help there!"

"Seems to me an Imperial Army crossed Thume back in the XVth Dynasty."

"And I can think of three that tried it and vanished without trace. Thume is totally unpredictable."

Shandie sighed. "Then Hushipi will have to handle the gnomes without me. Omnipotence . . . tell me about the caliph."

"What about the caliph?"

"Is it personal, his feud with the Impire? When my grandfather dies, will he relent? Gods know, I don't want a war with a united Zark!" Without looking around he said, "Sit down, Signifer."

Gratefully Ylo tottered over to a chest.

The warlock was shaking his head. "I don't think so. He's spent sixteen years making himself overlord. No one's ever managed to unite the djinns before, except after the Impire's invaded and they want to throw us out again. Yes, he has a personal grudge against your grandfather, but I don't think he'll stop now."

There was a moment's silence, and then Olybino chuckled. "After all, you were there, too."

Shandie looked startled. "Where?"

"In the Rotunda. You were only a child, but you were a witness when Emshandar insulted him."

"Stole away his wife, you mean?"

"Exactly. The woman who is now the queen of Krasnegar."

"And that's what's been driving the man all these years?"

"Djinns never forget an insult, and Caliph Azak is no ordinary djinn."

"No, he isn't," Shandie agreed mournfully. "The Impire is being stretched very thin, Omnipotence."

"A few more victories like today's and it will be stretched much thinner."

"Exactly!" the prince snarled. "As I said—you could have helped!"

Ylo held his breath, but the warlock merely smiled. He stretched like a great bear; lamplight flickered on the jewels of his cuirass and rippled on the muscles of his forearms. "Why should I help in every little feint?"

"*Feint?* Karthin was a feint?" Shandie leaped to his feet. "What's he up to?"

No more! Certainly Ylo would like to see the caliph taught a lesson, a real lesson, but not now. Not with this army. In a month or two, maybe . . .

Olybino was grinning big white teeth. "Ever heard of the Gauntlet?"

"No."

"It's a traders' pass through the foothills, just outside of Ullacarn. While you're licking your wounds here, the caliph is pushing his army through it. He'll take the city, cut you off . . . The harbor at Garpoon is all silted up, of course. Four legions—"

"God of Slaughter! Tell me!"

"I'm trying to, sonny! As far as I know, no one's ever brought an army through there, because it's got more good ambush sites than there are fleas on a camel, but the caliph happens to know it personally—"

Shandie stamped a foot. "We can intercept?"

Olybino rubbed his hands together in a gesture that seemed totally out of keeping with appearance, something an old man might do, not a youthful giant. "He'll be all strung out in column of route, and you can come in on a side track and cut him like a snake."

"A map! I need a map!"

The warlock shrugged and held out a roll of vellum that he had not been holding a moment earlier. Ylo's gut tightened at this evidence of sorcery.

Shandie took it, but he did not open it.

"Your Omnipotence, I ask a favor."

"I thought you might." The warlock's deadly gaze settled on Ylo, who cringed. He just could not take any more of this!

"It's his first battle," Shandie said. "He's beat, and I need him. I was hoping to go over his duties with him tonight, if you would help—and now I need him even more!"

Olybino chuckled. "Perk him up a bit, you mean?"

Aargh! Ylo sprang to his feet, feeling as if he'd been struck by lightning. The tent blazed brighter for him. Even the fur on his wolfskin seemed to crackle. A moment before he had been slumped down, trembling with exhaustion, and suddenly he was up and shaking with a fierce desire to *do* something, *fight* someone, *run* somewhere . . . His aches and weariness had vanished and he was as eager for action as a yearling colt.

Shandie looked him over, and smiled. "Thank you, Omnipotence. Signifer, get me the proconsul! I don't care how you do it, but get him here *now*!"

Ylo shouted, "Yessir!" and raced from the tent.

6

THREE DAYS AFTER THE BATTLE OF KARTHIN, AS THE CAL-
iph's forces threaded the deadly narrows of the Gauntlet,
the Imperial legions stole in on their flank under sorcerous
concealment, like an invisible razor moving to sever a sleep-
er's throat.

At the Keez Place, beyond the ranges, the old woman
Phain lay still a-dying.

The Blood Laws forbade anyone to remain within earshot
of the Departing, except the Watcher, but a woman knew
best where her own duty was. So Frial had found herself a
convenient stump at the edge of the clearing, and there she
sat and wove a basket. She had woven a heap of baskets
these last three days, until her fingers were sore and she had
denuded the area of withes. Her grandmother would die in
her own good time, no doubt, as the old dear had always
done everything in her own good time.

Frial did not need to be there. There were many relatives
and neighbors *more* than ready to keep an eye on little Thaïle
for her, and the Gods knew that there were enough chores
piling up back at the Gaib Place to keep her busy from
dawn till dusk—but she was going to remain here, where
Thaïle could see her anytime she wanted to look, and be
comforted.

The weather was remarkably good for so early in the year.
The rainy season seemed to have tailed off into scattered
showers, and there were thick trees to shield her from those.

It was a pleasant enough Place, with the stream chattering
and the great cottonwoods towering like guardians all
around. Beyond them, the wall of the Progistes formed a
jagged barrier against the sky, white on blue, and they were
a comforting sight. The forested slope of Kestrel Ridge
closed off the west. The glade was carpeted with cool ferns.
She liked the Gaib Place better, set in its own protective
little hollow, but she knew lots worse—cottages built out

in the open, even, visible for leagues. Gave her the shivers, some of them.

The Keez Place must have been even better, long years ago, when her grandfather had chosen it. A couple of others had crowded in since then, indecently close. Her own brother, Vool, now, and his snarly wife Wiek ... the Vool Place was far too close, barely out of sight over the rise. Shameful!

That same pestering brother had come to see how she was doing, hovering around her like a midge, sending out waves of discomfort. He'd been a fusspot as a child, Vool, and he was a fusspot now, at forty.

"It could be a long time yet, Frial." He had settled on a fallen log to be miserable in comfort.

"I'm sure it will seem longer to Thaïle," Frial said complacently. "She's a very sensitive child."

"Like you," he agreed. "You were always sensitive. Always the most sensitive of the family. Even before your Watch."

Vool himself wasn't sensitive, she thought, eyeing her own busy fingers. If he'd been the least bit sensitive, he would never have married that born-miserable, complaining wife of his. His face had taken on a morose look right after his marriage and never lost it.

"It's not always a blessing," she said. Like now, for instance.

Frial was not merely sensitive; she had the talent they called Feeling. She could Feel people's emotions farther than she could hear their voices, often. Right now she could mostly Feel Vool's misery. He was unhappy because he lived closest to the Keez Place, where old Phain lived—and was now dying—and that made him feel responsible, although he wasn't. He was unhappy because Frial was *here* and his irritable wife was just over *there*, and he knew they did not get along. And he was unhappy because he had two kids of his own who would be due for Death Watch very soon.

Over in that ramshackle cottage, little Thaïle was dozing,

most like. At any rate, she was less worried than she'd been for the last four days. The old woman was asleep, certainly, for Frial could Feel the confused, meaningless patterns of dreams.

And in the distance, her ill-tempered sister-in-law was worrying as hard as always, and probably about nothing. There were happy children somewhere down the hill, and they helped.

The cottage was a disgrace. Why hadn't some of the family kept it in better repair for the old woman? Frial herself would have, if she had lived near, and Gaib would have helped, too, just for her sake. Gaib helped out lots of neighbors, not even relatives, sometimes walking half a day to take supplies to an elderly friend or fresh food to an invalid. Gaib was a truly kind man. Of course a woman with Feeling couldn't have married any other sort. The thought of being married to a brooding type like Vool made her skin crawl.

And now he was dredging up one of his worries to share with her. She held out her basket to admire, but before she could draw his attention to it, he launched into one of his frequent complaints.

"I think all this is wrong! A kid shouldn't have to do a Death Watch on a relative. Makes it a lot harder."

"You know there was no one else in the area qualified. Lucky we'd dropped by, really."

He was not deterred. "Well, Thaïle shouldn't have to do a Watch anyway! It's a waste of words, and we ought to tell the recorders so."

Frial sighed, having heard all this before. He was brooding about his own brood. "The recorders know best, Vool."

"Maybe they do. Maybe they don't. Maybe they just think we'd be offended if our family was taken off the Gifted list. Maybe if we offered, they'd be glad to."

"Glad to what?" she muttered absently, wondering about the chickens back at the Gaib Place. They'd be laying all over the landscape at this time of year, and Gaib would be too engrossed with digging over the vegetable patch to give them a thought. When she got back, there'd be no eggs pickled, and the hawks too fat to fly.

"Glad to take our family off the list, of course! None of our relatives have shown any real Faculty for generations."

That wasn't true, she thought with a shiver. The recorders had been very interested in her Feeling. They'd eventually decided it wasn't quite strong enough to show she had a true Faculty, but for a while she'd been very worried, and her parents, also. They obviously hadn't told Vool, or else he'd conveniently forgotten. Vool himself had neither Faculty nor any special talent at all, except perhaps for fussing.

"If what you say is true, then we have nothing to care about."

"But it's a waste of magic!"

"That's recorders' business, Vool." Their worry, not his.

"You want to come over to our Place for some lunch?" he muttered, abandoning the argument.

And be close to that grouch of a sister-in-law? "No, thanks. But I'd sure appreciate a bite if you could bring one again, like before."

"It's sure to rain later," Vool muttered, glowering up at the cloudless sky. "You'll sleep at our Place tonight. All this sleeping out of doors'll give you rheumatics for certain."

Her worry, not his.

"I'll survive," she said, unwilling to admit to her sore hips. "And . . ."

Pain! She dropped the basket.

"What's wrong, Frial?"

"I think it's come," she mumbled, staring at the cottage. *Wake up, Thaïle!*

"Grammy?" Vool demanded nervously.

Frial nodded. The old woman was awake, and her pain and fear were rolling like thunder across the glade.

Then Frial Felt her daughter awake, also. Confusion! Alarm! *Oh, Thaïle, my darling!* Fear! Terror!

Terror from the dying Phain . . . terror from the child . . .

Frial clenched her fists, fighting the urge to rush to the aid of a daughter in distress.

Then calm intervening. Resolution. Sympathy. Thaïle was coping, good girl!

"It's going to be all right," she muttered, conscious of perspiration wetting her face, aware also of Vool's concern close to her. He jumped up and came across and hugged her, and for a moment his worry blanketed all the other sendings. She had never realized how much she mattered to him! She began to weep as the clamor of emotions rang again in her head.

Panic. *Agony!* She cried out.

Love, then, and help . . .

It was over. Confusion from little Thaïle as the word registered. Huge torrents of concern from Vool. Relief and peace and almost happiness fading as the old woman passed away . . .

"It's done!" Frial wiped her eyes and tried to stand up. Her brother held her down.

"Wait, love," he said. "You're shaky still. It isn't your Watch. Thaïle will do fine, I'm sure. We don't need to worry about Thaïle."

Fancy Vool talking like that! She felt guilty at having thought poorly of him for so long. He did care.

"Yes," she agreed, striving to relax. Old Grammy had passed on her word of power and gone to the last weighing, and the Gods would find much good in that kindly old soul, and very little evil. Her balance would join the Good, and . . . and . . . and Frial was weeping, which was silly and not like her. She ought to be concerned for her daughter, who had just had a shattering experience. But Vool was right; Thaïle was fourteen now, and a young woman, really, not a child anymore.

It would be all right. There was nothing to worry about. No one in their family had shown any real Faculty for generations, she reminded herself sternly. Of course she did have

Feeling, and Gaib had a wonderful gift for green things. But those were details, just talents. Everyone had some sort of talent, even if it was only for worrying. Nothing directly to do with Faculty.

They would have to wash the body now, and gather all the relatives for the wake, and . . .

Terror! Now what? Something new . . . Awful.

"Mother! Mother!"

Thaïle raced out of the cottage and came hurtling across the glade, long arms flailing for balance, close-cropped hair awry. Even at that distance, Frial could see the pallor on her face. She cried out and tore loose from her brother. She sprang up and ran to meet her daughter.

They collided into an embrace hard enough to knock the breath out of both of them. The child was sobbing, almost screaming. Hysterical. Terror and agony . . .

"Thaïle! Thaïle! What's wrong?"

The thin body was shuddering with pain. Stricken young eyes huge with terror . . . "Can't you Feel it?"

"Feel what?" Frial shouted. All she could Feel was her daughter's own freezing dread, so close.

Thaïle turned to stare at the towering ramparts of the Progistes. "Death! Murder!"

"What's wrong?" Vool demanded, arriving in blustering incomprehension. "What happened? What's wrong?"

"She's Feeling something!" Frial said. "Tell me! Tell me!"

"Thousands of men!" Thaïle cried. "Pain and death! A battle? Yes, it must be a battle. Oh, Mother, Mother! So much death! So much hate, and suffering!"

She buried her face in her mother's shoulder, shaking uncontrollably. Frial and Vool gazed at each other in horror.

If Thaïle was truly Feeling a battle, then it must be beyond the mountains, Outside, far away.

There were never any battles in Thume.

May the Keeper defend us!

Frial could Feel nothing at all.

Blow, bugle!
Blow, bugle, blow, set the wild echoes flying,
And answer echoes, answer, dying, dying, dying.
--TENNYSON, THE PRINCESS, IV

CHAPTER TWO

YOUTH COMES BACK

1

THE WELL-NAMED BATTLE OF BONE PASS CAME THREE DAYS after Karthin, and this time the outcome was never in doubt. The djinn army was cut into three portions and then systematically butchered, the caliph himself being wounded and many of his best generals slain. The legions herded away seven thousand prisoners, and no one counted the dead heaped in the wadis.

Pandemia was very big, and the Impire comprised more than half of it. Imperial couriers traveled faster than anyone else in the world, yet reports from outlying areas took weeks to reach the Opal Palace in Hub.

Sorcery was instantaneous. That same evening Warlock

Olybino materialized in the imperor's bedchamber and smugly told him the good news.

Many times throughout his long reign, Emshandar had been given secret tidings by one or other of the Four. Knowledge was power, and no one knew it better than he. He had often used such covert information to great advantage in the eternal ferment of Hubban politics, and only very rarely had he ever gone public with it before the mundane reports arrived—a good conjurer never shows all his pockets.

This time he made an exception. A man who will not see ninety again cherishes every minute the Gods grant him. Emshandar could not afford to wait a month or two. He considered holding off until his golden jubilee, just three weeks away, but even that seemed rash at his age. At dawn he summoned the Senate, and at noon had himself carried to the Rotunda to give it the news in person. He would not have been surprised to learn that it was the last time he would make such an appearance; he would have enjoyed the occasion anyway.

One of the main reasons the Impire had prevailed for three thousand years was that the imps were united and their enemies were not. Other peoples tended to fight among themselves, a habit the Impire encouraged and exploited. The djinns were even worse than most. Throughout history, the emirates and sultanates of Zark had squabbled like starving rats and thus been easy pickings whenever the imps felt an itch to loot and oppress someone.

Back in 2981, one of the petty kings had proclaimed himself caliph and set out to change the ancient pattern. Many others had tried in the past, but this caliph had turned out to be a military genius. He had succeeded where they had failed, welding the innumerable principalities into one ominously coherent and hostile state. No one doubted that when he had finished making himself overlord of all djinns, he would carry the black banner of Zark against the Impire. The caliph's ever-growing power had shadowed the closing years of Emshandar's reign like a rising thunderstorm.

Gaunt and stooped, palsied but triumphant, the imperor proclaimed his victory from the Opal Throne. He went on to predict that Bone Pass had broken the power of the upstart forever. The caliphate would collapse within weeks.

The senators cheered the old fox as they had not done in a generation, and ordered the bells of the Impire rung for three days. They almost carried a motion conferring the title of "the Glorious" on Shandie, but the imperor interrupted to announce that of course he would bestow a dukedom on Proconsul Iggipolo. The Senate took the hint and dropped any idea of honoring the commander of the XIIth above his fellow legates. Subsequent speakers were careful not to mention Shandie at all.

Which pleased his grandfather.

There was no need to give the lad any highfalutin ideas!

2

IN THE ENSUING DAYS THE SOUND OF BELLS RIPPLED OUT from the center, bearing the glad news to every corner of the Impire and eventually to lands beyond. By summer word of Bone Pass had traveled even as far as Nordland, in the far northeast. The jotnar had already made their contribution to the Year of Seven Victories, when a group of thanes had expanded the usual spring training into an ambitious looting expedition of the Winnipango and run into the XXIVth Legion by mistake.

The survivors badly needed an easier foe to restore their morale. Those who had not participated must demonstrate that they had not stayed home out of cowardice. Word of the caliph's downfall caused them all to raise their flaxen eyebrows and contemplate the prospect that the defenses of Zark might now fall back from their recent regrettable efficiency. Not much was said, but several longships began loading supplies and an ominous buzz among the steadings told of axes being sharpened.

By the time the harvests were ripening in the south, word of the Battle of Bone Pass came even to the other end of the world, to the tiny kingdom of Krasnegar in the far northwest, on the shores of the Winter Ocean. There was nowhere more remote than that.

It was brought there by a Captain Efflio, master of a grubby little cog named *Sea Beauty*. Although jotnar were far better sailors than imps could ever hope to be, they could not compete with them in business, so the coastal traders of the Impire were often owned by imps. Usually there would be jotnar among the crew—never too many, though, lest they be tempted by ambition.

Efflio was elderly, lazy, and asthmatic, but shrewd, even by impish standards. He was also a fair sailor, a trait he could reasonably assume was due to some jotunn blood in his veins, for any family that had lived for long within reach of the sea was likely to have had unfortunate experiences with raiders.

Having delivered a cargo of garlic and onions to the city of Shaldokan at a good profit, he wheezed his way along the docks to the nearest impish tavern and began eavesdropping on conversations. Within the hour he picked up word of a potential hire. Some rural duchess wanted some horses shipped to a place he had never heard of. Her agent was having trouble arranging the matter, because livestock was about the most unpopular haul on the four oceans. The garlic had already made *Sea Beauty* detectable for two leagues downwind, so Efflio had little to lose in that regard. He also knew that the secret of transporting animals was to starve them to within an inch of their lives—what doesn't go in can't come out. He set off in search of the broker.

Two days later, when he was almost ready to sail, he

summoned his bosun, Krushbark, who stood half as tall again as he did and was very anxious to raise anchor before some of his recent shore activities caught up with him.

"Gnomes," Efflio said sadly.

"What about 'em, sir?" Krushbark inquired through bruised lips. He was blinking blearily down at the captain as if there were too many of him on deck. His eyes had a heraldic appearance, sea-blue irises set in very red whites.

"Someone will have to muck out the hold," Efflio explained, taking it slowly and not speaking any louder than necessary. The duchess' agent had been very insistent that the horses arrive alive, so they would have to be fed *something* in the next month. "I tried to hire some gnomes to do that. Gnomes don't like cold places, and they won't sign on when I tell them we're headed north."

The bosun thought about that, then rubbed his eyes with fists like tree stumps.

The captain tried again. "You want to tell the lads they'll have to muck out?"

"Gnome work!" Krushbark said. "Gnomes don't mind that sort of work."

"But no gnomes will sign on."

"Ah." Krushbark ran fingers through his mop of barley-colored hair. "Gnomes! How many did you want, sir?"

"Two should be plenty," Efflio said patiently.

"Gnomes," Krushbark agreed. "Two gnomes."

"Good man," said the captain.

An hour or so later the bosun came back on board with a couple of gnomes under each arm. He'd brought extra, he explained, because he hadn't been sure how hard a gnome should be hit. Efflio made no comment about additional mouths to feed—gnomes were easily satisfied, and he preferred not to argue with his bosun unless he had to.

Sea Beauty set sail at once.

3

IT WAS LATE IN THE SEASON FOR A JOURNEY TO KRASNEGAR, but the Gods were lenient, and the cog made fast time. She encountered no ice. She lost no gnomes, and only two of the horses. The crew fared well then—especially the gnomes, who were willing to eat everything from the shoes up.

One sparkling morning with a fair breeze blowing, *Sea Beauty* sighted her destination. For days she had skirted a low, treeless land, a barren plain bereft of inhabitants or landmarks. The island peak of Krasnegar jumped up over the horizon so unexpectedly that Captain Efflio felt it should have shouted, "Boo!" As more and more of it came into sight, he began to feel very uneasy. Eventually his qualms grew strong enough that he ventured to climb the mast for a better view, a feat he had not attempted in the last ten years.

Then he could no longer doubt. He had been here before! The great rock like a slab of yellow cheese, the spiky black castle on top, and the little town running down one face— they were unmistakable. He had been second mate on *Champion* at the time. That had not been yesterday, nor the day before either, but even so he should have remembered the name or recognized the description. He never forgot a port he had visited, never! At the very least, no matter how long it had been, he should not have forgotten that landmark rock.

He remembered it now, of course . . . vaguely . . . a humble little outpost, despite its imposing castle. It was home to both imps and jotnar, which was very unusual, and an independent kingdom—probably remaining so only because neither thane nor imperor could see anything in it worth stealing. A nonentity of a place.

Nevertheless it was set all by itself in the bleak north, where there were no other good harbors. Why was it not better known and more talked about? Why had he forgotten it so completely? Not just him! Back in Shaldokan, he realized now, there had been surprisingly few people able to give him directions to this place, or tell him much about it.

Like all sailors, Efflio disliked any hint of the occult, and this uncanny anonymity certainly smacked of sorcery. He had heard tell once of something called an *inattention spell* that could produce such effects.

Wheezing nervously, he had barely started his descent before he detected a change in the creaking of the mast. To add to his alarm, then, he saw that the bosun was coming up after him. Efflio tried to shout at the dumb ox to belay that, but he had no breath left for shouting—or climbing back up to the crosstrees, either. So he stayed right where he was, wishing he had replaced the rope ladder the previous summer, when the hands had first begun griping about its condition.

A few moments later the jotunn arrived behind him, feet a rung or two lower. He wrapped an arm around both mast and captain and peered over his shoulder. A passing gull shrieked in derision at the sight.

"Krasnegar!" Efflio whispered, having trouble making any sound at all with his face being squashed against the ropes.

He felt the bosun's porcine grunt before the sound emerged beside his ear.

"You ever been here before?" he asked.

"Dunno," the giant said. "The dock looks kinda familiar."

The captain could not make out any details of the harbor yet, but jotunn long sight was notoriously sharp.

"And what's that?" Krushbark demanded, pointing seaward with his free arm and causing the mast to creak ominously.

"Fishing boat?" Efflio wheezed. By squinting hard, he could just make out a tiny speck in the far distance, bobbing on the long green swells.

"With kids in it?" the bosun demanded.

• • •

No imp could resist a mystery. By holding his next tack, Efflio had little trouble in closing on the dory. Then he hove to and studied the curious sight.

The cockleshell was indeed manned by two children, and it was barely big enough for both of them. The girl was an imp and the boy a jotunn. Normally that combination would suggest abduction and rape, but they were too young for that—twelve or thirteen, perhaps. Moreover the girl waved cheerfully, seeming undistressed. The boy just kept rowing. The tiny boat rode up and down over the swells.

Efflio had been a father in his time. He might very well be a grandfather by now—he had no way of knowing, having lost touch with his various offspring years before. He thought of himself as a kindly man, as long as kindness came cheap enough, and he did not enjoy the idea of these two waifs being blown away into the wastes of the Winter Ocean.

Furthermore, although the boy's ragged shirt and pants were unremarkable, the girl's green gown was a fine garment, lady's wear. Something shone very brightly in her hair. There might be a reward. There might even be salvage, although the little dinghy was not worth much. Efflio decided that his duty was to rescue this strange expedition.

"Throw them a line!" he ordered.

An absurd argument then developed. The boy stayed silent, leaning on his oars, while the girl refused the line, shouting that she did not want to be rescued. The sailors, having their orders, insisted.

Eventually the child yielded. The boat was pulled in; the two children climbed a rope ladder to *Sea Beauty*'s deck, and the dory was hauled aboard. The ship heeled over to the starboard tack, resuming her voyage to Krasnegar.

The girl came stamping aft to where the captain was watching, the boy trailing behind her. She was very angry. Her dress was a gorgeous thing of sea-green silk, now somewhat marred by salt water and fish scales, and perhaps a trifle small for her. If that miracle on her head was what it seemed, then it was worth a fortune. Those pearls around her neck couldn't possibly be real, could they? Efflio began to think more seriously of salvage. The day might turn out to be more profitable than most.

"Why did you interfere?" she demanded shrilly, eyes flashing. Her dark hair had been pinned high on her head, but it was now falling loose. The tiara had slipped to one side. She was gangly and flat-chested, but she already had the self-confidence of the stunning beauty she would be in another two or three years.

The boy was taller and heavy-looking, the sort of flaxen-haired jotunn brat that could be found by the score in any port in Pandemia. In two or three years he would be sprouting like a sunflower. Typically, he was scanning the ship and ignoring the people.

"First tell me who you are!" Efflio said.

The child tossed her head, and the wind shook more of her hair loose. "I am Allena the Fair, and this is Warlock Thraine."

Efflio remembered the ballads his mother had sung to him when he was a child. The mate and the helmsman and a couple of others were listening, and grinning. Feeling strangely nostalgic, he bowed.

"I have the honor to be your Majesty's most humble servant, Admiral Efflio, Master of *Sea Beauty* and Lord of the Winter Ocean. Allena the Fair, obviously. I ought to have recognized your Majesty at once. But Warlock Thraine was a pixie. Are you sure this one isn't an imposter?"

The boy did not seem to hear; the girl pouted. "A great sorcerer can look like a jotunn if he wants to!"

"That's true," Efflio agreed. "But a jotunn who claims to be a pixie in disguise is definitely not to be trusted! Are you quite sure he is Warlock Thraine, your Majesty?"

The girl flushed and dropped her eyes. "It was a game, but you needn't make fun of me!"

"You mean that boat isn't really the famous *Ark Noble* and that isn't Warth Redoubt I see ahead of me?"

The onlookers guffawed. The castle ahead was Krasnegar, and the name scrawled in red lead on the dory's bow was *STROMDANSR.*

"Of course not!" The girl had turned even redder. "Warth Redoubt was *much* bigger!"

"How many head?" asked the boy, sniffing the air.

"Twelve," Efflio said. "Your names? Real names?"

"I am Princess Kadie of Krasnegar. He's Gath, my brother."

About to lose his temper, Efflio caught the mate's eye, which was twinkling like a beacon.

"You should'ov piped them aboard, Skipper!"

"Or else I should throw them back!"

The girl tossed her head again. Oh, she was a vixen, that one! And she was obviously the brains of the pair. The boy was being very quiet, gazing blankly at the rigging, but he did not seem scared. He was probably just dull-witted, for her make-believe had left him doing all the rowing. Once she had perfected her techniques on her dumb brother, the minx would have males dancing to her tune for the rest of her life.

The boy completed his study of the lines and turned his steady stare on the captain. "How close to the wind will she sail?" he asked, and waited solemnly for an answer.

Efflio told him, taking a harder look. There was a surprising brightness in those big gray eyes—odd-colored eyes for a jotunn, quite a dark gray. When jotnar had gray eyes, they were a pale, foggy shade. And the kid's hair stuck up in golden spikes all over his head, which wasn't usual, either. So he was not purebred jotunn, and the girl's claim that he was her brother might be believable. Mixed bloods tended to favor one parent over the other. She might have meant "half brother" anyway.

She had breathtaking green eyes. How could Efflio have missed those? He had never seen such green eyes before in his life. So she was not pure imp, and she might well have jotunn blood in her, because her ridiculously inappropriate dress was a skimpy thing that left her arms and shoulders bare, yet she seemed unaware of the spray and the whistling wind. Efflio himself was swathed like a bear, and the gnomes had been huddled under blankets in the galley for days. The boy had bare arms and bare legs. He obviously felt the cold no more than did Krushbark, whose shirt was open to the waist.

Who were these two orphans of the sea? Again the captain felt uncomfortable prickles of superstition. If those were real emeralds in the crown-thing on her head, then he ought to throw the livestock overboard and head back to the Impire at once. He could live out his days in luxury on what he would get for that. He could buy off the crew with one pearl apiece from the necklace and send the kids home somehow.

But if there were occult forces at work, then the children might be something much closer to the mythical Allena and Thraine than they looked. And as for her being a princess— and the boy presumably a prince . . . well, who could say what was possible in this forgotten, eldritch outpost?

Then he felt a sudden shift in the motion of the ship as *Sea Beauty* entered the bay. The far end was closed by a splatter of small islands, forming one of the finest harbors Efflio had ever seen—certainly the finest he had ever forgotten. The great rock stood high on one side, its nearer face plastered with town. The landward shore bore only a few cottages and haystacks.

So it was too late to take the treasure and throw the horses overboard, even if he ever would have done such a thing. He shouted to the mate to shorten sail and laid course for the quay.

4

SORCERY OR NOT, KRASNEGAR MADE A GOOD FIRST IMPRESSion. It had a prosperous, contented air about it that Efflio could not quite identify. There were no trading vessels moored at the docks, only fishing smacks and a couple of small whalers. Lobster pots in stacks, nets drying over racks, blubber being rendered in cauldrons over fires . . . Women sat in rows and gossiped as they mended nets, while others cleaned fish and tossed a steady rain of them into the salt barrels. Men similarly wrangled while repairing oars and harpoons. It all seemed very healthy and normal.

It reminded him somehow of Impport, on Krul's Bay, where he had grown up, although Impport was much flatter. He had a daughter in Impport. He *probably* had a daughter in Impport. He hadn't been back there in twenty years.

He would never want to live in a town built on such a slope—not with his chest—but he could see little wrong with the place otherwise. He was beginning to remember it now. It had a well-organized, impish feel to it, and yet the people held their heads high and did not peer over their shoulders before they spoke. That might be the jotunn influence. Most of the people he could see at the moment were blond, but of course jotnar would gravitate to the docks, and the imps to the landlubber businesses within the town.

Krushbark hailed a man ashore, who shouted willingness; a line curled through the air. The man caught it expertly, looped it around a bollard, and threw it back. Then he went to the next bollard and the process was repeated. Hands began hauling the cable, as the helper waved cheerfully and went on about his business. In impish ports, he'd have demanded money for that trifling assistance. *Sea Beauty* nudged the dock, then nestled coyly in against it.

Without even waiting for the plank to be run out, a man vaulted over the side and came striding aft with the air of a predator thirsty for blood. Efflio took a step nearer the pin rack; Krushbark dropped the rope he had been coiling and moved quickly to the captain's side. But it was not the captain the newcomer was after—he came to a halt in front of the children. He put his fists on his hips and glared down at them.

The boy smiled shyly. The girl raised her chin and tried to project poise.

For a moment there was silence. Efflio wondered what other misfits he would find in Krasnegar—this man looked for all the world like a faun, but fauns rarely roamed far from the jungles of Sysanasso, far away in the Summer Seas. He was also much larger than any faun Efflio had ever seen, larger than most imps, even. Nevertheless, his face was a deep-tanned faun shade, his hair a brown tangle, and his nose looked as if it had been stepped on in his childhood. Faun.

His jaw was too big, though, especially now, being stuck out like that. Part jotunn, maybe?

Fauns were very good with animals. *If he is a faun,* Efflio thought, *then one gets you twenty he's a stockman, and he's come to get those stinking brutes out of my hold.* The newcomer wore ragged work clothes—and yes, his boots had been through a stable recently.

But that raised the problem of how this exiled faun could have known *Sea Beauty* was bringing the livestock. Again the uncanny tingled the captain's scalp. Much more of this and he would start jumping at shadows . . .

He had seen the dory on deck, and the children, of course.

"Hello, Papa," the girl said.

"And just *what* do you think you are doing with *those?*" the newcomer demanded.

"Which *those,* Papa?" the girl inquired sweetly.

"You know which *those,* and don't call me *that!*"

"But it's much more ladylike than 'Daddy' or 'Pop' or—"

The hostler growled dangerously. "What are you doing with your mother's jewelry?"

Efflio relaxed—he had still been secretly wondering if he had missed a good bet for instant wealth, but if the jewelry belonged to the wife of a man who wore such despicable stable rags, then they were certainly not real emeralds and pearls. Even fakes of such good quality would be worth a fair amount, though.

The girl was trying to seem unruffled. "She lets me borrow them when I dress up. I was being Allena the Fair, and Gath—"

"She never said you could wear them out in the town!" her father roared. "Or in a *boat!*"

"She never said I couldn't!" the girl protested, but she was starting to wilt before his anger.

"And look what you've done to your dress!"

"It's my old one. It's too small now! Oh, *Daddy* . . . Please don't be angry!" She sniffled, and an artful tear ran down her cheek. Her brother was watching in attentive silence, apparently unconcerned, or letting her do the negotiations.

"Angry?" the faun said. "I'm speechless!"

Perhaps that had been what the child intended, but now she tried another tack, with a dramatic gesture at the audience. "Daddy, these *pirates* captured us! They *forced* us to come aboard their ship and—"

"*Kadie!*" the man thundered. But he turned and made a quick scan of the onlookers. He picked out Efflio at once, although most would have guessed one of the jotnar. "Cap'n? Your pardon! My name's Rap." He held out a hand. "I have to thank you for rescuing these brats, I fear. And the skiff, of course."

Efflio introduced himself. "My pleasure, Master Rap. No harm done, and we'll waive transportation fees. Where do I go to lodge a claim for salvage?"

He had spoken mainly to amuse his own listening officers, but the stablehand did not reply with a blank stare as the captain had expected. He apparently caught on at once. A small smile puckered a corner of the big faun mouth, and the gray eyes twinkled.

"Imperial maritime law doesn't apply here, Cap'n. In any case, she had a crew aboard, surely? And she was underway? I think you'd have trouble getting her declared a derelict."

"That might be," Efflio admitted regretfully. It had been worth a try, though.

The faun laughed. "Indeed, my daughter's countersuit for piracy might take precedence—but I suspect the local admiralty court will award prize money of a few beers, at the least. Where exactly were they?"

"About three leagues along the coast."

"We were *not!*" the girl shouted.

"Hold your tongue, Kadie. I am very grateful to you, Cap'n, and of course their mother will be also."

"We were half a league out, Father," the boy said quietly. "The tide would have brought us back."

The hostler hesitated, then shrugged. "All the same, it was very foolish. Next time take a sailboat."

Efflio felt rather nettled that the boy's word was obviously being accepted over his, even if it was the truth.

"Sorry, Father. I won't do it again."

"Good. We'll discuss it later. Now, Cap'n, we've been starved for news lately. What word of the imperor? Is the old rogue still chopping off heads with wild abandon?"

Efflio had never been a loud-mouthed patriot, but he felt himself bristle at the man's impudence. Then he remembered that he had strayed beyond the bounds of the Impire. This disrespectful cowboy owed allegiance to the king of Krasnegar, up there in his castle, not to the imperor. Even so, his master ought to beat him for insulting his betters.

"The Gods continue to shower blessings upon his Imperial Majesty."

The faun chuckled. "They wouldn't dare not! Old Foxy would summon Them to his court and frighten Them to death!" He spoke as if he and Emshandar IV were old friends. Insolent, blasphemous peon!

"His arms have won several glorious victories of late,"

Efflio said stiffly. "The legions have struck a notable blow against the goblins at Pondague. They have retaken the pass and are building a wall across it, so the green vermin won't cause any more trouble with their raids."

The faun looked distressed. "You haven't heard the last of the goblins, Cap'n."

But of course Krasnegar itself must be on the borders of goblin country. Efflio scanned the dock quickly, wondering if he had overlooked any greenish faces. "Do they ever bother you here?" he asked uneasily.

"No. They need us for trade. We have loads of furs waiting to head south, if you're interested. A lot of them were brought in by goblins. Death Bird himself drops around once in a while. He has a taste for jotunn beer."

Efflio shuddered. "The monster himself? That murdering, torturing, green horror?"

The faun's gray eyes went strangely cold. "The same. The imps started the fight, you know, Cap'n . . . Never mind. What else is happening out there in the real world?"

For a stockman, he had a curious interest in politics.

"His Highness the prince imperial engaged the caliph in battle at a place called Bone Pass, and made great slaughter."

"Did he so!" The faun looked pleased. "Good for Shandie! I still think of him as just a kid, younger than Gath there. But he's only six or seven years younger than me . . ." The gray eyes glazed, as if their owner was calculating.

"The caliph was wounded. Very likely he has been knifed by his own supporters since."

The faun's attention returned at once. "No. No, I doubt that. Azak's probably another one the Impire hasn't heard the last of . . . But the queen will be eager to hear all your news. I'm sure she will invite you to dine one evening while you are here." Then a horse whinnied sadly, and the hostler reacted. "Someone is reminding me that you have cargo for me!"

"For the palace, Master Rap."

"They're still my problem." The man released another of

his faint smiles. "I'm sure you want rid of them as soon as possible, and I can catch the tide on the causeway if we unload right away. Then I'll be happy to stand you and your crew all the ale you can drink. Our beer has quite a reputation. Ah . . . excuse me, there's some good help going by right now!"

He leaned over the rail and bellowed, *"Krath!"* A jotunn walking along the dock road spun around, peering to locate the hail. The stockman beckoned. "Krath! Here!" He ran to the plank.

Efflio's impish curiosity was burning like a rash. What sort of stablehand discussed politics and was familiar with maritime law? For that matter, what sort of stablehand was so assertive and threw out royal dinner invitations? And were those jewels real or not?

He turned to the two children. "What's a faun doing in these parts?" he demanded.

The boy looked surprised.

The girl sniggered. "Doing?" she said. "Nothing much. He hangs around the palace . . . Looks after the royal horses, and so on."

"She's teasing you, Captain," the boy said solemnly. "He's the king."

5

SO CAPTAIN EFFLIO HAD SAVED THE LIVES OF A PRINCE AND princess. Well, maybe he hadn't, but he had tried, and that turned out to be a very fortunate occurrence indeed.

Because that disreputable stockman really was the king, and he really was a faun, or part faun, and all fauns had great empathy for animals, and when this one saw the condition of the rack-boned, starving beasts in *Sea Beauty*'s hold, then he lost his temper.

He was also part jotunn.

He displayed an astonishing fluency in nautical language. Soon he had lifted Captain Efflio bodily and was busily shaking him like a floor mat, and when Krushbark started to object, he was blocked by the king's friend Krath, who was even bigger, while a large number of enormous golden-haired locals heard the king's fury and came sauntering up the plank carrying harpoons and gutting knives and whatever else they had been working with, and it seemed *Sea Beauty* had been invaded by the Krasnegarian militia, and her captain was about to be taken apart, limb by limb, organ by organ.

Then Princess Kadie burst into tears. The madness faded from the gray eyes. The faun-jotunn put the captain down, and turned to pick up the girl and hug her, and comfort her. The boy was pale, also, but saying nothing.

The locals smirked and began drifting away again, regretful that the excitement was over without a drop spilled.

"Get them unloaded, Krath," the king said hoarsely, still cuddling the girl to him, his voice muffled by her hair. "All right, honey, all right! Daddy's not mad anymore."

"Did you ever kill a man, Father?" the boy asked, as if inquiring about horseracing, or model ship building.

His Majesty looked down at him coldly. "Yes, Gath. I did. Several. I once killed a thane with an ax." He peered around his daughter's head and looked meanly at the captain. "He deserved it."

He obviously thought Efflio did, too.

When all the horses had been assembled on the dock, shivering and complaining, the king came striding aft again, to where the master huddled within his frightened officers, trying to edge behind the sheltering bulk of Krushbark.

His Majesty was still in a poor humor.

"I think eleven of them will make it," he snapped. "I'll deliver the receipt before you leave. And if you ever bring us stock again, Cap'n, they had better be in better condition than those!" He glared.

"It was a miscalculation, sire. The fodder—"

"It certainly was! But you did pick up my two brats, and for that I am grateful. I said I would shout for the beer, and I'm a man of my word. Just tell them I said to put it on my slate."

"That's very generous of your Majesty," Efflio muttered, appalled to think what free beer would do to his crew.

"Don't worry about a watch. No one will touch your ship here." A hint of a smile softened the faun's anger. "For your jotnar I recommend the Beached Whale. Our locals will be happy to provide whatever sport they need, and there's a good bone-setter across the street. Imps may prefer the Southern Dream—but take your own dice. I notice you have some gnomes aboard. That's unusual hereabouts."

Gnomes? "Oh, yes, gnomes." He'd forgotten.

"I don't suppose they'll fancy beer?"

"I have no idea!" Efflio said. Never in his life had he spared a thought for gnomes' drinking habits.

"They lack the capacity," the king said knowledgeably. "Tell them I'll send down a couple of bottles of wine and a tasty bag of offal. If you can spare them for a day or two after you've cleaned up, I could use their help in the palace cellars." He scowled again. "Rats. And remember what I said about horses!"

He turned on his heel and strode away.

6

SEA BEAUTY NEEDED SEVERAL DAYS TO REFIT BEFORE SHE could load another cargo. Most of the crew needed several days to recover from the king's hospitality. Efflio passed the time in arranging a return hire: furs, narwhal ivory, and salted fish. Obviously the Krasnegar run could be profitable, which explained some of the trouble he had experienced obtaining information about it in Shaldokan.

The captain soon began to fret about the weather, for the season was late. He was also appalled to discover that his altercation with the king had been even more dangerous than he had realized, for the king was a sorcerer. So said all the locals he talked with in the saloons. He rarely used his power, they whispered, but there was no doubt that he was a great sorcerer.

The throne belonged to Queen Inosolan. Her father Holindarn had been king before her, and she was descended from the legendary Warlock Inisso, founder of the dynasty. The present king had been merely a stableboy in the palace—that was why he hated to use the title. He also denied being a sorcerer, but everyone knew . . .

That much was generally accepted, but thereafter the tales Efflio heard whispered in the dark and beery saloons were wildly divergent, all of them able to raise the few remaining hairs on his scalp. Transformations, disappearances, reappearances . . . The king was even identified with the mysterious faun sorcerer who had appeared in Hub many years ago and cured the imperor's sickness, thus ending the Ythbane regency. The bizarre end of the notorious Thane Kalkor was mentioned, the death of the wicked Warlock Zinixo, and Queen Inosolan's dramatic return from exile . . . Efflio listened and shivered and bought more ale to keep the tales coming. There were some talented raconteurs among the imps of Krasnegar.

But he was a good man, the king, they would conclude at last. He was much admired for his hard work and his honesty, and for the sake of his beloved queen. The whole town worshipped the queen and wished her well. And if anyone had a problem, he knew he had only to buttonhole the king on the street, and help would be forthcoming. A good man. A good queen.

A fine little town, Efflio concluded reluctantly. Apart from its Evil-begotten hills, of course.

But he vowed to stay well away from the royal family.

The royal family turned out to have other ideas. On *Sea Beauty*'s third morning in port, young Princess Kadie came strutting up the plank with her taciturn brother in tow. This time she was dressed more appropriately, in a fine fur-trimmed cloak and a sable hat too large for her. The weather was turning chilly. The skies lowered, and the wind smelled of snow.

She marched over to the captain and curtseyed, almost losing her borrowed hat in the process.

He bowed apprehensively.

"Good morning, Captain."

"Good morning, your Highness."

"Gath has a letter for you."

The boy was also better dressed than before, in long pants and a shirt without rips in it. He wore no coat or hat, though, and his shirt was inside out. He solemnly handed Efflio an envelope.

"Bow, dummy!" the princess said.

The boy's fair face reddened all the way to the roots of his spiky hair. He snatched back the envelope, bowed, and then thrust it at the captain again.

"Idiot!" his sister muttered.

The envelope contained an invitation to dine at the palace, inscribed in the queen's own hand.

Efflio gulped. This he did not want. "I shall write a reply, if you would be so kind as to wait?"

"That won't be necessary," Princess Kadie declared airily. "I'll tell her you got it. I bid you farewell, then, Captain, until the shadows lengthen and the humble plowman wends homeward."

"No!" Efflio said hastily. "I can't come!"

The child drew herself up to her full height, which wasn't much. Her green eyes flashed. "You dare refuse a royal summons, Captain?"

Efflio gritted his teeth, aware that the first mate and the coxswain were listening and smirking. He resisted a suicidal craving to take a rope's end to a certain royal backside.

"I shall explain in my reply to her Majesty that my health prevents me from climbing hills, your Highness."

The girl pouted, obviously at a loss. There was a pause, and Efflio was just about to head to his cabin when the boy spoke up for the first time.

"Mommy really does want to meet you, sir. I'm sure she will send a carriage." His face was full of earnest appeal.

Efflio could find no answer to that, except to accept.

Only twice in his life had the captain ever ridden in a carriage. He had never once visited a palace, and castles were places to shun. Even if the king of this land dressed like a peasant and herded his own livestock, the queen was of genuine royal blood and would probably hold court in proper style. The captain had no idea of the correct way to behave around queens or the assorted nobility who might be going to appear, and he certainly did not own any form of suitable court dress.

When the promised coach arrived just before sundown, therefore, he was almost relieved to see that it was a dusty, shabby old thing, its paintwork peeling and streaked with bird droppings.

He quite enjoyed the bone-rattling ride up the winding, vertiginous hill—a single very long street, twisting continuously back and forth, curling itself almost vertical on the bends. Often the way was as cramped as an alley, squeezed between tight-packed houses, flanked by poky little stores whose narrow, many-paned windows seemed more designed to keep secrets than display wares.

Eventually the carriage bounced and jangled up to the gates of the improbable castle, whose many sharp black towers pointed to the sky like a giant's pencil set. There was one man-at-arms leaning on his pike there, but he was so engrossed in a chat with a couple of pretty maids that he probably failed to notice the arrival at all. Echoes rang noisily as the vehicle rumbled through a long archway, and then it came to a halt in an inner courtyard.

No liveried and bewigged footmen appeared to greet the newcomer. After sitting expectantly for a moment, Efflio opened the door for himself and climbed down. The driver was attending to the horse. Several men and women were walking around—crossing the yard or going in and out of doors and up and down stairs—but they all seemed to have more important things on their minds than a visiting impish sailor. Some bore burdens as recognizable as laundry and trays of fresh pies.

What sort of way was this to greet a guest?

Then a treble voice said, "Hi."

Efflio turned to regard the young prince, Gath, cuddling a kitten and accompanied by a pack of inquisitive dogs. His shirt was right-way-out now.

"Ah, your Highness," the captain said. "Would you be so kind as to have her Majesty informed that I have arrived?"

The boy studied him earnestly for a few minutes. Then he draped the kitten over his flaxen head like a hat and seemed to ponder the question further. Finally he said, "Why not go and tell her yourself?"

"Because I don't know where she is!"

"Oh. She's in the parlor. This way."

The visitor was led to the royal presence by his Royal Highness Prince Gath assisted by six royal dogs and wearing a royal kitten.

7

IN MOMENTS, EFFLIO KNEW THAT QUEEN INOSOLAN OF Krasnegar was the most remarkable woman he had ever met. He had already learned that her ancestors had been both imp and jotunn. He could not have guessed, for she was one of a kind; he had never seen anyone like her. Her features lacked jotunn angularity, yet they were not pudgy like an imp's, and most impish women in their thirties were as plump as dumplings. Her coloring was unique—hair of a rich honey shade and eyes even greener than her daughter's—but he suspected that her undeniable beauty came mostly from within. She had poise without arrogance; she spoke gently without leaving any doubt at all that she was ruler of the kingdom. She had summoned him, and yet she put him at ease and stole his heart with a smile of welcome that seemed completely genuine. She was also glowing with forthcoming motherhood.

She apologized for the informality—avoiding formal functions during her confinement, she explained. She sat him down in a huge and comfortable chair beside a homely peat fire and inquired if he cared for mulled ale. The secret was to heat it with a red-hot poker, she explained, smiling, and demonstrated. He admitted that the result was the finest mulled ale he had tasted in years.

The queen herself sat opposite and at times she played with a sketch pad. Mostly she just talked, drawing him out, listening intently as if everything he said fascinated her. As soon as she sensed that he had revealed everything he knew on one topic, she would switch easily to another. Her questions were shrewd and her range of interests enormous—seamanship, the current state of agriculture in the Impire, fashion, trade, and of course politics. Her attention was the most flattering experience he had known in years.

Kadie swept in wearing a ballgown and her mother's tiara

again, and was firmly sent away. A younger jotunn girl named Eva appeared a couple of times to complain that Kadie was being *beastly* to her, utterly *horrid*, and the queen settled the matter each time with patient good humor. It was only much later that Efflio realized that the Gath boy had been sitting all the time in a corner, listening to the whole conversation without saying a word.

The queen apologized for her husband's absence—quite needlessly, had she only known . . . or perhaps she did. The king was on the mainland, inspecting the beehives, she explained. He had promised to return before the tide turned. Never would be too soon for Efflio.

He had rarely met a woman who cared a spit for politics, but then he had never met a queen before. Fortunately he had some interest in the subject. He found himself telling her of the goblins' raids and their defeat at the hands of the legions, of dwarf trouble in Dwanish and troll trouble in the Mosweeps—even the trolls seemed to be organizing these days, and who could ever have imagined that?—and especially of the djinns. He watched her nimble fingers and the play of shadows on her features until the light grew dim. The fire hissed and scented the room with its friendly smoke. At times he wondered about Impport, if the old place had changed much, and if he still had a daughter there, and whether she might even have a place near her hearth for an old retired sea captain.

Eventually Inosolan laid away her sketch pad with a mutter of annoyance. She clasped her hands and stared a while at the fire. There was a frown showing on those gold-inlay eyebrows. Then she looked up and smiled at him sadly.

"I know Bone Pass. It is a horrible place."

Zark and Krasnegar were about as far apart as it was possible to be in Pandemia.

"Er, I expect it is worse now, m'lady."

"Of course!" She sighed. "Why must men behave like that? I knew the caliph quite well. A very remarkable man."

Now that was pushing things a bit too far . . .

His face had given him away. She smiled mischievously. "I can be even more improbable. I was married to him!"

Efflio wondered what color he had turned now and hoped it would not show in the dimness.

She had turned her attention back to the smoldering peat. "The marriage was annulled by the imperor. In Hub, of course. Azak . . . he was only a sultan then. He went back to Zark, and I came on to Krasnegar. Later he proclaimed himself caliph and began his conquests. I have often wondered if the humiliation he suffered that night . . . More ale, Captain?"

Efflio declined, sure that he had already indulged unwisely. "You have traveled widely, ma'am."

"Yes. My husband even more widely." She frowned at the windows. "He is late. We shall have to eat without him if he does not come soon. I do hope he hasn't missed the tide."

"They say . . ."

The queen's smile seemed to sharpen. "That he is a sorcerer? He always denies it."

"Er, yes." That disposed of the subject without resolving much.

"I have never witnessed my husband using sorcery!" Inosolan said with a royal finality that sent a sudden shiver down his back. Her eyes flashed green in the gloom.

"I do not doubt you, ma'am!"

"Good." She relaxed to being just a beautiful woman again. "If he has missed the tide, Captain, then he has missed the tide. He won't walk across the waves, I promise you. What is the news of Prince Shandie?"

Efflio forked over his steaming brains. "I think I have told you everything I know, ma'am. He remains legate of the XIIth. Everyone thinks he should be a proconsul at least, but his grandfather . . ." This was not the Impire, so it was safe to say such things. ". . . his grandfather seems to be jealous of his success. He didn't recall him to Hub for the jubilee."

The queen nodded. "He must be incredibly old. He was old when I knew him, seventeen years ago."

"Just turned ninety-two, ma'am."

"With anyone else," she said thoughtfully, "one would assume that there was sorcery involved. But of course an imperor is exempt from sorcery by the Protocol."

Except that supposedly a sorcerer had been responsible for Emshandar's miraculous recovery when he had been near death seventeen years ago. A faun sorcerer. Perhaps his cure had been more effective than intended? The captain shivered, wishing he had accepted another tankard of that excellent mulled ale.

"Shandie will inherit soon enough," the queen said, laying aside her sewing. "I hope that all these victories spell a period of peace ahead for the Impire." She moved as if to rise, but there had been an odd note in her voice.

"Why should they not, ma'am?"

She hesitated. "There's an odd superstition about the year 3000. You must have heard it?"

"Old wives' tales, ma'am!"

She laughed. "And I am an old wife, so I can repeat them! All right, I know that wasn't what you meant! But they bother me. I never cared much for history, but I know this much. The Protocol regulates the use of magic. It protects the Impire, and all of Pandemia also. We all need the Protocol!"

"And twice it almost failed."

"Right. It broke down at the end of its first millennium, when the Third Dragon War broke out. Jiel restored it. A thousand years later it failed again, and there was the War of the Five Warlocks. That was when Thume became the Accursed Land and so on."

"There have always been wars, ma'am, and there always will be."

"But those were the worst, by far! Those were the only times that magic broke loose again like the Dark Times before Emine—dragons, and fire storms, and all the other horrors that sorcerers can inflict. And they seem to come every thousand years."

"Coincidence, surely?" the captain said uneasily. He had been hearing these stupid rumors for years, and he was astonished to hear them repeated by this apparently level-headed and practical lady.

"Maybe," she said softly.

"But . . . ?"

The queen bit her lip and turned her green eyes on the captain. "But my husband takes it all seriously! And that is not like him."

And her husband was a sorcerer!

Wasn't he?

Youth comes back:
> *Often I think of the beautiful town*
> *That is seated by the sea;*
> *Often in thought go up and down*
> *The pleasant streets of that dear old town,*
> *And my youth comes back to me.*
> —LONGFELLOW, *MY LOST YOUTH*

CHAPTER THREE

VOICES PROPHESYING

1

THE BATTLE OF BONE PASS DID NOT TOPPLE THE CALIPH AS the imperor had predicted it would, but it shattered his power. By midsummer the legions had advanced beyond Charkab against token opposition and a torrent of loot was flowing back to Hub to finance the war.

The XIIth was relieved then and withdrawn to its home base at Gaaze, in Qoble. Qoble was Impire. It was a strategic center from which forces could strike at Zark, or at the elves in Ilrane, or even at the merfolk of the Kerith Islands, although the Impire had never had much success fighting merfolk.

The XIIth was happy to be home. Gaaze was where the

men had their wives, their mistresses, and their children. Here they dwelt in permanent barracks instead of insect-ridden tents. Here they could heal and restore their numbers and train for the next conflict.

Ylo yearned for Hub, but he preferred Gaaze to battle-fields. He welcomed the civilized surroundings, the superb climate, the luxurious quarters. The women of Qoble were imps, not djinns. They wore pretty dresses instead of black shrouds. They were more visible and much more accessible.

In Gaaze Shandie was still legate of the XIIth, but he was also the prince imperial. Rich citizens fawned over him, in-viting him to an unending glitter of parties and balls. He declined whenever he could, but duty required him to attend many, and his signifer was always at his side. The blushing debutantes were presented and when they rose from their curtseys, their eyes would invariably fall on the prince's companion, the handsome one in the romantic wolfskin cape that was the badge of a hero.

Ylo enjoyed Gaaze. Gaaze was good to Ylo.

The year of victories was drawing to a close. In far-off Hub the weather would be turning foul and the days short. In Qoble the sun still shone ferociously.

Early one morning Ylo was at his desk as he always was early in the morning. He sat by the door and the big room was filled with the bowed heads of scriveners, copying out letters and reports in busy silence. There were twenty of them, and they were only a small part of the huge staff he commanded. At his back was the door to the prince's private study. He had a clear view of the antechamber, which was already starting to fill up with hopeful petitioners.

He had become an important person. Shandie's day would be filled with visitors and documents, but Ylo would choose who or what came first. He was the legate's right hand, his sword and his shield. He worked hard and loyally. Old dreams of murdering the heir to the throne were nothing now but nightmares to raise a sweat in the dark. He had fallen completely under Shandie's spell. He knew it and cared not at all.

When the imperor died and a new imperor sat upon the Opal Throne, then his signifer would be at his side and the fortunes of the Yllipo clan would be restored. Shandie had promised.

Meanwhile Ylo must justify the prince's trust and his judgment. He must also show the world that the Yllipos had owed their success to more than historical good fortune, and show them he would.

For the past hour he had been clicking the coding sticks, deciphering a missive from the imperor. He had whistled softly as the meaning began to emerge from the gibberish. And then—inevitably just as he was coming to the really interesting part—the text had degenerated into gibberish. Muttering curses, he checked his work. He found no error. That meant that the unknown clerk in Hub had made a miscalculation, or skipped a word in the key, or blundered in any one of a dozen ways. Ylo might need hours to find the glitch, by guess or by Gods. At worse, he would have to admit defeat and ask for a repeat, which might take weeks to arrive. God of Patience!

He leaned back and rubbed his eyes, then frowned around the big room, searching for similar signs of slackness or in-attention in his minions, but they all seemed suitably en-grossed. Sunshine streamed through the huge windows and soft sea breezes rustled the papers. Another beautiful day . . . he was long overdue for some time off.

"Good morning, Signifer," said a rustly, dry-leaves sort of voice.

Ylo jumped and then frowned at the unimpressive pres-ence of Shandie's political advisor. He did not rise—he was a soldier and Acopulo was not. "Morning."

Acopulo was a small, birdlike man, one of those impish zealots who refused to wear anything but standard Hubban dress, no matter what climate they might be inhabiting.

Now his silvery hair was plastered to his head by sweat and dark patches soaked his doublet. His legs within his hose were thin as rice stalks. He regarded Ylo with disapproval.

"Any mail for me?"

"None today."

"Ah well—patience is a divine virtue." The little scholar not only looked like a retired priest, he often sounded like one, also. He had an inexhaustible supply of platitudes. "Any news at all?"

"Well . . ." Ylo rubbed his chin, frowning at his inkstand. "Back in Hub . . . No, that's just hearsay. No value until it's confirmed."

"Suppose you do your job and let me do mine?"

"My responsibility is not to pass on rumors, Sir Acopulo."

"Tell me anyway."

Ylo tried to think of some other delaying tactic, but he was too sleepy this morning to play the game with real enthusiasm. "There's a report that Count Hangmore is to be the new consul."

The little man's mouth twisted in a grimace. "I predicted that weeks ago. Have you nothing better than that to offer?"

Ylo gritted his teeth. "Nothing I am at liberty to reveal."

"You mean nothing at all, then." Acopulo had been a teacher, one of Shandie's childhood tutors, and at times he treated Ylo like an excessively stupid pupil. "From the expression on your face when I approached, you have a garbled cipher to unscramble. I shall leave you to it." He stalked away, leaving an angry signifer glaring after him.

Ylo bent back to the accursed message. He had made no progress when another, more extensive, form shadowed his desk.

Chief of Protocol Lord Umpily would probably have melted into a puddle of pure oil had he tried to wear a doublet in Qoble. Instead he was robed in a loose Zarkian kibr of unbleached cotton that made him resemble a runaway tent. Nevertheless, the dark eyes that peered out through the rolls of fat were sharp—and exceedingly inquisitive as he inspected Ylo for signs of wear.

"Which was it? The succulent Opia, or the luscious Effi?"

Pretending to ponder, Ylo rested his arms across the paper in front of him, because he strongly suspected that Umpily could read words upside down. "I'm afraid I have no idea to what your Lordship refers!"

It had been both, actually. He felt very good this morning. A little weary, perhaps, but very good overall.

Umpily sighed wistfully, jowls quivering. "Enjoy it while you're young, my boy."

"Oh . . . I do, I do!" Ylo said with a satisfied smirk.

Umpily looked at him thoughtfully and lowered his voice. "You know Legate Arkily?"

"Not well."

"His sister?"

"The young one?" Ylo said with some enthusiasm. "Not nearly as well as I should like."

"Her husband has left town again, and I don't know where he's gone."

"You think he's up to no good?"

"Acopulo does. I think he's just smuggling."

Ylo reflected on Legate Arkily's sprightly sister. "If my duty requires me to stoop to undercover work, then I suppose I must."

"You think you can get to the heart of the matter?"

"At least reveal the bare facts."

Umpily waggled a cucumber finger. "Business before pleasure, now!"

"No. Regrettably, the pleasure has to come first. It doesn't work otherwise." Ylo exchanged smirks with the chief of protocol, then reached for a small sack under the desk. "You have a full net this morning, my Lord."

Umpily seemed to correspond with half the imperor's

subjects and thousands of other folk, as well. He was a one-man gossip factory. Beaming happily, he rolled away with his loot and again Ylo returned to the coding sticks.

Any day now Shandie would become imperor. Then Umpily would almost certainly be put in charge of the Bureau of Statistics, which was the intelligence arm of the secret police. Acopulo was probably hoping to be Secretary of State. And Ylo . . . Ah, what joys would the future hold for young Ylo? Any day now. It could not be long.

Then he heard a rustle of excitement out in the antechamber. Muttering complaints to the Gods, he looked up to scan the big room. He located Centurion Hardgraa easily enough, and a handful of his swordsmen, but he could not see Shandie. Puzzled, he rose to his feet and scanned twice more before he spied the prince. He was wearing civilian doublet and cloak, which was unusual, but the remarkable thing about Shandie out of uniform was that there was absolutely nothing remarkable about him. He could have been any well-dressed young man in the whole Impire.

Ylo had been hoping for more time to work on the cipher. He hated reporting incomplete work, but he would have to mention what he had discovered. He watched as Shandie moved through the crowd of well-wishers, flashing greetings just cordial enough not to offend yet formal enough to deter conversation. His memory for names and faces was unfailing. In a few minutes he had escaped from the jungle and came striding in, to pause at Ylo's desk.

Ylo saluted.

"Morning, Signifer."

"Good morning, Highness."

As usual, Shandie's face gave away no more than a dwarf's, but he registered Ylo's excitement. "And you've got something important!"

"Yes, sir—"

"My wife? She's coming?"

"Er . . . No, sir. 'Fraid not."

The prince sighed and frowned. For months he had been

begging his grandfather to let Princess Eshiala come and join him here in Gaaze, but the old man would not even acknowledge the requests anymore. "Did I ever mention that she is the most beautiful woman in the world?"

"I think you did, sir."

Oddly, though, that was about all he ever did say of her. He had never said that she enjoyed dancing or music or travel—or anything. Nor that she disliked them, for that matter. Shandie seemed curiously blind to women. At the previous night's dance, for example, at least six had indicated their availability, yet he had shown no sign of even noticing the signals. He was a great leader of men, but either his extraordinary self-discipline controlled even his love life, or he was just unbelievably innocent. Had he been anyone else, Ylo might have offered him a few lessons.

"What's the big news, then?"

"The second half is garbled, sir. The first half is your promotion to proconsul." Ylo presumed upon his growing sense of friendship to add, "Congratulations!"

Shandie had inhuman self-control, or perhaps such an honor meant little to a man destined to be imperor. "Thank you. Let me know when you have it worked out. Until then, we'll carry on as usual."

"I'll be as quick as I can."

"I know you will. Any clues so far?"

"I think it's another campaign, sir. Against the elves this time."

The prince muttered something crude, spun around in a swirl of cloak, and stalked away into his own office.

Ylo was left with his mouth hanging open.

His ears had deceived him, hadn't they? Surely the prince could not have referred to his liege lord and grandfather, Imperor Emshandar IV, as a bloodthirsty senile old bastard?

2

PRINCESS ESHIALA DETESTED FORMAL DINNER PARTIES.
She turned down most invitations automatically, but she
could not refuse the imperor. Fortunately this was a very
modest affair, strictly family. Emshandar never threw ban-
quets anymore; he was rarely seen in public at all. Tonight
there were only eight around the table. His elderly cousin,
Marquise Affaladi, was being squired by the Guardsman
with whom she had been creating such a scandal lately. The
old man had assumed that the brash youngster was one of
her grandsons, and no one dared correct his error. His own
grandson Prince Emthoro had brought a current mistress,
who had the face of a child and the poise of a centurion.

The guests of honor, though, were Senator Oupshiny and
his new bride, the lovely Ashia. Ashia qualified as a member
of the imperial family because she was Eshiala's sister. She
was also Duchess Ashia of Hileen now, Oupshiny being a
duke as well as a senator. Her first husband had been a shoe-
maker's apprentice, and undoubtedly still was.

Candles blazed, gold plate glittered, and an army of servants moved like white ghosts in the background. The little
orchestra behind the screen played very softly, not interfer-
ing with conversation.

The cost of the guests' attire and adornments would have
outfitted a legion and kept it in the field for a year. Old
Emshandar had become quite eccentric in his dress lately,
but tonight his doublet was as lavish and sumptuous as any,
loaded with jewels and orders.

Eshiala was the sole exception, as usual. She wore a simple
white kirtle with a gold trim and almost no jewelry. When
she had first come to court she had been ignorant of the
madcap carousel of fashion, so she had disregarded it and
gone her own way. That had been her first and only rebellion, and it had been forced upon her because she had been
quite unable to manage hooped dresses and haystack hair-

styles and heels like stilts. Shandie had told her she could wear anything she wanted, and the imperor had said she looked gorgeous and that had been that.

Anyone else would have been ostracized for such presumption, for anyone who did not join in the game could be suspected of mocking it. A lady was expected to spend a fortune every month on her wardrobe and furnishings; many had one attendant to look after earrings and another for shoes and so on, just as a gentleman might have one special valet to tie his cravat. Every week saw some new fad in fans or lace or sleeves, and anyone who did not adopt the latest craze instantly would be suspected of *economizing*. That was utter ruin. One whiff of frugality would do more harm to a reputation than would open incest.

But the court could not just ignore the wife of the prince imperial. They could not reasonably whisper that her husband was falling on hard times and must be out of favor. Her lowly origin was common knowledge, so it could not be maligned further—she was beyond the reach of the dowagers' claws. They dared not make an open enemy of the future impress. They detested her, but they tolerated her because they had to. She had no friends, though.

At times she would catch the eye of one of the other diners and read the contempt in it and the hatred. *Peasant go home!*

She was glad to see that Emshandar was having one of his better days—on a bad day he looked as if he had been dead a month. Tonight, maybe a week. He nibbled listlessly and sipped sparingly. His teeth were all gone, so that his nose and chin almost met. There was nothing at all between his bones and his skin, and he could not recognize a face at arm's length. His eyes lurked in tunnels and twisted around erratically as he struggled to follow the talk.

She almost liked the old man. He was the only person in the court who said whatever he liked. She was perhaps the only person in the court who did not fear him. She was loyal to the Impire and did her duty, and her conscience was clear.

To her immediate right, the old senator was flushed and raucous, his white hair tousled and his face shiny. He welcomed all the innuendoes and topped them, laughing loudly at his own vulgarity.

Opposite him, his lovely young wife was flirting with everyone—even the imperor, which was no mean feat—enchanting the men and infuriating the women. Ashia had mastered fashion, or thought she had. No one commented when she mispronounced a word or misunderstood an allusion, especially not her besotted husband. No one asked her what the old fool's grandchildren thought of her.

How could two sisters be so unalike? Ashia was the real beauty of the family. Eshiala had always known that. She was taciturn and timid, Ashia vivacious and voluptuous.

Eshiala was being quiet, as was her way. She responded courteously to her neighbors' conversation and was careful to use the tableware exactly as the true aristocrats did. She did not let her words wander onto dangerous topics or reprimand her sister for behaving like a trollop. She projected calm and reticence, raising her voice only when addressing the deaf old mummy across the table from her, and everyone had to yell for the imperor.

None of them would know how her head throbbed, or how terrified she was that she might throw up. She detested being on display. At the moment she was supposed to be eating some tiny bird-thing concealed in a rich sauce, dissecting it like a surgeon, when she could not even see it properly. Everyone else seemed to be managing. The imperor had been given something he could eat with a spoon.

She watched her ebullient sister perform like a one-woman circus in her gems and silks and could think only that the two of them had done very well, for the daughters of a provincial grocer.

Marriage with commoners had become a tradition in the dynasty. Emshandar himself had married the daughter of a humble scholar at some small-town university and his son

Emthoro a soldier's daughter, whom the court had dismissed as a camp follower. Shandie had chosen the younger daughter of a grocer.

"And how is Uomaya the First?" her left-hand neighbor inquired.

Her left-hand neighbor was Prince Emthoro, Shandie's cousin. He was a dark man, gaunt and saturnine, with a sharp nose that twitched when he was being malicious. He frightened her. His brown eyes were restless and shiny, and oddly slanted. She feared the ambition behind them, for he was third in line to the throne, after her child. Somehow she had come to believe that Emthoro, more than anyone, was likely to rip away her disguise and denounce her as the fraud she was.

But he was third in line; she granted him her fourth smile of the evening. "Maya is very well, thank you."

"Growing like a troll, I suppose?"

"Growing *as fast* as a troll."

The prince chuckled. "I did not mean to imply that she was growing to look like a troll. I'm sure that would be sedition. How soon will you join Shandie in Qoble?"

Her stomach knotted. "That is entirely up to his Majesty to decide. He knows how Shandie and I feel."

Eshiala was by nature a recluse. Six weeks after their wedding, Shandie had gone off to the wars, and at times now she thought she had forgotten what he looked like. She had nightmares of being reunited with him and curtseying to the wrong man. Fortunately he had left her pregnant, and a princess was allowed to disappear from view during her confinement. Even after that excuse had been exhausted, she had continued to refuse as many invitations as she dared. After two years she was still a stranger at court.

The last ten months she had spent blissfully rearing her baby. Although she had been forbidden to nurse her, she doted on little Maya. She would cheerfully just sit and hold her for hours. But now Shandie had been appointed proconsul in Qoble and he wanted her to join him there. Maya would have to stay behind in Hub. She was too young, too vulnerable, too important, to go journeying.

Emthoro must be reading her thoughts. "A woman's place is with her husband, surely?" he asked in his silkiest voice.

"Of course," she lied. Why, why must she give up her baby to go and live with a man she hardly knew?

"Eh?" the imperor bellowed. "What's that you're saying?" The rest of the table fell absolutely silent.

The prince rolled his eyes almost imperceptibly, just enough that the other diners would see, but not Emshandar, of course. He raised his voice to a bellow. "We were talking about Eshiala going to join her husband, Sire! In Qoble."

"Shandie?" The old man worked his mouth for a moment. "He'll survive, I'm sure. Lots of pretty girls in Qoble! A mother's place is with her child!"

Emthoro's nose twitched. "That's exactly what I was telling Eshiala, Sire!" he shouted back, and without a blush.

Then the imperor pulled something out of his mouth and turned to the servants to demand that they take away this plate of unchewable tasteless rubbish and bring him another bowl of soup, with more spice in it this time. The other diners, deciding that he had nothing else to say, picked up their conversations again.

Emthoro had not finished with Eshiala. "Have you ever visited the Imperial Library, Cousin?"

She could not recall. The Opal Palace was so huge that she could not remember what parts she had been shown and what not. "I don't know," she admitted miserably.

"Oh, I think you would have remembered. There's a great hall with rows and rows of balconies and a huge rose window at one end."

"Then I'm sure that I've never been there."

Emthoro smiled mysteriously. "You haven't heard of the Puin'lyn statues?"

"Should I have?" He was obviously going to talk to her

at length, so she would have to try to listen and eat at the same time. She resumed her attack on the lark, or whatever it was.

"The Imperor Umpily III wanted some statues," the prince explained, expertly dissecting a slice of flesh from the tiny carcass before him. "For somewhere public . . . I forget where . . . and commissioned the greatest sculptor of the day, Puin'lyn. That's an elvish name."

She knew that, of course, but she merely nodded.

"There were to be five male and five female figures," Emthoro continued, with the air of someone coming to a humorous part of a story. "Umpily's five immediate predecessors and their wives, carved in Tewper marble, which is a sort of pinkish-brown color and fine-grained. It gives a statue a very lifelike texture. Apparently there was some disagreement about terms . . . I forget the details. And the contract had not said how the figures were to be garbed. At any rate, when Puin'lyn delivered her promised statues, they were ten nudes and . . ." He chuckled. ". . . not the sort of nudes that could be left around in public, either!"

Eshiala smiled politely, not sure what the point of all this could possibly be. Emthoro laid down his knife and fork, and a footman whipped away his plate.

"Great art, of course, but erotic as you could imagine. Perhaps more so, mm? So the Puin'lyn statues were hastily moved to the Imperial Library and there they have been hidden ever since. Fortunately most of the scholars who work there are too old and decrepit to be distracted from their studies."

"You are warning me to avoid the library, then, lest they bring a blush to my cheek?"

"Oh, I wasn't suggesting that. Their real appeal is to adolescent boys, of course. When Ralp and I were kids, we used to come to Hub once or twice a year and the statues in the Imperial Library were the highlight of the trip. Shandie knew a way to get in without the curator knowing. We always had plans to take paints along and touch up some of the details, but fortunately we never quite found the courage."

She had no idea why he was telling her all this, or what sort of reaction was expected of her. Everyone else had finished this course and she had barely started. She laid down her knife and fork in defeat. The plate mercifully vanished.

Emthoro chuckled. "They raised hopes in us that time failed to satisfy—males and females both."

"I fail to see . . ." She was supposed to fail to see whatever was coming.

"Shandie," the prince said, with a twitch of his nose, "was especially enamored of the central figure among the females. He told us on several occasions that he would marry a woman as beautiful as that."

What had she ever done to Emthoro that he should seek to wound her like this? She had produced an heir, of course, and thereby demoted Emthoro from second in line to third. She knew her face was burning and that others were noticing and listening; and enjoying.

"Are you telling me that I remind you of a statue, my lord?"

"A little. There is certainly a facial resemblance. Mayhap we could visit the library some time and see? Shandie must have . . . but perhaps it is just my imagination." He smiled meanly.

"Statues," Eshiala said icily, "do not produce babies."

Emthoro showed his teeth in surprise. "True," he said, and turned to speak to the marquise.

Eshiala relaxed with a sigh of relief that she hoped was inaudible. Another gold plate was laid before her.

Across the table, Ashia was howling with mirth at some quip she could not possibly understand.

Eshiala wondered if perhaps Prince Emthoro was closer to the truth than he knew. She was a fraud. She was here only because she had told Shandie that she loved him and she didn't.

One day she had been slicing ham in her father's store, back in Thumble, when a group of soldiers had wandered in, all sweaty and smelling of horse. She had noticed one of them staring at her oddly. Of course she could not remember a time when men had not tried to flirt with her, but she had sensed the difference in Shandie's attention even then, that first day. On his way home from the battle, a month later, he had stopped in Thumble again and stayed a whole week. On the third day he had told her he loved her. On the fifth, he had proposed.

Her mother had told her not to be a fool; she would never make a better match than an imperial legate. Her father had insisted that to decline a proposal from a high imperial officer was close to treason. Ashia had turned purple and screamed that she owed it to her family.

Eshiala had asked her suitor for more time to think and get to know him. On the seventh day, he had let slip who he really was. That had settled the matter, of course. All imps were loyal to the Impire and the imperor.

She did not think she loved her husband. She suspected she was incapable of loving any man. She did not dislike him. She was grateful for Maya. She disliked Hub and the court, but she had consented to those. She detested pomp and public displays and ceremony. She had consented to those, also.

She did her duty, as a loyal subject of the Impire, and as a wife. And as a statue? And very soon she was going to find herself being hailed as impress.

3

AT KRASNEGAR, THE BRIEF NORTHERN SUMMER DREW TO ITS close. Wagons rolled on the causeway, bringing in the harvest. Old Foronod the factor was still official tallier. He sat in his office every day, throwing papers around and shouting at his clerks and generally making a confounded nuisance of himself. The real work of creating order out of chaos was done by the king himself in the great annual rush, when twelve months' supply of crops and meat and peat must be collected and transported and stored in two or three weeks' continuous toil. Krasnegar had many very hungry mouths to feed now, sixteen years after being struck by a wave of babies.

This year Rap noticed an astonishing improvement. Things rushed along at a great pace; the harvest almost seemed to gather itself, and the job was complete a week before he had expected it to be. That great crop of youngsters had suddenly grown up enough to become useful and they were all available to help, giving him about four times as many hands as he had ever had before. They were inexperienced and often clumsy, but they were willing and cheerful and so convinced they were adults now and having fun that everyone around them had fun, also.

So all went well and when the Big One arrived, the first blizzard of the winter, Krasnegar was well prepared. The shutters were closed, the boats safe, and the gates barred against bears. Now there was little to do except eat and drink, dance and party, study and teach, brawl and make love. And give birth.

"I won't drop this, you know," the king said firmly, but his hands were unsteady as the midwife passed him the precious bundle. He was always astonished how incredibly tiny these fragile miracles were when they first appeared. Tucking the babe in the crook of his left elbow, he adjusted the edge of the blanket around its face and headed for the door.

Of course this was the middle of the night—when else did babies arrive? Lamplight reflected like a halo from the flood of rich gold hair on the pillow. Inos was paler than usual and her lower lip was swollen, but she was smiling proudly, as indeed she should.

Two of each, now.

Rap knelt by the bed, leaned very carefully over his new son, and kissed her. "Clever girl," he murmured.

"I had some very expert help."

"It was a pleasure. Nice of you to put it that way, though."

"I didn't mean at the beginning. A frantic roughhouse, I expect . . ." She smiled knowingly. "I mean at the end."

"We all do what we can," he said softly.

"Thanks anyway, love."

"Don't mention it." The midwife would gossip, of course. Nothing he could do to stop gossip. He chuckled and changed the subject. "This is the finest Winterfest present a man ever received."

"Then don't refer to it as 'this' . . . I mean, call it 'him.' "

" 'Him'? That's not much of a name! Let's see. Can't tell much from his coloring yet, but I think he's going to be more imp than jotunn."

"I thought that, too. But he's got your nose, love."

Rap peered crossly at the diminutive face, screwed up in a frown, but fast asleep. "They all have my nose at that age! Or perhaps he just squished it on the door frame."

"Don't be crude!" the queen said from her pillow. "What will you name your son, my lord?"

"You decide!"

There was a brief argument about precedence.

"Holindarn," Rap said at last.

"Kadie and Eva are named after my family. It's your family's turn. Why not name him after your father? What was he called, anyway?"

"Grossnuk."

Inos said, "Oh?" with little enthusiasm.

"I don't remember him much." The king poked the baby's chin with a finger. "Hey, Grossy! We want you to grow up like your grandpapa the slaver! The drunken raider who fell off a dock in the dark. Big and mean and strong like the murdering, raping, wife-beating—"

"On the other hand," the queen said thoughtfully, "if he is going to have impish looks, then perhaps an impish name would be more appropriate."

"There you go, changing your mind again!" the king said. "Women!" He gave her another kiss. "Hi there, Holi!" He kissed the baby, too. It scowled but did not wake. "Be half the man your namesake was and you'll do fine."

"Holi it is, then." Inos yawned—a monstrous, unladylike, queen-size yawn.

"Get some sleep now, love," Rap said, and stood up. "What time would you like the bell to start?"

Inos groaned. "Must we? I always associate it with funerals."

"No. Think of celebrations and weddings and life!"

"I expect they'll ring it whether we want them to or not," she agreed sleepily. "Keep Holi a state secret till lunchtime if you can."

"Tell him that!" the king said. He departed, taking their son and the lamp.

4

HE LEFT BABY PRINCE HOLINDARN WITH THE WOMEN AND wandered off by himself, much too excited to sleep. There might still be life down the hill, in the taverns, but he had no desire to be mobbed by a bunch of drunks. Tomorrow, maybe. All his friends were long since abed. It would be unkind to waken them just to explain about this incredibly beautiful and intelligent new baby. He had the rest of the night to himself, and he was going to enjoy every minute of it.

The present king and queen had abandoned the ancient

tradition whereby the reigning monarch slept at the top of the great tower. There were many more convenient rooms available and much warmer.

He opened a door and stepped silently within. A small lamp flickered high on a shelf, illuminating three beds and three young faces on three pillows.

Nearest the door was Eva, flaxen hair, ivory winter skin. The king adjusted her quilts.

Hello there, little one, he thought. You have a baby brother now. You won't be able to pull all those tricks any more. Life is hell, Baby Eva! Now you've got to face it squarely, without being the family pet. Eight years old, supplanted and rejected already! How awful. How you will suffer! I'll try to remember that, though, and I'm sure your mother will.

He crossed the room to the twins.

The dark-haired one . . . Princess, you have a baby brother. Someone else for you to organize, imp. Another thrall to serve your whims and dance to your tune. As he did not speak aloud, the child could not hear and yet she fretted briefly on the pillow.

Dreaming, Kadie? What on earth do you dream about? Your day is one long dream, so far as I can see. Your life is filled with Allena the Fair and the White Lady of Tower Perilous and the Wild Riders of the Sea Wind . . . Your life is one endless romance. You never have time just to be yourself, Kadie. Is that what you do in your dreams? Do you dream all hard and practical and plain, while the rest of us dream frills and fancy? He chuckled, still silent. Dream on then, little beauty. And if you can rid your life of realities by night and keep your days as one long dream always, then you will indeed be blesséd of the Gods.

Gath, with shards of hair protruding everywhere like a golden porcupine . . . You have a brother now, my son. You are much older and will have to be an example for him. I'll explain that tomorrow. On your birthday, we're going to make some changes, lad. You and your sister will have your own rooms from then on, and this time there will be no argument. You're a good team, I know. You do all the heavy digging and she does all the thinking. I don't know how to stop that, Gath. It worries me a little. You never do anything on your own, not that I can see, and I can't understand that, because I was on my own a lot at your age. Oh, I had friends, but by my thirteenth birthday I was a working man and had been for years. If you're not following after Kadie, then you're following me, or your mother. What goes on in that silent head of yours? What kind of a jotunn never loses his temper? You're certainly not an imp, because you mind your own business. Are you perhaps a faun on the inside?

Rap knew very little about fauns. They were said to be stubborn, though, and Gath was never stubborn. Gath was the most obliging person in the world. It didn't fit the patterns. And it didn't seem healthy, somehow.

The king wandered aimlessly along dark corridors and eventually found himself in the great hall, trellised by moonlight, silent and haunted. Starting to feel chilled, he headed for the cavernous fireplaces at the kitchen end. Even if the last embers had burned away, there would be heat left in the stones. He found a deserted bench standing almost within the ashes, so some other night bird had been there before him. A few fragments of driftwood still glowed like the eyes of rodents. He sat down and absorbed the radiating warmth, sniffing the old familiar smells of peat and ash and ancient grease, listening to the casements rattle in the wind.

This was what he remembered best of his childhood. He could recall almost nothing of the earliest years, before his father died and his mother moved into the castle. At ten he'd started work in the stables, but in retrospect it seemed that much of his youth before that had been spent huddling close to these gigantic hearths.

Behind him, at the far end of the hall, was the dais. That

was where he sat these days, beside the queen, playing at being king because it pleased her. He still did not feel like a king.

Of all the men and women who ruled in Pandemia, or who had ever ruled in Pandemia, he thought Inos came closest to ruling by the love of her subjects. Not a man or woman in the kingdom had a word to say against her. And, although she insisted that he was the king, he regarded himself as merely the first of her subjects.

None loved her more. After all, he was the one who was allowed to sleep with her. What had he ever done to deserve that? He would do anything for her.

The townsfolk accepted him now. They pretended that they had forgotten all about sorcery, and he was sure that was because of Inos. The world was incredibly kind. He was so happy he couldn't believe it. He had done nothing to deserve all this happiness. From stableboy to king. From shovel to scepter.

Life was so good that it felt wrong, somehow.

Good before bad and bad before good. He shivered. That had been one of his mother's sayings. It seemed to imply that big good came before big bad, and—

Something moved and he jumped. A gnome crept in from the shadows, looking for warmth as he was. It was heavily swathed in fur, probably not too pleasant to get close to.

When *Sea Beauty* had sailed away from Krasnegar, she had left her gnomes behind. Rap had shown the four all the wonderfully musty cellars below the castle, and they had eagerly decided to brave the climate and take service as royal rat-catchers. Being nocturnal by preference, they had rarely been seen since.

"You startled me!" Rap said. "Er . . . Tush, is it?"

"Pish," the gnome said. "Why is a day man awake now?"

"I've been having a baby."

Firelight shone on the shiny black buttons of the little man's eyes. "You jest, King?"

"Yes, I jest. It was the queen who did all the work. But I have a new son. About this big."

"I was at least five before I was that size," Pish said dryly. "Please give Queen our best wishes." The small people seemed to have little grasp of ranks or titles, or how they differed from personal names.

"I shall and I thank you for them. I've been wanting to speak to you. You and the others are doing very well. We've noticed a big improvement."

"We have reduced the numbers almost below the safety level," the gnome agreed, rubbing his hands to warm them. Pish was about Rap's age, although no taller than Eva, and he had even less nose than Rap did. Tush and the two women were younger. The gnome population of Krasnegar was certain to increase from now on, and that might bring new problems . . .

"What safety level?"

"If we kill off too many, they won't be able to keep up their numbers. Of course there are still plenty in the lower buildings, which you said do not belong to you."

"I can probably arrange for you to . . . er, work there, as well," Rap said, wondering how Krasnegarians were going to adjust to gnomes, or how he could persuade the gnomes to eliminate the rats and mice altogether.

"We already do," Pish said. "The big people are always willing to let us come in and remove the rodents for them."

"Well, that's great! The palace servants must have passed the word. You will have trouble getting around the town in this weather, though?"

"Not at all," the little man said smugly. "The tunnels serve very well and are quite warm."

Tunnels? Rap knew of no tunnels in Krasnegar. Then he realized that there must be sewers, although he had never thought of them before. His stomach lurched.

"Oh, that's good," he said quickly. "Any . . . er, anti-gnome feelings?"

The gnome chuckled. "They are so ignorant in this town!

They have never seen gnomes before! They treat us like real people and speak politely to us. They even give us money."

"Er, quite. Well, I'm glad I was able to help. There is one thing, though, Pish."

"What's that, King?"

"Cats. Not the cats, Pish."

"You do not need the cats now," the gnome protested, suddenly shrill. "Not when we are here to do the work!"

"Not for that, but a lot of people like cats around to . . ." Why did people like cats around? "They like cats."

"We like cats, too!"

"Not in the same way. And the dogs, also."

"Dogs we don't meddle with if they don't meddle with us."

"Good. But leave the cats."

"Oh, very well! I'll tell the others. What should we do with the money, King?"

"Hang on to it until you have a problem."

"What problems can gnomes have?" the little voice asked.

Before Rap could think of an answer, the gnome had gone. Nothing remained except a hint of a something in the air. Pity about that! Gnomes were fine people once you got past that. Rap had explained washing to them and they had promised to consider the matter—next summer or the one after. Certainly not in winter. Still, there were some day folk in Krasnegar not a whole lot better.

What problems could gnomes have?

What problems could a king have?

Sorcery, maybe.

He was starting to feel sleepy. He rose and began to pace through the echoing gloom of the castle. His castle. King Rap of Krasnegar! Even after all these years, he could not adjust to that. When the imperor wrote, he hailed Rap as his royal cousin.

Royal sorcerer.

He hated being a sorcerer and always had. He hated being able to manipulate people, or seeing people as toys, and to a sorcerer they were nothing more. Inos had destroyed his power once, but it had returned in part. He was not all-powerful, as he once had been, but he was still a sorcerer.

So he had found a way out. He had cast a magic shield around himself, like the invisible shield Inisso had cast centuries before over the whole castle. His powers were contained, then. He could neither sense with them, nor use them.

Of course no sorcerer could cast a spell too strong for his own powers to break, but Rap had restored his power only three times. Once for the twins, once for Eva, and tonight for Holi . . . He savored the thought again—new son, new joy.

And while the women had been washing the baby, he had put himself back in his bottle. Now he was mundane once more, a mundane king. Perhaps it was the memory of that brief glory that was making him so restless now.

Being a sorcerer was dangerous, of course. The use of power rippled the ambience and the greater the power used, the greater the distance at which it could be detected. The wardens, or indeed any more powerful sorcerer, might hunt down the user and imprint him with a loyalty spell. Over the years, the four wardens had all acquired votaries to serve them—Bright Water had dozens of them. Many sorcerers chose not to use their power for that reason, and probably many of them hid within the same sort of cloaking spell as Rap did. He had not invented anything new.

But the ethics of sorcery bothered him far more than the dangers. If he could ease his own wife's torment in childbirth, then why not other men's wives'? Why not cure the sick, repair fire damage, heal wounds? Why not reform the drunks, raise the dying, warn the sailors of the storm?

Why not be a God?

Where would it end?

And why stop at Krasnegar?

Once he had been offered a wardenship. He could have been warlock of the west, mightiest of the Four, judge and ruler of all Pandemia, greater even than the imperor. He had declined the honor, a decision he had never regretted.

That was a path that had no sane ending. Wardens lived for centuries, running the world for their private comfort and amusement. Fortunately he no longer had that option. He was not the demigod he once had been. Inos, oh, Inos! My love, my queen!

He had arrived at a door he almost never visited. So that was what was on his mind?

Why not? On impulse, he opened it. It creaked.

The little chapel was icy cold, but not quite dark. A smear of snow lay unmelted before the other door, blown in through invisible cracks by the arctic wind. On the table at the far end, a single lamp glimmered. The other lamp beside it was dark. One window showed a faint trace of moonlight; its partner was opaque and always black . . . the Good and the Evil—the Powers, whom even the Gods must serve.

He was not a praying man; not religious. He joined in the ceremonies Inos insisted were required of sovereigns, but only by going through the motions. He never opened his heart to the Gods. The one time he had spoken with Them, the discourse had not been amicable.

Amused to think how astonished his wife would be, he stalked up the aisle until he had passed all the pews and stood before the table. It was covered with a splendid silk cloth, he noted. Inos spent a fortune on such trivia, for some reason.

He went down on his knees. So much happiness! He bowed his head. *Thanks!* he thought. That didn't feel quite right, somehow. Self-conscious, he said aloud, "Thank you." A notable occasion! He had probably not spoken a true prayer to the Gods since his mother died.

"About time," a male voice said.

He overbalanced with shock and almost fell, steadying himself with a hand on the floor. He caught a momentary glimpse of bare feet blazing in splendor, bright as the sun and yet without heat, and then his eyes closed in watery agony. The image of those feet was still there on the insides of his eyelids, and he could still sense the brightness before him.

"You summoned me?" Anger mingled with his fear.

"Perhaps. Or you felt repentant. At least you came to give thanks, not demand favors. You came because you were happy, not because you were in need of something. We appreciate that. Be happy while you can, King Rap."

"Oh, of course!" he snapped. "You can't bear to see a mortal being happy, can You? Tonight my heart is overflowing, so You have to come and spoil it!"

He heard a sigh and when the voice spoke again above him it was female, sadly tuneful as an old lament. *"Time and advancement have not improved your disposition. Can you not give Us the benefit of the doubt just for once?"*

He squirmed, unable to think of an answer to that divine rebuke. He looked up, shielding his face with his hand and trying to open his eyes a hairsbreadth. Useless—one glimpse of that stabbing brilliance made them flood with tears. Yet the rest of the chapel was dark, untouched by the glory.

When the Gods spoke again, They were still in Their female aspect. *"Why do you not use your powers to help your people, King Rap? Why do you not divert storms from Krasnegar, fill the larders single-handed, stamp out disease? You could make your town a paradise."*

Had the Gods been eavesdropping on his thoughts?

"Is that Your command to me?"

"No. But We demand an answer."

"Because . . . Because I think I would produce a nation of idlers and degenerates! I should end up doing all the work and probably gain small thanks for it in the end, when everyone began taking my blessings for granted."

After a moment he added, "People value happiness by what it costs."

"Would they understand if you explained that to them?"

"Probably not," he admitted. "But I think they would

not be happier, in the long run. I really do have their own good at heart, I think."

Then he saw that mortals should not argue with Gods.

"And so it is with Us. We also must sometimes act or decline to act, from motives that you may not comprehend."

"I am sorry," he muttered.

For a moment the chapel was silent and he wondered if They had gone. He shivered as the cold bit through his garments. The floor was hard and cold on his knees.

"Then try to understand now. We bring a warning. You will have to lose one of the children."

No! No! No! Something seemed to grip his throat until he thought he would choke. "Which one?"

"It would be even more unkind to tell you that." A long sigh seemed to drift around the chapel like a lost soul.

"I suppose it would. But why tell me anything at all? Just to torture me? If I wanted to know the future, I could use my powers—foresight or premonition." At the moment all he could see was the green afterimage inside his eyelids. His eyes still hurt.

"But you do not use those powers! And in spite of your efforts to remain ignorant, you have already sensed the approach of evil."

"The year 3000?"

The voice became stern again and male, dark with overtones of power and duty. It thundered, yet it woke no echoes in the little chapel. *"That is part of it. The times were vulnerable and you blundered, Rap."*

"Me?"

"Yes, you! You interfered with the order of the world and because the millennia were poised, the consequences will be grave beyond imagining. Already the fabric trembles."

Rap had a low opinion of the Gods, but did he believe They would lie to him? Yes, he decided, They might if it suited Their purpose. Not all Gods served the Good. Or if they did, the distinction was not always evident to mortal eyes.

"What must I do?" he demanded angrily. He wanted to curse Them and he did not know how to curse Gods.

"Nothing," They said. "There is nothing you can do. You erred, and the least cost of that error must be one of your children."

"Take me! Take me instead."

"That may be necessary, also. The penalty may be much, much greater than We said. We cannot save you from the price of your own folly."

"Tell me what I must do! Anything! Anything!"

"Nothing. You will have happy days for a while. Cherish them as mortals should. And when the sacrifice is needed, try to understand that good intentions are never an excuse. Godhood is not all joy, Rap. Power brings sorrows as well as joys. You know that."

"Tell me!" he screamed.

This time there was no reply. The Gods had gone. Rap stayed there until he was almost frozen, begging on his knees or prostrate on the icy flags, but They did not return. The chapel stayed silent except for the echoes of his sobs and the wailing of the wind, and all his happiness had shattered into dust.

5

THE YEAR OF VICTORIES WAS ALMOST OVER; YLO WAS CARrying a white flag.

In three more days the world would celebrate Winterfest with dancing and feasting. He was walking to his death with a madman.

This should be a time of peace and merrymaking, but the God of War was still reaping. Many, many men would die before the year did.

Madness! Suicidal madness . . .

The light was failing and the rain had not let up all day; fine, cold, pitiless rain that fell straight down and soaked into everything. The air was gray. Thin mud made the trail treacherous underfoot, slapping up with every step, and Ylo was actually glad of his wolfskin hood, for the first time in . . . how long? . . . ten or eleven months? It must be that long since he had become signifer to this maniac, and this was the first time he'd truly appreciated the furry absurdity as a rain cover. As a sunshade, fine—he'd often been grateful for it as a sunshade. As a girl attractor . . . well, it did help there. And now it made a good waterproof, except that it smelled bad and seemed to weigh as much as it would if it still had a wolf in it.

The hillside was tufted with shrubbery and little copses, sinister, misty patches that might hide a hundred armed warriors and probably did. He held the flag in one hand and a lantern in the other, a yellow eye within a fuzzy corona of rain. Reflections sparkled from puddles as he led the prince imperial deeper and deeper into his own trap.

Ylo was convinced it was a trap. Back at the camp he had actually dared question his orders—an Imperial soldier did not do that very often and live. Madness to go alone to the rendezvous, he had said. The heir to the Opal Throne had no right to risk the future welfare of the Impire by such insane rashness.

A lesser man might have chopped off his head for insolence, but not Shandie. He had just shrugged and said quietly that it would be madness to trust anyone else in such circumstances, but elves spurned treachery once they had given their word. He had also said that Centurion Hardgraa would accompany him if Ylo did not want to. That had settled the matter, of course, as he had known it would.

And so here the two of them were, slithering and sliding down this Evil-spawned path across this doom-haunted hillside, heading for a vague speck of lamplight and a parlay.

Somewhere over the ridge behind them the legions shivered in their sodden bivouac—eating cold food, huddling inside wet clothes; and no doubt cursing fluently and vowing that someone was going to pay for this.

Somewhere over the ridge ahead was an elvish army,

probably doing all the same things and swearing all the same oaths.

Somewhere off to the right but invisible, the Qoble Range reached snowy ramparts to the roof of heaven. Doubtless the peaks would be a spectacular sight when the rain stopped, for those alive to see it.

And somewhere in the neighborhood lay the border between Qoble and Ilrane. Every few centuries the boundary moved. Qoble was a fragment of the Impire cut off by the mountains. A winter road around the western end of those mountains had been a priority of the imps since before history. Many times they had spilled a sea of blood to get one, but they had never been able to hold it for long, because the elves prized this miserable little tract of land, also, for aesthetic reasons.

On the maps the gap between the Nefer and Qoble ranges were marked as Nefer Moor. Perhaps it had been open country when it was named, but now it was mainly dense forest. Wooded terrain favored the nimble elves over the cumbersome legions, and yet all these weeks of marching in the rain had brought success at last. Shandie had cornered the elves brilliantly. This time they could not escape. The history texts listed seven Battles of Nefer Moor; the eighth would be a rout.

Rain and falling darkness and cold and mud.

"Is that a light ahead, or just mud in my eye?" Shandie asked at his back.

"It's a light, sir." The bait in the trap.

His tone must have revealed his thoughts, because Shandie said, "You still don't believe we can trust them, do you?"

"No, sir. I might trust them with anyone else, but you're too valuable."

A chuckle. "I'm worth more to them alive than dead, Ylo. One thing you must never do in warfare is create causes! Understand what I'm getting at?"

Ylo said, "No, sir," just as his foot slid on the slick grass and he flailed wildly off balance. He steadied himself with the flagstaff, feeling a dozen new trickles of icy water launch themselves down his skin. His sandals were sodden.

"This is just a sordid little border squabble," the prince said. "Politics and nothing more. The elves know that. But if they kill me, I become a martyr. They rouse the whole Impire to fury! Ilrane would be overrun from one end to the other. Worst thing they could do."

No one had ever accused elves of being logical before, so far as Ylo knew. And what if they took Shandie hostage?

"Why negotiate at all?" he asked. "You've got it all now! You've nailed their ears to the chopping block!"

The prince actually laughed, as if he were on a summer stroll, not a funeral march. "The second-best time to negotiate, Ylo, is when you know you can win. Gives you a chance to get it all for free. That's why we're here."

That wasn't what his commission required of him, though. Ylo had decoded those orders and he knew that they demanded *stern measures*. That was a nice way of saying that the imperor wanted a massacre or two. Take no prisoners! Teach the slanty-eyes a lesson! Emshandar would emphatically not approve of a parlay when the enemy was helpless.

Ylo couldn't say that. Shandie was a considerate and long-suffering commander, but Ylo could hardly throw the man's own orders in his face.

"What's first-best time to negotiate?" he asked.

"When you're certain to lose. Then you may salvage something, right? And that's why *they're* here!"

"Think they'll surrender . . ." Ylo asked, and added, "sir?" as he realized he was questioning a proconsul.

"I hope so. They should!" Shandie sighed. "I just hope they haven't gone into one of their suicidal sulks, that's all."

The elves' lantern was clearly visible now, sitting on a stump in an open glade. Two men stood beside it. How many hundreds lurked in the undergrowth, all around?

Ylo turned aside from the path, trudging through the long wet grass toward those two still figures. Tall and slim, they looked like boys, both bare-headed, with elvish curls shining in the rain as if they wore golden helmets. One of them held a white flag. Neither seemed to be armed.

Indeed, only one was wearing armor under his cloak and only chain mail at that. In the murky evening light, the colors of their garb were muddied and indistinct, but undoubtedly more somber than elves' usual riotous display.

This was a strange setting for a historical meeting! Ylo might feel proud of having a part in it, were he not so accursedly wet and cold. He strode to the stump and laid his lantern beside the other. Then he backed off a pace and planted the staff in proper military style. Shandie stood at his side. The elves watched in wary silence. Lit from below, their faces were cryptic masks of beaten gold, their oversize eyes sparkling in the ever-changing hues of opals.

Ylo had known a few elves back in Hub, long ago. He hadn't liked them much, although he had nothing really specific against them. There was no way to tell an elf's age, which was always disconcerting. They tended to be artistic people, absurdly impractical, but they could fight when they wanted to. History was littered with the bones of impish generals who had underestimated elves. He hoped Shandie was not going to be another.

The elf in the armor raised his hand in greeting. "Welcome, your Highness!"

The voice was high and sweet. Gods! A woman! Ylo glanced at her companion and decided that one was male.

"Greetings to you," Shandie said harshly. He removed his helmet, to be on equal terms with the opposition. He wiped his face with a wet arm. "I am Proconsul Emshandar, Governor of Qoble, Legate of the XIIth legion."

"I am Puil'stor, Sirdar of the Army of Justice, President of the Council for the Emergency, War Chief of Aliath Gens, Deputy Syndic and Presenter of Aims of Stor Clan, Exarch of Aniel Sept."

Under other circumstances, Ylo would have laughed at that gibberish, but he continued to play statue. He was only a decoration at this meeting, not a negotiator. The history books would not mention his name, unfortunately—unless, of course, he became famous later. *The prince, accompanied by the future Consul Ylo . . .* His fingers around the pole were growing numb.

"You have strayed outside your jurisdiction, Proconsul."

"That is what we are about to decide, isn't it?"

The elf laughed and the bell-like sound was an obscenity in such morbid surroundings. "Nicely put, Prince! Now, the evening is inclement, so let us be brief and begone. I have a song to study, one I would fain sing on the morrow."

It had better be a lament.

"You called for this parlay," she said. "What do you offer to earn our mercy?"

"I find your humor inappropriate," Shandie said. "I seek to avert bloodshed. You have seven thousand men—"

"Five. Two thousand are women."

"You have seven thousand warriors, then, and they are trapped. I have four legions at my back and two more at yours. The lake road is blocked. Your famed elvish archers are useless in this weather. Pardon the cliché, Sirdar, but you are at my mercy."

She did not dispute the facts. "And your offer?"

"I shall allow you to withdraw, upon your parole."

Having been expecting a demand for surrender, Ylo barely choked back a gasp. The imperor would have his grandson's head in a bucket for this!

The woman showed little surprise. She arched a shiny golden eyebrow. "Parole? What means that? And what happens after?"

"I ask only your word that all your warriors will disperse and return to their homes, until after Winterfest. They may keep their weapons. I shall occupy Fairgan, but I give you my word I shall go no farther. The valley of the Linder will be the border, as it used to be."

Shandie! The Old Man will make a doormat of your hide!

Puil'stor considered, putting her head on one side like a bird. "And if we refuse your terms?"

"My orders are to butcher you."

She rubbed her cheek with slender fingers. Ylo could not imagine her as a soldier, although common sense said she must be, and a good one. She was a looker, and under other circumstances he would have been planning an effort to advance his education in elvish matters.

"It's tempting," she said.

Tempting? She should have her words bronzed. It was insane generosity, that's what it was.

"Nothing you can do can stop me taking what I want," Shandie said. "I dislike unnecessary bloodshed, that's all."

"I suspect you have more scruples than you admit, Highness. You are a fine soldier. You outmaneuvered me splendidly. We elves always assume that imps are unimaginative. It is often our downfall."

"We frequently underrate the tenacity of elves."

"Of course the warden of the east has revealed all our secrets to you?"

Shandie hesitated. "Of course."

The sirdar smiled ruefully. Ylo wondered what Warlock Olybino was thinking of this parlay. He enjoyed bloodshed, that one, as long as "his" legions won in the end. He had appeared at least three times in Shandie's tent on this campaign and perhaps at other times, also, when Ylo had not been present.

Shandie was a superlative leader of men because he could inspire loyalty. Ylo knew that better than any. But Ylo knew also what perhaps no one else did—that the prince's reputation as a military genius rested entirely on the occult help he received from the warden of the east. Without Olybino, he would be only another legate.

So what was the warlock thinking of this meeting?

"I was afraid you might have some such offer to make," Puil'stor said sadly. "I was hoping, though, that the prince imperial might be a man of greater honor."

"Ma'am!"

"Your cause is flawed, Prince! This campaign was provoked by treachery."

"It certainly was not!"

Oh yes it was, Ylo thought.

"Come!" the elf said. "We are alone here. Let us be honest in the presence of death. There was no elvish attack on Fort Exern. The garrison was not destroyed by elves, but by Imperial duplicity. I suspect—I hope—that the bodies were those of common felons, for I wouldst not believe the Impire capable of—"

"What you are suggesting is not what was reported to me!" Shandie shouted. Ylo stole a sideways glance at him; the tricky light made his rain-washed face seem strangely haggard.

"You are not a simpleton!" The woman's voice was so inflected with tragedy and her face so rain-soaked that she might be weeping; it was impossible to know. "Tell me that you believe that trumped-up farrago?"

"I am a soldier, ma'am. I obey orders."

"You were not obeying your orders when you came here."

She was right, of course. She had guessed at Shandie's gnawing guilt, as Ylo had not. That was why Shandie had offered such extravagant terms. Ridiculous terms.

"Even if what you suggest were the case, Sirdar, I can do no more than I have already done. I can offer no more than I have already offered. Take your lives at my hand and go in peace, lest the Evil prosper more than It need."

Ylo had never heard Shandie's voice quaver like that before. He glanced at the second elf, the boy, but he was watching his leader intently and the uncanny underlighting threw a strange, unholy radiance on his golden features. *One of their suicidal sulks,* Shandie had said. Oh, God of Slaughter! Ylo hoped that it was the bite of the cold at his bones that was causing him to shiver so. The land would run with blood.

Puil'stor lowered her gaze to stare at the lanterns flickering and hissing in the rain. She wrung her hands. "Had you any trace of justice on your side, I should accept your terms gladly, for they are generous beyond belief. But I cannot acquiesce in the triumph of so perverted a cause."

Discipline forgotten, Ylo was frankly staring at Shandie and he saw the legate's features twist in pain.

"Ma'am, I beg you to reconsider."

She shook her head with a great sadness. "I shall not withdraw. Perform your slaughter, Prince Emshandar."

"This madness will gain you nothing."

"That may be, but we must all be true to the songs our souls sing. I shall proclaim that any who wish to accept your offer may do so, but I know that none will."

And if seven thousand elves fought to the last man, how many imps would die with them? God of Slaughter! The first casualty was going to be a certain signifer, frozen to death before the battle even started.

Shandie replaced his helmet. "Their blood is upon your head, ma'am."

"Nay, upon yours, for you ride a curséd road. What is conceived in evil must breed more evil." The sirdar paused and glanced at the boy beside her. "I would ask one favor, though."

"Ask!" Shandie said.

"Joal is a minstrel of renown. Let him accompany you tonight and pass freely from this field of sorrows, so that at least one witness may return to the tree of my ancestors and record our passing."

Shandie bowed his head. "If that is your wish."

What did a man feel when he was chosen as Only Survivor—unspeakable relief or utter shame? Ylo looked curiously at the boyish face, but it showed no expression at all. Joal must therefore be older than he looked. He might, of course, be as old as the imperor. One never knew with elves.

For a moment the only sound was the hiss of rain on the

grass. Then Joal said, "No!" His voice was a chord struck on a harp in a vaulted basilica.

The sirdar turned to him in dismay. "My love! For the children!"

He did not look at her; he was as unmoving as an Imperial sentry, although his knuckles were white on the staff of his flag. "No," he repeated.

She sighed and faced Shandie again. "Then our business is completed, Proconsul."

"You will not reconsider?" Shandie asked in a hoarse whisper.

The sirdar shook her head.

The parlay was over; Shandie saluted. The imperor would get his massacre, the Eighth Battle of Nefer Moor, and it would do him no good. He would have committed the error Shandie had warned of not twenty minutes ago—he would have created a cause.

"Dragons!" said a new voice.

Reflexes jerked Ylo back a step. He almost dropped the flag. His heart fell clear to his boots.

Another elf stood beside the other two. He wore a shimmering silver cloak and a jaunty cap. The glade was not yet dark enough for him to have approached unseen. He had not risen out of the grass.

Shandie also had recoiled a pace. Now he saluted, his face suddenly grimmer than ever.

"Will your legions fight *dragons*?" the newcomer demanded angrily.

He looked about fifteen. A dandy. A runt.

The past months had made Ylo very blasé about the Four, although he had met none of them except Olybino. He had studied what was generally known of them and collected a few confidential hints from Shandie. He knew that Olybino had been East for forty-four years, so he was a much older man than his occult demeanor suggested. He knew that the warden of the south was an elf and he had held the Blue

Throne for twice as long as Olybino had held the Gold. South must therefore be more than a hundred years old, and his prerogative was occult control of the dwindled population of dragons that still dwelt within Dragon Reach.

This kid looked to be about fifteen, but he was threatening Shandie with dragons. He was the warlock of the south.

Dragon Reach was not very far away—as a dragon flew.

May the Good preserve us!

"You know who I am?"

Shandie had recovered from the shock. "Warlock Lith'rian. I remember you."

The kid smiled contemptuously. "I should hope so! And I asked if you were prepared to fight dragons tomorrow?"

Ylo sneaked a look around, hoping to find Warlock Olybino. Lith'rian must be bluffing, surely? Certainly he could use dragons as a weapon if he wished—and no one else must—but not in this war! Not against the Imperial Army. The legions were sacrosanct. Even humble Ylo in his wet and smelly signifer's wolfskin was sacrosanct. Why, then, was the humble Ylo feeling so naked and mortal?

Shandie said quietly, "I rely on the Protocol to protect me from dragons, your Omnipotence."

"Then you will be disappointed! I am tired of this diet of blood the old monster craves in his dotage. I despise his warped methods and devious aims." The warlock looked at the woman. "I applaud the sirdar's decision! She shows us that there is still honor in the world."

She bowed. "Your Omnipotence honors me."

"You honor our race and the Gods. Help is on its way."

Dragons.

Ylo could barely stop his teeth from chattering. He hoped Shandie would understand that the cold and rain were doing that to him; that fear was only a small part of it.

"And what of the Protocol, your Omnipotence?" Shandie asked.

"What of it?" Lith'rian snarled. "You dare invoke its

name? You cosset it when it aids you and rape it when it doesn't!"

"I have done nothing to—"

"Legally, no! You stay within the letter and you foul the spirit. Emine never intended the Protocol to sustain such noxious ventures as yours."

Shandie straightened his shoulders. "I had nothing to do with whatever happened at Fort Exern. I have done my duty as a soldier until tonight. Tonight I exceeded my orders in an effort to spare men's lives. Women's, also."

"So you will feel better when you celebrate your triumph in Hub?"

The prince sighed. "I suppose so."

"And I ask you again if you are prepared to fight dragons?"

"Yes," Shandie said. "If I must. Tomorrow I will enter the valley of the Linder and occupy Fairgan, or I will die trying."

He meant it.

God of Madness! Now it was the imps who were turning suicidal.

Lith'rian adjusted the silvery cloak on his shoulders. It seemed dry, despite the rain. "I suppose you expect help from that playboy soldier in the yellow helmet? You think he will take care of my dragons for you while you savage the elves? I advise you not to count on him. Olybino has never been much of a sorcerer and he knows it. Don't count on him, Prince Emshandar. I invited him to this meeting. I invited him to my sector. *And he was too frightened to come!*"

"I am here now," Olybino said, appearing at Shandie's side.

Lith'rian sneered. "Not much of you."

The image of a giant young warrior was transparent. Rain was falling through him. "I am disinclined to trust a man who seeks to overthrow the rule of law. The Protocol is our shield and you will destroy it!"

The elf looked nauseated. "You pompous mirage! I say that the Protocol was designed to protect the world from the political use of sorcery and that you have been abusing it by turning that spotty-faced prince of yours into a world conqueror! I say that the Protocol does not justify such criminal fakery as Exern, nor the massacre your royal hero plans for tomorrow. You seek to buy his friendship so that he will take your part in the council when he sits on the Opal Throne."

Shandie drew breath as if to speak, then seemed to think better of it.

"Your elvish wits are muddled, as usual!" Olybino's voice held strange echoes, like shouting in a cathedral. "You know that the wheels of history begin to turn and the knell of the millennium is sounding. And what of the Covin, Brother? Never has there been greater danger, greater need for us to stand together. Call off your worms!"

"Call off your legions!" Lith'rian cried, his elvish treble as plaintive as the rain song in the forest night.

"You imperil the Protocol itself at such a time?" East boomed. "What folly is this, my brother of the south?"

"It is not I who imperils the Protocol, it is you who have perverted it! Your bronze bullies are a stain upon my lands—clean it up or I will burn it off!"

"You are crazy! You destroy us all!"

"Then be it so!" Lith'rian folded his arms in defiance.

What was going on here? Glancing around all the faces, Ylo could see nothing helpful in any of them. Sorcerers fought duels—according to the ancient tales—and the stronger destroyed or enslaved the weaker. They might call up armies of occult votaries and unleash hellfire and horror. The city of Ginlish was under a mountain now . . . But the principle behind the Protocol was that the four most powerful sorcerers in the world would regulate one another and together control all others. They had means to achieve consensus—why were they not being invoked? And East seemed to be hinting at even greater dangers. There were unexplained mysteries here. Just as his thoughts had struggled that far, Shandie put the question into words.

"My Lords, what of your associates? In such a grave matter, should not the Four take counsel together?"

"Ah!" Lith'rian said, never taking his eyes from the ghostly shape of Olybino. "As of this morning, we are but Three."

"The warden of the north is dead," the other warlock added.

Witch Bright Water had been centuries old, Ylo knew. Her departure was hardly surprising and probably not to be regretted, if half the stories about her were true.

Shandie whistled. "You have not yet appointed a successor?"

"Not yet." South's strange elvish eyes still watched East intently.

"Then the matter may be decided by a simple vote, surely? May I ask where the warden of the west is?"

"You presume far, Little Prince!" Lith'rian snapped, although he looked to be ten years younger than Shandie. "You are not yet imperor!"

"I make no claim to have rights in this! I am only trying to help."

"The mundane is wiser than we are, Brother South." Olybino's tone was as magisterial as ever, yet Ylo thought it concealed a whine of appeal. "Let us place our differences before our sister of the west."

Lith'rian scowled, pulling his cloak tight about him. His anger was directed at Shandie, but on him anger seemed too much like juvenile petulance. "Withdraw your legions, Princeling!"

"Your Omnipotence, I am sworn to obey my grandfather the imperor."

Flunky! The warlock spat the word. "Accomplice!" Then he faded away and there was only falling rain where he had stood. The grass there did not seem displaced.

"This has been an evil night's work!" Olybino said. "See

what your foolish scruples have wrought?" Then he also was gone.

The four mundanes stood alone in the sodden clearing— but had the warlocks ever been truly present? Darkness had settled in utterly, so that nothing was visible beyond the lamps' comforting glow, not even the treetops against the sky. Ylo had a strange sensation of awakening from a nightmare.

The sirdar made a wordless sound of relief. "Well!" She smiled grimly. "You chose a poor time to invade Ilrane, Prince!"

"Perhaps!" Shandie said. "I think Lith'rian is bluffing, though. Even if he is a match for the other two, he would be criminally stupid to abrogate the Protocol as he threatens. They will appoint a successor for Bright Water soon enough and restore the balance."

She shrugged. "Tomorrow we shall see who is bluffing and who is not, Highness. Until then—farewell!"

"Farewell, Sirdar. I still hope that you will change your mind and seek to promote the Good."

"And I hope the same of you, Proconsul."

"Let us go, Signifer," Shandie said.

The night was an opaque blackness, swallowing the lantern's feeble glow. Stumbling and slipping, Ylo led the way up the track, worrying about straying off the feeble path, worrying about falling and extinguishing the lamp . . . just worrying in general. And shivering. And feeling horribly insignificant.

His dreams of taking part in historical events were bitter memories now. The Four always got what they wanted, his father had said. A humble signifer had never been important in the sweep of strategy, and apparently a prince was of little more account when the wardens intervened. *Dragons?*

But now the Four had become the Three and the balance was overthrown. Without the Protocol to ban political use of magic, the world would be plunged back into the Dark Times, before Emine. Three thousand years of civilization would be overturned. War would again be fought with sorcery, with fire and earthquake—and with dragons.

"East was correct," Shandie said suddenly. "This has been an evil night's work. Was I wrong to offer mercy, Ylo?"

Ylo stopped in astonishment and raised the lamp to see his legate's face. "You are asking my opinion, sir?"

Shandie had halted, also. He rubbed his face with his hands—wiping his eyes or else concealing his expression. "I suppose I am. Give it."

"I . . ." Ylo almost panicked, trying to find words.

"Better keep moving," Shandie said, "else we freeze to death. Obviously you doubt."

Ylo began to walk again. "I am not qualified to judge, sir. No one is. 'Might have been' is a game for the Gods."

Shandie followed. "I think perhaps I was wrong. Had I demanded surrender, they would have spurned it, but they might have broken before our charge tomorrow and run. Now they will not. Had I not parlayed at all, they might have tried to break out and I could have let them go. By seeking to save all of them, I have condemned them all. Stubborn, yellow crackpots! Elves are the most twisted thinkers in all Pandemia. And I have angered the warlock of the east."

Ylo made a noncommittal noise and concentrated on finding the way. If Shandie needed to talk, then this was a safer place for him to unburden himself than in the camp, where ears abounded.

"Worse. I have made a bad enemy in South!"

Yes, that might be the nastiest wasp in the nest. History told of many imperors who had alienated wardens and paid dearly for it.

For a moment Shandie muttered inaudibly. Ylo walked on, watching the sparkle of reflections on the water that cascaded down the track in front of his boots.

"Sir? What's the Covin?"

"No idea," Shandie said absently. "Covin's a legal term for conspiracy."

"But . . ." Perhaps Ylo had misheard. He'd thought that Olybino had used the word. In fact, he'd even thought the warlock had used it as if it were the name of something frightening. Absurd! What could possibly frighten a warlock?

Shandie's mind was on other things. "Lith'rian thinks straighter than most elves, I think, Ylo. I shall resign my commission."

"Sir?"

"I don't know what has gotten into my grandfather lately. He was never a warmonger. He prided himself on being a man of peace. And this last year . . . My place is in Hub."

That was the most cheerful remark Ylo had heard for weeks. Yes, Hub would be a very pleasant change from this.

"The time for obeying orders may be past," Shandie said.

God of Mercy! What was he planning? That was not a good thought at all. Shandie had a daughter back in the capital, a daughter he had never seen. A daughter could carry on the dynasty if . . . if Shandie tried a rebellion and failed. *Good be with us!* Was he thinking of trying to usurp the throne? Ylo did not want to think such things. He did not want to hear such things. He had escaped the executioner's ax once by an eyelash.

"It's stopped raining!" he said loudly. "That's good!"

"No!" Shandie said. "That's bad. That's very bad. I was afraid that might happen."

6

THE RAIN HAD STOPPED. AS YLO AND SHANDIE WERE BEING challenged by the outposts, the wind was rising. By the time they reached the commander's compound, it was rushing along the lines of tents in noisy ripples and tearing the clouds off the stars.

The legions were on battle alert; there had been no fires since sundown. Rank had its comforts, though, and those included a couple of dim lamps and a charcoal brazier. Centurion Hardgraa was busily producing hot drinks for cold officers, having nothing better to do and being one of those perpetually active people Ylo could never understand. It was impossible to imagine that human lumberyard ever putting his arm around a woman and just relaxing. He fussed over Shandie like an armored hen, especially when they were in the field, where military procedures recognized no place for personal bodyguards. Relief flooded the centurion's gnarled face as he saw that his beloved prince had returned unharmed, but he said nothing. Instead he thrust out a branch with a tankard that steamed invitingly.

Shandie muttered thanks, passed the draft to Ylo, and waited for the next. That was typical Shandie.

The mug was wonderfully warm in freezing fingers, smelling of fragrant herbs. It tasted of spice and honey. Ylo burned his mouth and didn't care. He thought he could hear ice crystals crackling inside him as the hot stuff went down, and all the little hairs on his arms stood up in celebration.

The tent was filling up. Armor clinked. The air grew thick with the smells of wet leather, wet horsehair, wet men. Wet wolf, locally.

Shandie passed back his empty mug, glancing around the dim faces cramped in on all sides. The tent roof flapped loudly, which meant the ropes were drying out already and the wind was still rising. God of Mercy!

The proconsul spoke up then, in the harsh voice of authority. "Everyone here? Very well. I offered terms. They were refused." He paused, as if waiting for comment, or picking his next words with care. "So the plan remains the same, gentlemen . . . with two minor additions. First—no quarter."

One or two drew breath audibly. Perhaps it was just his imagination, but Ylo thought there was a change in the silence after that. Butchery was never popular, if only because it meant that the other side would not be taking prisoners, either.

The tent billowed and creaked.

"Second. There may be a change of plan, either before or after battle is joined. I am aware that we are facing a defeated, encircled, outnumbered rabble of elves, gentlemen. But there could be unexpected developments, is that clear? Whatever orders I send, *don't* write me a letter to ask if my signifer's been partying."

A few of the men chuckled, as he must have known they would.

"Something funny?"

Silence.

"You will not question any signal whatsoever! I hope there is no confusion over that? Then try to get some sleep, all of you. May the Good be with us."

Nicely done, Ylo thought—as always. Shandie had given as much warning as he dared. Of course he'd left the signifers exposed, no queries, no repeats. Ylo'd better not get his right hand mixed up with his left in this one.

The visitors departed, all but Legate Arkily of the XXVth. Ignoring him, Shandie began stripping off his armor and Ylo went to assist. It would all have to go on again right after, but a good toweling would help. Arkily was hanging around because he was second in command and therefore had the right to know everything Shandie knew.

But nothing in the world would start Shandie babbling lunacy about dragons, not even to Arkily.

During battle alert, Ylo slept on a cot in the commander's tent. Ylo could always sleep, even in damp chain mail in a rising gale on battle alert—it was a gift. He also had the ability to waken instantly, as he did when Shandie lifted the flap to look out, at first light.

The signifer raised his head and sniffed. Impossible! Then he was on his feet beside the proconsul, staggering slightly, shivering with dawn chill. Sniffing again.

"He's bluffing!" Shandie muttered furiously. "He wouldn't dare!"

It seemed as if the warlock would dare, though.

Rain had been falling for weeks, all over Nefer Moor. The streams were bank full, brown torrents. The trees, the grass, even the soil—they were all saturated, and yet the smell of woodsmoke was unmistakable. The elvish army lay to the west and the wind was out of the west. Ylo made an audible gulping noise as the implications fell all over him.

Shandie growled in frustration. "It's a bluff!"

Maybe it was. Maybe the fire was only an illusion. Maybe it was a real fire and had been started by mundane human hands, impossible as that seemed. But the only way to call that bluff would be to march a detachment of men into the blaze. If the Protocol still held, then no sorcery would harm them. The elves would, of course. Even mundane flames would.

If it wasn't a bluff, there were dragons between the two forces and the scouting party would be melted.

Dragons sought metal. Gold for preference, but bronze would do. Four legions in this camp—twenty thousand men in helmets and chain mail, with swords and shields, officers in cuirasses . . . several hundred tons of metal. A dragon would go insane on a single taste of metal, and waste the countryside.

"If there are dragons out there," Ylo mumbled through a sour, dry mouth, "can he keep them under control? Can even a warlock keep them under control?"

"That's what we'll have to discover, isn't it?"

And Shandie was the sort of commander who might think to put himself at the head of the First Cohort and investigate in person. If he did that, Ylo would be lead man.

That might get his name in the history books.

If there were any more history books.

Drumbeats throbbed through the camp and armored men poured from the tents into the half-light. Even seasoned campaigners woke easily on the morning of a battle, and it was no secret that the legions had brought the elves to bay at last. The weeks of marching in circles on Nefer Moor were over.

Reveille was the worst time of the day for Ylo, when all his varied responsibilities seemed to scream for his attention at the same moment. He had to attend to his own toilet, dress himself, help Shandie with his armor, see that the necessary signals were being issued, and wrestle a dozen lesser snakes before he could even give a thought to breakfast. The most important task of all was the trooping of the standards. All the lesser signifers of cohort and maniple brought their own standards to be blessed, as well, but it was Ylo who saluted the Gods each dawn, Ylo who swore that the legion would serve the Good—a commitment that he always felt should more fittingly be made by the legate who would give the orders. In this camp, he was senior of four legionary signifers and everything took four times as long.

The bunting on the standards snapped impatiently in the gale. Halfway through the invocation, he began to cough. His eyes had been tingling for some time. In the distance, horses were screaming in terror. Wet wood generates much smoke.

He was facing northwest, toward Hub. He could see the snowy majesty of the Qobles out of the corner of his eye. They were even more spectacular than he had expected. He could detect very little but smoke to his left, but at times he was sure there were flickers of fire visible there now—no dragons in sight yet, thank the Gods! He could hear the roar of flames, hear trees exploding in the heat. That soggy glade where he had met the warlocks might be ablaze already. *Cough!* He was many days' march into a forest and downwind from an inferno.

He had been worrying about the dragons themselves. He had forgotten the intense heat a dragon gave out.

Cough!

"Signifer!"

Ylo blinked tears away and spun around in astonishment. To interrupt the invocation of the Gods was a major break in discipline, whatever else it was, and not something he would have expected of Shandie. "Sir?"

"Strike camp!" the prince commanded, and then he, also, was convulsed with coughing.

Ylo grabbed the standard from its socket and made the signal. Legates and tribunes and signifers were running already.

The warlock had won.

Shandie strode back to his tent with a face black as a cave. Perhaps, like Ylo, he was wondering how many days' march lay between the legions and the edge of Nefer Moor. True, not all the Moor was heavily wooded, but most of it was. Forest fires traveled at night, as well as by day.

Would Warlock Lith'rian offer quarter, or would the elf do to the imps what they had planned for the elves?

A runt. He had looked about fifteen.

The roar of flames was quite audible now, the fire visible. Whole trees were exploding into flame. Where was Warlock Olybino?

Shandie charged into his tent and headed for the chests where the secret documents were kept. He threw up the lid and then began to cough again. Even within the tent, the smoke was thick enough to see.

He turned to Ylo. "Get a bugler!" Ylo ran, almost colliding with Centurion Hardgraa as he led up the proconsul's horse. Despite its blindfold, it was struggling and thrashing, insane with terror. Normally a horse wrestling Hardgraa would be an interesting match to watch.

Striking camp in a gale was never easy; it was impossible in a choking fog of woodsmoke. The mules were as terrified as the horses and could not be loaded. Shandie probably recognized the inevitable as fast as any man there and admitted it much sooner than most commanders would. He abandoned the baggage, called for column of route. Even then he was too late.

Withdrawal became retreat. Retreat became rout.

The flames were coming faster than a man could walk; the smoke alone was a killer. Before the dull red sun was clear of the horizon, four legions had been reduced to a panic-stricken rabble, fleeing eastward. Time and again men found their way blocked by flooded streams. Time and again men crested a safely grassy hilltop only to see fingers of fire already curling into the valley ahead. Some claimed to have seen dragons, but the claims were doubted—in that brutal smoke, a man did well to see his own boots. Whatever was making the forest burn, the fire alone was enough to save the elves.

No Imperial Army had faced sorcery since the War of the Five Warlocks. The casualties were surprisingly few, but the survivors staggered back to Qoble in tatters, a starving mob half crazed by terror. The other two legions were attacked by the elves under Sirdar Puil'stor and driven from Ilrane with heavy losses.

The Seven Victories had been followed by a crashing defeat. For the first time in nearly a thousand years, the Protocol had failed the legions.

Voices prophesying:
> *And 'mid this tumult Kubla heard from far*
> *Ancestral voices, prophesying war!*
> —COLERIDGE, *KUBLA KHAN*

CHAPTER FOUR

DESTINY OBSCURE

1

THE GAIB PLACE, ON THE WESTERN FLANKS OF THE PROGISTE Mountains, was known to everybody as one of the best there was. It had its own spring, which failed only in the driest of summers, and it was tightly enclosed by steep slopes on three sides. The only way to it was along a path winding through the plantation of coffee trees that Gaib tended so carefully. The Place also grew beans and pumpkins, sweet potato and bananas, corn and melons and a thousand other things—more variety than any other Place in the district.

The only fault the neighbors could ever find with the Gaib Place was its isolation, for there were no other Places within a quarter day's walk. In Thume that was a very unusual criticism. Pixies were a shy and reclusive people, prizing privacy above all else.

The very center of the Gaib Place was marked by a gnarled gray boulder about the size of a chair. When Gaib and Frial had built the first room of the cottage, they had enclosed that boulder within it, because it marked the exact spot where they had consummated their joining and thereby consecrated the Place to be their dwelling ever after. As Gaib had added other rooms around it, that one had remained their bedchamber. They slept there always, on a fragrant heap of fern fronds, laid on the packed clay floor. Such was the way of the pixies.

As their family had grown, the cottage had eventually sprawled out into an untidy collection of four rooms. The construction was skimpy and patchy even by local standards, for Gaib was much more inclined to nurture trees than to cut them down and he had tried to make do with deadfall as far as possible. The poles of the walls were too narrow to hold chinking properly and the shingles leaked in the rainy season. So the cottage was nothing much, but it was a good Place.

Gaib and Frial were distant cousins. Their family was recorded as Gifted, but that had never been a problem for them. Gaib had an undoubted talent for green things. When Gaib planted something, it grew. Some of that was experience, which he would share when asked. He could explain with great patience how one must transplant a coffee seedling with its taproot straight, else it would die before it even flowered, but sometimes his success was inexplicable, uncanny. The neighbors joked that Gaib could talk a sick tree better, or make an old ax handle sprout and bear fruit.

Frial had Feeling, which was both a blessing and a curse to her and might explain why she had accepted a Place so remote from the clamor of others' emotions.

Despite their respective abilities, neither she nor Gaib had ever been recorded as having Faculty, nor any of their ancestors, either, as far back as the great-great-grandparents they had in common. Oral traditional could reach no farther than that, but the recorders insisted that the family was Gifted.

Three children they had reared there. Feen, their son, had gone off in his time and found a Place of his own amid the cedar groves of Kestrel Ridge, and found a good woman to share it with him. Sheel, their older daughter, had toyed with several suitors until her easy-tempered childhood friend Wide had taken her to see a fine spot he had discovered some two days' walk to the north. She had accepted him there. Frial and Gaib saw little of Sheel now, but she was known to have at least one child.

Now only Thaïle remained at home. She was fifteen, gangly and awkward yet, but a loving, lovable girl, a joy to her aging parents. A year ago Thaïle had kept Death Watch for Phain of the Keez Place and had received her word. That was when fear had entered their lives for the first time.

The rainy season was almost over. Winter still ruled the high country, but the cool season was the most pleasant part of the year in Thume. The day was sunny and calm, although storm clouds hid the palisade of the Progistes, that comforting barrier against the terrors of Outside. The aromatic scent of coffee blossom had gone now, but there was a rich sort of greenish, growing feel to the air around the Gaib Place. Pigeons were purring tenderly to each other.

Gaib had killed a pig that morning to replenish the dwindling larder. He sat on the bench by the door, enjoying the sunshine and scraping the porker's skin with a split rock. Frial was making sausage in the tiny kitchen.

She came out carrying a bowl of offal and took it across to tip in the midden pit. Chickens rushed over to investigate the treat; they began games of grab and chase. As she came back, Frial stopped suddenly and stared off to where the path wound away into the trees. A shadow seemed to fall over her, although the rest of the clearing was filled with sunshine.

Gaib said nothing, for he was a slow-spoken man, but he ceased his work on the hide and watched. She was still a fine woman in his eyes, although younger men might have remarked on her thickening body and the streaks of gray in the nut-brown hair tied tight about her head. Her woolen robe she had woven herself, the wool having come in trade from a neighbor in return for coffee. It was a dusty brown shade, coffee colored.

Her chin was not as pointed as it once had been, or her neck as slender. The face that had once glowed with the innocence of spring dew had creased into lines of sadness as she aged, but that was the price of having Feeling—to sense the darknesses that lurked within everyone she met, as well as the joys and loves. Despite that burden, she was a happy-spoken person and still eager on the ferns beside the boulder.

She came hurrying back to the door. "I think I shall go to the Feen Place," she said a little breathlessly. "Take them a hock and perhaps some ribs."

Her eyes said more, then she glanced again at the path.

"You will not make it back by dark," Gaib said softly.

"You remember to coop the chickens, then!" She vanished into the cottage.

Gaib frowned and continued his work on the hide. In a remarkably few moments, Frial came bustling out with her warm cloak on, and shoes, and a bonnet still untied. She had a basket on her arm. She bent to kiss his forehead and he reached up and touched her with the back of his wrist, which was clean. She scurried across to the trees and disappeared. She would double around to the path when she Felt it was safe.

Trouble coming. He rose and tossed the hide up on the roof for safety. Then he went to the spring to wash the blood off his hands—noticing, as he so often did, that the water seemed warmer in winter than it did in summer. He liked to think that was a secret sign of approval from the Gods, a private little blessing on the Place.

He strolled back to the door and seated himself on the bench to await the unwanted visitor's arrival. Meanwhile, he could listen to the whisper of the leaves and the remarks of birds passing through, hunting nesting sites.

He did not know who the visitor would be. Frial would not, either, but clearly she had Felt unwelcome emotion on its way and they could both make guesses. There was an elderly widower who had lascivious ideas about Thaïle; there were a couple of grouchy old women. None of those normally inspired Frial to quit the Place and none would likely come calling at this hour on a winter's day at the dark of the moon.

Gaib never considered the possibility of violence or danger. He owned nothing worth stealing except perhaps food, all of which he would willingly share with a stranger. Any pixie would know that and none would outstay a welcome.

The visitor came into sight on the path—a man, tall and slim, striding with an easy, youthful gait. His jerkin and pants were green, as was his broad-brimmed hat; his cloak was brown with fur trim. He bore a recorder's satchel slung on his shoulder. That was what Frial had feared, of course.

He stopped and looked around the Place before addressing the owner. "Goodman Gaib?"

Gaib bowed awkwardly. He had spoken with recorders maybe five times in his life and felt ill at ease with them. "I am Gaib and welcome you to the Gaib Place."

"I am Jain of the College."

Gaib tendered the bench, or food, or refreshment. The newcomer accepted only the bench and a dipper of water. He praised the Place, as was to be expected, but briefly. He chose the far end of the bench, where he would not bloody his boots with the results of the pigskin scraping; he removed his hat and laid it beside him, revealing curly brown hair and ears as pointed as Gaib's own.

"Please sit, Goodman Gaib. You will forgive me if I go

at once to our business? You will forgive me also if I mention that your Place is far from my planned path. I envy you the solitude, of course, but I hope to return to the Grike Place by sundown."

That was a long way, Gaib rejoined politely, repeating his offer of hospitality for the night. He salted his words with a hint of reproof at the unseemly impatience of youth.

"I hope that will not be necessary." Jain's eyes were less slanted than most people's, amber colored and very bright. He smiled at his host for a moment, then tugged the satchel around to his lap and unlaced the cover.

Gaib knew that recorders were supposed to have strange powers, but he was not a worrying man. He waited placidly. Jain produced papers and perused them. Reading, that was called.

"I do not wish to disrupt your family life any more than needs must, but it would speed our talk if Goodwife Frial and the child Thaïle could join us." Again the bright amber inspection . . .

"My goodwife has gone to visit our son and his family."

"Ah? She left long ago?"

He was pushing a little too hard, even for a recorder. Gaib considered the question for a while.

"Some time ago. I don't know if she'll be back before tomorrow."

Jain nodded thoughtfully, pursing his lips tight enough to make grooves in the youthful smoothness of his face. "And the child?"

"She shouts when we call her a child. Loudly."

"Come, now! I am sure you bring up your children to be more respectful of their elders than that." The recorder took another look at his bundle of papers. They were shabby and well worn. "Not much over fifteen. Well, I shall be considerate of her feelings when we speak."

"She went wandering off around lunchtime," Gaib said truthfully. Thaïle might well have left for the same reason as her mother had; her Feeling had a much greater range.

"She did not say where she was going. It is possible that she, also, has gone to visit someone."

That last remark was so unlikely that it could be classed as a lie, and lying to recorders was unwise. The visitor was obviously trying to overawe him with his education and his wisdom. Gaib was very glad that the women had left. This was man's business.

"You know what children are," he added. "Always rushing off to call on one another."

"A moment ago you told me she was not a child any longer."

"I said she did not think she was, sir. Not that I did not think so."

Oh, this smart-aleck youngster thought he was very grand, with his important satchel and his College ways. Maybe he did know a lot of things and maybe he even had occult powers, but had he ever skinned a pig, or delivered piglets, or laid out coffee to dry in the sun? Had he ever built a home or raised children? Ever buried a baby? What was he compared to a real man, a loving father, a provider? Had he ever planted a crop of anything?

Gaib could tell if a melon was ripe without cutting it open, and he had never met anyone else who could do *that*.

The recorder sighed, staring across the clearing to where a rooster had just emerged from the undergrowth near the midden pit. It looked up from its foraging and began strutting purposefully toward him. When it drew near, he held out a hand at knee level. The bird hopped up on his wrist and cocked its head to study him with an eye as bright and yellow as his own. He stroked the shiny mahogany feathers of its breast. Then it jumped off and streaked away in alarm, wings spread and head out in front, appalled at what it had just done.

Jain turned his gaze back on Gaib.

The afternoon seemed much colder than it had before that demonstration. Gaib could not recall having felt so uncomfortable in many years. Perhaps never.

"Where is she?" the visitor asked.

"Up the hill, I expect."

Jain frowned and raised his eyes to the encircling banks. Gaib thought of the rooster, his heart beating fast.

"A long way!" the recorder muttered. "A very long way!"

He stuffed the papers back in the satchel.

"A year ago she kept Death Watch for a woman named Phain."

"Yes, sir."

"Her grandmother."

"Great-grandmother."

"Of course, forgive me." The recorder looked annoyed at his slip. "It is unusual to assign a relative for a Death Watch. A Watch is hard enough on a child without that."

"She and her mother just happened to be visiting relatives nearby." Gaib tried to make the matter seem unimportant. "When the old crone began to fail, there was the usual hunt for a suitable Watcher and she was the only one close. There are few Gifted families in the district. None of them had a child of the right age, except one boy, and he had already gained a word."

Jain smiled. The smile was curiously sinister. "She *just happened* to be visiting? Whose idea was the visit?"

"I . . . I do not recall. It was a year ago."

"You are quite sure you do not recall?"

"Quite sure. Her mother's, I expect." In spite of the chill, Gaib was sweating. Why did such trouble have to enter his life now, at his age? What had he done wrong? He thanked the Gods every morning for Their blessings; he aided the old and the sick as he could. He wondered if Thaïle was Feeling his fear, in her secret place, far away up the hill. He wondered if Jain could Feel his very thoughts. Lying to recorders was unwise. Everybody knew that.

"And what talent did she manifest when she had been told the old woman's word of power?"

"Nothing special, or we should have sent word to the

College, of course. We would have sent word. I mean, if she had displayed any Faculty."

"We judge who has Faculty!"

"But . . . Of course, sir."

"What talent?"

"She seems to have her mother's knack of Feeling. Not as strong, though!"

"Ah? Not as strong?"

"No. Not nearly as strong."

Jain shook his head in bored disbelief. He pulled out his papers again and rustled them, like a snake rustling on dry leaves. "Goodwife Frial has a borderline Faculty—her talent is well developed. You have traces. Seeing the fertility of your Place, even in winter, I wonder if your ability was underestimated. Green thumbs are hard to gauge. The word is weak."

"Weak? Word? I don't understand."

The recorder closed his eyes as if repeating a lesson to a very dull child. "Almost everyone has some talent or other, some ability. A few have more than one. Tell such a person a word of power and that talent is raised to the level of genius."

"Only if he has Faculty," Gaib said stubbornly.

The amber eyes flicked open. "No. Not normally, Goodman Gaib. It is true in your experience, I admit, but only because the words you are aware of are all very weak. Each one is known to a great many people and thus its power is very diluted. Spread thin, you see. Surely you were taught this?"

"I must have forgotten."

"Mmm? Just a stupid peasant? I think you underestimate me, and that is truly stupid. But it is true that these words rarely produce much effect. We call them 'background' words and we keep track of them very carefully. Because they are weak, when they do augment a talent, then we can assume that the person involved has Faculty, a Gift for magic itself. Otherwise, the effect is negligible, I agree. It is curious that your daughter *just happened* to be in the area when the woman Phain was about to die."

It had not merely been curious, Gaib thought, it had been disastrous.

The recorder stuffed the papers back in the satchel and began lacing it up. With relief, Gaib decided the man was leaving. The next remark stopped his heart.

"At the Vool Place, I was told that your daughter Felt a battle in progress Outside, beyond the mountains."

"That was right after the old woman died, my daughter had never seen death before, she had just discovered a talent she did not know about, she was hysterical, she was imagining . . ." He was babbling like a child.

"There was a battle."

The Good preserve us!

The recorder had known everything, all along.

Jain stretched his legs, folded his arms, leaned back against the wall of the cottage, relaxed—and smiled thinly. "The Keeper knew of the battle, of course. And your daughter did. Only those two, in all Thume. And you tell me that her Feeling is weaker than her mother's?"

Gaib said nothing, watching his hands rub together, hearing his skin making raspy noises.

"I trust that you are loyal to the Keeper, Goodman Gaib?"

"Of course," Gaib said hoarsely.

"Perhaps you have forgotten your catechism? Let us see if you can remember it. Stand up. No, hands behind you. Head up, back straight. That's better. Now, Goodman Gaib. *What lies Outside?*"

"Death and torture and slavery."

"Who waits Outside?"

Gaib was a child again, standing before his father. "The red-haired demons, the white-haired demons, the gold-haired demons, the blue-haired demons, and the brown-haired—"

"Wrong!"

"The dark-haired demons."

"Right. *How do the demons come?*"

"Over the mountains and over the sea."

"Who defends us from them?"

"The Keeper and the College."

"Whom do we serve?"

"The Keeper and the College."

"Who never sleeps?"

"The Keeper."

The recorder gathered his long legs and rose, clutching his satchel. He donned his hat. After a minute Gaib raised his eyes and met that bright gaze. He felt very small and stupid. And frightened.

"I shall go and talk with your daughter now. I judge that she has Faculty. You will send her to the College before her sixteenth birthday. This is your duty to the Keeper and the College."

God of Pity! Gaib mumbled something.

"I beg your pardon?"

"Yes, sir."

"And how do you keep her until then?"

"Away from death."

"Correct. Look at your left hand."

Gaib obeyed. His hand was shaking as he had never seen it shake before, but that was not what mattered. Although he had felt nothing, the third and fourth fingers were now grown together. He cried out and tried to separate them. Then he tried with his other hand, but they had become one broad finger with two nails.

"You must blame your own stupidity," Jain said in a sad, weary voice. "I don't enjoy mutilating people, but you need a reminder of where your loyalty lies. Forget it in future and you will have to suffer such worse."

He brushed past Gaib as if he were a bush and strode across the clearing, heading away from the path, toward the hill. In a moment he had vanished amid the trees on the slope.

Gaib ran into the cottage and found his metal knife, the one he killed pigs with. He tried to push the point between the two halves of that hideous finger, but he found bone there. By the time he had made sure it was bone all the way across, the grotesque double finger was hurting and bleeding a lot. He wrapped a scrap of cloth around it.

He went through to his Place beside the boulder and threw himself down on the heaped fern fronds. He pulled the blanket up, covering even his face, and just lay there, curled small and shivering. He wished Frial were beside him, holding him.

2

IT WENT WITHOUT SAYING THAT ALL PIXIE CHILDREN HAD secret places of their own. Thaïle had shared a family secret place with Feen and Sheel, which they had shown her as soon as she was old enough to keep the secret, and another they took their friends to when they came to visit. She also had one of her own. She even knew now where Sheel's secret place had been, now that her sister had departed, and it was not *nearly* as good as her own. She had never discovered Feen's place, but boys were supposed to be better at finding good places than girls were. So Feen had told her, anyway.

As a small child she had changed her secret place several times as she had ranged farther afield and grown more discriminating, but her final choice had lasted her for several years and she did not expect to change it before she went away to a real Place and a man. In fact, a year or so ago she'd thought her days of playing childish hiding games were over. Then she'd learned a word of power and nothing had been quite right after that.

Hours ago she had Felt an unfamiliar mind coming closer

to the Gaib Place. Contempt, she had Felt, and a sort of stern anger. Frightened, Thaïle had slipped away from the cottage and hurried to her secret place. She had been there a long time.

Her place was halfway up a green cliff, in among the largest trees. You climbed a shabby old eucalyptus, crawled out on a wide branch, and scrambled across to the top of a big mossy rock. Then you squeezed between the two rocks it was leaning against and ducked under a massive dead trunk and you were there. The secret place itself was as large as one of the rooms in the cottage, a strangely angled grotto of flat, smooth rocks lined with moss and creepers. Most of it was open to the forest canopy, but there was a wide overhang to sit under when the rain came and a nook to store precious things in.

There she kept a stuffed dragon her mother had made for her ages ago, which had been her special favorite companion when she was small, some extra-beautiful pebbles she had picked up from time to time, strings of melon seeds to wear as necklaces, a man's elbow carved in stone, several bright snail shells and even brighter fragments of pottery, some bronze rings that must have been links in a soldier's armor once and were all green now but probably quite valuable, a half-finished feather hat, and a couple of lopsided baskets she had made herself.

Lately she had added a rolling pin and a well-polished bowl made from a gourd. Gaith had given her the bowl and Shoop the pin. She had given them her most gracious thanks in return. Gaith was bearable, so he'd also gotten a kiss, but Shoop hadn't, because he wasn't.

In the very safest, darkest corner, carefully wrapped in banana leaves, she hoarded some scraps of leather, a right-hand glove and the beginnings of a left-hand glove; also a needle and some thongs. A year ago she'd been hoping she would find the courage to give the finished gloves to Phoon, who was as old as her brother; he had a wonderful laugh and bulgy muscles in his arms, but then Phoon had found a

Place and offered it—and himself—to some girl he'd met on his explorations. She'd accepted both, so Thaïle's gloves had never been finished. Another day, some other boy . . .

And about this time last year, Thaïle had kept Death Watch for Grammy, because the family was Gifted. So she had learned the old woman's word of power. That had brought her Feeling and Feeling had spoiled everything.

It was bad enough here at the Gaib Place, remote though it was. She could Feel what everyone in the district was feeling—love, anger, happiness, boredom, and stranger things, too. To go and visit the neighbors' Places was torment, because the Feelings were stronger at close quarters, and she could not help but learn to recognize each person's own Feelings. That made it all worse. Even from here, she knew when Looth made love to his wife, or Heem raged at his children. Sometimes at night she would be wakened by thunderclaps of passion from her father in the next room. They terrified and disgusted her, although they were not so nauseating as the underlying slithery hypocrisy of her mother's acceptance. She'd always thought her mother was the loving one and her father stolid.

Behind all the Feelings of the district lay a never-ending murmur of thousands of other Feelings from far away. Sometimes she thought she could Feel the whole world, all the people of Thume, and all the demons who lived Outside, as well.

Today she had Felt the stranger coming and had run up to her secret place and crouched there for hours. She'd Felt her mother's alarm begin when she'd detected the approach of the unknown, also. And then her father's lower, slower emotions had turned to alarm, too.

Her mother must have gone away, because her feelings had faded even as the stranger's grew stronger. Thaïle had wished then that she had done what Frial had likely done, heading over the ridge to visit the Wide Place, or the Heem Place, or somewhere. She should not have stayed here at all.

By the time her father's sudden terror struck, she had

become too paralyzed to do anything except hunker down as small as she could, like a baby bird in its nest. Then the stranger's spite and anger had stopped abruptly, cut off all at once. That had been almost worse, because after that she could not place him—she was quite certain, somehow, that it was a man who was visiting the Gaib Place and he was still there.

After a little while, she Felt *pain* from her father, real pain. She whimpered in sympathy. She had never known Gaib to react like that, even when he'd dropped the log on his toe last month and limped for days. No, no! What was the stranger doing to him? She began to pray—to the God of Places, the God of Mercy, the Keeper . . .

Without warning, a blast of amusement surged over her, very strong, very close. Someone was laughing. Someone was extraordinarily happy about something. Her terror faded before it and she discovered that she was starting to smile in sympathy. Whatever could be so incredibly funny?

"Thaïle!" cried an unfamiliar voice, not far off. "Thaïle, come out wherever you are!" The voice was full of the same laughter she had been sensing.

Obviously it was the stranger, although how he could have come up from the cottage so quickly she could not imagine. He no longer Felt dangerous at all; the contempt and anger were all gone now. There was only that wonderfully reassuring hilarity. If she didn't go out to him, then he might come looking for her. He was probably a sorcerer and could find her secret place if he wanted to. So there was no use refusing him.

Thaïle wiped her eyes with the backs of her hands, ran fingers through the tangle of her curls, and scrambled under the fallen tree that barred the exit—all legs and arms, like the climbing frog her mother called her sometimes.

He was a slender, lanky man in green, sitting on a brown blanket, which he had spread in a sunlit spot below an airy acacia tree. He was laying out things on the blanket, and she stood behind a bush for a moment to watch. She saw plates and bowls, but she could not see where he was getting them from. The blanket, she realized, must be a cloak, for it had a fur collar and very few blankets had collars. She could feel a snigger coming on, like a need to sneeze.

He raised his head and looked right at her. He waved an arm cheerfully. "Come on! I'm not going to hurt you!"

Grinning shyly, she walked through the trees to his patch of brightness. He was really quite good-looking, she decided, with curly brown hair and extremely pointy ears. His clothes were beautiful and his smile melted all the prickly fears inside her.

"Sit down, Thaïle. I'm Jain of the College."

"You're a sorcerer!" She ought to be frightened out of her wits. She wondered why she felt so happy instead.

He grinned. "Not quite. I'm only a mage—but that doesn't matter just now. I expect you're hungry? I know you're hungry! So am I. How about some icy-cold orange juice to start with?"

She sat down, tucking her legs as far out of sight as she could, because they were all scratched and dirty, and very skinny legs anyway. Her frock was torn and full of burrs. She drank from the shiny metal cup he gave her. It was astonishingly heavy. She wondered why she could not Feel anything from him, being so close, but all she sensed was that bubbling, laughing amusement, the sort of happiness you want to share with someone else. That was all. Funny! Most men put out scary *want-you* Feelings when they were near her, even quite young boys; and most male adolescents were unbearable at close quarters now, because of that. Although she hated to think of it, she Felt that *want-you* even from Wide, her sister's man . . . and even her own father sometimes had traces of it. It was a man thing men couldn't help, she'd assumed. So either this Jain sorcerer was not a normal man at all, or he was capable of hiding his real feelings from her.

"You can speak, can't you?"

"Yes, sir. I'm sorry."

He looked at her squarely. "Call me Jain. I want to be friends and you have absolutely nothing to fear from me. I'm a recorder, from the College. I'm not a monster. Not a freak. Just an ordinary sort of man. I have a Place of my own and a goodwife who shares it with me and I'm not going to do anything nasty at all. All right?"

If he had a Place of his own, then why wasn't he at home in it, growing something, as a man should?

"What did you do to Gaib?" she muttered.

Jain's bony face grew sad. "He lied to me, Thaïle. He knew I'm a recorder, yet he told me lies. That's forbidden by the Blood Laws, you know."

She nodded dumbly, aware of tiny veins of fear within her wanting-to-laugh feelings.

"I punished him a little. Don't worry; he'll be all right. You won't lie to me. And I won't lie to you. I have to tell you some things. But first, eat up!"

She looked over the dishes he had laid out and her mouth began watering so hard that she couldn't have spoken anyway. There were bowls of fruit, steaming rice, juicy pork chops, bright vegetables—plus all sorts of other things she couldn't even identify. She stared at them, unable to believe that all this was just for the two of them.

Jain was watching her with a wry smile. "Don't know where to start, do you? Look, just for fun, try this first. It's cake and I don't suppose you've ever tasted anything like it in your life."

Cake, Thaïle decided quickly, was perfect bliss. She began to eat as if she had not eaten in a year or more.

Jain himself nibbled on a fig, although it had to be a sorcerous fig at this time of year. It was all sorcerous.

"You eat," he said pensively, "and I'll talk. First, I have to tell you some history. Maybe you've heard this, maybe not. Doesn't matter. This lovely land of ours is called Thume, right? It lies between two lots of mountains—those up there, the Progistes, and the Qobles, far away. It has sea on the other two sides—big, big water. Over the mountains and over the seas live other people. You've heard of the red-haired demons and so on. Well, they're not really demons, they're just people, but they're very violent people, most of them."

She nodded with her mouth full, to show that she was listening. Jain would be better looking if his eyes had more slant to them, she thought.

"You Felt one of their battles, didn't you?" he said. "Yes, I know about that. Don't worry! The Keeper knows about it, too. It was she who told me. There were thousands of men killed that day, at a place called Bone Pass. The dark-haired men killed the red-haired men, mostly." He sighed and took another fig.

Jain knew the Keeper herself! Thaïle almost choked when she realized that. She hadn't known that anyone ever spoke with the Keeper. And she'd always thought the Keeper was a man.

Jain did not seem to have noticed her surprise. "Often, in ancient times, these other races would bring their wars into Thume and then we pixies had to fight them to save our-selves from being killed or enslaved or brutalized in horrible ways. It happened over and over and over. And about a thousand years ago, there was a really terrible war. It's known as the War of the Five Warlocks, but that's just a name. It was started by a very great sorcerer named Ulien'quith. He was an elf, one of the golden-haired demons, and he had a whole army of other sorcerers to help him. Votaries, they're called. Their enemies chased them here, to Thume, and Ulien made himself king of Thume, by sorcery. He made the pix-ies fight his enemies when they came after him."

Thaïle had thought that she'd drunk all the orange juice, but the golden cup was full again, so she took another drink. It was very strange to be eating all these wonderful things with a sorcerer. She wished Gaib and Frial were there to enjoy the meal, also. They had probably never seen its like in their lives. She knew she hadn't.

"Try this," Jain muttered, pushing a golden plate over. "It was a very terrible war and we pixies got the worst of it, until we almost died out altogether. It wasn't just armies that caused the trouble. Both sides used huge amounts of sorcery. There were dragons and storms of fire and monsters. Plagues of snakes. The ground opened and swallowed whole cities. Over there—" He pointed toward her secret place. "—are ruins of a great castle. You can't see anything now except the tumbled stones, but once it was a vast fortress."

His eyes twinkled, hinting that he knew of her secret place and knew she hadn't guessed what it was made of.

"The war went on for many years, until Ulien died. He was succeeded by a pixie, named Keef. Keef stopped the war and sent all the Outsiders away. Keef founded the College. Keef was the first Keeper!"

Thaïle nodded again. She wondered what all this history had to do with her. It was sort of interesting, though, and oddly exciting, in a way she could not quite place.

"Ever since then," Jain said, "for a thousand years, there has been a Keeper at the College. The Keeper keeps the demons out—the other races out. We live in peace, here in Thume, because of the Keeper. You know all that, of course."

He stopped smiling for the first time since he'd started his lecture. "For example. That battle you Felt last year—the Keeper Felt it also. It didn't concern her, or us. What the darks and the reds do to each other is their business. But a lot of the losers ran away into the mountains. Many died of wounds, or the cold, but a few days later the survivors started dribbling through the passes, down into Thume."

Thaïle paused with a piece of juicy mango halfway to her mouth.

"Alarmed?" he said. "Yes, it should alarm you. There

were hundreds of men, all starving and all armed. All violent men, warriors. If they'd had the chance, they would have brought death and rape . . . do you know what rape is?"

She nodded quickly.

And he nodded, also. "Even pixies do that, I'm afraid. But not often. Not like what would have happened . . . Anyway, the Keeper dealt with them. They never arrived in Thume, Thaïle. Not one. It's not nice, but it's necessary. Understand?"

"Yes. I think so."

Jain smiled again, comfortingly. "Well, that's the bad side of the Keeper's job. Fortunately, it doesn't happen very often. Like to see some magic?"

Not being sure she did, she said, "Isn't all this food magic?"

"Yes, it is. Of course it is. But I'm going to show you something—someone. About a month ago an imp . . . that's the name for the dark-haired demons, or some of the dark-haired demons. This imp came wandering into Thume on his own. Actually on a horse, but not with anyone else."

He paused until she timorously asked, "Why?"

Jain chuckled and wiped his fingers on the grass. "Just out of nosiness. Nobody Outside knows what happens in Thume. They know people disappear here, but they don't know why. The Keeper's power prevents them from finding out. And this man is an imp and imps are extremely inquisitive people. Worse than jackdaws, imps. So I'm told. Anyway, at the moment he's about four or five days' walk north of here, still riding his horse, exploring Thume. I'll show you! Watch."

He pointed and a mist seemed to form within the trees where he pointed. Then there was a sunlit clearing there, where there hadn't been a moment before, and a man on a horse, ambling along.

She gasped and was about to jump up.

"It's all right," the recorder said. "He can't see you. He's a long way away, really, like I said. That's a demon for you."

She sank back to stare at the rider. His horse continued to plod, without ever going anywhere. The man was strumming on a lute, but she couldn't hear any music—nor the horse's hooves, she realized. The horse was heavy laden, the man lightly dressed in a bright-colored shirt and brown pants.

The man looked very ugly, but not especially evil. He had black hair and a stubbly black beard. His nose was long and pointy, his ears small and rounded. He seemed chubby all over, and he sat in the saddle like a sack of yams. The strangest, ugliest thing about him was his eyes. They were shaped like melon seeds and set level, in a straight line across his face.

"Ugh!" she said. "I don't think I like demons."

Jain laughed. The vision faded away. "That one's harmless enough. His name's Uliopo, not that it matters. He's a minstrel and a very bad one. He's harmless."

She thought about that, eating a piece of cake she had missed earlier. "What's going to happen to him?"

"That's up to the Keeper, but she's let him live this long, so I expect he'll continue to go around in circles for another month or two and then arrive at where he wants to go."

"Circles?"

Her companion laughed again, reaching for a tall silver bottle to pour himself a drink. "Yes. He came from the north and I think he wants to go south, but he's been going round and round and round. He doesn't know that. He hasn't seen anyone at all, or any signs of people." He peered quizzically at Thaïle over the rim of his silver cup.

"The Keeper is playing games with him?"

He chuckled. "I suppose so. The Keeper does what she wants and I don't question her! I just wanted you to know that the Keeper is merciful sometimes."

Thaïle wiped her mouth on her arm. She could not have eaten another crumb. "Why do you want me to know that?"

"Because you have Faculty."

That was what she'd been afraid of.

The wanting-to-laugh feeling had gone, but she wasn't frightened. Perhaps that was more magic, or else she'd accepted that this strange man wasn't going to harm her. She still couldn't detect any Feelings from him. Down at the Place, her father was still very unhappy, but her mother was hurrying back. That was good.

"Listen," Jain said softly. "I'm just like you. I was born at the Hoos Place, which you won't ever have heard of, because it's very far away, on the other side of Thume. My folks were just as poor as yours. Well, almost as poor—we did own an ox. My family is Gifted, like yours is, so when I began to warble and get fuzzy-lipped, I had to keep a Death Watch, as you did. An old man died, as Phain did, and told me his word of power, as she told you hers. I'd always had a talent of sorts and suddenly I was a genius with it—because I have Faculty. I have a Gift for occult power. As you do."

She studied him for a moment, then said, "What sort of talent? I didn't have Feeling before."

"No. But you must have been a very sympathetic sort of person, keyed in to people's moods. With a word of power, that became Feeling."

"What's your talent?" she demanded, thinking he wanted her to ask.

She'd been right—he grinned. "Lying! I'd always been a sly little beggar. After I got the word, I could talk anyone into believing anything! I could convince my dad the sky was green, if I wanted to."

To her astonishment, she was smiling back at him. "That doesn't 'zactly give me lots of confidence in what you're telling me, you know."

He chuckled. "I told you—I'm a mage now. Now I could make you believe it without actually saying anything." He became serious again. "One word of power makes a genius of you. Two words of power makes an adept. That lets you be good at almost any mundane skill, a sort of superperson. Sometimes, if you have a real Faculty, you start to pick up some occult abilities then, too. I had found I had a fair insight. That means I could read people's thoughts. Usually only a mage or a sorcerer can do that. Don't worry—I rarely do."

She thought this had been one of the rare times, though. If he read that thought, he didn't reply to it.

"And three words make you a mage. I told you I'm a mage. I know three words. I can do magic, like showing you that imp. Probably I'll be told a fourth word, when one becomes available. Four words make a full-blown sorcerer."

Thaïle noticed another piece of cake she had overlooked and decided she might just be able to squeeze it in. She was feeling that odd sort of excitement again.

"And me?" she asked with her mouth full.

Jain turned to look where the sun was slipping low in the western sky. He pointed that way, then stretched his arms overhead and rubbed them, as if he were growing stiff with sitting. "You have Faculty, without a doubt. You have to come to the College before your next birthday."

Which was what she'd feared ever since the Death Watch. She didn't want to go to the College, whatever and wherever it was. She wanted to find a good spot to be a Place and then a good man to share it with. Usually the boys liked to find the Place, but it wasn't unknown for girls to, well, sort of lead them to likely sites. She wouldn't mind the other way, either, if a quiet young man with wide shoulders and thick arms and a kind smile came by and said he'd found a great Place and would she come with him and look at it . . .

That was what life was for. A pixie was a flower that rooted in a place and grew and blossomed there and sent out its seeds in the wind to root in places of their own.

This College Jain talked of must hold dozens of people—recorders and mages and sorcerers and Gods-knew what else. A seed couldn't root in a patch all crowded with weeds!

"I didn't want to, either," Jain said sympathetically. "I

was a little older than you. I had a Place all picked out already and I'd even shown it to a girl or two. But I had to go. That's the law. I was mad and rebellious and sorry for myself. When I got to the College, I realized what I'd been missing all my life. And now—now I can't bear the thought of ever leaving. Oh, Thaïle! Human beings don't have to live in chicken coops. At the College you'll wash in hot water and wear fine dresses and eat fine food! Cake, even! You'll sleep in real beds, you'll . . . I don't suppose you have the faintest idea what a real bed looks like, do you?"

She shook her head, pouting.

"Then trust me. Trust the Keeper! You will be very, very happy and never have any regrets." His yellow eyes narrowed wolfishly. "And you haven't any choice, anyway, remember! The Keeper knows of you; the Keeper never sleeps. Don't try anything foolish, because it won't work."

She cringed before his slitted gaze.

"Not me," he said. "I'm only a mage. I couldn't put a compulsion on you that would last until you got to the College. But the Keeper will not be defied, Thaïle. And stay away from old people, or sick people. Understand why?"

She shook her head, trying to edge backward off the cloak, away from him.

"Can you remember the word the old woman told you?"

She nodded. It was a long, gibberishly thing that didn't seem to mean anything, but she hadn't forgotten it.

"Can you repeat it?"

She licked her lips and said, "That's not allowed."

He smiled. "Right. It isn't. But even if it were, you probably couldn't. Words are very hard to say, except when you're dying. That's why we have Death Watches. Whose idea was it to go visit at the Vool Place?"

His rapid changes of subject bewildered her. "Idea? I don't know! That was ages ago."

He scowled. "Maybe it was only coincidence, then. But at the College there's tales of a Faculty so strong it can actually seek out words. That's very rare, if it's even possible. The most powerful of sorcerers can't detect words directly! So maybe your case was just coincidence."

She didn't think he thought it was, though.

"Just in case," he said, "you must stay away from old people and sick people. You don't want to go picking up any more trash words. Can't lose a word, once you know it!"

He smiled again, but then her attention was grabbed away by a huge explosion of terror and pity from Frial and an upwelling of anger and pain from Gaib.

"Your mother's home," Jain remarked, rising.

Thaïle sprang up also and backed away a few steps, nauseated by her parents' distress. "Tell me! Tell me what you did to him!"

The recorder snapped his fingers and his cloak floated up from the ground to adjust itself on his shoulders. The dishes and food had all vanished without Thaïle noticing.

"You'll be working party tricks of your own in a year or two, you know." He smirked cheerfully and placed a broad-brimmed hat on his head at a jaunty angle.

"What did you do to my father?" she shouted.

"I gave him a fright," Jain said sulkily. "If you want to cheer him up, you can tell him that it'll wear off by morning. I'm only a mage and that's the best I can do on transformations. *Thaïle!*"

She had started to run. His command seemed to root her toes in the turf, but she did not turn.

He came closer, right behind her, and she began to shake. She had become so used to Feeling other people's emotions that he frightened her, because he was masked from her. She could smell a strange flowery scent about him, mixed with sweat.

"Forget them, Thaïle. Your father is an ignorant, small-minded peasant. Your mother can't be much better, if she has tolerated that oaf all her life. They live like beasts and they've brought you up to think that's the right way to live. Well, it's not! Come to the College as soon as you can.

Don't wait until you're sixteen. Come soon. Come and learn how to be a human being. Come and learn your destiny. Forget these churls."

Forget her family, her home? Never!

"There is more to life than rearing babies, Thaïle!"

She listened to the silence for a whole minute before she realized that the recorder had disappeared and she was alone.

She took off down the hill as fast as she could run.

――――――――――

Destiny obscure:
> *Let not ambition mock their useful toil,*
> *Their homely joys, and destiny obscure;*
> *Nor grandeur hear with a disdainful smile*
> *The short and simple annals of the poor.*
> —GRAY, *ELEGY WRITTEN*
> *IN A COUNTRY CHURCHYARD*

CHAPTER FIVE

HOSTAGES TO FORTUNE

1

THE SUN WAS RETURNING TO KRASNEGAR.

In midwinter there was almost no daylight at all. Sunlight appeared as a bright blur in the south for a short while at noon and then was gone, like a brief candle in a crypt. At the dark of the moon, the sky was an iron bowl bearing only a glitter of stars and the nightmare twitch of aurora. Those were too arrogant to illuminate human affairs, as if the sins of the climate were none of their business.

A full moon, though, never set. The stars and aurora fled before it. It soared through the sky, big as a silver plate, shedding a helpful blue light on the snow, so that men could emerge briefly from their lairs to view the stricken world.

The second full moon after midwinter was the traditional date of the Timber Meet, a custom that had developed in Inos' reign. She had instituted winter expeditions to obtain lumber from the forests to the south, using horse sleds to bring the trunks over the bare hills to Krasnegar. Unfortunately, the forests belonged to the goblins. Goblins, as Rap had been known to remark, were green but not stupid. By the time he had married the queen and taken charge of such masculine matters as tree-cutting expeditions, the goblins had awakened to the value of lumber as a trade item.

That winter the first Krasnegarian team to venture south was quietly surrounded by about five times as many goblins, all armed with spears or bows and anxious to discuss the matter of stumpage. Goblins' well-deserved reputation for being enthusiastic torturers added a certain urgency to the negotiations.

A mutually acceptable method of payment was devised, and it had since evolved into an annual event. The goblins themselves were far more efficient in the cold than even jotnar, worlds better than either imps or horses. Teams of goblins cut the trees, then hauled the sleds by moonlight to Krasnegar. Rarely a blizzard would cause postponement, but if the weather behaved itself, the goblins would come to the Timber Meet without fail. They scarcely seemed to notice the cold, although it could burn a man's lungs. The sled teams were rumored to hold a nonstop three-day race all the way from the edge of the forest. The token prizes awarded in that annual event were said to be fingernails, or ears.

As Rap trotted across the causeway, the sun was a brilliant blur in the ice fog, low to the south. The moon would rise right after sunset. His path wound among a nightmare jumble of ice floes, but the bay itself was worse, with the added danger of falling through to certain death.

Ahead of him, a single line of smoke rose vertically from

one of the little cottages that marked the shore. Three sleds of lumber stood waiting for unloading, and forty or fifty goblins formed a dark pattern against the whiteness. Some of them were moving, but most were just sitting in the snow, talking. If Rap tried that, he would be dead in ten minutes.

Panting hard, he reached the shore, where the going was easier. Across the bay, the improbable peak of Krasnegar jutted skyward, blurred by all the smoke from its chimneys, crowned by its castle. His castle. The town seemed to shine in the watery sunlight, glittering behind the ice haze.

A group of three men had separated from the others and he headed toward them, wondering if the one in the middle could be Death Bird himself.

Yes, there were times that Rap regretted his decision not to be a sorcerer. Even with the feeble powers that were all he could summon now, he would know at once whether the middle goblin was Death Bird. Of course he would also know what the man was thinking and that would take all the fun out of the negotiations. He sometimes wondered how long his resolution would last if a meeting such as this one ever turned nasty. Did he have the courage to die a mundane as a matter of principle?

He came to a puffing halt, blowing outrageous clouds of steam and running sweat under his furs—he was not as young as he used to be. Three sets of unfriendly, oddly angular eyes regarded him through the slits of the buckskin masks. Of course they could see no more of him than he could of them. They were short, broad, hard men; none of the three was tall enough to be Death Bird.

Rap dragged up his memories of the rasping goblin dialect. "Am Flat Nose. Speak for town."

"Speak chief!" the middle goblin snapped.

"Am chief."

Mollified, the spokesman announced himself, "Blood Needle of Porcupines." He and Rap each advanced a pace and embraced. Rap winced at the pressure, almost gagging at the reek of the bear grease that goblins used as winter underwear.

Blood Needle introduced Silver Flash of Salmon Totem and Busy Tooth of the Beavers . . . more bone-grinding hugs and stomach-turning whiffs of rancid fat. Although they must have ordered the fire lit in the nearest cottage, they were not inviting Rap into the warmth. That meant the negotiations must be completed quickly.

"Have seen trade goods?"

"Trash!" Blood Needle unhooked his mask for a moment so he could spit in disgust. Rap thought he saw the spittle bounce on the ice.

"Good salt!" he said. "Fine glass. Rich spices. Useful buckles . . ." He paused, running through a mental list of the goods he had left stacked in the cottage the previous fall. His feet were chilled already.

"Need swords!" the goblin said, stepping forward a pace. "Axes. Many many heads for arrows."

This was where things always got sticky. Krasnegar was bound by treaty with the Impire not to give the goblins weapons. If Rap abrogated that pact, then the Imperial trade would be shut off and the town would soon wither away, even if it did not starve in the first winter. If he angered the goblins, on the other hand, then Krasnegar might vanish overnight in a storm of blood. Long ago, as a sorcerer, he had made the causeway goblin-repellent, and goblins disliked water, but that did not mean they couldn't grit their big teeth long enough to charge across the ice. Whatever geography might say, economically his kingdom lay directly between the two sides.

"Have no swords. Imps keep swords." His goblinish was rusty. "Not trade us swords." He went back to extolling the virtues of his offerings.

Blood Needle kept calling them trash and offal and worse. "Wolverine scats!" he concluded definitively, folding his arms.

"Are not. Will not speak more." Rap folded his own. Despite all he could do, he had begun to shiver.

The goblins' angular eyes flashed. "Will keep trees and take trash, too!"

"Are thieves?"

"Will take trash and chief, too! Trade back to town for swords."

Blood Needle was a hard bargainer, obviously. Kidnapping and ransom and next he would be threatening to burn the town, no doubt. Rap decided he had played the stupid game long enough. His teeth were chattering.

"Will ask Death Bird if thief!" He spun around on frozen toes and crunched off to the cottage where the fire burned. He marched in and slammed the door. It was only a box of four stone walls with a hearth and a couple of small windows. It contained nothing except Death Bird and a tub of grease.

Stripped to a rag, the goblin king was sitting on the dirt floor, anointing his feet with bear fat. The stench of it would make a man's eyes water. On the hearth a driftwood fire blazed and crackled cheerfully. He was staying well away from it, but its glow made him shine slickly green all over.

"Playing tricks!" Rap said, by habit stamping his boots to remove the snow. Even in here, his breath smoked. He moved over to the fire and stood as close as he dared, gasping with relief as he thawed.

The goblin chuckled, a low, brutal sound, full of menace. "Are not sorcerer? See through walls?"

"Not see through walls . . . Oh, let's speak impish, you big lunk! I didn't need sorcery. I knew you must be around somewhere because Raven Totem owns the trees and there was no spokesman from the Ravens. How are you, you ugly green horror?"

Death Bird laughed at the compliment and scrambled to his feet. He was big for a goblin and growing bigger year by year. He was shorter than Rap, but with the muscles of a troll. His black hair was greased into a rope that hung over his left shoulder, dangling to his bulging belly, and he had much more mustache than most. His eyes seemed almost square, although that was partly an effect of the tattoos around them. Grinning a set of tusks like a timber wolf's, he strode forward to embrace his old friend. Rap threw all his strength into the hug, but he felt his ribs creak.

The first king of the goblins.

A man with a destiny decreed by the Gods.

Reflecting that he would have to burn his soiled furs as soon as he got home, Rap squatted down by the fire and smiled at his former slave. Death Bird moved away from the heat to begin replacing the grease he had deposited on Rap.

"You're getting fat!" Rap remarked smugly, aware that his own midriff was well concealed.

The angular eyes narrowed. "Want to try a best of three?"

"Not likely!"

"You put some beer in with that junk you want to palm off on me?"

"No, but I'll send over a few bags of beer for you." Rap knew who would drink it when it was thawed out. Nobody else would get as much as a sniff at it. "Mostly I gave you alum."

The goblin grunted, although that might have been less a comment than just the result of trying to reach an awkward part of his anatomy. "Why alum? I got no use for alum. Don't know what anyone does with alum!" He shot Rap a suspicious glance.

"Something to do with dyes. But I'm told the dwarves prize it highly, and who makes better swords than they?"

The goblin interrupted his toilet to stare at Rap with an obvious anger that would likely have terrified anyone else. And even Rap had known more pleasant experiences.

"You still claim you're not a sorcerer?"

Warned by a smell of burning fur, Rap edged away from the fire. "No sorcery. I hear the imps are building a wall across Pondague Pass."

Again the big tusks flashed. "Keeps them out of mischief."

"While you trade with Dwanish! Come on, Death Bird! It's obvious. You've been feinting at Pondague all these years until you've got the Impire convinced that there's no other way across the mountains. But you'll never persuade me that you haven't scouted out a few more passes by now! Moreover, the dwarves are your natural allies. That's no big secret, either. When do you strike?"

Death Bird was glaring. "You're the one who told me of my destiny. Prophesy for yourself."

Rap had not really expected to be taken into his confidence. It could not be long now, though. Death Bird had picked up just enough impish culture to become a deadly foe to the Impire. He had spent seventeen years uniting his people and preparing his war. All the border struggles that the Impire had considered important had all just been training for the big one. This year? Or next? Or the year 3000?

Rap shivered. "It so happens I do have a prophecy for you. There's an old belief that Emine's Protocol will fail at the end of the millennium. That's in two more years. I am informed on excellent authority that there's something to it."

The goblin chortled, giving away nothing at all. Satisfied with his grease coat, he began pulling on his buckskins. "Be nice to see Hub again. Throw a party for them. Er, with them, I mean."

"You just may. But it means sorcery trouble."

"Bright Water's dead, you know that?"

"No. Hardly surprising." The mad old loon had been witch of the north since 2682. "Who's her successor?"

Death Bird's square eyes twinkled amid their tattoos. Somehow his face seemed even greener with the rest of him covered in buckskin. "A dwarf, named Raspnex."

"The one we met?"

"Zinixo's uncle," the goblin agreed, grinning like a hyena.

Of course he would be pleased to have a dwarf on the White Throne if he'd been making treaties with the dwarves.

North's official prerogative was the jotnar raiders, but Bright Water had favored her goblins, also, although she'd been too crazy to be reliable.

Rap thought back to his days of sorcery. "I wouldn't have judged Raspnex's heft to be quite up to warlock standard, but he's not a bad man. He was the strongest of Zinixo's votaries in Faerie. After I broke Zinixo and went back there, he hadn't tried to imprint any of them. I was impressed."

South, of course, was an elf. Elves and dwarves were born enemies, so there would be trouble within the Four again. Face it—there was always trouble within the Four! The witch of the west was a troll, Grunth. She was not especially powerful. Nor was Olybino, warlock of the east. Lith'rian was probably the strongest now, so it was odd he'd agreed to Raspnex . . .

Rap shrugged and left the matter to simmer on the back of his mind while he tackled other things—like his smoking left leg, for instance. He shifted around.

"How's that little lovely you had with you last summer—Bluebell?"

"Fine. Not so little now."

"How many wives does that make?"

Death Bird became cagy. "Several."

"How many children?"

The goblin grinned. "State secret. How is your woman?"

"Oh, she's fine," Rap said. "Just had the cutest little son. We think he's going to be sort of fair-haired impish, which is fine because we have a jotunn son already and one of our daughters is impish and the other is jotunn and thank the Gods none of them really looks like me, but just let me tell you what Kadie did the other day . . ."

Death Bird waited with ill-concealed impatience until Rap's tale was complete. Without even a smile at the punch-line, he launched into a dull and pointless account of how his oldest son, Blood Beak, had killed his first bear.

2

EVEN A PIXIE COULD BE LONELY, AND A PIXIE WITH NO PLACE of her own was a lost soul. As the dry season grew drier and hotter, Thaïle felt the call of the faraway College more strongly every day. Already it seemed to have stolen her from her friends, her family, and her familiar surroundings. Already it had enfolded her in its own occult, invisible embrace. She could make no plans; she could think no farther ahead than the onset of the next rainy season, because by then she would be sixteen and somewhere else and a different person, leading a wholly different life, which she could not even now imagine. The Gaib Place was no longer her home. The road ahead disappeared over a cliff.

Before the recorder came, she had just begun to join in the preliminary steps of courtship, the shy exchange of gifts to indicate interest. Jain's visit ended that. The neighbors all knew of it. Suddenly she was a stranger to her friends, excluded from those rituals. No man was going to waste a sample of his handiwork by giving it to a woman who had to go away soon. Thaïle, likewise, need not spend time crafting hats or gloves or any of the usual garment gifts that women produced for men—they would merely be refused with the traditional kindly fiction that they did not fit.

Only three of the boys she knew were of any interest, anyway, and they had all gone off on their explorations already.

Even her parents had reacted to her new destiny with a sort of rejection. It was certainly not deliberate and Thaïle might not even have noticed it had she not had Feeling, but somehow Gaib and Frial seemed to have accepted that she was lost to them, as their other two children were lost to Places of their own. They had moved closer to each other in some subtle way, as if filling a gap. That might be just a part of life, a form of self-defense for the old, who should not spend their declining years in fruitless pining. But in this case, the lost child had not gone yet; she had no Place of her own for shelter and no replacement love.

Thaïle had reluctantly concluded that her old life was ruined; she might as well embark on the new as soon as possible. To leave soon might be kinder to her parents than hanging around until the last minute. The coffee harvest was the busiest part of the year. She would stay and help with that and then depart. Meanwhile, as the beginning of summer was an easy time and her help not needed, she would start her farewells by going to visit her sister. It would be the first time she had ever been to the Wide Place, and almost certainly it would be the last.

As a father should, Gaib reacted to her announcement with predictably ponderous protests about the dangers of getting lost, raped, or eaten by bears. Frial considered the problem in her usual matter-of-fact way and said she didn't think anyone with Thaïle's Feeling could ever get lost and would have to be incredibly stupid to get herself raped. And there weren't any more bears there than there were here. Gaib reluctantly acquiesced in her decision, as he always did.

Thaïle's problem then was that what they said wasn't what they felt. Underneath their affectionate concern, they felt guilty at having failed their child, angry that they didn't know what they had done wrong, relieved that she would not be around for a little while to remind them of that failure, and then much more guilt for feeling that relief. At close quarters, with all their worries showing, people were unbearable.

The visit was not a success. The Wide Place was fair enough in itself, lurking in dim coolness below massive boughs. The air was heady with the smell of cedars, and nowhere could have been more private. The necessary compliments came easily.

And yet, within two minutes of her arrival, Thaïle knew

that she would not be staying long. Sheel was far more interested in her newborn second son than in a half-forgotten
sister, and Wide was far more interested in the sister than
he should have been. His fingers were all round her like
mosquitoes. His erotic cravings seemed to fill the air like the
aromatic scent of the trees or the warning hum of bees.

Within an hour Thaïle knew that her sister regretted her
choice. Wide had turned out to be a poor provider, lazy and
shiftless. He hunted when he should have been harvesting,
chased women when he should have been planting, and most
of the rest of the time, also. Sheel admitted none of this, but
her emotions did.

Later on the first evening, things turned even worse.
Thaïle mentioned the College. Apparently Sheel had never
told Wide that her family was Gifted. He was not pleased
to learn that his children would have to keep a Death Watch
one day and might be stolen away by the College if they
displayed Faculty.

One good thing—when he heard about Thaïle's occult
talents, he stopped pawing her thigh under the table for a
while.

Thaïle withstood the head-splitting tension for two days
and then said farewell. Even home was better than the Wide
Place.

Noon on the second day of her return journey found her
trudging along by herself through long grass by the Big
River. There was no real path to follow, because pixies seldom saw the need to go anywhere. She wandered between
thorn bushes and tufty thickets of bamboo. The sun was
brutal.

Some distance off to her right, behind a hedge of tall reeds,
the river oozed back and forth across the plain, dark and
mysterious, broad and oily, reputedly full of deadly croco-
diles. It also contained snakes. To her left, the edge of the
forest seemed even more sinister, but over the treetops

loomed the rocky peaks of the Progistes, blue in the haze. They were the only landmark familiar to a hill-country girl here in the muggy lowland.

The previous night she had stayed at the Shoom Place, granted shelter by a friendly old couple with no children still at home. Tonight she wanted to sleep on her own pile of ferns, at the Gaib Place, and she had far to go.

She was hot, she was tired. Her feet ached, her legs ached, and the flies were driving her mad. The highlands were hot in the dry season; noon in the valleys was an ordeal to be endured. All sensible people would be lying under a tree somewhere with no clothes on.

A pouch at her belt held some slices of heavy bread and a fat leg of chicken, generously provided by Shoom and his goodwife, but Thaïle was too hot to think of eating. She was haunted by the problem of the College. She had the other problem, too, of what to tell her parents about Sheel. No one could lie to Frial.

However, at the moment she was very intrigued by a Feeling. There was someone ahead of her, coming her way, someone who was bubbling over with good cheer. She had Felt her—or possibly him—for over an hour now. She wanted to meet whoever this happy person was and find out what could possibly be so pleasurable on such an airless, stifling day. That was a more attractive puzzle than her own worries.

It was unfortunate that they were not traveling in the same direction, so that they might walk together and she might share the other's bliss. But if they had been going the same way they would not have met, of course.

Strangers could be dangerous. A young woman traveling alone was never truly safe, not anywhere. Thaïle knew the risk as a theoretical thing that in practice never applied to her or anyone she knew, like being struck by lightning. She ignored such absurd concerns as being beneath a woman's dignity.

The unknown's feelings drew close and then seemed to

stop. Most likely the woman—or man—had halted for a noontime rest, which would give Thaïle a chance to creep up unseen and inspect her. Or possibly him. Feeling was not directional enough to use for stalking, but straight ahead stood a single tiny clump of exactly three trees, apparently all alone in this wasteland of grass. There would be shade there. That would make a good place to aim for.

Abruptly there was change. Rapture became rage, howls of pain came drifting through the hot air from the trees. Thaïle teetered for a moment on the lip of flight until she realized that she was not Feeling fear but fury. A bear or a lion or even a snake would have provoked much worse than that. She ran to help.

The screams guided her. She dashed around a last high clump of bamboo and stopped dead. Her quarry was dancing madly around in the nude, beating himself with a cloth that was probably his pants, yelling incoherently. A straw hat and a pair of sandals and some lunch lay forgotten in the trees' shade. Even at that distance, Thaïle could see the ants streaming over them—big red ants.

The victim came to a panting halt and began inspecting himself with care. His emotions settled down into a lower range, anger mingled with regret and a dash of self-contempt. Satisfied at last that he had dislodged all his assailants, he looked up and discovered his audience. He shrieked in horror and jumped vertically, while attempting both to turn his back and put on his pants before he came down again. In consequence, he collapsed on the ground in a squirming heap of extreme embarrassment. Thaïle gave way to helpless laughter.

In a few moments she realized that the mortification and some real physical pain she was Feeling from the man were mixed with amusement, also. Apparently he could see the joke, and that seemed an unlikely male reaction under the circumstances. She choked down the rest of her laughter as he came over to her, respectable in his shorts but still breathless, streaked by dust and sweat from his exertions.

"I'm Leéb of the Leet Place," he announced, "and . . . and . . . Oh, my! *Oh . . . my!*" He fell silent, staring at her open-mouthed. A wave of astonishment and happiness almost knocked her over.

He was only a boy, about her own age. He was short and bony and somehow comical. His mousy-brown hair was wavy instead of curled; it hung limp in sweaty straggles. His ears were very large, not at all pointy, and they stuck out absurdly. His nose was much too small for him.

But his eyes were pure gold and wide with wonder.

"I'm Thaïle of the Gaib Place," she said hesitantly.

He said, "Oh!" again faintly. "Oh!"

"What's wrong?" she cried, disconcerted.

"You're . . . You're beautiful!"

Then his face turned bright red below its deep tan, all the way from his collar bones to the tips of his absurd ears, and again she Felt embarrassment, but it did not mask his joy and amazement. She felt her own face redden, also. She looked away quickly.

No one had ever called her beautiful before like that and meant it, and he did mean it.

Want you! his emotions said. *Want you! Want you!*

Even the lustful Wide had not projected desire as strong as that, and she thought it should have repelled her when coming from this Leéb as much as it had from him. But it didn't. It wasn't the same. It wasn't Wide's *want-you-to-make-me-happy.* It was different and it reminded her of the *wanting* she had felt from Sheel when she cuddled and nursed her baby. It was a *want-you-to-make-you-happy* wanting—tenderness! She had never felt that from any man before. A little from her mother, maybe. But not the same.

When she dared look up, Leéb was staring at the ground, awkwardly scratching the swelling ant bites on his bony ribs. The *wanting* was overlain by continuing embarrassment and self-contempt at what he had said—but it was still there.

"If you can rescue your sandals," she said, "and your hat—I've got some food we can share."

He blinked at her. "Thaïle? Thaïle, you said?"

She nodded.

"That's a lovely name . . ." He was regarding her short hair with hope. "Goodwife Thaïle?"

"No. Just Thaïle."

He closed his eyes as if saying a prayer to the Gods.

"Get your shoes, Leéb," she said. "And tell me about it."

They sat in the burning sunlight and chewed the bread together. They took turns biting chunks off the chicken leg; and Leéb talked. And talked and talked and talked.

There was only one thing he could talk about, the Place he had found. It was by the river, he said, on a hidden backwater. There were trees of all sorts. There was a very ancient well that he could easily clean out. There was open ground that had once been a rice paddy and could be again and would feed a huge family all by itself. There were fish galore! There was firewood and masses of withes to make wicker, which was all that was needed for a house in the valley. He was very good at weaving and he would make a *big* house! There were fruit trees running wild, and berry bushes. There was sweet grass for goats to give milk for, er, kids—he turned red again at that point—and an old couple lived about half an hour away, who would be pleased to have a young family in the neighborhood and who would lend them an ax and all sorts of other things to help them get started and probably leave them most of their household goods when they died, because their children all lived a long way away now . . .

It was perfect, he said. It would make the finest Place in all Thume. And his Feelings said that she would fit right in.

"Look out for the ones that fall in love quickly," her mother had once told her, "because they can fall out again just as fast."

Not Leéb, she thought. She had Feeling and she knew that what he was suffering wasn't just lust, although there was certainly a flattering amount of that included. Leéb was sure that he had found the perfect place to be the Leéb Place and then he had found the perfect woman to share it with, the very next day. If a man believed in the Gods, he must believe in this.

At last Leéb ran out of superlatives, and after that he just sat and stared at her in blissful wonder.

She explained that she had been visiting her sister and was on her way home.

"But you'll come and see my Pl—come and see the place?" he begged.

He wasn't what she had ever imagined. He did not have bulgy arms and broad shoulders. He was skimpy and far from handsome. Homely at best! But she had Feeling and she had never Felt a man like him, or at least not one who felt what he did, for her. A gentle, loving boy, who laughed when he should have been angry. A boy who did not take himself seriously, but took her very seriously indeed and wanted to make her happy.

She wanted to weep. She could not bear to tell him about the College, or tell him that she must soon go away.

She shook her head.

Again he blushed. "Oh, I know we've just met!" he said. "I wouldn't expect . . . Not so soon . . . I mean, all I wanted was to let you see. And think about it, of course. I don't expect . . . *that!*"

She shook her head again. *That* wasn't the problem at all. If he showed her this Place and it was one-tenth as good as he said it was, she was going to accept Leéb right there— bare bodies on the grass. She was sure of it. And that would never do, not when she had to go away.

But she could not bring herself to tell him the terrible truth, because then he would go out of her life forever and she thought she had found something as precious as the Place he had found, even if she could not keep it very long.

When in doubt, ask your mother. That was another of her mother's sayings.

"Why not come to the Gaib Place and meet my parents?" she said at last.

For Leéb, that was the second-best thing she could have said. Long before evening, they were walking hand in hand.

3

PRINCE HOLINDARN OF KRASNEGAR WAS HAVING BREAK-fast, again. He liked to have several breakfasts, to prepare him for as many lunches as he could persuade his mother to provide. If greed was the criterion, Holi was definitely impish.

Looking down at him as he sucked busily and kneaded her breasts with his tiny fists, Inos was trying to decide whether his nose was really faunish, or if that was just a normal baby nose. As usual, she decided that she neither knew nor especially cared. He would definitely do. Impish or not, he was growing like a jotunn. It was all these breakfasts.

Whatever illusions the rest of the world might have about springtime, Krasnegar knew better. The days were growing longer, but arctic winter still held the castle in its dark embrace. Yet another blizzard was howling around the castle, and once in a while the great fireplace would puff out an eye-stinging cloud of smoke. The queen was sitting with her feet almost in the hearth, her back turned to the great hall for privacy. Meanwhile the life of the palace went on around her, servants coming and going, everybody carefully pretending not to notice what her Majesty was doing.

She wondered how many reigning monarchs behaved so casually and managed to get away with it. Her parents, even, would have been shocked, and they had never been known to stand on ceremony. Queen Evanaire had certainly never nursed Princess Inosolan in public like this.

The source of all the informality was sitting beside her on the bench, facing the other way and supposedly watching what was going on at the far end of the great chamber, but once in a while sneaking admiring looks at her bodice. He was quite within his rights to do so, and she enjoyed his attention.

Rap had returned the previous day from a seal hunt—beating the blizzard to the door by about three hours—and it was wonderful to have him back. She was also glad to see that he was in a cheerful mood. Something had been bothering him ever since Winterfest. Rap was not normally a brooding type. She wished he would get it off his chest, but she was not going to pry. He would speak up when he was ready.

He hated playing monarch, but he did not look too abominably scruffy today. His jerkin was quite respectable, even if his boots were not.

"No! No! No!" a shrill voice cried from the dais. "You have to put more *feeling* in it! Try again!"

"You are the most beautiful woman in the whole world!" an angry boyish treble snarled.

"That's a little better. But you still should sound more impressed."

King and queen exchanged grins. The castle children were being rehearsed without mercy in a forthcoming dramatic presentation, *The Terrible Revenge of Allena the Fair*, written, directed, and produced by Princess Kadie. Starring, of course, Princess Kadie in the title role.

Amateur theatricals were an ancient Krasnegarian tradition, one of the many ways the inhabitants made merry during their long winter captivity. Dancing and madrigal singing and concerts and assorted game tournaments were others. Whether a man's taste ran to bare-knuckle brawling or lute playing, he could always find something of interest going on.

Krasnegar held some remarkable talents, for its size. Inos could think of four or five superb singers, a juggler, two or three dancers, and a half-dozen musicians, any of whom would have won acclaim within the Impire. It had not always been so. The change could be traced back to a certain act of insanity by Inos herself, way back in . . . Gods! Where did the years go? Kadie and Gath were thirteen now, so . . .

"Why so troubled, love?" Rap said softly. "Is the little monster sucking all the life out of you?"

Holi stopped work and rolled his eyes to see where the voice had come from. Inos grabbed the chance to detach him and lay him against her shoulder. "Hook me up, will you, love?"

"Actually," Rap said with a gleam in his eye, "I'm much better at *un*hooking."

"Then you need the practice!" she said.

He sighed and fastened her bodice for her.

Inos adjusted Holi on her shoulder. "As for being troubled, I was just thinking . . . Next year will be too early for Kinvale, won't it? Maybe the year after?"

Rap scowled. "The year 3000? Does she have to go at all?"

Surprised by that response, Inos went back to first principles and reconsidered the matter. She had always assumed that Kadie must be packed off to Kinvale one of these days, as she had been, to learn decorum and Imperial manners.

How she missed Aunt Kade! It was over a year now since the dear old lady had peacefully failed to awaken one morning, her soul gone to join the Good. Aquiala had sent word through the magic portal and Inos and Rap had gone incognito to the funeral, but she still missed her dear, brave aunt. Kinvale would never be the same without her.

"I suppose we had better settle the succession first, hadn't we?" she said. "You want Gath to succeed?"

Now it was Rap's turn to look surprised. He glanced around to make sure no one was listening; perhaps he was considering that a commons fireplace was not the most suitable location for discussing such weighty matters. Or maybe that wouldn't occur to him. "Is there a law?" he asked. "Kadie's older."

"Only by twenty minutes! Just custom—the oldest boy. It's the Imperial way and the way Krasnegar's always done it. Sisters get traded off for treaties, younger sons are sent to the wars to be killed, and the oldest son inherits. It's brutal, but it stops argument. I had an older brother, you know. He died in infancy."

"Yes, I knew that." Rap smiled. "What a lot of bother he could have saved us if he'd lived!"

She pulled a face at him and was distracted by a contented burp from Holi. One of these days they would have to discuss the succession in the council—but Rap was still musing.

"I have trouble," he said softly, "imagining Gath imposing his will on the kingdom!"

True, Gath was extraordinarily placid.

"On the other hand," the king added, "it is considerably harder to imagine the kingdom ever tolerating Kadie longer than the first week." He grinned to take the sting out of his words. "Perhaps we should send Kadie to the Imperial Military College in Hub and send Gath to Kinvale, to learn how to be a gentleman."

"I think Gath is a born gentleman. That's the trouble!"

"Truly. Gath ruling jotnar just doesn't fit on the page, does it?" He sighed, no doubt thinking of the bruises and broken bones he had suffered while establishing his own right to be taken seriously as a king in Krasnegar. "But Kadie's a born tyrant." He dropped his voice. "Careful. Company!"

"Papa!" the imperious voice of a born tyrant said as Kadie rustled up behind Inos in her Allena-the-Fair gown. "This will not work!"

"What won't work, sweet?"

Allena the Fair stamped her foot. "Iggi as Warlock Thraine. He can no more act than a horse!"

Rap said, "I have known horses with considerable dramatic ability."

"You know what I mean!"

"Well, why don't you play Warlock Thraine and I'll stand in as Allena the Fair?"

Kadie uttered a royal scream of fury that upset her younger brother. Inos soothed him and scolded her daughter. Rap looked sick to his stomach, which was what always happened when he was trying not to laugh.

"I need Gath!" Kadie declaimed, plumping down between her parents to sulk. Being respectably clad now, Inos moved around to the other side of the bench so she could face the hall and broil her back for a change. Besides, the royal family should set a good example of domestic harmony by all pointing in the same direction. She noticed that her jewel box had been raided again and Allena the Fair's gown of purple velvet bore an ominous resemblance to the drapes in the best guest bedroom.

Rap had been inspecting the theatrical company, which was now being shooed away by servants wanting to lay tables. "Where is Gath?"

"I don't know! He won't say."

The king's eyes widened. "He's not going to be in your play?"

"No." Kadie continued to pout. "He won't! He disappears half the day and won't say where he's been! And Mom won't let me follow him to find out!"

Rap whistled silently and then said, "Hey, Pret!"

A passing footman flashed the king a smile and detoured closer so that Rap could grab a tankard from his tray.

"If Holi can drink all day long, then I don't see why I shouldn't!" Rap raised the tankard in a toast before he drank, grinning at Inos. She wondered what had made him so gleeful all of a sudden.

"There isn't going to be any stupid play!" Kadie said. "With Iggi being Thraine, everyone would laugh at us! So it's canceled."

"That's a shame, dear," Inos said tactfully. "Perhaps you could rewrite the Thraine part so that Iggi can handle it?"

"No! It's hopeless!" The princess sulked in silence for a moment, apparently contemplating the void thus left in the cultural life of the kingdom. But then she said sweetly, "Daddy?"

"When you call me that, like that, I know you want something you know I know you shouldn't have!" Rap took another swig of ale and smacked his lips. "Yes, my beloved?"

"Is Corporal Isyrano the best swordsman in the kingdom?"

Her father shot Inos a perplexed glance over the top of Kadie's head. "Without a doubt," he said warily.

"Better than you?"

"Me? Kadie, as a swordsman, I make a fair bandmaster! I'm no fencer! But Isyrano's very good indeed, so far as I can judge."

"I want you to tell him to give me fencing lessons."

"Fencing lessons." Rap considered the matter, looking somewhat dazed. "May I ask why you want fencing lessons?"

"Does a girl need more reason than a boy would?"

The two of them could keep this up for hours. Inos adjusted Holi's blanket while she waited to see who was going to give up first. She wondered if Rap realized that Corporal Isyrano was the sort of man a girl might find good-looking. She wondered if Kadie was starting *that* already. She wondered if Rap appreciated that his Kadie troubles had barely begun.

The king was redeploying on more strategic ground. "Well, I don't see why not. Very good exercise. By all means ask the corporal to give you fencing lessons."

"I did. He won't."

"Ah. Did you ask politely?"

"Of course!" Kadie said, much too quickly.

"Or did you try to order him to give you fencing lessons? Kadie, I have told you a hundred times that you are not to go around throwing orders at everybody! You don't give orders to anyone, no one at all! And I have told everyone in the kingdom that they are not to obey you if you try! Everyone!"

Ignoring the opportunities presented by this obvious exaggeration, Kadie said grumpily, "Then how do I get fencing lessons?"

"You ask. Politely."

"Can I say you said he—"

"No. You don't mention me at all."

"Then he still won't!" Kadie cried despairingly. She jumped up from the bench and went rushing away as fast as she could move in the velvet drapes.

"God of Madness," Rap muttered, raising the tankard. It stopped halfway as he turned to his grinning wife. "Fencing?"

"The Elven Queen in *The Valor of Giapen*, I expect."

"Ah, my literary ignorance showing again . . . And what's this about Gath? He has finally broken free from bondage?"

She thought she'd told him. Motherhood was making her forgetful, perhaps. "Before you left. Gath has taken up good works."

"Now I have heard everything. What sort of good works?"

"What I usually do. Hot soup to the sick and so on. He came and said that since I wasn't able to do it while Holi was still small, then maybe he should."

The king swelled with pride. "His own idea?"

"Apparently. He's been doing it for about two weeks now, I suppose."

"That's wonderful," Rap said, looking awed. "He thought it up all by himself? And didn't ask his sister's approval? And he's sticking with it—you are making sure the soup goes where it's supposed to, aren't you?"

"Of course! I have learned *something* in thirteen years of mothering."

"Great!" Rap said. "That's great! I must congratulate him."

"Yes, you should show approval," Inos said. "He was a bit upset yesterday. Old Thrippy is dying and—"

"*God of Fools!*" Rap's tankard crashed to the floor, sending frothing ale everywhere. He stared at Inos in horror. His face had gone ashen, as if he had just seen a dragon.

4

RAP PACED TO AND FRO. INOS SETTLED HERSELF IN ONE OF the big leather chairs by the fireplace and waited until he calmed down enough to speak. They had cleaned up the beer, handed Holi over to the nursemaid before he woke up demanding his first lunch, and retreated to their private parlor. Now Rap was presumably going to explain. The peat glowed, and the room was toasty warm, a rarity in Krasnegar in winter.

She studied him, being careful not to let him notice. He always seemed big, unless there were jotnar present. Clumsy, almost. A cautious, well-meaning man, unaware of his own strengths. Very few former stableboys could ever have persuaded a kingdom to accept him as a ruler, but Rap had, and she was certain he had done it without using sorcery. Very few men could have refused what he had refused—godhood, infinite power. She owed everything to Rap and she thanked the Gods daily for him.

If Gath was a born gentleman, then he had inherited the trait from his father.

"Corporal Isyrano," Rap said, still pacing. "He went off to the Impire . . . when? Ten years ago? Got homesick and came back . . . last year?"

"Year before."

"Right." Rap fixed a beady look on Inos. "Did you know he'd deserted from the Imperial Army?"

She'd suspected. "Does it matter?"

"Not at all. Bleeding smart thing to do. I would." He began to pace again. "He was in one of the good legions, though. And he was on the fencing team! And he's no aristocrat, either."

Rap was probably just working it all out in his own head, not deliberately trying to be mysterious.

"Yes?" she prompted.

"Legionaries don't fence. They throw their javelins and then they bash things with their swords, but they don't fence."

"No, dear." What did the corporal have to do with Gath?

"But every legion has its fencing team. They have tournaments and people gamble thousands on them. To get on a legionary fencing team *you have to be damned good!*"

"Yes, dear."

"Damned good," Rap muttered to himself. "Gentlemen, most of them, of course, but I think Isyrano was the lead man on his team. Brunrag left her husband and went south . . . don't remember when. She's been back three years, or is it four? You're more qualified than me—how's her singing?"

"Hub would fall at her feet."

The king threw himself down in the other big chair, dislodging a cloud of dust. "I wonder how many didn't get homesick? How many have we lost forever?"

"It's all my fault, you mean?"

"Of course it isn't your *fault*, but it was your doing. You're the one who scattered magic everywhere."

Inos shivered at the memory of the day she had been a sorceress—for about an hour. As soon as she had bullied Rap into telling her four words of power, she had summoned her loyal subjects to the castle and shouted the words for all to hear. It had been the worst experience of her life. The pain had almost killed her, but she had done it.

The lamps flickered faintly and one of the casements rattled. Snow was packed tight over the glass.

"It didn't work for long, of course," Rap said. "You know that."

They had never discussed it, but she had guessed, then wormed the story out of her aunt. "Kade told me, roughly."

"I've been lying, all these years," he said glumly. "I keep insisting I'm not a sorcerer. But that's like a man saying he hasn't any money, meaning he left it all at home today. What I mean is 'I'm not a sorcerer just at the moment.' I'm an out-and-out liar!"

"No, you're not! You just avoid the question—I've heard you do it. It's nobody's business but yours."

If he'd ever once admitted to having magic powers, then people would have always been bringing him sick babies and dying relatives and they would have shunned him the rest of the time, because the simple folk of Krasnegar feared magic.

"It almost worked," he said. "You did destroy one of them—Little Chicken's. It was so weakened that it just stopped existing. I don't know why, because it was probably the strongest. You shattered the others. They had so little power left that people forgot them. Most people."

His face was drawn and stiff already. The sorcerous suffered when they talked of magic.

"Not you."

"No. I have this knack for magic, so I remembered them better than others. As they recovered their strength, I was the one who remembered best. They homed in on me. So I am a sorcerer, after a fashion. A very weak sorcerer, though, because the words are spread so thin. I have three ghost words and one good one—the one I got from Sagorn, the one I didn't tell you."

"And where does Corporal Isyrano come in?" she asked, although she was fairly sure she knew the answer now.

"He must have been present in the bailey when you did your big scene. He would only have been a kid then. He remembered one of the words."

"And he already had a knack for swordsmanship?"

Rap nodded. "Plus a knack for magic, like me. So he remembered a word. He became an occultly gifted swordsman. Once he discovered his ability, of course, then he headed off to the Impire to get coaching, because nobody here could teach him properly."

And how many others? Brunrag the singer and a dozen or two more she could think of. And, as Rap had said, maybe others who had traveled south and had not returned.

"We may have adepts and mages, as well? Maybe even a sorcerer or two?"

Rap was staring glumly at the red glow of the peat. "No sorcerers. You spoke four words and one seems to have died. So only three survived. I haven't noticed any mages or adepts around, but they could be lying low. If they have any sense they are."

Inos rose and went across to sit on the arm of his chair. She stroked his tangled hair. "And now they're dying off?"

"Some of them. Words are passed on deathbeds. Anyone may have one. For all I know, old Thrippy has one. Now you see the problem?"

"You think Gath is trying to learn a word of power?"

Rap groaned and rubbed his temples.

"Maybe. Someone may have told him about them—Gods know who may know about them. It's just . . . I don't know. Gath's always seemed such an honest, open kid."

She didn't say what they were both thinking—that Rap's son might have inherited his gift for magic.

"Could he be doing it by instinct, do you suppose?" she asked.

"Doesn't sound likely. Even powerful sorcerers, even the wardens, can't detect power unless it is being used. So how could he be attracted to it by instinct?"

For a moment they sat in silence. Rap leaned his head against her, weary with worry.

"Is it so serious, though, love?" she said. "Even if he picks up all three and becomes a mage—is that so terrible? You'll pass on your words to the children when you die, won't you?"

"Hadn't planned on dying yet, but I suppose so. I might do what Inisso did and give one to each child. Gath's far too young to be trusted with power. But that's not the point."

She had missed something and obviously it was serious. "What is the point, then?"

"The point is that they're very weak words. Yes, three will make a mage, but a very weak mage."

"What can a very weak mage do?"

"Not much, I suspect. If he tried to turn you into a frog, you'd just go green, or something. I don't know."

"So?"

"So he'd be a pushover for any good sorcerer who came along, who could sense his use of power and enslave him; make a votary of him."

"Then you'll have to have a serious talk with your son!"

"I suppose so."

"Leave Kadie out of it!" Inos said firmly. "If she finds out, she'll pester all the old folk in the kingdom to death."

Rap sighed. "I never knew my father. I'm no good at this being-a-father thing."

That was absurd. The children worshipped him and so did all the dozens of other children around the palace.

"I'm sure you can handle it, dear," Inos said sweetly. "Compared to killing Thane Kalkor, it won't be difficult at all."

5

IT WAS ALL WRONG, FRIAL THOUGHT, WRONG, WRONG, wrong! What should have been a precious, once-or-twice-in-a-lifetime joy had been soured by the curse of Faculty and turned to tragedy. A priceless moment had become a torment.

The roiling Feelings had given her a skull-splitting headache. She was angry at Thaïle, who should have told the boy the truth right away and should never have brought him home to the Gaib Place. She was angry at Gaib, who was being awkward and stubborn because he was frightened and wouldn't admit it. She was even angry with that love-sick runt of a boy with his ridiculous batwing ears—especially angry with him, for being so utterly, witlessly smitten by her daughter. Angry because he looked so wrong and Felt so right.

Angry, also, at the news Thaïle had brought back. That shiftless Wide had never Felt right to her, but Sheel had refused to listen. Now what had her stupidity brought her? Any girl should trust her mother's feelings, especially if they were Feelings, as hers were. But Sheel was another problem, to be suffered later, at leisure.

The sun was just setting behind Kestrel Ridge, the moon just rising over the mountains, golden and almost full. It was a beautiful evening; even the bugs were tolerable. Only the Feelings were wrong. If they were giving her a headache, what must they be doing to Thaïle?

Four people sitting outside the cottage, in misery—she and Gaib on the bench with their backs to the wall, the young lovers cross-legged on the ground opposite, close but not quite touching.

He had found his dream Place and wanted a dream girl to share it with. She wanted to hide from the recorders . . .

Leéb had never even heard of Gifted families, or Faculty,

until now. Gaib had explained, very clumsily. Frial herself had gone over it all again.

The boy was distraught. Thaïle was close to tears.

As she should be!

Now Gaib had fallen into angry, baffled silence, out of his depth. He kept twitching, as if he expected the Jain sorcerer-recorder to materialize out of the trees.

"How long until your birthday?" Leéb asked, turning to Thaïle.

She sniffed. "Half a year. First new moon of the rainy season."

He nodded glumly and picked at a blister on his toe.

"Yours?" she asked tremulously.

"Another month. I'll be eighteen."

He looked younger, but he gave off no Feelings of lying. He was giving off nothing but massive frustration, plus the underlying infatuation, of course.

"Mother!" Thaïle moaned. "What are we to do?"

"Do? You know quite well what you have to do! You have to wait here for another month or two and then we'll take you to the College." Frial tried to imagine Gaib going on a long journey away from the Place. Her mind shied like a startled doe. "Or we'll find someone to go with you. Goodman Leéb will stay the night here and tomorrow he'll be on his way."

Twin blasts of pain threatened to tear her head apart.

Leéb reached out and took Thaïle's hand defiantly.

That didn't help any.

"There are lots of pretty girls in the world, lad," Frial said coldly.

More pain.

"This Place of his," Gaib growled. His anger was growing stronger, hotter. "You've not seen it yet?"

"No, Father," Thaïle said patiently. They'd explained that several times. "But I believe what Leéb says about it."

"Lots of bugs down in the valley," Gaib mused. He'd never been there, of course.

"I'm a lowlander, sir," the boy said nervously. "I know some things about bugs."

Frial bit back an angry comment. Anyone would think bugs were the problem.

"Long way," Gaib muttered. Under his plank exterior, he was more angry than she could ever remember Feeling him. She hoped he wouldn't hurt the boy, who'd done nothing worse than fall in love, which was his duty.

"Yes, it's a long way, Goodman," she snapped. "What difference does that make?"

"Might never find them," he said quietly.

Outbursts of Feelings all around made her wince—hope and fear and astonishment. The astonishment was her own, she realized. And some of the fear.

"The recorders will find them!" Recorders came around every year or two, asking about new Places and who lived in them.

"Ah, there's that," Gaib agreed.

"I never heard of recorders!" Leéb said suddenly. "Well, I'd heard of them, but they never came near the Leet Place. Never that I heard of. Seems it's only where there's these Gifted families around that they bother much." His excitement began to boil up like milk.

Frial felt a deep surge of satisfaction from her goodman.

"There, then," Gaib said. "Maybe they won't find you at all. Any rate, you've got half a year, lass. Ain't breaking the law until then. Half a year in a good Place with a good man would be worth taking, I'd think. Gods give some folks a lot less."

Frial was stunned. She had forgotten he could be like this. She had forgotten that there had been a spark there once. Jain of the College had wakened something in old Gaib.

"What about us, when they ask us?" she demanded, suddenly fearful.

Gaib turned and leered at her with what teeth he had left. "You know where this Place of theirs is?"

"Not exactly."

"Me, neither."

"Oh, Goodman!" she said. She wanted to laugh and cry at the same time.

Thaïle and Leéb were staring at each other.

"Oh, would you?" Leéb said. "Would you?"

Thaïle didn't say a word. She just laid a hand on his knee and the two of them seemed to fall together at the same moment, into a tight embrace. Then they toppled backward in a flurry of straightening legs, locked in each other's arms.

Frial felt dazzled by the waves of joy.

"Here, now!" Gaib barked. "Remember your manners! Time enough for that tomorrow, when you get there. Or whenever you get there . . ."

The lovers broke apart reluctantly, flushed and starry-eyed.

"Now, Goodwife," he said. "What can we give them to get them started? I've got a spare spade and a mallet and I think Phoan's got an ax he'd trade for a brace of piglets . . ."

Thaïle scrambled to her feet and ran to hug her father. Leéb rose more circumspectly and came to Frial, hesitant . . . wondering if she approved. His eyes were pure gold.

May the Gods be with us!

She spread her arms to hug him also and let her tears flow.

6

A LEGION HAD ITS OWN STANDARD. SO DID EVERY ONE OF its ten cohorts and every one of its thirty maniples. Add in the cavalry and the specialty troops and the total came to well over fifty standards, each one sacred, each borne by its own signifer.

When Shandie's four legions were routed by dragons on Nefer Moor, the imperor's official report to the Senate described the incident as a rapid withdrawal, necessitated by forest fires. Militarily the results were not too serious. A lot of equipment had been abandoned, of course, but the loss of life was surprisingly low. Nor had there been any loss of territory—"The integrity of the Impire's borders had not been jeopardized," as the communiqué put it, carefully not mentioning that the legions had been trespassing in Ilrane at the time.

Forest fires in the middle of the rainy season?

The army itself knew better and word spread through the legions like an epidemic, from Julgistro to Zark and from Pithmot to Guwush, seeming to travel instantaneously, as only bad news could. Dragons were mentioned, but dragons were almost too fearful to discuss, unthinkable. What really caught the army's attention was the rumor that almost two hundred standards had been lost. Many other battles had cost more lives or lost much ground, but for sheer humiliation Nefer Moor had not been equaled in centuries. The army could guess what sort of *rapid withdrawal* had led to the loss of two hundred standards.

Of the four legionary standards themselves, only two were among the saved. The XXVth's had been rescued from a flooding river by a young legionary named Ishilo, who had thereby become something of a hero. Its signifer was later apprehended and put to death with traditional cruelty. The other legionary signifers were condemned *in absentia* to suffer the same fate, and many lesser signifers did.

Only the XIIth's had returned to Qoble in the hands of its own signifer, as it should. Ylo had not planned any heroics. He knew that he was never motivated by heroism. He had mostly been staying close to Shandie, in the belief that close-to-Shandie was the safest place to be. Staying close to Shandie, he had never had an option about lugging the fuddling standard along, because if he'd thrown it away, Shandie would just have made him pick it up again. So he'd still been holding the blank-blankety thing when they staggered out of the forest. Besides, he'd twisted his ankle early in the flight and the pole had been useful as a staff.

He was given no chance to explain that and was too smart to try. Shandie was in eclipse, having been routed on his first independent command, but the army desperately needed a hero. Shandie's signifer was available.

"Don't let it go to your head," Shandie warned him, but Ylo could not see why not. It wouldn't last long, so why not enjoy it?

The surviving troops of the XIIth voted him one day's pay apiece for saving them from disgrace.

From ancient Marshal Ithy in Hub came a signifer's cape of pure white wolfskin, an honor not granted since the previous dynasty.

Patriotic citizens sent him purses of gold, and the councillors of Gaaze presented him with an illuminated scroll.

By day troops cheered him whenever they got the chance.

By night he found himself fighting off girls—not all of them, of course, just the plainer ones.

He let it go to his head. He let it go wherever it wanted.

Which was all very fine, Ylo reflected sleepily, but it wouldn't save him from the imperor himself.

The old man had probably never realized that his grandson's signifer was an Yllipo, the last surviving member of an attaindered clan. Shandie had not told him. Ylo had handled the reports on Karthin and Bone Pass and he knew what had been said—Prince Ralpnie had died in action and his replacement was a legionary named Ylo. That was all.

But now that Ylo was a one-day wonder, the old tyrant would certainly find out. There would be plenty of sly lips in Hub willing to shout the truth in the deaf imperial ear.

And Shandie was on the brink of rebellion. He might not lose his own head, but he was very likely to lose Ylo's.

There it was in his own handwriting on Ylo's desk:

My dearest and most revered Grandfather,
Much as it grieves me to address you in these blunt terms,
I find myself driven to drastic measures. I have beseeched
you for many months now to grant leave for my dear

wife to join me here in Gaaze so that I may no longer be deprived of her love and comfort . . .

If Eshiala was not allowed to come at once, Shandie wrote, then he would resign his commission forthwith and deliver that resignation personally, in Hub.

Defiance! Treason! The blood-soaked old despot would have a homicidal fit. No one had sassed him like that in fifty years.

Shandie's trouble, Ylo decided with a yawn, was monogamy. Gods! The man could have all the women he could handle if he chose to, right here in Gaaze. Principle could be carried too far. Much too far. What could possibly be so wonderful about one particular woman?

Heirs were a consideration, of course, and an important one to a future imperor, but Shandie already had a daughter. Another child could wait, surely?

Home life might possibly have some appeal—Ylo had never tried it and had no wish to do so at the moment.

And as for recreation, variety was a large part of it. Why sing the same song every night when there were so many beautiful melodies around to try?

Of course Shandie had political reasons for wanting to be back in the capital. The old man was showing increasing signs of irrationality, and he certainly could not last much longer. But return to Hub was not what the prince was demanding.

Ylo blinked again at the terrible document and read it through again. He glanced longingly at the door to Shandie's office, wondering if he dared go and reason with the maniac. He reluctantly decided that a future decapitation in Hub was worth two immediate decapitations in Gaaze. Shandie would brook such gross insubordination no better than his grandfather did.

The scribbled note at the top was meant for Ylo. It said merely, "Confidential. Transcribe personally."

The final document would be specially sealed and go in its own bag, weighted with lead in case the ship sank. It would arrive unopened in Emshandar's hands. No one else would ever know that his grandson had delivered an ultimatum.

But the old man was almost blind. Personal letters had to be written with a special brush and a special black ink, in huge letters like a poster, a dozen or so words to the page. That was Ylo's job.

So the imperor would know that at least one man was witness to his shame. That was possibly a death warrant all by itself, and if the imperor was aware that the flunky in question was a hated Yllipo, his vengeance would be certain. The letter was Ylo's death warrant, just for reading it.

Ah, duty! The perils of a military career! With a sigh, he reached for his brush and the ink bottle, selected the largest sheet of vellum he could find in his drawer.

Life had been unspeakably hectic in the two months since the XIIth had limped into Gaaze, scorched, filthy, and exhausted. Ylo had been exhausted ever since. With his army disarmed and scattered, Shandie had been faced with the enormous task of refitting it in winter, when the passes were closed, while trying to guard against an elvish counterattack, which fortunately had not materialized. He had rebuilt everything from the bottom up, even as rumors of dragons sparked desertions on an enormous scale. Shandie had worked himself to a shadow and his staff to less than that.

And Shandie slept nights. Ylo didn't, much.

Ylo had his own grand office in the proconsular palace. A side door led through to Shandie's office. The main door led out into a hall where a hundred scribes labored. Unofficially, he was probably the second most powerful man in Qoble.

Oddly enough, he had not been using his power for his own gain. There just had not been time in his life and he had no need for money at the moment anyway. He hoped the wraiths of his more notorious ancestors were not too ashamed of him. Later, when Shandie was installed on the Opal Throne and appointed him praetor of a city somewhere, then he would loot the place and become rich. It was what was expected. It was the way things were done, and all Yllipos were born with a talent for jobbery. Meanwhile, he politely refused all bribes, moving the would-be donors to the bottom of the list. He had created considerable confusion in local affairs thereby, because no one had any experience of dealing with honest officials.

He yawned again.

"Sleeping sickness?" a waspish voice demanded. Little Sir Acopulo was standing in the doorway, pouting like a maiden aunt.

"No, it's just that I was up all night." Ylo displayed his most cherubic smile.

The pout grew to a scowl. "Signifer, you suffer from a complete lack of moral probity!"

"*Suffer* from it? I enjoy it enormously!"

The scowl became a grimace. "Have you received any mail?"

"Two invitations to balls, one threatening note from a husband, and three thank-you letters, but I think I can handle—"

"Don't play dumb, Signifer. Your performance is much too convincing."

"I don't understand what you mean, sir." Ylo widened his eyes to indicate bewilderment. Their daily sparring had become a tradition. He suspected that the prudish political advisor took it much more seriously than he did.

"I was inquiring if there had been any mail for me?"

Ylo scratched his head. "Yes, there was something addressed to you . . . No, maybe that was yesterday, or the day before." He yawned as widely as he could.

The scholar glared and seemed about to depart. "Try to get more sleep, boy. You're quite confused at times."

"Ah! I recall. The prince asked me to ask you if 'Raspnex' is a dwarvish name."

Acopulo's little eyes narrowed. "Why does he want to know that?" He much preferred to converse with Shandie in private and hated reporting through Ylo.

Ylo shrugged, smiled innocently, and waited.

The scholar admitted defeat. "Yes, it is."

"Thank you. I'll tell him." Ylo picked up his brush again, as if the conversation were over. He knew it wasn't.

"Why did he want to know?"

"I can't remember."

"I shall ask him myself, then," the little man said suspiciously.

Ylo smirked. "Go ahead." Meaning he had not invented the question, of course.

Acopulo snorted and turned to leave.

"Trade?" Ylo said softly.

"What does that mean?"

"I answer your question, you answer one of mine?"

"I am always willing to advance your education, as the need is so obvious."

"Mm. I recall now that Lord Umpily had heard a rumor that Raspnex is the name of the new warden of the north."

The little man nodded. "I half expected something like that."

Ylo wanted to ask him to prove it, but that would not be politic. "Now, my question! Dwarves and elves fight like dogs and cats. Why would Warlock Lith'rian ever have agreed to accept a dwarf on the White Throne?"

"He may just have been outvoted."

"But he was strong enough to use his dragons against the legions in spite of the other two! So why would he let them foist a dwarf on him?"

"Bah! He accepted Raspnex in exchange for the dragons, of course. Obviously Raspnex was the price the elf paid to have the others let him chase you out of Ilrane." Acopulo's thin lips pulled back in a sort of smile. "Cheap at the price, maybe?" He disappeared from the doorway.

He was still guessing, though. No one would ever know for certain. Ylo sighed and set to work with his brush.

He put an enormous blot on the third word. He blanked out the first two, tossed the vellum aside, and reached for another sheet.

A tap on the door interrupted him. He looked up and squinted at a young tesserary nervously clutching a mail sack.

"Well, bring it!" Ylo snapped irritably. "I can't read 'em from there!"

The youngster hurried across the big room.

"Sorry," Ylo muttered, remembering that Shandie never lost his temper, no matter how tired or overworked he was. "Forgive me. You open it and pick out the important stuff."

Beaming at the honor thus granted, the kid pulled his sword to cut the seals. He unlaced the bag, tipped the contents out on the floor, and knelt down. One by one, letters and reports began lining up along the edge of the desk. Finally the tesserary rose.

"There's a lot of others here, Signifer."

"That's fine, Huil," Ylo said, pleased at recalling the lad's name. "Thanks. That will be all."

The kid saluted and marched to the door.

Come to think of it, Huil was probably older than Ylo. Ylo just felt old today, that was it.

Aha! Top priority! His practiced eye picked out the private seal of Princess Eshiala. He grabbed up the package and strode over to the inner door.

The proconsul's office was a small ballroom. Ylo marched across a meadowland of mosaic floor to the desk in the center, where Shandie was in conference with some civic officials. He glanced up, frowning, then smiled as he saw the seal. He muttered his excuses to the visitors and slit open the letter.

Ylo had barely reached the door when he heard a yell and spun around. Shandie the Inscrutable? Shandie the Imperturbable?

"Ylo! Look at this!" Shandie the Inscrutable came racing across the great room, waving his letter, civic dignitaries forgotten. He thrust it under his signifer's nose. "Recall!" he whispered urgently. "See? She says the old villain's recalling me! As soon as my replacement . . . It's right here, Ylo! At last!" He thumped his signifer on the back hard enough to make him stagger.

Ylo had never known the prince so excited. "Congratulations, sir. Then that letter to his Majesty . . ."

"What letter?" Shandie was hastily scanning the rest of
his wife's news and did not look up.

"Your letter to the imperor threatening . . . I mean, asking . . ."

"Oh that? Burn it, for the Gods' sake! We're going back
to Hub, Ylo!" He grinned in triumph.

The news penetrated Ylo's fog-filled brain. Hub! At last!
Great!

"My wife!" Shandie sighed. "Did I ever mention that she
is the most beautiful girl in the world?"

"I think you did remark on that, sir." A million times.

There were a million beautiful girls in Hub. Shandie could
certainly have that one, if Ylo could have all the rest.

7

THIS WAS GOING TO BE A BAD ONE; GATH JUST KNEW IT. HE
wasn't sure how he knew it, but he did. Funny thing was,
though, that he hadn't been up to anything he shouldn't've.

He couldn't even think of anything in his past that might
have caught up with him, except the molasses he and Kadie
had spread on the seats in the kitchen staff toilets—but that had
been two years back and was long forgotten. He still felt
bad about it, though.

The room was dim, full of jumping shadows, lit only by
the lantern in Dad's hand and little red worms of glow
among the peat. It was cool, too, and smelled of smoke.

Gath went and sat in his mother's chair, while Dad laid
the lantern on the high mantel and poked at the fire.

"You sit there," Dad said, waving a hand without looking around.

Gath hated to think of his dad being upset, especially if it was his fault. He knew that other boys' dads beat them, because they'd shown him the welts—Jar and Kliff and Brak. His dad had never struck him once, not ever, but he was the king and he could look very fierce sometimes. It wasn't a beating that was the trouble tonight, just being unhappy. He was sure Dad was unhappy, or would be unhappy soon, although he wasn't sure why.

Over in the corner was the big chest where the crowns were kept. Long ago he'd used to come in here with Kadie and Kadie would pick the lock and they would play at trying the crowns on, but he hadn't done that in a long time. So it wasn't that. Unless Kadie was still doing it. He hoped he wouldn't get asked about that.

He'd done awfully bad in yesterday's spelling test. It might be that.

Or it might be his swollen eye.

Dad flopped down in the other chair. Not fierce, but rather solemn.

"It got punched, sir." Gath didn't have to call Dad "sir." No one had ever told him to, but everyone else did and he rather liked to. Reminded him that his dad was the king. And a wonderful dad, too, of course.

"What happened to . . . I can see that. You're going to have a great shiner!"

Gath sniggered. "No, I didn't."

"I can see your knuckles, too, but I don't suppose you punched yourself, did you?"

"It was Brak."

"Who was it and . . ." The king scratched his hair. It was the only hair in the kingdom untidier than his, Mom always said. "Brak? Redhead jotunn? The blacksmith's son?"

Gath just nodded. He was feeling a little *mixed up* again. He'd felt *mixed up* a couple of times this afternoon. Maybe he'd banged his head when Brak knocked him down.

Dad said, "You ought to pick on someone your own size. Not more than twice as big, anyway. Who started it?"

Gath considered the question. Was the one who started it the one who swung the first punch, or the one who called your father a sorcerer?

"Who hit who first?" his father demanded in a royal sort of voice.

"I hit him first. I punched him on the chest."

"Idiot-stupid place to punch. What had he said?"

Gath didn't want to answer that, but something told him he should. While he was still debating, his father made an impatient noise. "You're not a kid anymore, Gath. This is a man-to-man talk we're having, remember? So, please tell me what he said."

"He said you were a sorcerer."

"Oh!" the king said, and did not look pleased.

After a moment he said, "Did you ever ask me if I was a sorcerer?"

"Kadie did. When we were little."

"And what did I say?"

"You said that it was a very impertinent question."

"I did?" His father looked happier. "Thank the Gods for that, then. And why should it matter if Brak thinks I'm a sorcerer?"

Gath thought about that. "It doesn't seem to matter much now, Dad, but it did then. It was the way he said it."

His father laughed quietly. "Well, I know you're not the sort who goes around picking fights. Tomorrow . . . no, I'm judging the knife-throwing contest in the morning. Before supper tomorrow, we'll go down to the gym and I'll show you a few things."

"What sort of things?" Gath demanded, feeling very excited all of a sudden.

"Did you know I once had a fight with Brak's father?"

"And lived?" Gath said in astonishment. He didn't think Kratharkran the smith had ever actually killed anyone, but he was *huge*! Maybe Dad really was a sorcerer. Kadie said he was, but Kadie said all kinds of things. Gath thought he might be, but he wouldn't say so, or admit it to Brak and the others.

He was the finest dad in the world, as well as being a king. Gath wouldn't trade him for anyone else's dad.

His dad was grinning, his teeth shiny in the shadow. "Don't recall dying. We squabbled when we were kids, of course, and he always won. But once I beat him fairly in a real stand-up, grown-up, knockdown fight. Once! Now *don't* go and brag about that to Brak, you hear? Krath would be after me like lightning, and I might not be so lucky next time. But there's a few things I can show you about defending yourself. I know you'll not abuse them."

He sighed and then added, "Fighting's a pretty stupid pastime, I think. But this is Krasnegar. Now . . . that wasn't really why I wanted to talk to you."

Gath pulled his mind off the prospect of beating Brak. He didn't really want to beat Brak, anyway. But it would be nice to stop him calling Dad a sorcerer.

"I'm very proud of you for what you've been doing, Gath."

Oh, *wow*! "Doing what, sir?"

"Helping sick people and old people. Why did you decide to do that?"

Gath felt his face going all hot. He'd begun to think he'd been very stupid. The other kids had laughed at him—he'd walked away from several near-fights over that, and after the first few days it had become an awful bore, but of course he hadn't been able to stop then in case the others thought it was because of what they'd been saying. But if it pleased Dad, then he'd keep on, of course. Wonderful!

Now he had to answer the question, and that was tricky. Really he'd thought it would be a good idea to help people because Dad did it sometimes and it was the only thing he could think of that Dad did as a king that he might be able to help with. He'd have to be a king himself someday, probably, so he might as well get started learning, he'd thought. But he didn't want to say so.

"Well, Mom can't just now, with Holi so little."

"Mmph. That's all? Well, never mind."

The king scratched his head again, as if the conversation

was getting difficult. "It could present a problem, Gath. It's hard to explain. Have you ever heard of—"

"Yes, sir."

"Gath!"

"They're secret words that sorcerers know. And if you can make a sorcerer tell you his words of power, then you become a sorcerer, too."

"Not bad!" Dad said in an odd voice. "Who told—"

"Guys," Gath said vaguely. It was one of the things boys talked about, like girls.

He had to wait a bit for the next question, and when his dad spoke it wasn't a question.

"Gath, I'm going to tell you a secret. Quite a lot of secrets. I know you won't tell anyone if I ask you—will you?"

Gath shook his head. He especially wouldn't tell chatterbox Kadie! He didn't understand why his dad seemed so cheerful when he was going to be so unhappy. This wasn't working out right, somehow, although he didn't know how, or why he thought that.

He was starting to feel *mixed up* again.

"I really am a sorcerer, Gath. When I want to be. Surprised?"

"No, sir. I sort of thought you were."

His father laughed. "You're a good boy, Gath! All right, it's a long story. My mother was born a very long way from here, in a place called Sys—"

"What sort of seer?" Gath said, excitedly.

"Oh, you'd heard that, had you?"

"No, sir."

There was an odd sort of pause, then, until Dad said, "Then why did you ask about your grandmother being a seer?"

"I wanted you to tell me more . . ." Gath had a horrible certainty that he was going to start weeping in a few minutes, which was all wrong for a man of thirteen and a half and would upset Dad, except Dad was really upset about Thrippy, or was going to be upset. Had he said that yet?

What was there to cry about anyway? He was ever so *mixed up* and big guys didn't sob all over their dads' chests . . .

"I haven't really told you anything yet, Gath."

"Sorry, Dad. I'm trying not to."

"Not to what?"

"Interrupt. Was he a *real* raider? Did he kill people and burn towns and . . . What's the matter, Dad?"

His father was looking awful solemn—the *unhappy* starting. "I don't know, Gath. You seem to be getting ahead of me."

Gath sniffed, feeling a lump starting in his throat. "Ever since this morning, I think."

"You not feeling well?"

"Oh, it's just Thrippy!"

"Something bothering you?"

"But, honestly, Dad, I didn't know the silly old man was going to throw an arm around me and I didn't really hear what he said and she'll make an awful scene!"

"I think we'd better get your mother . . . Gath, what did you just say?"

He *knew* he was going to cry, so he decided he might as well get it over with. He jumped up and across to his father's chair and was falling into his arms, except that Dad hadn't started to hold them out to him, but they soon got that straightened around . . .

He wept, or would weep, and was held, or would be held, or had been held . . . He had felt, would feel, better after his weep, when they would go to Mom and he was telling them about Thrippy and what he'd whispered and of course they would know the old man had died would die was dying . . .

He was *ever so* mixed up.

8

INOS MARCHED INTO THE PARLOR AND SHUT THE DOOR.
The fire had shrunk to a few glowing ashes; the room was
chill. Some of the candles had gone out and the others were
guttering.

Rap lay sprawled in one of the big pillowed chairs, looking
as long as a jotunn. He glanced up at her gloomily. "Well?"

"He's sleeping now," she said. "He was pretty distraught
there for a while, but I think he'll be all right."

Rap grunted in misery.

"Not much we can do, really," she said, "except hold him
tight and love him and stay cheerful."

Rap turned his mournful gaze back to the ashes in the
grate. "No."

She perched on the arm of his chair. She had never seen
Rap give in to despair before, and she was not going to
allow it now.

"I know he's big," she said, "but he's only thirteen. A
thirteen-year-old in trouble needs his mother."

Rap took a moment to react, then he looked up at her
inquiringly. "I know that."

"Oh, good. I thought perhaps you were sulking and feeling rejected."

But that did not win the indignant response she had hoped
for. Rap just said, "No," and went back to brooding.

She tried again. "You have a kingdom to run. You can't
spend all your time nursing children. If it was anyone's fault,
it was mine, because I was supposed to be minding the kids
while you were away."

"It wasn't anyone's fault," Rap told the fireplace.

She tousled his hair thoughtfully. Obviously there was
more wrong than she knew and obviously Rap had given
up pretending that there wasn't, or he would be trying to
seem more cheerful. It must be bad, if he was taking this
long to get around to it. Something had happened back

about Winterfest, around the time Holi was born. Rap had been wading deep waters ever since.

"It wasn't deliberate," she said. "I'm sure of that. Gath wasn't deliberately trying to learn a word of power. He says he wasn't and he's not lying. He didn't know that Thrippy knew a word of power. How could he? No one did. Thrippy's never shown any occult ability at all that I know of. In fact, a little magic might have improved his work considerably." Thrippy had been a palace servant so long that she could not remember when he had not been old.

Rap showed no amusement. "I went down there," he said. "He's in a coma now, and sinking. They don't think he'll live till morning."

Poor old Thrippy!

But the word that had done nothing for the old man had shattered the boy. Gath must have inherited his father's knack for magic, just as he had inherited his porcupine hair. Different-colored hair; different talent.

"So Gath has a sort of foresight? Your mother was a seer?"

She waited a long time and finally Rap said, "So they say. I got the impression Gath was kind of a few minutes ahead of me all the time. He was answering questions before I asked them."

"That's when he's upset. When he calms down, he's all right. I think he'll cope. When he gets used to it."

"Yes."

"It does take some getting used to," she said. "Magic does. I remember. You must remember that. It takes time."

No reply.

"Rap!"

"I was even younger," he muttered. "I blocked it out altogether, somehow. I didn't know I had any power at all until I was older than he is."

"Well, that was you. This is Gath."

"It's tough enough on adults. It must be a hundred times worse for a kid." He shivered. "How can he live at more than one time? He'll go crazy!"

"Phooey!" Inos said. "Children bounce like balls. He'll be all right, love. It's not him I'm worried about."

Rap sighed very deeply. "Sorry. I'm just tired. Let's go to bed."

He tried to pull himself up in the chair and she pushed him back.

"There's more to this than you're letting on! What are you hiding?"

He rolled his eyes to stare up at her in abject misery. "I've never kept secrets from you, Inos."

"Good. Why start now? Out with it."

"There's nothing to 'out' with."

"Rap, I'm tired, too, but you don't get out of this chair till you talk. You may start losing eyes or skin very shortly. And don't just say, 'There's more bad news but you'd be happier not knowing!' That's a sure way to make me fear the worst. Speak!"

He clasped her hand and squeezed. "You couldn't fear the worst!"

"Tell me anyway."

"I made an error, darling."

"When? How?"

"That's the trouble—I don't know when. Or how. But somewhere in our adventures, when we were kids, I fouled up badly. And now the ravens are coming home to roost."

She felt a tremor of real fear. "What ravens?"

"Don't know that, either. Something to do with the end of the millennium." Rap looked up at her bleakly. "The night Holi was born, I talked with a God and They said . . . They told me . . . They said that one of the children . . . now I think They were talking about Gath . . ."

Hostages to Fortune:
He that hath wife and children hath
given hostages to fortune.
　　　　　　　　　　　　—FRANCIS BACON, *ESSAYS*

INTERLUDE

ALL OVER PANDEMIA, SPRING RIPENED INTO SUMMER.

In Krasnegar the king spent less time on the mainland than was his custom at that season, and more with his children. Gradually a certain very frightened boy began to adjust to his uncanny new talent. He did not go insane, as his father had feared.

In the splendor of the Opal Palace the imperor clung to life, weakening steadily and rarely seen. Rumor—and there was always rumor in Hub—contended that he was failing and could no longer cope with the immense workload he had always handled so easily. Recalling an unhappy regency eighteen years previously, the wags whispered jokes about a pressing need for faun sorcerers.

Princess Eshiala continued to decline almost all social invitations, while pursuing her studies in elocution, music, deportment, jurisprudence, literature, equitation, poetry, history, interior design, piscation, geography, constitutional law, theology, venery, and all the many other matters with which a future impress was expected to be conversant.

The curious term "covin" came into more general use, although no one would admit to knowing to what it applied, or even whether its new popularity derived from some particular conspiracy.

In Qoble the prince imperial fretted. Agonizing months passed after Eshiala's note told him of his grandfather's decision. When the old man did finally issue a formal recall and appoint a successor, he was adamant that Shandie must not return by ship. That refusal was both inexplicable and ominous.

Admittedly the sea routes from Qoble led around either Zark or Ilrane. Shandie knew he must not set foot in either, but shipwreck was a rare thing. Any decent sorcerer could raise a storm, of course, but to do so against the heir apparent would be a flagrant breach of the Protocol, which should call down the wrath of the Four. No sane sorcerer would dare. So what did the imperor fear? Was he totally senile?

Unseasonable blizzards in the Qoble Range kept the passes closed far later than usual.

In Thume a boy and girl had consecrated their Place in the way of the pixies and begun to build their cottage. For them the days were filled with joy and the nights with love. Time flowed by unnoticed, and no one came near to disturb their idyll.

In Zark the legions continued their slow retreat before the advance of the caliph's rebuilt army.

The harvest ripened and brought thoughts of fall. In retrospect, the Impire was to look back on that last summer of Emshandar's reign with longing.

CHAPTER SIX

STRANGE INTELLIGENCE

1

THE CLOUDS WERE DAZZLING WHITE ON LIMITLESS BLUE AND they trailed their shadows over the sunlit hills. Below them, straight as an arrow, the Great East Way ran onward to the horizon, pointing the way to Hub. It was the most welcome sight Shandie had seen in months. The horse's hard muscles moved smoothly between his legs, iron shoes rang on the stones, and the wind cooled his face. At the end of the road was home, with his wife and the daughter he had never seen and soon the Opal Throne.

Up front rode Ylo with the shining standard. Hardgraa followed, flanked by two others. Then came Shandie and fifty on his tail. Other traffic heard the hooves and saw the glitter of bronze and made way. As the company thundered through hamlets or toll gates, small boys waved and citizens cheered. Probably few of them noticed his emblem on the standard; perhaps few even knew that he wore a legate's insignia. They were cheering the idea of Impire.

He was going home at last!

The passes had opened at last, and Shandie's party had been the first to cross, fighting through drifts. Unwelcome business in South Shimlundok had delayed him another month, but now he had reached the Great East Way, which ran from Hub to the Morning Sea— "a thousand leagues without a bend," one of his ancestors had boasted. That was an exaggeration, but not much of one. Only five hundred leagues separated him from Eshiala now.

Already the fields on either hand were turning gold and the hay had been gathered . . . a good crop, too.

Eshiala, with her serenity, her sweet voice, her perfect features! Her body was smooth as a rockdove's breast and flawless. There was not a mole on her skin anywhere. *Her hair is black as the raven's wing* . . . He had never seen a woman move as she did—she floated.

His favorite memory of her was the first time she came to court. Amid all the frippery and ostentation, she had worn a simple apricot-colored sheath and a thin coronet of diamonds. She had drifted through the aristocrat rabble in all their finery and she had cut them down like a scythe.

Others might think her cold, but he knew she was merely shy. She was not a passionate person, but then neither was he. Passion made him uncomfortable; fire and ice would not do well together. They were well matched and they had shown they could make children together, which was what mattered, especially for a future imperor. And perhaps there would be a little passion when they were reunited . . .

Common sense said he should be taking his time on this journey, inspecting the cities and garrisons, because it might be years before he could make a personal tour through these parts. Common sense be damned!

• • •

As soon as Shandie shouted to him, Hardgraa seemed to know why. He let his mount drop back and the two cantered side by side. The centurion was scowling already.

"You're going to make a run for it?"

"Did you ever doubt I would?" A company of fifty could not travel at top speed, for no post ever held fifty good mounts. Tonight Shandie was going to push on ahead with just a handful of men.

"You're being predictable," Hardgraa growled, "and that's asking for trouble."

All his life Shandie had been guarded and it was true that there had been attempts on his life, although never anything very efficient. On the road he was far more vulnerable than he was in camp or palace. A couple of times he had outwitted conspiracies accidentally, by sheer speed, only to learn of them later. But now he had a reputation for speed.

"How much warning would you need to set up an ambush against a troop like this?" he demanded, shouting over the hooves.

Hardgraa spat while he thought over the problem. "Don't need to. Just one good bowman."

"Good suicidal bowmen are scarce. But it would still need time and a fair idea of when I'm due to ride underneath, wouldn't it? You can't keep bow or man strung tight for days on end."

Hardgraa grudgingly nodded agreement to that. "So?"

"So we'll outrun our news."

Even the imperturbable centurion was shaken by that suggestion. "Outrun the mail?"

A fit rider with money and good weather could ride three posts a day. If he was desperate enough, he could even four-post, although few could keep that up for long. By law the imperial posting inns were supposed to stand eight leagues apart, and on average they did. A man on foot could walk from one post to the next in a day, and even a pack train could usually manage two. Four-posting meant more than thirty leagues a day, usually employing eight or even twelve horses; it was fast travel and slow suicide.

The Imperial Mail went faster than that, but a mail pouch changed men as well as horses. A courier blew his post horn to warn of his arrival, and another rider grabbed his sack before he even slowed down. No mundane rider could out-run the mail.

"State of emergency," Shandie said with a grin. "A pro-consul can stop the mail."

What he was suggesting was so close to blasphemy that he seemed to have shocked his chief of security, for the first time ever. Shandie jerked a thumb to indicate the men fol-lowing. "You think Okratee can handle it?"

Hardgraa nodded confidently. Optio Okratee was his hand-picked deputy, so of course he could handle anything. "How long?"

"Three or four days will do it," Shandie said. "Then the government stuff will take precedence, so any private letters will be held up longer."

The centurion was grinning now, as the idea seized his imagination. "Who do we take?"

"Sir Acopulo and Lord Umpily, of course."

Neither looked capable of surviving one of Shandie's mad rides, but he knew them of old.

Acopulo, his political advisor, was a small, birdlike man, but his white hair made him look older than he really was, and he had one of the sharpest minds in the Impire. He could trace a strand of spider web a thousand leagues and name the spider. Acopulo could read all the patterns.

Umpily, the chief of protocol, was twice Acopulo's size. He was riding near the rear, with the billows of his gray cloak making him look even more bladderlike than usual. The fat man had more curious sources of information than the entire imperial bureaucracy in Hub. Young Ylo thought he knew everything that was happening in the Impire be-cause he read all the official correspondence, but those told only the official facts. Shandie learned many more important facts from Umpily's gossip, just as he learned what those facts really meant from Acopulo's devious reasoning. The flabby Umpily would find the trip hard, but he was much tougher than he appeared.

"And me?" Hardgraa said, suddenly wary.

"Of course."

Shandie would not omit his bodyguard and chief of security, nor a couple of good swordsmen to back him up. They should not be required to do anything except look dangerous, but to travel with no guards at all would be plain stupidity—and also unkind to Hardgraa, the paradigm of the fighting man, old campaigner, ex-gladiator and loyal as they came. He ate granite for breakfast and bronze for lunch.

"And Ylo."

"Him?" Hardgraa barked, astonished and obviously wanting to add, "Why?"

"Think of him as a mascot," Shandie said, smiling.

Ylo was undoubtedly enjoying himself up front, holding the standard high and letting the ends of his white wolfskin flap in the breeze. The promiscuous young demon reveled in his good looks and his reputation for heroism because they brought him women. He probably did not realize how his legend inspired the legions, also, and thereby aided Shandie. If he did know, he did not care. There were very few things Ylo did care about, except Ylo. Ylo was loyal because he chose to be, but Shandie had some thoughts about using Ylo when they returned to Hub.

Hardgraa, Acopulo, Umpily, Ylo. Yes, those few. At the next posting inn Shandie would stop the mail and leave Okratee and the troop behind to see that it stayed stopped. He would carry on with his chosen few and Evil take the saddle sores!

These same few were going to be the nucleus of the next imperor's court, the inner circle. The Impire was moribund and due for a shakeup such as it had not known since the morning his great-great grandmother Abnila threatened to abolish the Senate. Shandie was ready to do the shaking, with the help of his friends. He would start by winning justice for Ylo, so that there could be no doubts about what the next imperor stood for.

The chosen few.

A handful of men.

2

O A K H O U S E , OFFICIAL RESIDENCE OF THE PRINCE IMPERIAL, was located just within the northern wall of the palace complex, on the edge of a steep scarp. Its balconies offered a magnificent view of the city, with the ghostly towers of the White Palace in the distance and a silver glint of Cenmere on the horizon beyond. Eshiala had counted twenty-two temples visible from there, but she might have missed dozens more. Half of Hub lay spread out before her like a marble forest and it was very splendid, if one cared for great cities.

She was not looking at the view at the moment, though. She was leaning on the balustrade with her sister and being nagged as usual.

Ashia's idea of a suitable gown for a summer afternoon involved incredible quantities of taffeta and lace and whalebone. It represented months of work by skilled seamstresses. It was encrusted with pearls and intricate embroidery. Naturally, a lady could wear such a dress only once and must then discard it. Her hair was emblazoned with seashells and silk bows and more gems.

The summer day was baking hot. Eshiala wore a simple cotton shift, with almost nothing underneath it, although no one knew that but she.

"You do realize," Ashia said in her most venomous tone, "that when you become impress, everyone will have to dress as you do?"

Eshiala mulled over the question and decided it was non-sensical. "No, I don't see that at all."

"Well, you should! It is obvious."

"Then let them. What I wear is a great deal more comfortable, I'm sure."

Her sister drew a deep breath of disbelief. Whalebone creaked. "Comfort is not the point! If everyone takes to dressing like a grocer's daughter, then what happens to all the maids and seamstresses? What happens to the hairdressers and jewelers? You'll ruin half the workers of Hub!"

Eshiala had no answer to that, never having considered the problem. She privately considered that Ashia herself would look a great deal better in something simple, instead of being primped and painted like a figurine. She had always been on the plump side, but surely she did not need quite so much scaffolding to contain her figure. She seemed to flow out of it at the top. Perhaps that was the idea, though.

Maya would waken from her nap soon. She was always brought to her mother then; today she would be a welcome distraction from her nagging aunt.

"You know what *they* think of you, don't you?" Ashia inquired snidely, gesturing with a thumb to indicate the door from the balcony. "Your gaggle of goslings?" She was referring, of course, to Eshiala's maids of honor. Those genteel maidens were at the moment waiting for the princess and duchess to return to the tea party and undoubtedly having a good gossip about the pair of them in the meantime.

"I know very well what they think of me," Eshiala said patiently. "They think I am a grocer's daughter." They undoubtedly thought the same of her sister, of course.

"Pah! They wonder why you insist on *behaving* like a grocer's daughter."

The maids of honor were perhaps the worst of Eshiala's burdens, in the continued absence of her husband. Of course a princess and future impress must be attended by maids of honor, however much she might prefer not to be. Normally being a lady-in-waiting was a great honor, and the lady so attended would see that the girls chosen were taught the ultimate refinements in courtly behavior. When their duenna was little older than they were and knew a great deal less about the curriculum, the relationship became sadly skewed. They disapproved of Eshiala because their matronly mothers did, and they sniggered behind their fans at her.

She was miserably aware that she was failing them and doing an atrociously bad job of keeping them virtuous and safe from the predatory attentions of their male counterparts, the gentleman dandies of the court. Two had been forced to leave her household in disgrace already, and she was astonished that it was only two.

"They're even worse than they were when I was here," Ashia commented with a satisfied smirk.

"You were a great help." Certainly, those first terrible months in Hub, Eshiala had been glad of her sister's company. On the whole, though, life had been easier since Ashia's marriage to the old senator.

"You know what they call you? The Ice Impress."

Eshiala did not care what her maids of honor called her behind her back, but she said nothing. Surely Maya must be awake by now?

"Tell me," Ashia said, turning in a swirl of taffeta, "how painful is labor?"

"Darling! You're not! How wonderful!"

"No, I'm not!" her sister admitted, looking slightly abashed—which was a great rarity for her. "But I have been advised that 'nativity would be fiscally expedient.' "

"Fiscally?" Eshiala repeated, bewildered.

Ashia smiled as a cat might show its claws. "When the old goat dies, the entailed estates will go to his son, naturally, and there is going to be a battle imperial over what is and what is not entailed! If I have provided another heir, the courts will look upon my arguments with more favor. I shall expect considerable pressure to be applied from above, of course, darling, but even so."

Eshiala was appalled. "Interfere with a court of justice?"

"Oh, *don't* be so tiresome and provincial! I'm sure Shandie will understand, even if you don't. But, *just* as insurance, I think I may have to make the necessary sacrifice and produce a son for Old Frosty."

Eshiala knew her face was turning pink. "Is it, er, possible?"

Ashia roared with laughter, momentarily forgetting the courtly demeanor she cultivated so painstakingly. "In the way you mean, it's . . . well, 'improbable' would be a charitable description. But there are other ways to arrange such things and I'm sure he won't query."

"You wouldn't dare!"

"Oh, you poor innocent! Well, never mind. You survived the consequences, so I'm sure I can. Revolting, messy business, undoubtedly. Better to travel hopefully than arrive."

"Ashia! You wouldn't!"

The duchess rolled her eyes mysteriously. "I not only would—I have! But no luck so far. You don't imagine I'd want a child as ugly as that old bastard anyway? His grandchildren look like baboons."

It was ironic that Ashia, who genuinely seemed to enjoy bedroom intimacies, should have trouble, when Eshiala had conceived so quickly. "But think of the scandal!"

Ashia sighed and patted Eshiala's shoulder. "There will be no scandal, dear. The course of events would have to be much more obvious to cause a scandal—like Shandie coming back and finding another prince on the way. *You* have been careful, I hope?"

"Extremely careful!"

"Sh! They'll hear us!"

Ashia gave her an odd look. "You are looking forward to having him back, aren't you?"

"Of course I am."

"Gods save me! Don't try to lie to me, darling. Oh, you poor thing!"

"What do you mean?"

"You know what I mean!" Ashia sighed. "I don't know . . .

I did give you a demonstration once. I can't do any better than I did then, I'm sure. Didn't it help?"

"It . . . That sounds like Maya coming." Eshiala had no need to be reminded of that horrible afternoon when she had spent two disgusting hours behind a drape watching her sister, naked on a bed with a stalwart young hussar. She had never been able to bring herself to do any of those grotesque things, and certainly never would. She was certain that Shandie would be terribly shocked if she even tried. That had been just a few weeks after her marriage; ironically, she had probably already been with child by then.

Ashia ignored the diversion. "Any more word on when he arrives?"

Eshiala repressed a shudder. "No word. He will outrun his news, I expect."

Her sister gave her a careful, pitying stare. "I wonder if he's the one who needs the lessons? Let's hope he picked up some finesse from the fair maids of Qoble or somewhere. Now let's go back in the farmyard and set an example of ladylike behavior for the goslings, shall we?"

3

IT WAS TROLL WEATHER. THE COUNTRYSIDE WAS WILD AND uncultivated. Clouds had been building all day in the west as the seven horsemen sped along the highway. Just before dark brought travel to a halt, their destination post inn came into view in the far distance—and at that moment the skies exploded. By the time the weary wayfarers reined in at the door, they were drenched and half frozen. Shandie could not recall being so wet and morose since the night the dragons came.

The law specified that every post inn must provide at least twelve beds. It did not say how many wayfarers might be packed into each, though.

As the door opened, the noise and smell together were enough to knock a man over. The tavern was jammed with wet and weary travelers, sitting, standing, eating, drinking, arguing in near darkness. Smoky lamps swung from the rafters, but their only purpose seemed to be to reveal their own presence so that a soldier did not bang them with his helmet. Apart from the rain and a sense of moorland isolation, this could have been any one of the previous sixteen nights. Two more nights should do it.

Hardgraa went first, his armored menace clearing a trail wide enough for the others to follow. Reaching a corner under a lamp, he thumped a heavy hand on a man's shoulder and rumbled some cheerful platitudes about patriotism and support for our gallant fighting men. The table was quickly vacated.

Shandie sank gingerly onto a rough stool, wondering why he so enjoyed doing that when he had been sitting all day. His head still throbbed with the rhythm of hooves, but he kept his helmet on because there was nowhere else to put it. He leaned elbows on the table and watched the rain dribble down his arms. Military uniform was designed to deflect steel, not water.

Acopulo settled beside him, with a wince of relief, silver hair shining in the gloom. His civilian clothes would have given him better protection from the weather. For the moment there were only the two of them—Hardgraa had disappeared on his usual wary tour of inspection, and Ylo would have gone to arrange accommodation. Most likely Umpily was already deep in conversation with someone, extracting information like a bee sipping nectar.

"I fear we older ones are holding you back," Acopulo sighed. He liked to exploit his frail appearance, but despite his prematurely white hair and his sparrow build, he could be tough as rawhide when he wanted. Now he was weary and fishing for a compliment. Shandie assured him that he was at the end of his own tether and quite amazed how well everyone was holding up, especially Acopulo, but he should have remembered how Acopulo had ridden them all into the ground on the dash to Highscarp . . . and so on.

Mollified, the political advisor assumed his most censorious priestly voice and went straight to business. "Why have we had no report of dwarf trouble?"

Shandie gathered up his road-deadened wits. At times the little man behaved as if Shandie were still his peach-faced student, who must be instructed in the powers of logic as well as the political structure of the Impire. He had now had a whole day to grind his mental millstones undisturbed. Fortunately, he rarely put on this professorial performance in front of witnesses.

"Is there dwarf trouble?"

"Certainly. The price of flax has plummeted. Olive oil is cheap as water."

"So the Dwanishian border is closed again?"

"Excellent!" The sly old scholar sounded disappointed. "But why were you not informed, mm?"

The deduction had not been difficult. When relations with Dwanish were strained, the dwarves cut off the supply of swords. The Impire then blocked sales of strategic materials and a glut forced down prices. The disaster on Nefer Moor had been followed by half a year of peace, but that situation was too good to last.

Shandie was not going to discuss his grandfather's actions, even with Acopulo. "I have one for you," he said. "Umpily has been picking up more stories of troll trouble down in the Mosweeps—bands of outlaws emerging from the jungle and attacking the villages, killing the defenders, and driving off the inhabitants."

"Bah! What you call villages are actually labor camps, the defenders are legionaries, and the inhabitants are serfs, who are delighted to be freed."

"They're slaves, but I'm not supposed to admit that," Shandie said angrily. "It will be one of the first matters I attend to when . . . But why this, now?"

His political advisor drummed scholarly fingers on the table. "It's very unusual behavior for trolls, I grant you. They're usually much more placid."

"You've missed the point, my lord . . ." Shandie smiled up at the mud-splattered face of his signifer. "Yes, Ylo?"

"One room with four beds, sir?"

"Guess who gets a bed to himself? Yes, that'll do." Shandie watched the wolf hood vanishing into the mob. A woman smiled hopefully at him, but he shook his head. Two more nights until he was back with Eshiala!

Umpily's bean-bag bulk emerged from the throng and squeezed onto another of the stools, sighing deeply.

"Not a word of complaint!" Shandie warned. "You've got more padding than all of us put together."

"It's the padding that hurts!" The chief of protocol twisted his flabby face in dramatic agony.

This is the last time, Shandie thought. He might never again travel a highway like this, riding the wind with a few friends and a token escort. As imperor, he would take the entire Praetorian Guard with him when he sallied forth from Hub and possibly a regular legion or two, as well. For ten years he had roamed the impire like a bird of prey, but soon he would be chained to his perch. Fatigued and cold and hungry as he was, he felt a perverse nostalgia for a life about to end. And next month he would be twenty-eight years old! Youth had slipped away, squandered on a dozen battlefields and a hundred highways.

He despised brooding. He turned back to his political advisor. "Trolls?"

"The operative word in your query," Acopulo said testily, "was 'more.' You said, 'more stories,' but I think you meant 'stories of more incidents.' Am I correct?"

"Probably I meant both."

"Ah. Terminological exactitude is a prerequisite for apperception, as dear old Doctor Sagorn used to say. So you are asking why trolls should be turning to violence now, at this point in time?" The old man was cross that Shandie might have seen something he had not. He was also tired by a hard day, of course, and he was twice Shandie's age.

"I am asking why the culprits have not been apprehended."

"Yes, that is worrisome, isn't it?" Even in the deep shadows, the little man was visibly intrigued at so meaty a problem.

Umpily had been listening but was not much interested. "The Mosweeps are all rain forest, that's why! I need beer!"

"If I know Ylo, beer's on its way," Shandie said. "They use dogs to hunt down escaped serfs. Abducted agricultural workers, I mean. The army uses dogs."

"It fits with the dragons, doesn't it?" Acopulo said. "If the dogs were finding the serfs, then the perpetrators would have been found also and stopped. But the attacks continue, so the dogs are being blocked. The army's being blocked and there's another hole in the Protocol."

A white wolf head loomed over the crowd, which parted to emit Ylo and a buxom waitress almost as tall as he and much thicker. Her fists clutched four foaming tankards like small buckets, displaying arm muscles that would not have shamed a troll. She thumped the drinks down on the table, having to stoop to do so without tipping them. Ylo clapped her on the rump like a horse.

"Four stews and four more steins to follow, Ootha, my love!" He flashed his smile at her. She simpered and pushed off into the crowd, working her elbows vigorously.

"Ah, what a challenge that would be!" he said longingly, settling down beside the others. "A wild mare!"

"How can you even think of such things?" Umpily moaned. His jowls quivered emotionally. "After sixteen hours in the saddle?"

Ylo wiped froth from his lips, smearing the dried mud around them. He glanced briefly at Shandie to make sure the meeting was informal, then told Umpily, "I've thought of nothing else all day, my Lord."

"Do you ever?"

"Only right after."

Acopulo seemed to have retreated into thought. Hard-graa and his two henchmen had arrived and commandeered an adjacent table. Ylo was certainly the freshest of them all.

Shandie sat in limp silence for a while, and his companions took their cue from him. They all knew one another well enough that they did not need to fill every awkward second with conversation. Then . . .

"Er, sir?"

"Yes, Ylo?"

"I keep wondering . . . Why you don't just clear the civilians out and take what you need?"

"I assume you did that."

"I demanded the minimum I thought you might accept. Most legates would have sent me back for seven beds, or even seven rooms."

"You underestimate yourself. If you were serving such a man, you would have gotten what he wanted, as you did for me. You judged my wants exactly. One room will do us, because we're leaving at moonrise. Four hours at the most. We're also outnumbered twenty to one—why risk a riot?"

Ylo nodded, but he did not look convinced. Undoubtedly most officers would do as he suggested. Shandie did not want to draw attention to himself, just in case he was recognized. Perhaps Ylo was right and he was making himself more noticeable by being abnormally considerate of the civilians.

Then the robust Ootha reappeared with four bowls of thick stew, contriving to jostle Ylo as she did so and win another pat. The men fumbled in their pouches for their spoons. The messy stuff was mostly water and vegetables, of course, but better than many such repasts Shandie had known. He made a mental note to congratulate the innkeeper personally.

Conversation ended completely, but the troll problem remained.

Warlock Lith'rian had flagrantly violated the Protocol by loosing his dragons to block the army on Nefer Moor; someone was using subtle sorcery to block it in the Mosweeps. Emshandar had refused to let Shandie return by sea, so perhaps he put credence in the persistent rumors of a Nordland fleet shipwrecked on the coast of Zark. Jotnar were the prerogative of the warden of the north. Of course shipwreck was uncertain evidence of sorcery, but it was all beginning to add up.

Shandie would dearly like to know what game the Four were playing at the moment. His grandfather was the only mundane who might have information on that, and sometimes he did not hear from the wardens for years at a time, or so he claimed. To inherit the throne at a time when the Council of Four was squabbling . . .

Ylo had been eating at an incredible rate. He stopped suddenly, with his bowl still half full. "I'm stuffed!"

Glancing at the others, Shandie saw an amusement he could never quite share. He was a prude, he supposed. "I don't expect any of us will be done here for at least fifteen minutes."

"You will excuse me, then?" Ylo was on his feet and away into the crowd at once.

"He can't possibly!" Umpily said, rolling his eyes.

"Of course he can!" Acopulo snapped. "He set it up. He told the innkeeper that the legate would settle for one room if a woman was provided. The innkeeper would assume that the legate himself . . . There they go now, up the stairs!" He sounded as outraged as the sort of fussy old priest he so much resembled.

"I meant fifteen minutes not possibly!" the fat man muttered. He sighed wistfully. "Can he?"

"Easily. Ylo is my organizer," Shandie said firmly. "If he couldn't organize that, I should think less of him, as it obviously matters so much to him." However much he personally disapproved of the signifer's promiscuity, he would not tolerate bickering within the group.

"Lechery will be his downfall!" the political advisor said snappily.

"Not unless I want it to be!"

Acopulo muttered a sulky apology and went on with his meal. He had the arrogance of a philosopher. Being convinced he could think better than everybody else, he wanted to do everybody else's thinking for them. Given the chance, he would guide Shandie to remake the world according to Acopulo's designs.

Shandie knew that. He never lacked for willing helpers, but he liked to know their motives.

To Umpily, power was knowledge and knowledge power. He lacked the will to use it. Power used was power spent—announce an appointment, for example, and you made one friend and a dozen enemies. Unlike Acopulo, Umpily had no reformist agenda. Curiosity satisfied was enough. The fat man was a true imp, now busily finishing Ylo's meal.

Hardgraa was motivated by old-fashioned loyalty and honor and patriotism, very unimpish.

And Ylo? Ylo was motivated by Ylo and only Ylo. Shandie had seen that on the first day, when the lad reeled into his tent, exhausted and out of his mind with battle shock. Offered a chance to escape the living death of the ranks, anyone would have grabbed it without question. But even then Ylo had begun dreaming of his own advancement.

Shandie had thought to use him more or less as a signal that he disapproved of injustice. Out of interest, he had scratched and seen the glint of valuable metal. So he had scratched harder and uncovered a huge capacity for work and a superb attention to detail. If Ylo had been proving his worth to clear his family name, then he had succeeded beyond question. He would continue to serve Shandie loyally as long as Shandie would advance him—which was a traditional impish arrangement that worked both ways. It just

seemed unfortunate that so likable and talented a man should
be so narrow. Ylo cared only for Ylo, as the buxom Ootha
was no doubt now discovering.

And Shandie? What motivated him? His love for Eshiala,
of course, but what else? Pride in his inheritance, yes. A
dedication to honest, fair government and justice. A sense
of duty. A hatred of war . . . what a dull list! But then he
was a dull man, he supposed.

Thunder seemed to shake the building. The roar of voices
faded briefly, frightened horses shrilled in the stable. Gradually the racket picked up again.

"Moonrise?" Acopulo muttered hopefully. "We shan't see
our horses' manes before dawn."

"It's only a storm," Shandie said. "It'll pass."

"Prince Emshandar!" a new voice said and he reached for
his sword.

It was a woman—Shandie relaxed slightly. She faced him,
standing directly behind Umpily. She was enveloped in a
dark garment, one hem draped over her head as a hood, and
in that gloom nothing showed of her face but a glint of eyes.
One bare arm protruded, its hand holding the cloak closed
at her neck. Her other hand was inside, clasping the cloth
tight below the elbow. The visible arm was old and bony,
the skin loose and wrinkled from wrist to elbow. Her fingers were long and knotted with age, yet she stood erect
and proud within her shroud of homespun. It seemed to be
dry, which was uncanny on such a night. He could tell
nothing of what lay within—she might have been clothed
in rich silks or utterly naked.

Conversation buzzed on all around him. Acopulo and
Umpily continued eating unaware, and that had to be sorcery.

"You have the advantage of me, ma'am."

"My name would mean nothing to you. Have you heard

of Wold Hall?" Her voice was creaky with age and heavily accented, but he could not place it.

Unheeding, Acopulo finished his sparrow-pecking and pushed his bowl over to Umpily, who began shoveling its contents into his mouth as enthusiastically as a pig at a trough. Shandie's skin crawled with a sense of the occult. Who? The witch of the west he had never met, but she was a troll. This woman was no troll.

"You are rash to exert your powers around me, ma'am."

"I do not fear the wardens." Her tone implied that she feared something else. "I asked if you knew of Wold Hall?"

"The name is familiar."

"There is a preflecting pool there. It is old and will not work by day, but it should give good counsel in moonlight."

He thought her eyes were elvish—large and slanted—but they did not flicker with the opal fires. The skin of her arm and hand was the same leather-brown shade as his own, not the gold of an elf's. He could not identify her race and that was bothersome. Halfbreeds always favored one parent over the other, yet she was nothing he could identify.

Already she was turning away, as if her task was done.

"Wait!" he said. "Tell me more."

"Place one foot in the pool," that curiously alien croak said. "Right foot to see what you should seek; left to see what you must shun."

"I believe my duty is to avoid sorcery, ma'am," he said suspiciously. Could this be some devious scheme to disqualify him from the succession?

"A foreseeing would not contravene that obligation. There are precedents."

"May I ask your purpose in telling me this?"

She looked back at him with those strangely angled eyes glinting out of the dark. "Ask not the price of gifts, Prince Emshandar. Times are troubled. I . . . Just say I am applying a random factor in the hope of diverting certain events that seem to be well-nigh inevitable. I may not do more." She seemed to shiver.

"Is this the millennium business again?"

She sighed. "Truly. Now I must go. These are sad times, your Highness, and like to become sadder."

"Tell me more!"

She shook her head within the cowl. "I may have already transgressed the Gods' interdict."

Again she seemed about to leave. He leaped up and reached overhead to twist the lantern, flashing a faint beam into her hood. He caught a glimpse of a face as ancient as war, deeply lined with age and pain. He sensed suffering. Her pupils were a pale shade and large. Her nose was wide, like a faun's. Elvish, yet not elvish. Sadness and pity.

She turned quickly away into the crowd and was gone, although he was not sure how, or where. He sat down, perplexed.

"Ugh!" Umpily said, picking something out of his bowl. "What beast did this come from?"

In the wavering gloom, Acopulo peered at the object with scholarly interest. "It appears to be the jawbone of a hippogryph."

"Hippogryphs don't have jawbones!"

"It was delicious anyway," Ylo said, resuming his seat. His wolfskin was draped over one shoulder. His hair was tousled; he was pink and breathless. "Oh! I didn't think I had eaten quite so much." He glanced reproachfully at Umpily.

"I'm astonished," Acopulo said dryly. "You have exhausted neither the fifteen minutes allotted nor yourself, apparently. Is that not remarkable, Legate?"

"Commendable," Shandie said. His heartbeat was slowly returning to normal. Obviously his companions had heard nothing of the bizarre conversation. "Very efficient. What do you know of Wold Hall, gentlemen?"

"The Treaty of Wold Hall?" Acopulo said, frowning. "Signed in . . . around . . . 2900. Dwarves."

"It was a hunting lodge," Umpily said, "favored by the Impress Abnila. Used for secret conferences sometimes. Somewhere on the Great East Way, I believe."

There are precedents. If the Impress Abnila had consulted a preflecting pool, then her great-great-grandson certainly could.

"It may be around here, then," Shandie said. "Can you find out for me?"

Surprised, Umpily nodded. "If it is in the neighborhood." He pushed away his bowl and drained the tankard. Then he licked his spoon to tuck it back in his pouch. "I think I saw a selection of cheeses over there on the bar." He heaved his bulk up and pushed away through the mob.

"What do you know of preflecting pools?" Shandie asked.

Acopulo's scrawny face narrowed in astonishment. "As much as any, which is little. The dear doctor made a study of such devices and discovered almost nothing. I have heard opinions that preflecting pools are more dependable than magic casements, which promote only the interests of the house. The pools may be more limited in scope, but less devious. They supposedly give honest answers to the inquirer. Talking statues, of course, are something else again . . ."

"Thank you," Shandie said quickly. "I was told once that there was a preflecting pool at Wold Hall."

The priestly face lit up with interest. "If that is so, then it would be worth a visit."

"Exactly what I was thinking," Shandie said.

"Shall we be staying here awhile, then?" Ylo asked thoughtfully.

4

WOLD HALL, OR WHAT WAS LEFT OF IT, STOOD IN A RUGGED glen about a league west of the inn—so the innkeeper had reported, and the travelers found the turnoff without trouble. The rain had gone and a quarter moon floated among silver clouds, but dawn could not be far off. An ancient military road wandered away over the hills, then plunged steeply down into woodland. The horses soon became as jumpy as fleas.

It was hard to blame them, for the wind rustled leaves overhead, spattering cold drops of water at random, while the footing was a treacherous medley of rocks and mud and puddles.

The obvious danger was making Hardgraa petulant. Had the centurion known of the mysterious shrouded woman, he would have become mutinous, but everyone assumed that Shandie had dreamed up the expedition on his own and had been planning it for some time.

They all wanted to wait until daylight, of course, but that would have meant staying on all night, as well, to see the pool by moonlight. The moon might not be visible the next night; there might be no pool at all. The whole thing could even be a well-organized assassination plot, but Shandie hated reversing a decision once he had made it. He knew that streak of stubbornness might land him in trouble one day; he just hoped this was not the day.

Then an owl glided overhead, spooking Ylo's horse, which was the most skittish. Skilled rider though he was, he almost went into the mud. Shandie called a halt. The legionaries were left to tend the mounts and the others set off on foot. Most of those feet were in boots, but Ylo and Hardgraa wore only regulation army sandals.

A half hour's misery brought them to an imposing wall, of standard military construction—when the legions weren't fighting, they were always kept busy building something. It was in sad disrepair, showing evidence that the locals had been quarrying it for building stone. The gates were missing, doubtless long since melted down; Shandie led the way through the gap, into a tangle of unkempt forest.

Numerous jagged walls within the undergrowth hinted at

former farm buildings and remains of guard barracks, all roofless now and decayed among the encroaching jungle. The whole complex would likely have held a population of several hundred in its days of glory.

Eventually the half-buried path led to a clearing before the main building itself, stark in the moonlight. One end was obviously very old, the other could be dated by its pointed arches to about the time of the great impress. It had all been gutted by fire. Its windows were gaunt as sockets in a skull.

The sky was already growing brighter.

"Let's split up," Shandie suggested. "The pool must be somewhere around here."

"Sir!" Hardgraa rumbled warningly. He had been carrying his sword in his hand since leaving the horses. "You have no idea who or what may live here!"

"Whoever it is, it doesn't trample weeds." Shandie strode off to begin exploring.

No squatters were discovered before a shout from the portly Umpily brought the others to inspect his find. He was standing on a terrace, overshadowed by trees. Weeds and roots had thrust up the paving stones and the flanking balustrade was half in ruin. A flight of stone stairs led down to a gleam of water directly below.

"Not very impressive," Acopulo remarked with a disparaging sniff. "I certainly don't recommend drinking from it."

"I wouldn't water a horse at it," Shandie agreed, scowling at silvery scum and odd wisps of mist that drifted over the surface.

"You couldn't get a horse to it."

And that was obviously true. The pool was smaller than he had expected, but its edges were concealed by trailing shrubs and willow trees, so it might be larger than it seemed. The sides of the hollow rose steeply, the steps being the only visible access.

"What does one do?" Umpily inquired, coughing in the morning damp. The air was cool and everyone was shivery with lack of sleep. "Chant at it, or invoke it, or jump in?" He sounded unwilling to do any of those things.

"You put one foot in it," Shandie explained, trying to sound more confident than he felt. "Right foot to see what you should seek, left foot to see what you should shun." No one asked where he had learned such flummery—they all knew that he spoke with warlocks.

"One prophecy per customer?" Acopulo said.

"Sounds like that." Shandie headed for the top of the stairway. The woman had implied that the pool was in magical disrepair. There might only be one prophecy per night, and if so he intended to have it for himself. More likely nothing at all would happen and he was going to make a fool of himself.

The steps were unsteady, caked in loam, masked in shadow. He felt his way down very cautiously, one uneven tread at a time, while steadying himself with a hand on the mossy blocks of the wall. Unless the construction was a faked antique, this part of the complex predated Abnila by centuries. It might have been a mundane pool at first, of course, and been ensorceled later.

He almost stepped into water before he realized, for the steps continued on, under the surface.

From the last dry slab he looked across a dark and oily expanse much larger than it had seemed from up high. The wind did not penetrate into the hollow. The slowly writhing traces of mist were more obvious at this level, as unpleasantly eerie as the pallid patches of scum. There was no color in the moonlight. He could see the moon reflected, of course, and the silvered edge of clouds and the trees. No water weeds or lilies, but there was an odd scent—not decay, but almost sweet, like a hint of incense.

Leaning over, he could make out his own reflection, his helmet shining. The heads of his companions stood out against the sky, as they peered over the balustrade to watch him. He hoped they did not lean too hard and bring it all crashing down.

Dawn was advancing, so he must make a move. Did he want to know of danger—the face, perhaps, of a future assassin, or a traitor? He was well protected always and would be even better protected in future. Every man must die at last, and he certainly did not want to view his own death. Nor would there be much value in a prophecy of some catastrophe in the far future—he assumed he would live to a ripe antiquity, like his grandfather.

To ask to see the good news might merely produce an image of his beloved Eshiala, of course. That might not be an earth-shattering revelation, but at least it would make the side trip worthwhile. And he had so many reforms he wanted to introduce when he mounted the throne—perhaps this sorcery could help him decide where to start? He leaned against the wall and removed his right sandal. Then he put his bare foot in the water.

The next step was deeper than he had expected. Furthermore, the water was warm, when he had expected coldness. That surprised him so much that he almost toppled in bodily. Steadying himself with a hand on the wall again, he rested his weight on the slimy slab and waited until the widening ripples died away. Warm water explained the mist, on a cold morning.

The surface cleared very slowly, surprisingly slowly. Gradually the reflections steadied—the moon, the clouds, the mists. Trees. His own face. All dark and indistinct.

Except that the moon was now full.

No, it was a pale image of the sun. All the random shapes of mist and scum and shadows and reflections had subtly reformed into a meaningful pattern—an indistinct, alien landscape. He was seeing a daylight view darkened as by smoky glass. First, he made out a distant castle, on a peak. Then he picked out the summer cloud behind it, dimmed to patches of pale gray. The stretch of water in the foreground must be the sea, for waves were running onto a beach. So that angular rock was an island, and now he saw that there was a town on the slope below the towers.

Where was this? What use was a prophecy that he couldn't identify? Just as he was about to call out to ask the others if they knew the place, he realized that what he had thought to be his own reflection was someone else. He was staring into the puzzled eyes of a boy, a young jotunn in the shabby work clothes of a fisherman or farmhand. He was standing in the foreground with his hands in his pockets.

Startled, Shandie moved. Ripples flowed out from his shin; the image was gone. Tight with excitement, he waited for it to re-form. This time the water stilled more quickly, but the moon was again at the quarter and there was no castle, no boy. The magic show was over.

He retrieved his right foot, removed the other sandal, and tried with his left foot. The water seemed much colder and the ripples faded swiftly; he was going to be shown nothing more. One prophecy to a customer.

Carrying his sandals, he walked up the stair, feeling exceedingly frustrated. Perhaps the poor old thing had tried its best for him, but its best had been unsatisfying. His journey had been wasted. At the same time, he felt uneasy at the spookiness of sorcery. He was much more familiar with the occult than most mundanes. As a child, he had once watched the wardens all materialize in Emine's Rotunda, and that same evening he had seen a sorcerer vanish in a pillar of fire. He had sat in the visitors' gallery when Witch Grunth appeared in the Senate chamber to receive the address of welcome upon her accession. Olybino had been a frequent visitor during his military days. But he was not so familiar with the occult that he could feel blasé about it.

"You came a long way to wash your feet," Acopulo remarked snidely, "if I may say so!" He was the only one of the group who might say so and he knew it. Even so, he was presuming far.

Shandie ignored the irreverence. "You saw nothing?"

"You did?" the scholar demanded.

The others had not made a sound, but their silent shock was unquestionable.

"Yes, I saw a vision of a castle and a town, but where it was I have no idea. And I saw a boy. Fifteen or sixteen, maybe." Shandie thought for a moment. "A jotunn, but an odd face. His eyes seemed dark, although it was hard to tell colors. His hair needed a good brushing . . . reminded me of someone, but I don't know who. And you saw nothing?"

No, they all said, they had seen nothing.

"And my other foot got nothing, so it is one per person. One of you try, then. By the way—the water is quite warm. It shocked me so much I almost fell in."

The others exchanged uneasy glances, none willing to claim precedence.

"Dawn will be here shortly," Acopulo said. "You go first, Signifer, and we grown-ups can take our time on the stairs."

With a glance to Shandie for his consent, Ylo hurried off. The two civilian advisors followed.

Shandie put on his sandals. Then he leaned on the crumbling balustrade with Hardgraa and watched the procession going down. "You will not venture, Centurion?"

"Not unless you want me to, sir. I'd rather not know."

"Sensible man! All I've gotten out of this is an Evil-begotten mystery that will probably worry me for years. Every time I go near the sea, I shall wonder. Our young friend is going to go with the right foot, also. I expect he will see cohorts of gorgeous women."

Hardgraa grunted. "Probably! The other foot would show legions of angry husbands."

Shandie chuckled. He was always taken unaware when the gruff old campaigner chose to reveal his sense of humor. "More'n likely!"

The ripples were barely visible from the terrace, Shandie noticed. He could see nothing unusual happening in the pool.

Ylo seemed to have witnessed something, though, for he made a remark to Acopulo, who had now reached the bottom. The two exchanged a few words. The little man laughed. He sat down carefully and Ylo helped him remove his boot—his right boot. The signifer came trotting up the stairs, slowing only to pass the wide bulk of Umpily.

"Well?" Shandie said as Ylo reached the top. "The most beautiful woman in the world?"

"Oh, yes! You saw her?" The brightening sky gave enough light now to show the excitement on the signifer's face.

"No. I was just guessing. Really? That's what you saw?"

Ylo nodded agreement so vigorously that his wolf ears flapped. "Yes, your Highness! Absolutely . . . Beyond description!"

"Lying naked on a bed?"

"In a garden, but, yes. Naked." Ylo sighed deeply. "Incredible!"

Well, he ought to be a good judge.

Hardgraa made a soft snorting noise. "I hope you noted her features so you'll recognize her when you meet in public?"

"I'll know her anywhere!" Ylo promised.

Shandie wished he was as confident about his own vision. When he got back to Hub, he would crack a whip over the Imperial bureaucracy and demand a list of all offshore islands with castles on them. The sun had been low behind the island, so it must lie off either the east coast or the west, not north or south. The search would keep the quill-pushers out of trouble for a while. But it would not explain the strange woman who had initiated this seance, a woman who claimed she did not fear the wardens.

Down below, Umpily was gingerly lowering his left foot into the water. Acopulo was mounting the steps, carrying his right boot.

"Any luck?" Shandie called.

"I saw something," the little man said, but he added nothing more until he had reached the terrace. "But not very helpful."

"You wish to tell me in private?"

"No. It's certainly not worth keeping secret." The political advisor sat down stiffly on a section of fallen balustrade and pulled on his boot. "I saw my old mentor, the venerated Doctor Sagorn." He sniffed.

During his student years, Shandie had heard Acopulo relate many tales of the great sage, too many tales. "Is he still alive, then?"

"I don't see how he can possibly be. He was old as the Protocol when I knew him, and that was thirty years ago." Acopulo screwed up his wizened features. "I seem to have been granted a retroactive prophecy! One should trust in the Gods and not such sorcerous gimcrackery." He had already forgotten that he had recommended the experiment himself.

"His Lordship is going with the left foot," Hardgraa remarked thoughtfully.

Acopulo lowered his voice. "He may be seeking news of his dear wife! I suspect a lack of trust!" He snickered maliciously.

"His wife died almost a year ago," Shandie said. "You didn't know?"

The scholar choked and began spluttering apologies. Feeling that he had been rather malicious himself, Shandie pulled a face and turned away to wait for the fat man. Umpily had sat down on the stairs to replace his boot. He took his time coming up. The sky was blue and the moon a faint smudge now, half hidden in cloud.

"Well?" Shandie demanded.

"Not well, Highness," Umpily puffed. "I . . . I saw no vision at all." His flabby features seemed unusually rigid and pale.

"That was unfortunate," Shandie said cautiously. "I expect the light was wrong, or the pool exhausted by its efforts. Let us be on our way, gentlemen. We have a long, hard journey ahead of us."

Strange intelligence:
>*Say from whence*
>*You owe this strange intelligence? or why*
>*Upon this blasted heath you stop our way*
>*With such prophetic greeting? Speak, I charge you.*
>>—SHAKESPEARE, *MACBETH*, I, III

CHAPTER SEVEN

CURRENTS TURN AWRY

1

"WELL, I DON'T THINK IT'S FAIR!"

The king and queen of Krasnegar were eating breakfast and Princess Kadie was adjusting the universe to fit her needs and wants, as usual.

There was no one else in the great hall. As always in early summer, the whole castle seemed deserted. Almost everyone was over on the mainland or gone fishing. Rap had been spending much time in the hills, checking on the livestock, but he'd taken a night off to come home and get to know his family again.

He awoke from a reverie, realizing that Inos had not answered Kadie's comment and so must be leaving it for him.

Someone had eaten all his porridge . . . didn't matter, he wasn't hungry now.

"Sorry! I was daydreaming. What was the question?"

His daughter impaled him with a disapproving expression she had inherited from her mother. "I don't think the corporal should be allowed to have Gath on his team!"

Several responses were available: *What team?* for example, or *Why not?* or even *What corporal?* although that one would probably prompt a screaming fit—except that he hadn't witnessed any fits from Kadie for a while. The twins were growing up, and she was doing it faster than her brother, which was to be expected. Kadie was thirteen and a half going on thirty. This morning she was dressed as if to attend a wedding, which was normal.

"Why isn't it fair?" he asked.

His daughter tossed her black mane in exasperation. "Really, Daddy! A fencing contest where one of the players is . . . uses . . . Well!"

He must be behaving very stupidly if he was *Daddy*. "Uses what, Kadie?" he said, applying a parental glare of moderate intensity.

She dropped her eyes. "Well, everyone knows!" she muttered.

"Knows what?"

"That Gath is a seer, of course! That's why it won't be fair to let him be on the boys' team. No one can ever lay a button on him. *Not even the corporal!*"

Rap glanced at Inos and saw a flicker of the distress she showed every time Gath's powers were discussed. She blamed herself, of course, which was stupid.

And this argument was unnecessary at the moment. Summer had barely opened the causeway again and yet Kadie was planning a winter fencing carnival. Kadie had become a complete fanatic about fencing, predictably infecting all her friends. Rap still had not adjusted to the idea of girls fencing, but he had certainly learned not to laugh at it when Inos was within earshot.

"I didn't know Gath had even been near the gym," he said. "I certainly didn't know he'd taken up fencing."

"He hasn't. Not like the rest of us."

"Well, that helps even out the odds, surely? If he doesn't practice, it does. I can guess what his defense is like. How's his attack?"

"Awful! The corporal says he isn't aggressive enough."

"There you are then. It cancels out."

Kadie rose with great dignity. "I see. Fairness is relative! Boys are different. Of course! Now, if you will excuse me, dear Mama, darling Papa, I have an appointment with my *coiffeuse*. But I still consider it very . . . er, unfair . . . to permit occult abilities in mundane athletics!"

"Kadie!"

Again the princess tossed her hair—Rap wondered what Inos would say if he proposed a law making long hair illegal in the kingdom. No, he wouldn't risk it.

Kadie sat down in a sulk. "Just because you won't let me talk about them doesn't mean that everyone else doesn't know."

"Now, wait a moment, love," Rap said. This ought to be investigated. He knew how he had suffered from having a reputation for magic in Krasnegar, and he had been several years older than his son was now. "What exactly does everyone know?"

His daughter pouted. "They know you can't sneak up behind Gath. Throw something and he isn't there. Flip a coin and he'll call it right a dozen times in a row!"

"Gath will really show off like that?"

"Yes!" Kadie said. Then she added, "Sometimes." That probably meant, "Once."

"Then I apologize and I agree he shouldn't be allowed on a fencing team."

Kadie bounced up jubilantly and withdrew, flouncing off along the great hall.

"Sounds like Gath's adjusting," Rap said hopefully.

Inos nibbled a piece of crusty roll, eyeing him with a fond smile in her so-green eyes. "Oh, I think so. Remember telling me once that all occult talents had a mundane equivalent?"

"No. Did I say that? Sounds like a pretty dumb remark."

"One of your best, dear. But I think in Gath's case it may be true. He's always had a sort of talent for staying out of trouble."

"Kadie makes up for it."

Inos shook her head. "Kadie's normal. Gath . . . He hasn't come to me with a bleeding knee since he was a toddler, and some days I seem to spend half my time being court nurse, bandaging battered children. It's very rare for Gath to be involved when the gang of them gets into really serious mischief. He's always just somewhere else."

There might be some truth in that. Troublemakers were noticed, but good behavior tended to be overlooked. Gath had never been a problem. "He's got too much sense," Rap said.

"He's not stupid," Inos agreed, "but he's no mental giant, either. At his age it can't be experience, so what is it?" She reached across the plank table and clasped her husband's hand. "He's managing, that's what matters!"

"If he's showing off for the other kids, then he must be."

"His friends are starting to adjust, too. You look! Quite often now he wanders around with that dreamy old smile of his as if he hasn't a care in the world."

"Or can avoid it if he has?" Rap hated to think about foresight and premonition, because they always tied his mind in knots. Even as a sorcerer, he had never completely understood them, and much of that arcane understanding was now lost to him. His mother had been a seer, able to foretell such things as the sex of babies. Or so he'd been told—he didn't remember her very well. Gath's talent was different, though. At times he seemed to be living a few minutes ahead of everyone else.

"Here he comes now," Inos said. "And what did I tell you?"

Gath was sauntering along the room toward them, a gangling boy with his hands in his pockets as usual and his hair a silver bird's nest. His expression suggested that he was finding the world interesting but not threatening.

Kadie wasn't the only one starting to sprout. Gath had always been tall for his age, and of course it was the big ones who went over the wall first. He was still a kid, but he was almost as tall as his mother, all spindly arms and legs.

He sprawled on a bench, stretching out his oversized feet. "It will be soon," he told his father solemnly.

Rap swallowed the greeting he had been about to pronounce. "What will be what soon?"

"A good morning."

Rap glanced up at the windows. Rain in Krasnegar was a rare event, but there was certainly rain falling now. And that was fortunate, because he had a whole mountain of bills of lading to inspect. The first ships had arrived. If there was anything missing, anything Krasnegar might need over the coming winter, then the orders must be sent back at once or there would be no time for delivery before the ice came in again. The rain would keep him dutifully working indoors, not wasting time in frivolous pursuits.

"It stops in about half an hour," Gath explained seriously.

Rap gave him a baffled look. He suspected he had just noted a twinkle in those deep gray eyes, but he wasn't sure. A thirteen-year-old should not be inscrutable like that! "I have a pile of accounts to go over this morning with Master Gracker."

"No, sir. You and me go down to the docks."

Now, that was a specific prophecy! Whatever powers his faun grandmother might have had, Gath's range seemed to be little over an hour, or two at the most. Moreover, as far as Rap had been able to discover, he was limited to knowing things before he should know them. He apparently could not prophesy for others. He knew the rain would stop because he would see it stop.

So what happened if Rap rushed him down to the dungeons and locked him up there for an hour, so that when the rain did stop he couldn't know that the rain had stopped? That would mean he couldn't have made the statement he'd just made, wouldn't it?

Except that Rap would never do any such thing.

And now the boy had just come out with another extremely specific, verifiable prophecy, something he rarely did. What happened if Rap refused to go down to the docks? This was going to be interesting, because Rap had no intention of going down to the docks this morning. He had far too much work to do. Why should he . . .

"To see Captain Efflio," Gath explained.

"Give me one good reason . . . The one who brought the horses last year?"

Gath nodded. "No. Mostly rope this time. He thinks you can trade it to the goblins."

Rap took a deep breath. "Even the prospect of a shipload of rope will not—"

"Something to do with . . . Shandie?" Gath said, screwing up his eyes. "It's not clear yet, but . . . Shandie? Who's Shandie?"

"What are you talking about?"

"News from Captain Efflio. Yes, he is."

"Is he going to . . ."

Rap abandoned the question. Inos was watching the exchange with barely suppressed laughter. Efflio had been much better informed about the current news in the Impire than most sailors who called at Krasnegar, so a talk with him was an attractive prospect. It almost justified taking the morning off work. And Gath's shoulders were damp! That meant—

A flicker of uneasiness crossed the boy's face. "There's

something about the castle gate, Dad . . . I have to go outside before I know what's going to happen outside."

So he'd discovered the shielding? Never mind Captain Efflio! The time had come for another father-and-son . . .

"I knew you would!" Gath said happily, and now there
was no denying the gleam in his eyes, or the smile of triumph he was trying to hide.

Rap pulled a ferocious mock scowl at his son's glee, hiding his own relief. Obviously Gath had adjusted to his new
talent to the point where he enjoyed showing off with it, as
Inos had said. That man-to-man talk was overdue. But if
Rap was going down to the harbor with Gath, then he
needn't trouble Master Gracker. "Run and—"

"I already told him," Gath said smugly.

As king and prince left the barbican and hurried across the
courtyard outside, Rap noticed with amusement that his
lanky companion was taking strides as long as his own, although he had to strain to do so. The rain was definitely
relenting, blue sky showing to the west, but man and boy
headed for Royal Wynd, which was one of the town's many
covered ways. The first stretch was very steep and at present
deserted, so they let their feet run away with them, leaning
back for balance, footsteps drumming eerily in the shadows.

They slowed down for the first stairs, grinning at each
other. Gath was glowing with wordless bliss at being with
his father, which raised a question Rap had been considering
for some time. The citizens of Krasnegar all started work as
children. Princes and princesses had schoolwork to occupy
their childhood, but those were suspended during the summer. There was no reason why he should not take Gath with
him when he returned to the mainland, at least for a week
or two. It would be dull for him, and wearying, but perhaps
also a glimpse of his own future. When Royal Wynd entered
Pirates' Walk, Rap turned to the boy to ask if he would like
to come—and saw the answer already on his face.

"What am I going to ask you?"

Gath's happiness flickered briefly. "Don't know the words. We're going to talk about me coming with you to the mainland."

Rap nodded, while his mind worked that out. He could not shake the feeling that there was an impossible paradox lurking somewhere in Gath's odd talent and yet he could not corner it. In this case, Gath had known what Rap was going to say and then Rap had not said it. But the paradox escaped again, because Gath had brought up the subject . . . or did it?

Gath was soon insisting that he would not mind sleeping in tents, missing meals, riding all day, being drenched, burned, frozen, or any of the other horrors Rap described. He seemed to welcome such prospects. He insisted he had no plans for the next few weeks, nor would he mind leaving his friends.

His father felt a twinge of uneasiness at that, but he agreed he would take an apprentice along on his next trip to the mainland. He was fairly certain that his son had known all about that decision when he entered the great hall an hour ago.

Less than a year had gone by since Rap had worried that Gath never seemed to do anything on his own. Now he was concerned that the boy had become a loner. Truly parenthood was a course in gratuitous anxiety!

Two women locked in a corner gossip broke off long enough to bob their respects to the king. The king greeted them both by name, wishing them good morrow. Man and boy crossed the wagon road then and the rain was barely noticeable. They continued by way of One Weaver's Steps.

"Gath?"

"Yes, sir?" There was a guarded expression on the boyish face now.

"You mind talking about your . . . talent, premonition, whatever it is?"

"No. 'Cept it's hard to explain."

"Well, don't worry if you can't put it in words. I'm just curious to know how you see the future. When I'm being a sorcerer, I can do some of it, of course."

"Oh! You can? You really can?"

Rap should have told him so sooner. The poor kid was showing large quantities of relief, just because he'd been told he wasn't any more of a freak than his father.

"For me it's a real effort. You seem to do it all the time."

Gath nodded. "Can't help it."

"I know of two ways. I can use premonition, where I just think about doing something, then about doing something else, and then decide which one feels better. That only works on me myself, though . . ."

Gath was already shaking his head.

"The other way is foresight," Rap said. "But that takes a huge effort and usually you see so many possibilities that you can't make any of them out clearly. That works best on other people. Once in a while you run into a destiny, where the Gods have decreed that . . ."

He choked into silence, remembering the terrible prophecy he had been given. Fortunately Gath had not noticed his confusion.

"Not like that, either, sir," he said. "I don't think I can see destinies."

That was one blessing, anyway.

"The only way I can tell you," Gath went on, scowling at his feet as he walked, "is it's like having a candle in the dark. Other people seem to be walking with their eyes closed, falling into puddles and tripping over rocks. I can see the road ahead, for a little way."

"Hey, that's a good description! So you can go around the puddles?"

"Sometimes. Sometimes they're unavoidable, like algebra. Sometimes I run into things I didn't expect, or didn't see in time. It's nothing much, really, Dad."

"I think what you have is called *prescience*. I never tried that, but I suppose I could have if I'd wanted to. The name's not important. What matters is that it's a great gift! Be proud of it and use it well. Don't use it to aid the Evil."

Being thirteen, Gath of course wanted to know how his prescience could be used to aid the Evil. A few moments later Rap was able to change the subject and talk about the castle shielding.

He stopped where the way divided. "Let's run a test here," he said. "We can go on down Peddlar Alley, or we can walk on the wagon road, since it's stopped raining. Can you say who we'll meet in either case?"

Gath was staring down the rain-wet street. "If you go that way, Dad, you're going to run into the bishop."

"God of Horrors!" Rap said. "You're right. Quick!" He dived into Peddlar Alley with his son at his heels, and they did no further experimentation in the occult before they reached the harbor.

2

DURING THE PREVIOUS WINTER, CAPTAIN EFFLIO HAD TAKEN *Sea Beauty* south and revisited Impport, his childhood home. He had even located his long-lost daughter. But Impport had failed to live up to his memories of it, and his daughter's household had been a madhouse of rampaging children whose antics had done terrible things to his asthma. His son-in-law was a hair-raising religious fanatic. Efflio had abandoned dreams of a quiet retirement there.

Then a profitable cargo had brought him north again to Pamdo Gulf in the spring and another idea had germinated. He had encountered an ambitious jotunn sailor named Bithbal, who had some money to invest—jotnar and money were an unusual combination. The final straw had come aboard when Efflio had mentioned to Krushbark that he was considering a voyage to Krasnegar. The big man had just said, "Where?" with a totally blank expression. Krushbark's devastated face quite frequently wore a blank expression, but the discovery that the bosun had already forgotten that peculiar little town settled the matter for Efflio. One thing an imp could not resist was a mystery.

So here he was back in Krasnegar. It had not changed at all, although the harbor was busier, this early in the season. Purely on spec, he had brought a cargo of hemp, with some idea that it might be profitable. He had also brought Bithbal.

Bithbal and Krushbark had become enemies at first sight. Jotunn tradition prohibited brawling at sea, although in this case it had barely succeeded in keeping the peace between those two. Now that *Sea Beauty* was safely tied up, they were preparing to adjourn their hostility to a convenient tavern. At least one of them would be carried back to the ship unconscious. Then they would both feel happier and would work together better in future.

The early morning rain was just ending. As the two big men marched down the plank, Efflio was not at all surprised to see the faunish king approaching along the quay. He suppressed quivers of unease at the memories of sorcery, but he noticed that he had started to wheeze already.

The king trotted up on deck, accompanied by a young jotunn. The boy looked at Efflio and inexplicably blushed to the roots of his spiky hair.

"Good morning, Cap'n," the king said.

Efflio bowed. "Good morning to you, Sire . . . And to you, your Highness! Why, you've grown about two cable lengths!" He might as well put the king in a good mood. That sort of comment always pleased fathers.

The faun swelled proudly. "Hasn't he? He's going to make me look like a gnome when he's full grown. Who was that sailor we passed? He seemed familiar."

"Bosun Krushbark, Sire? Or Purser Bithbal?"

The king shook his head, looking puzzled. "Don't recall

the names. The second one? I'm sure I met him once, a long time ago. He didn't seem to know me . . . Never mind. No more horses?" He smiled menacingly.

"No, your Majesty. I brought a cargo of rope."

King Rap grinned mysteriously at his son, who grinned back shyly. "What made you think we would want rope?"

Efflio leaned comfortably against the rail and prepared to enjoy the trading. If an imp could not outhaggle a faun, then he was definitely due to retire. "The Dwanishian border has been closed, by order of the imperor."

"So rope is cheap just now?"

He was not supposed to know that! "So the dwarves would be very interested in buying rope, Sire."

"We have no trade with the dwarves." The king leaned against the mast. The boy settled himself on a bollard, watching his father with the doting gaze of a pet dog.

"But you trade with goblins," Efflio said.

He shivered at the long stare the king gave him.

"You are a perceptive man, Captain."

"Thank you, Sire."

"I'll think about it. The crown might be interested in acquiring your cargo, as you presumed."

That sounded very promising! Efflio wondered how best to open inquiries about taking up residence. He must be discreet, obviously. He might be expected to swear fealty to the throne of Krasnegar. He'd never been a great imperial patriot, but . . .

"He wants to stay here," the boy said.

"You keep out of this!" his father snapped.

"Just saving time, Dad. Sorry."

Efflio uttered a nervous wheeze. Was the son a sorcerer, also? "Indeed, your Majesty, he is correct. I have been thinking of retiring for some years . . ." How had the kid known that?

"Our winters are long, you know."

"But your hearts are warm. This seems a very friendly

little town. I can't manage hills, but I thought I would look around for some comfortable lodgings close to the docks."

The king nodded thoughtfully. "I know of several widows who could use a little extra income and might appreciate a lodger for company. You would have money, of course?"

If the rope sold and Bithbal bought the ship as planned, then Efflio would have plenty of money. Normally he would have denied the fact vehemently, but now he nodded. He was inclined to trust this strange ruler, this sorcerer-faun-king. He was beginning to feel quite excited at the prospect.

"I'll give you a couple of names," the king said, "but you're not to say I sent you!"

"Not if you do not wish it, Sire . . . Why not, though?"

The faun smiled faintly. "Because they'll do it to please me and that wouldn't be fair." He scratched his tangled hair thoughtfully. "You know, Cap'n, a well-traveled, knowledgeable man like yourself might be a valuable voice on our royal council. Would you be interested? There is a small honorarium, of course."

"That would be a very great honor, Sire!" Efflio said, astonished. Such an appointment would also add some interest to his retirement and let him meet the most influential citizens—merchants, for example. He wondered how large the honorarium would be.

"Then I suggest you apply for resident status."

The sailor thought unhappily of the rapacious bureaucrats of the Impire. "I require a permit?"

"Oh, no. Just my approval, or my wife's." The king laughed and held out a hand to shake. "Like this! Welcome aboard! But if you are going to remain with us, Captain, then why dispose of your cargo through a middleman? You could set yourself up as a merchant and trade the rope to the goblins directly."

Efflio whistled his longest, loudest wheeze yet.

"Oh, you wouldn't need to do the negotiating yourself if

you preferred not to." The faun's gray eyes twinkled. "Although there would be a commission. And of course you would have to store the merchandise. I can rent you some space in one of the royal warehouses at very reasonable rates."

"Most generous of your Majesty!"

"Think about it! I expect you would feel more comfortable with your life savings in the form of goods in storage than in a bag under the mattress? There is a token tax, of course, to cover the upkeep of the royal fire brigade."

The twinkle had become quite sinister. This was certainly one faun who was no pushover at haggling. The cash price of hemp had obviously dropped appreciably in the last few minutes.

The king chuckled and straightened up. "Come and dine with us tonight, Cap'n. Gath, here, can bring the chaise for you, or I can. And you can tell us all the news of the Impire."

3

EVIDENTLY THE WARM HEARTS OF KRASNEGAR WERE NOT its only attraction for Captain Efflio—he enjoyed its warm beer, also. Awash with mulled ale, he was assisted back to his ship around midnight by the king himself. A couple of crewmen took him in hand and steered him off to his cabin, their attitude suggesting that they had done this many times before. Still, Rap thought, he was a pleasant enough old rogue.

The sun had dipped out of sight, but the sky was still blue and there were still some people about. Work never stopped in summer. Gulls, waves, and people were always busy.

Rap drove the chaise slowly up the long winding hill, letting Patches take it easy. He needed time to think and time for the blustery salt air to clear his head. Time to think over what he had heard that evening.

Dragons! Lith'rian had been known to use his dragons before, for elves could be surprisingly vindictive. In his long reign as South, he had loosed them three or four times. But to turn them against East's legions! Olybino must have had an apoplectic fit.

When Rap had known those two warlocks, they had been reluctant allies. Lith'rian had been contemptuous of the pompous imp and his glorified visions of war; but Lith'rian was contemptuous of most people. Alliances within the Four were always shaky.

The imperor would have been deeply shocked, also, but Emshandar was reputedly almost senile now. He would have died years ago had Rap not cured his sickness.

That had been a violation of the Protocol and perhaps even the error that the God had mentioned. Had Rap warped the course of history by extending the old man's life? Or had he merely established a dangerous precedent? The Four had acquitted him on the charge of wrongful sorcery, and somehow he thought a world-shaking failure should be something more significant than that trivial kindness.

Efflio had brought other ominous news also—jotunn raiders shipwrecked in a freak storm and trolls raiding in the Mosweeps. Those were only the stories that had reached to distant Krasnegar. What else was happening that Rap did not know of?

The key to all this was Shandie, he decided. The boy he had known briefly was a celebrated soldier now, destined to be imperor very soon. He would know as much of current events as anyone, and he should be told the rest. Rap had a moral duty to advise the prince of the Gods' prophecy. He ought to write a letter.

By the time the chaise was clattering over the cobbles of the bailie, though, he had realized that a letter would not do it. He had no idea where Shandie was. A letter would vanish in the labyrinth of the Opal Palace, or fall into the wrong hands.

There was Sagorn, also. The old man was no sorcerer, but

he was probably still one of the sharpest thinkers in Pandemia. Rap decided to write to Sagorn instead.

The stables were echoingly empty in summer, with most of the royal herd away cavorting on the hills, but they were always one of Rap's favorite places in the kingdom, for he had spent much of his childhood here. At one time the horses had been his only friends. Even yet he often came to visit them when he needed peace to think. As he was rubbing down Patches, he considered the possible results of writing to Sagorn, and he discarded that idea, also. The scholar and his sequential companions might be traveling again, anywhere in the world, and a letter to them would be even more likely to be intercepted.

Rap could use sorcery, of course. He had no idea if his remaining powers were enough to fly him to Hub, but he could certainly rattle the ambience enough to attract the attention of the wardens. Now there was a crazy, suicidal idea!

Efflio had confirmed that Raspnex was the new North, which Rap had known for months. Raspnex had seemed like an honorable man once . . . but to trust a dwarf? In his new post of warlock Raspnex might be much more eager to acquire votaries than he had been in Faerie, when he had just been granted his own release. And Rap, who had once been a demigod, more powerful than any sorcerer in the world, would be no match for Raspnex now.

As he led Patches to her stall, he knew he would have to go in person. He was a king, he knew people in Hub. He could win admittance to Shandie and the prince would surely listen to him, for old time's sake.

But not yet.

Rap's place was here, in Krasnegar. The God had implied that nothing was going to happen immediately. The millennium was still more than a year away. A king's first duty was to his people. Rap must see the harvest gathered and safely stowed. He wanted to keep an eye on Gath, too, and help the boy all he could as he adjusted to his occult premonition. Inos still had her hands full with a half-year-old

imp named Holindarn. And little Eva was suffering from
lack of attention.

Not now. He would go in the fall.

There would still be time.

4

HAIL THE CONQUERING HERO COMES!

There were two heroes. As the prince's cavalcade roared
along the avenues of Hub, the crowds' cheers were all for
Shandie. The soldiers' salutes were all for Shandie. The
flowers were being thrown for Shandie, the bugles played
for Shandie. The rarely used Great Gate of the Opal Palace
swung open for Shandie.

Ylo knew that, but in his own eyes he was a returning
hero, also—and who else's eyes really matter but one's own?
His transient Qobel fame had faded, as he had known it
would. He was only the prince's signifer and after today
Shandie would have no military role to play; he would have
small need for a signifer from now on.

So no one was especially noticing Ylo, except Ylo. Three
and a half years ago he had left Hub as a virtual prisoner,
being escorted south to the barracks of the XXth. Today he
returned victorious. By courage and persistence and the
grace of the Gods he had triumphed. In his heart, Ylo accepted the cheers as meant for Ylo. Ylo's horse trampled the
flowers first and was first through the Great Gate. Ylo
brought Shandie home.

Someone in the chain of command could think. When Shandie had cantered up to First Post, which marked the start of
the Great East Way, he found a company of Praetorian Hussars that had been standing by for the last week. As prince
and companions attended to their toilet, word sped ahead of

them to the palace. It was the first time news of their coming had outrun them.

The Praetorian Hussars would escort the prince through the city no matter what anyone said, but even they could not take precedence away from the prince's signifer. However much those lofty, dandified young men might hate it, they would have to let Ylo lead them. They were much less worried about the prince's reputation than about their own.

They provided Ylo with a new standard, its emblems and battle honors wrought in real gold and silver, all polished to exacting Praetorian specifications, until even the wood shone and the metal had almost melted. They had brought experts along to make certain that the signifer was worthy of it, and he was treated like a child about to be put on display—stripped, washed, dried, perfumed, and then dressed again. He was given shave, shampoo, pedicure, and manicure, all at the same time. The effects of three weeks' continuous riding were soothed away with a massage, so that he would sit straight in the saddle. Someone had even thought to provide the pure white wolfskin that only this signifer might wear. They threw in a jet-black horse to match. When the whole ordeal was over, everything about Ylo was brand new and every eyebrow-hair was in regulation position.

A guardsman cupped hands for his sandal when he mounted. No one had done that for him in years—not since the day he was thrown out of the Praetorian Guard, in fact.

Oh, how sweet it was!

The cheering began before they left the post. Rumors of the prince's impending return had been circulating for weeks, and the crowds seemed to spring out of the stones. Word spread over the city like a peal of thunder. The demonstration was spontaneous, an outburst of relief. Hub was the nexus of the Impire, responsive to every nerve, tuned to every note and overtone. Hub knew that something was wrong, the center was failing. The old man's grip had loosened at last. The tiller needed a new hand—and here it came! The aristocracy summoned its carriages and raced to the palace. The populace took to the streets and cheered. *Hail the conquering hero!*

West they rode, along the huge expanse of the Avenue Abnila, thronged with roaring multitudes, through the City of the Gods, the City of Five Hills. Soon Olybino's palace came into sight on their right, glittering gold on its eminence. They passed below that, heading for the majestic Opal Palace itself, shining over them all, catching distant glimpses of sinister blue towers to the south and white to the north, the abode of other wardens. And the crowds surged everywhere, like a wild tide.

Ah, but then!

Then, after that ride of a lifetime through the cheering streets, came the march of a lifetime, as Ylo led the prince into the palace.

Fanfares of trumpets . . . Up the great marble steps . . . Guards saluting . . . Along the vaulted hallways . . . Gentlemen sweeping the floor with plumed hats in low bows . . . Ladies drooping submissively in curtseys, showing their cleavage and soft, round arms . . . The measured tread of boots behind him as Shandie followed with his guard . . .

How very, very sweet!

The Throne Room was the daytime heart of the Impire. Ylo had seen it only once. A few days before his eighteenth birthday, his father had brought him there to present him to the imperor. They had kissed the bloodthirsty old monster's hand. They had received imperial approval for Ylo to join the Guard. Three days later he had done so. Three months later Emshandar had ground Ylo's family into dog food.

The Throne Room was larger than most ballrooms. It sparkled with art and high windows and statuary and some of the finest frescoed ceilings ever conceived. Any day the imperor was in residence, a hundred ladies and gentlemen would be found loitering in the Throne Room.

There was a throne there, but it was rarely used, for the big events took place in the Rotunda. The Throne Room was where the everyday scheming was done. The imperor himself would certainly appear there at some point in the day. Important persons with petitions or appointments would await the imperial pleasure here in the Throne Room and not in any dingy antechamber with the common herd. Aristocrats departing or arriving would call to pay their respects, or just to see and be seen. Anyone without right of access to the Throne Room was no one.

As Ylo marched in, still bearing the standard, he was suddenly at a loss. Far ahead of him stood the throne itself, under a purple canopy, empty. On either hand, ladies and gentlemen were arranged in clumps as if they had been engaged in idle conversation. They bowed or curtseyed as he passed. There was no sign of the imperor. Shandie was at his heels and Ylo was lost. *God of Sailors!* where did he go from here?

If the prince went one way and his signifer went the other, then his career was over before it had begun.

Off to one side of the throne, though, Praetorian Guardsmen stood rigid, flanking an unmarked door. Saved! Ylo continued on down the length of the great hall, veered past the throne, and came to a halt at last.

It had been an Evilish long journey from Qoble.

An Evilish long journey since he was last in this room.

5

THE DOOR OPENED AND THE PRINCE IMPERIAL ENTERED.

The door closed.

A Praetorian tribune was eyeing Centurion Hardgraa and his two henchmen with mortal challenge in his eye. If the interlopers attempted to take up positions by the door, as they would normally do when Shandie was within, then there was going to be a pitched battle. The palace was Praetorian pasture.

"What do we do now?" Ylo whispered out of the corner of his mouth.

"We wait," came the reply, soft as wind rustling oak leaves. "And ogle the pretty girls."

"Show me how to do that," Ylo muttered, but he had spotted a socket close by one of those menacing sentinels. He marched over, set his standard in it, stepped back and saluted. Then he turned away as if he had just gone off duty. Apparently he was on the right track, because Hardgraa dismissed his two subordinates, thanking them for a long ride and a job well done.

Lots of women to ogle, not many girls. The conversations were starting up again, but Ylo was acutely aware of being watched. He wandered a tactful distance away from that potent doorway and Hardgraa paced at his side. Bystanders drifted out of their path.

Comprehension came like a dagger stroke. He was an Yllipo, the only Yllipo. All the two hundred or so courtiers present were politicos to their painted toenails. They all knew his background and who he was, every one of them. They would not dare address him until they knew how things stood between him and the imperor. Shandie was not cock of the roost yet.

Awkward minutes dragged by. Courtiers learned patience above all else. They might stand here until midnight.

Ylo noted an incongruous pair wandering in through the great main door—a fat man and a small, birdlike man, Umpily and Acopulo, who had followed the military procession in a carriage. They separated, joyfully greeting old friends.

Then a guardsman came striding through the crowd,

heading for Ylo like an arrow. His centurion's breastplate shone as bright as all the jewels and glitter of the courtiers and his plume floated higher than most of the hussars', even.

Well, well! Sweeter yet.

The Praetorian stamped to a halt and saluted. Ylo responded. Technically their relative rank was something of a military mystery, but there was no doubt who was the effective superior now.

The man's face was rigid. He was taking a risk and he knew it—but he was also covering his flanks and they both knew that. "I came to offer my congratulations, Signifer." He had always been a gentleman.

"Very kind of you, Centurion." For the life of him, Ylo could not recall the man's name. One of the Hathinos. It would come, when he needed it.

"Just wanted you to know, er, Signifer . . . That was the most unpleasant job I ever had to do."

"I did not enjoy it, either."

"No. Well, we must all obey orders. Nothing personal?"

"Nothing personal," Ylo agreed, noticing a hint of relief that the disciplined mask could not quite conceal.

He watched in satisfaction as his former superior marched away again. The audience was whispering. Nothing personal—but one day he would make that man lick his sandal, just on principle. Hithi, that was his name. Remember it!

"An old friend?" Hardgraa inquired dryly.

"Not exactly." *He smiled as he threw me to the sharks.*

"Well, try not to kill him in public," Hardgraa remarked cheerfully. Then he added, with the air of a man being deliberately relaxed, "Er, Signifer?"

"Yes, Centurion?"

"Don't look now, but one of the pictures on the eastern wall is of some interest."

Since when had that human battering ram ever cared for art? Ylo raised his eyebrows to convey his surprise and then slowly surveyed the entire room. "Oh, well done!" he said when he had finished. "Bravely done!"

The works of art in the Throne Room would have ransomed a fair city: sculptures, tapestries, paintings. The picture Hardgraa had spotted did not seem noteworthy in itself, at least not at this distance, but its subject was. Sunlit green waves in the foreground blew spume, and a majestic galleon heeled under full canvas. In the distance, balancing the composition, a conical rock bore a town on its slopes and a spiky castle at its peak. It was exactly as Shandie had described his vision in the preflecting pool.

For the last year and a half, Ylo had been anticipating the prince's every want. He could sense them now before Shandie was even aware of them himself. Hardgraa had the trained observation of a bodyguard, but he lacked the courtly guile to proceed from here. To march over to that painting and read its inscription, if it had one, would alert the entire court. The next step was up to Ylo.

He glanced around and located a footman hovering by the wall. He was no callow youth, either, but an old retainer, who should be well versed in palace lore. A flick of an eye brought the man to him, in a deft, unhurried glide. He bowed with the respect proper to Ylo's rank—which was giddily high at the moment—and he waited cautiously to hear what this enigma wanted.

What was the correct question? The palace art collection would doubtless be the responsibility of some ineffectual noble. There would be an underling to run things, but he would be a professional bureaucrat who spent most of his time playing palace politics. The real work would be done by his staff.

Ylo made a stab at the appropriate title. "The Assistant Deputy Curator of the Royal Paintings," he said loftily, and watched the flunky twitch with astonishment. "I want to see him. Now."

It worked like a sword through the heart. The man bowed and withdrew. This sort of authority could easily become addictive!

Hardgraa had drifted away and was deep in conversation

with a tribune of the VIIth, apparently an old friend. The room was gradually filling up as latecomers arrived to view the excitement. Here and there Ylo recognized a familiar face—notable political figures, friends of his parents. Still he stood in isolation, the untrusted Yllipo.

And what of the Yllipo's revenge? For a year and a half he had served the prince imperial with all his strength, served him loyally and well. He had not stuck a knife in his ribs, although the opportunities had been legion.

So now what? The old man must die soon. Until then there would be nothing to do but wait. Shandie would be generous—Ylo had no doubts of that, because he knew that generosity to one aide bought loyalty from all the others. When Emshandar V was proclaimed imperor and sat secure on the Opal Throne, then his former signifer would receive advancement. A seat in the Assembly to start with, likely. A title, then a few sinecure offices to pad his pockets, then a praetorship to make him rich. In a few years, perhaps a consulship.

And meanwhile, just wait. Wait and woo the women of Hub, the beauties of the Impire. His eyes had been scanning the talent without waiting for orders. One or two were not bad, but most were much too old for his taste. It was their daughters he was after.

Not one of them would compare to the goddess he had seen in the pool. The image had bewitched him. He had thought of little else for two days. Perfection! He suspected no other woman would ever quite satisfy him again. As soon as he had gotten her clothes off her, he would be comparing her with that vision, the goddess of the pool—and she would not compare.

He eyed the tables of refreshments. He had not eaten for hours and he might wait here many hours yet, but he decided to wait a while and let them all stare. He stared back, unconcerned.

Then a dark, slim man came strolling toward him. His doublet sparkled with the jeweled stars and the sash of the

Order of Agraine, his hose were of the finest silk. His arrogance would have provoked a conclave of bishops to murder. Ylo ought to know him, obviously. Every eye in the room was on the two of them. The hall fell silent.

"Signifer Ylo?"

Ylo saluted the sash, to be on the safe side. "My Lord?"

"Prince Emthoro of Leesoft."

Execration! Shandie's cousin! Third in line.

"Your Royal Highness! I beg pardon. I should have—"

The prince shrugged off the gaffe. "No matter. Your predecessor was my brother."

"Yes, Highness."

"You were present when he died." Emthoro displayed surprise, as if the question need not be asked. "I would hear the story."

"I hardly saw, sir. There was much confusion . . ."

Shandie's heir was a babe in arms. This man must inevitably be his chief opposition. Whatever their personal relationship, politics would dictate a rivalry. *Careful!* He was lean and quick and dangerous. His eyes held some of the fire that burned in Shandie's . . . curiously slanted eyes, almost elvish.

Ylo's voice was narrating the story of Ralpnie's death at Karthin, mostly from hearsay. Suddenly it dried up.

There she was!

"Signifer?" the prince prompted.

She had just arrived, with a couple of attendants. People were bowing as she advanced from the door. She wore a simple gown of sea blue. She floated rather than walked, acknowledging the onlookers with barely perceptible nods. Cold, slim, and regal, the ultimate in womanhood, carved from a block of diamond. Her miracle black hair was adorned with a simple coronet of rubies. Her features were as perfect as the Gods could achieve in fashioning beauty.

"Who is *that?*" Ylo demanded breathlessly.

"Who?" the prince inquired in a languid tone, and turned to look. "The one in blue?"

Danger! People were bowing to her! *Idiot!*

"Of course not!" Ylo croaked, sweat bursting from every pore. "The woman in peach."

"One of the Ullithini girls, I think." Emthoro regarded him with sinister curiosity. "I thought you meant Princess Eshiala."

Aghast, Ylo could only shake his head.

She was gorgeous. Shandie had called her *the most beautiful woman in the world*, and he had been flattering all others when he said so. Her features were perfection. Ylo had seen her naked body in the preflecting pool's vision.

He had thought of little else for the last two days.

He had concluded that no other woman would ever satisfy him again. And there she was, in the flesh.

His face must be red as a strawberry.

She was heading his way.

"Confine your attentions to the Ullithini woman, Signifer," Prince Emthoro said with a faint sneer. "It would be safer."

He turned and strolled off to meet the princess. Of course it was he she had been approaching. She did not know Ylo existed.

God of Fools!

Shandie's wife! He had been shown a vision of Shandie's wife!

A cough at his elbow dragged him back from the volcano. He turned to find himself being studied by a pair of huge opalescent eyes, glittering in rose and viridian. They looked very puzzled.

"You wish to see me, Signifer?"

Of course the Assistant Deputy Curator of the Royal Pictures would be an elf. Every elf was a born artist, and by comparison imps knew nothing of things artistic. This one looked like a boy of sixteen, but he might be a grandfather. His clothes were a blaze of silver and ultramarine; although they were beautifully made, they would not have purchased one lace cravat on anyone else in the room. He was shivering with anxiety at being summoned to this chamber.

Ylo thumped his thoughts into shape like a baker kneading dough.

"Ah, yes. I note that there are several landscapes included in the pictures here. I want to know about them."

The kid's golden jaw dropped. Ylo was not acting as impish soldiers were supposed to act.

"The places they represent . . . and the artists . . . and when they were acquired." That ought to do it. He could tell Shandie to expect the report in a day or two.

The assistant deputy curator gulped. "Of course, Signifer. The mountain scene to the left of that door is a view of the Mosweeps from Jedmuse, painted in oil on canvas by Jio'sys and acquired by confiscation of the estate of Duke Yllipo in 2995. The one to the left . . ."

Elves were fanatics at performing duties, and this one proceeded to reel off information like a human cyclopedia. Grudgingly impressed, Ylo listened as the catalog unrolled. Barely pausing for breath, the curator continued until he reached the only one that held any interest at all for his audience.

"The seascape is a fanciful rendition of the royal vessel *Golden Swan* in tempera, depicted by the artist Jalon, commissioned by Emthar II in the year 2936—"

"The place!" Ylo said. "That castle? Where is it?"

The elf stuttered. "I think it is just a fantasy background, Signifer. The catalog gives no detail on that."

"No inscription on the frame, or the picture?"

"No, Signifer."

"Ah. Excuse my interruption. Pray continue."

The trail had ended. The rocky island was not a fantasy— any more than Princess Eshiala was a fantasy—but the only way to identify it would be to ask the artist. The painting had been acquired sixty years ago. The artist must be long in his grave by now.

The deputy curator was waxing enthusiastic about the Ambel farm scene when a voice intruded.

"Ylo!"

Ylo swung around. The door had opened and the prince himself was standing there. His dark eyes blazed with a fury such as Ylo had seldom seen in them. Ylo strode forward at once. Behind him, the court stood aghast at the sight of the prince imperial acting as his own footman . . . And ignoring the wife he had not seen for more than two years.

6

THEY CROSSED A SMALL HALLWAY AND ENTERED ANOTHER room, bright and large and cluttered. Ylo took in no detail but one—a gangling old man sprawled forward on a table, his face on his arms. The back of his head was smooth as a skull, splotched with brown patches like lichen on an ancient rock, fringed with straggles of white hair. His rope-thin neck protruded from a collar far too large. Without question, it was the imperor himself, and he was apparently sobbing.

Shandie slammed the door behind him and headed straight to the side of his chair. "Grandsire, I have the honor to present—"

"No!" howled a broken, ragged voice. "No, no! Take him away. I won't look!" He twisted his head to the side and raised his arms as a fence to hide behind. The sleeves of his doublet fell back to reveal wrists like yellow twigs.

Shandie turned his furious gaze on Ylo again. "His Majesty has accepted that certain injustices have been done. He acknowledges that there was absolutely no evidence against yourself in the matter and that . . . that certain others may not have been granted a fair trial."

Ylo gasped aloud and his world reeled. Not revenge, but retribution?

"The titles, of course, can be restored," Shandie said, his voice hard and very loud, "and purged of ignominy. Some of the estates have been sold; some consolidated with other properties. The Dukedom of Rivermead itself is available and others can be added—including any that have particular sentimental value to you, of course. You will be granted an honorable discharge, with the rank of legate. You will be one of the largest landowners in the Impire." He paused, studying Ylo's reaction. "As liege of Rivermead, you will hold in gift five or six seats in the People's Assembly and may appoint yourself to one of them, if you wish. Dukes are automatically appointed to the Senate, but senatorship is normally restricted to persons who have reached the age of thirty. The Senate would doubtless consider this a special case, if so requested."

He meant *ordered*, of course. Ordered by the imperor.

Emshandar whimpered, but he had twisted away in his chair and did not look around.

Restitution? Vast wealth . . . Ylo would own personally much of what had previously been shared by many.

Retribution! By signing the warrants, Emshandar would be publicly acknowledging his injustice. Small wonder the old monster was sniveling like a whipped child! Utter humiliation!

Shandie was waiting.

Ylo knew the man as he knew his own fingernails. There was more to come.

"Or?"

A hint of something else dulled the anger for a moment, perhaps a flicker of admiration for Ylo's perception. "Look at this," the prince said, dropping his voice. He stalked over to the far side of the room and Ylo staggered after him, shaking as if he had been clubbed. Wealth! Power! Women galore!

Shandie gestured at a table. There, clearly, was the real cause of his rage. It was heaped head-high with books and scrolls. Baskets and boxes full of papers filled the space below it and flanked it on either side. Dozens lay loose on the rug also. Thousands of them, in all, a mountain.

"Look at it! Just look at it!" The prince's voice was soft, yet bitter as lye. "And this is only the priority stuff! Many of his staff have died and never been replaced. The rest are all as old as he is and they're so terrified of him now that they won't sharpen a quill without his say-so. It must have been piling up for months. Half the army is waiting for its pay . . . judgments to be approved, promotions, laws awaiting signatures . . . Gods! I don't know what all may be in here."

Then he looked at Ylo, who did not know what to say, or what was expected of him.

He was appalled by the pile of documents. It would be a nightmare to sort out. Everything would have to be catalogued, because one half would contradict or supersede the other half. Even if they could be approved and issued, there would not be enough couriers in the Impire to deliver them.

"I have lived too long!" wailed the ancient invalid at the far end of the room. "Let me die!"

Shandie raised his voice again. "I told his Majesty that I only knew one man in the realm who could ever straighten out a mess such as this."

And his eyes threw the challenge right at his signifer.

"I . . . I can't do both!"

"No, you certainly can't do both!"

It was obvious. Even if a duke could be a clerk—which he couldn't—to take over a property like Rivermead and perhaps others would be a full-time task. Ylo would be busy for years to come just running his own estates, no matter how many managers he might hire. He could not do both.

And Rivermead was a long way from Hub.

At times Shandie was totally incomprehensible. Why offer a man the world and then expect him to take on a mind-crippling ordeal instead? He must think that Ylo was crazy.

"I don't understand! I'm still a soldier. If you want me to clean up this stable, then you can order me to do it!"

A strange look came over the prince's face. "Yes, I could."

Duke Yllipo! Duke of Rivermead! One of the largest landowners in the Impire. An old and honored name.

It was not fair!

In the background, the imperor howled. "Give his pig-swill dukedom and get him out of here!"

Shandie shrugged, turning away restlessly. "You need time to think about it."

"No, sir," Ylo said hoarsely. "The Senate can wait."

The prince's face lit up with disbelief. "You'll do it? You'll try? The Powers know it's a hellish awful job ..." He glanced at the monstrous pile. "I don't even know where you can start."

"I'll need two or three good assistants," Ylo said, thinking longingly of the team he had trained back in Qoble. "More than that and we'll spend all our time passing stuff back and forth ..." Then he had a sudden inspiration. "We'll need extra couriers at the least—hussars?"

"Why not? Give them something to do for once."

"So let's keep the whole thing military, this part, too; keep the word from getting out. How about Praetorians?"

"Now that's brilliant!" Shandie said quietly. "Excellent!"

"I know a good centurion." Oh, sweet!

"I'll assign anyone you want." The prince grabbed Ylo's hand and pumped it wildly. "Good man! You have no idea what this means to me, Ylo! You have no idea what this will mean to the Impire!" He hesitated, as if embarrassed. "Frankly, I'm surprised. You're turning down a lot."

"I'll hold you to it, one day, sir." Ylo was being a fool. He should take the dukedom and run.

Shandie glanced along the room at the whimpering old wreck at the table. Another day the settlement would not include the satisfaction it would bear now, coming with Emshandar's personal seal on it.

"It's yours when you want it. Tell me why, though?" The

dark eyes studied Ylo narrowly—obviously the prince had expected to be refused.

"Proud to serve, sir," Ylo said hastily.

He wasn't going to say why.

Rivermead was weeks away from the capital, but Shandie's personal signifer would reside in the prince's own residence. Ylo had seen a vision in a preflecting pool, a prophecy.

A promise.

7

OUT IN THE THRONE ROOM, ESHIALA WAS RAPIDLY SPIRALING into panic. All these eyes! She should never have come here. She should have waited at Oak House. But the goslings, her maids of honor, had heard the cheering and persuaded her. Of course they had just wanted to be in on the excitement.

They should be here beside her now, and they had scattered all over the hall. Gods knew who they were talking to, or what plans they were making. And everyone seemed to be staring at her.

Shandie was back. Her husband. The man she was supposed to love. Tonight he would claim his marital rights. All very well to say that it was no more than her duty, but it had been a very long time since she had had to endure that. And from now on she would not be able to avoid the pomp and ceremony. Every day she would be on display at his side. Every night she would have to pull up her nightgown for him. She shivered.

A group of the senior courtiers had closed in around her so she couldn't escape, and now she was being baited by Emthoro—gaunt, saturnine, quietly vicious, jabbing at her with sly little hints and innuendos, enjoying her terror.

"Dear little Maya is almost two now, isn't she?"

"Nineteen months."

"Close enough," the prince said. She saw his nose twitch and waited for the spite. "Two and a half or three years is a very good spacing between children, I always think. I expect you're both hoping for a son next time?" He must know exactly what was troubling her. Were her fears so obvious? Did everyone know?

"Whatever the Gods choose to give me, Highness."

The long nose twitched again. "The Gods? Oh, I thought that was Shandie's job!"

Laughter all round—the consul and his wife were enjoying the sport and so were the other onlookers, a dozen or more of them now. She felt like a bear in a bearpit.

Then, thanks be to the Gods! Ashia arrived.

Eshiala had never been so glad to see her sister—gems, bows, lace, brocade, whalebone, and all. Ashia was no taller than she, but she was more buxom and she somehow managed to convey *irresistibility*, like a galleon under full sail or a runaway hay wain. Heels clicking, fan flailing, she swirled into the fray with a rustle of fabric to envelope her younger sister in a bearhug, crushing her against armored corset and overflowing bosom, whispering urgently in her ear, "Smile, you idiot!"

Then she pirouetted on a grand scale, easing Eshiala aside and scattering the group so that it was no longer a bearpit around her. Eshiala wondered why she could never achieve such outrageous maneuvers.

Ashia surveyed the bewildered survivors. "Prince!" she chirruped as Emthoro sardonically bowed to her. "Is it true, then?" She fluttered eyelashes like fly swatters.

His narrow face grew wary. "Is what true, ma'am?"

"That they're drawing up the deed of abdication?" Ashia beamed around the ring of startled faces. "Well, whatever else can be keeping them so long?"

"Apparently they are consulting with the Yllipo signifer."

"Well, perhaps they need a fourth for a game of *thali*?" Ashia countered quickly, and won a snigger. She whirled back to Eshiala without a pause. "Darling, I am as dry as a desert. Do let's find some refreshment!" And she whirled her sister off to one of the side tables.

"What in the name of virginity is wrong with you?" she demanded. "Cholera from the looks of you."

"Shandie's back!" Eshiala moaned.

"I know that! Everyone knows that! You should be glowing with joy and anticipation!"

"It's been so long!"

How could she explain, even to her sister? She had been married for barely six weeks when her husband had left her. Now, more than two years later, he was back. He would expect her to do her duty tonight. Every night. "I feel I hardly know him!" she whispered.

"Keep smiling!" Ashia said through her teeth. She snatched up two glasses of wine, pressed one into Eshiala's hand, and clinked them together in a toast.

"I warned you to stay in practice," she muttered, beaming for the benefit of watchers. "You want to be wooed all over again, I suppose?"

"Perhaps that's it," Eshiala agreed, forcing a meaningless smile that felt as unnatural on her face as a full beard and mustache. Would she know wooing if she met it?

"Tell him it's the wrong time of the month. Well, your Eminence! Isn't this exciting!"

No, Eshiala thought, she would not lie to Shandie. He had rights, and she had a duty—a duty to her husband and a duty to the Impire. Other women survived it. With luck she would conceive again right away, just as she had the last time.

The senior courtiers were collecting around her again. She had never known the Throne Room so crowded. Ashia screamed with laughter at some witty remark or other and threw a question to the senator on the far side of Eshiala, effectively dropping a conversational barricade in front of her.

The hall hushed as a herald appeared with his staff and

his many-hued tabard. He headed for Eshiala, making her knees knock even harder. She held her head high as she followed him from the room, ignoring all the eyes and the whispers.

She crossed the hallway and was ushered into the Cabinet, large and bright and normally a pleasant room to visit, for she was fond of Emshandar and he of her. She had never seen it without him present, though. For a moment she thought the place was empty.

Then she saw a soldier riffling through an enormous tip of documents that filled the far end of the room. He had no helmet on, which was curious. He turned at the sound of the door closing and of course it was Shandie.

For a moment they just stared at each other. Then he coughed and came forward uncertainly. "You really are as beautiful as I remembered!"

Was that all he could say? Unsure how to answer, she sank into a curtsey instead.

He sighed and raised her. "Ah, my lovely marble queen," he said. "I, too, have my armor on, as you can see. I can't embrace you properly in armor." He pecked at her cheek uncertainly.

"Welcome back," she whispered. "Er . . . How did you manage to arrive so unexpectedly?"

"Oh, there are ways."

"A good journey? Did you have a good trip?"

"It was long, and tiring."

"I expect so."

"The child is well?"

"She's very well, thank you."

"Ah." He swallowed a few times. "Your accent's much better. You don't sound like Thumble now."

"Oh. I'm glad." Gods knew she had worked hard enough at her elocution lessons—why did she not feel happier that she had pleased him?

"I brought you some presents. I brought you pearls from the Sea of Sorrows and the finest Kerithian rubies."

Rubies? Pearls? What use had she for those? "They sound wonderful. You are very kind."

"Perdition!" he said. "I forget! I left them with the baggage—they'll be here in a week or so."

They stared at each other, and then both looked away.

"This Evilish armor—" he muttered. "I could take it off, of course . . . ?"

She looked at him in bewilderment, but he was studying a big, ugly couch.

"If I were Ylo I would," he mumbled.

Who? She felt lost. What was he talking about?

"There's an awful lot of people waiting outside," she said.

"Yes. I expect there are. Well, let's go out and be sociable, then. Darling."

Currents turn awry:
> *Thus conscience doth make cowards of us all;*
> *And thus the native hue of resolution,*
> *Is sicklied o'er with the pale cast of thought,*
> *And enterprises of great pith and moment,*
> *With this regard their currents turn awry,*
> *And lose the name of action.*
> —SHAKESPEARE, *HAMLET*, III, 1

CHAPTER EIGHT

GATHER YE ROSEBUDS

1

THE FIRST RAIN HAD COME TO BREAK THE HEAT, AND IT drummed loudly on the thatched leaves of the roof, muffling even the nightly frogs' chorus. It might be just a stray summer storm, for it seemed early, but Thaïle knew it meant that the next new moon would mark her birthday, when she was supposed to be at the College. The half year her father had promised was almost over.

Even with the rain, the night was hot and sticky. She lay contentedly in Leéb's arms on a thick, soft couch of reeds. He was asleep and she could Feel the confused eddies of his dreams. Fear and anger and hunger—they didn't mean anything. Everyone dreamed such things. He was slickly wet, just as she was herself. She could smell his personal scent, made up of woodsmoke, loam, and green things, man and sweat and even the fish he had caught that day—all familiar to her now after so many nights like this, mingled with odors of reeds and the house. She loved it, the smell of love and home and safety.

There had been no signs of the recorders. There had been no signs of anyone—the Leéb Place was a heaven for pixies. She could Feel the presence of other people at Places in the distance, but none of them had come snooping, and next year would be time enough to go visiting. They had seen no one at all since the day they arrived, except for the neighbors upriver, Boosh and Neeth of the Neeth Place. Neeth said no recorders had come by the district in many years.

As Leéb had promised, the old couple had been very happy to have new neighbors at a respectable distance and they had helped a lot. They had freely showered advice and lessons on a hill-country girl who did not know many of the things that grew in the valley. Even Leéb had learned from them about crops he had not met before, like taro and murunga pods.

Boosh was going to have to be more helpful yet, in a few months. She had already been helpful, confirming what Thaïle had suspected, advising her.

Tonight, to celebrate the rain, she had told Leéb that he was going to be a father. He had been so happy at the news that she had started to weep, just from the strength of his Feelings. Then one thing had led easily to another. That was why he was sleeping so soundly.

As a Placemaker, he had been as good as his word. He was a wonderful weaver, and he had woven two big rooms of their house already. There was not one drop of rain coming in, either, not one! She could have six or seven rooms if she wanted, he said, and she had laughed and asked what in the world a woman would want so many rooms for. For children, of course, he had said. Most couples never had more than two, but she had already explained that Gifted families often had more than two and then he had begun talking of having dozens.

Easy for him! But he liked babies, he said, and she believed him. He was so gentle and yet so strong. Had any woman in the whole world ever been so much in love?

Leéb had made a coop for the chickens and a stall for the kid. A wonderful fisherman, he was making a boat. He had taught Thaïle to swim—sometimes they wore no clothes for days at a time.

She had never eaten so well in her life. She had grown plumper already, even before the baby had started. The woods were packed with things to eat: berries, wild onions, roots, and herbs. Breadfruit trees were as common as frogs; and one big breadfruit tree would feed a family all year round. There were many other trees that gave edible fruit— palms, ebony, nutmeg, mango . . . the list was endless. She had grown some rice and taro and beans. She had gathered wild cotton and started spinning.

She had gourds and a cook pot and a good stone knife. She could think of nothing she might possibly want that she did not have. She listened to the rain and felt safe and secure in the arms of her man.

But the next new moon . . . Would the recorders come for her? Could they find her? Would they punish her parents?

Surely even the recorders could not be so cruel as to take her away from the Leéb Place now? A pixie must be born where it was conceived, for that was the way of the people. One day she would clear away the reeds for a while and squat on the earth itself to produce her baby. Her *first* baby. Right here, in the Leéb Place.

The hunger in Leéb's dreams was changing to *want*—to love. She felt his body stir against her. She could almost imagine she saw herself in those Feelings, they were so strong and she was so close. Boosh had said it would be safe for months yet.

Thaïle kissed the end of that silly snub nose and Felt her man awaken. He moved damply against her.

She touched her lips to his. Tongue found tongue, his hand slid to her breast, and a thrill ran through her at once. Had any woman ever been so happy?

2

THE GREAT IMPERIAL BEDROOM HAD BEEN DESIGNED FOR the Impress Abnila and Lord Umpily knew some scandalous tales on the subject that were amusing, if not very probable. Of course probability did not ensure accuracy in historical matters, any more than it did in domestic gossip; or vice versa. Lord Umpily was carefully keeping a diary of his own experiences as chief of protocol for the prince imperial. He would never dare to publish it in his lifetime, but future historians would certainly relish some of his stories—and what could be more improbable than what he was witnessing now? This scene—here, today. Whatever would the Impire say if it knew how it was being governed?

And whatever would Abnila say if she could see what had been done to her bedroom now? The great chamber had been turned into a commissariat, or a scriptorium. Its erstwhile elegance was utterly disfigured by a horseshoe of tables around the bed. It reminded Umpily of a cockpit, with the spectators clustered around, laying bets, watching the long tussle between Emshandar and the God of Death enter its final round. The place reeked of candles and sealing wax and too many people.

Beyond the great crystal windows, a few leaves were starting to turn on the beeches. The vases on the dressers held chrysanthemums. Summer was aging.

In the center of all the activity, the imperor lay like a corpse, his vellum-coated skull on a silken pillow: toothless, eyes closed. Thus had his dominion shrunk. Now he did not rule even as far as his hands would reach, those spidery, misshapen fingers. Now he did not reign even as far as the edges of his bed, else he would surely make everyone go away and leave him to die in peace.

To the left of the bed, Centurion Hithi pulled another scroll from the hamper at his side. There was an *extremely* interesting rumor going around about that centurion! Umpily had not been able to confirm it yet. The man had been Ylo's superior, years ago, and now he was Ylo's assistant. Gossip whispered that Ylo had told the man he was going to remain a common clerk until he knelt and kissed Ylo's sandal! If true, that was an exquisite revenge. No Praetorian centurion was going to kneel to any man before the Gods died!

"Sentence of banishment against the earl of Wastock," the centurion muttered, passing the scroll to Shandie.

Umpily pricked up his ears. All documents relating to punitive matters had supposedly been removed and set aside for Shandie's personal confirmation, for the old man had been far too vindictive with his proscriptions in the final few months.

Frowning, Shandie checked carefully for Ylo's initial, then he unrolled the top and scanned the text. Umpily waited with anticipation and felt glee as he saw the prince's shocked reaction. Banishment was leniency in the Wastock affair. It had been a clear case of abuse of a ward, with many titillating messy details; Emshandar had wanted to hush up the scandal. Ylo had verified the facts with Umpily—a very thorough young man, that Ylo.

"Another one, Grandsire!" Shandie held out the scroll.

The sunken eyes opened. The old man started awake. He took the roll in a trembling, blue-veined hand, and passed it across to the legionary, who proceeded to affix the seal. Done.

It was all legal, if barely so.

Documents passed from hamper to centurion, from centurion to prince, from prince to the old man in his bed, and across the bed to the legionary clerks, and then into another hamper. The imperor had approved another law, edict, warrant, or something. It was legal.

"Recall of Proconsul Ionfeu."

"Grandsire?"

That was new business—Umpily and Acopulo had proposed Ionfeu as one of next year's consuls and Shandie had agreed. It was time to start working some of his own people into the administration. The imperor might not have noticed; he passed the scroll on to be sealed.

Umpily sat at the foot of the bed, with Sir Acopulo and Marshal Ithy. They had a table also, littered with papers. When Shandie had doubts about a document, he would refer it to his advisors. Thus was the business of the Impire transacted, in the dying time of Emshandar IV. Thus was the Impire governed. One day Umpily's memoirs would reveal it all.

It was six weeks since the prince had returned, just in time to avert a complete collapse of the realm, six weeks since Umpily had seen that unthinkable vision in the preflecting pool . . . and lied about it.

The great backlog was shrinking slowly, and Ylo now reported that nothing truly urgent remained. The onrush of new matters left little time for catch-up, but the pile was dwindling. Umpily had nightmares when he thought what would have happened without that remarkable young lecher and his brainwave of using Praetorians as scriveners. Of course the unfortunate victims had come close to mutiny— there was even a rumor of an attempted suicide—but the prince had insisted. And the motivation was superb. They were said to be working all day and half the night in their haste to clear up the work and be released from the humiliation. Ylo had already let one go, just to spur the others on. Civilian clerks would have made a life's work of it.

Eventually there would be only the centurion himself left—and Ylo's sandal unkissed! That was a marvelous rumor, but Umpily just could not think of a way to verify it. In fact, he wasn't sure who could have started it, except maybe Ylo himself.

"Charter for the Polity of Gurp," the centurion said with schooled impassivity.

Shandie did not bother to look at that one. Doubtless someone had paid well for it, although a few more crowns might have bought them a better name for their city.

"Another, Grandsire!"

"No! Tired. It's 'nough." The skull-like face on the pillow did not even open its eyes, but it clenched its gums stubbornly.

Shandie frowned and glanced at the ornate dwarvish clock on the mantel. "We'll take a break and do some more later. A quarter of an hour, gentlemen?"

The Praetorians rose and stalked for the door, the centurion trailing an empty hamper, the two guardsmen clutching full ones. Shandie rose and stretched and then wandered over to the coffeepot. The others rose also and went to join him.

Umpily could certainly use something to brighten up his wits. Shandie had a luncheon meeting scheduled with the Ilranian commissioners. If there was one thing calculated to drive a chief of protocol out of his mind, it was elves. Nordland, now, dealt with the Impire through a single ambassador. If he could not speak for individual thanes, at least he would say so. But elves! A dozen of them would twitter like fledglings in a dozen different directions and you never knew which one to listen to, although there would usually be one there with enough authority to negotiate seriously, if you could only figure out which. Even if you knew what their absurd rigmarole titles meant, you never knew whether they represented the real distribution of power. A fair rule of thumb was that the one in the most subdued clothing was the senior and the brightest dressed the least important, but if they knew you knew that, they would certainly switch the order. And their thought processes would madden the

Gods. Umpily's mouth watered at the thought of elvish cuisine. The portions were always too small, though. Jotnar, now, ate little except fish, usually boiled tasteless, but they did know how to heap a platter . . .

The marshal was clutching papers in both hands. "These are all right, Highness. These I recommend you reconsider."

Shandie smiled at him over the lip of a steaming cup. "I gave you only two choices, you old rascal."

"Chuck them, then!" Ithy attempted to smile back. He was a sick man. His face was swollen and hideously discolored by some recent dentistry and must be very painful. He wore civilian clothes, which was just as well. He would look like a turtle in a breastplate. Ithy had been trying to retire for years. Shandie would grant him his release as soon as things were settled.

As soon as things were settled—that phrase cropped up a lot these days. What it meant was *when Emshandar dies.*

The old wreck became hysterically incoherent if anyone suggested a regency. Shandie could make formal application, of course, and the Senate and Assembly would appoint him in less time than it took a clerk to dip a quill, but Shandie absolutely refused to do so. Evidently he couldn't bring himself to submit the old man to that last humiliation. Sentiment was a very poor basis for government, but his grandfather had been father to him and half a mother as well.

And—as even Umpily would admit—for most of fifty years Emshandar had been a fine imperor. Not great, but better than most. In the six weeks since Shandie's return, he had rarely left his bed.

But they could cope. They could run the world like this for a while yet. It wouldn't be long now, *until things were settled.*

Umpily thought they could cope. Shandie thought they could cope. Acopulo wasn't so sure. Yesterday he'd been pointing out that the caliph was rattling his scimitar again in Zark, stronger than ever, the dwarves were being ever more impossible than usual, and the goblins threatening.

Even the fauns of Sysanasso were starting to cause trouble and they'd been quiet for a century. The harvest had failed in the east. A severe earthquake had shaken Ambel. Not one but two comets burned in the northern sky every night, and everyone knew that comets foretold the death of imperors. Even the least superstitious were counting the days until the end of the millennium.

The Impire, the scholar said, was shaking on its foundations. He had given Umpily a very shrewd inspection as he said it, almost as if he knew what Umpily had seen in the preflecting pool. Acopulo didn't believe that Umpily had seen nothing, no matter how much he insisted. He himself didn't even think about it. A dwarf! It was unthinkable. The pool had been malfunctioning, or the whole thing had been a hoax.

Shandie had been touching his toes and flexing his arms. He hated sitting still and he was having to do a lot of that now. Suddenly he asked, "Marshal? Do you ever hear from Warlock Olybino?"

The old soldier started and instinctively glanced toward the bed and the unmoving figure within it. He found no guidance there. "No, Highness. Not for months."

"Since Nefer Moor?"

"Nothing!" Ithy shook his head somberly. "Has his Majesty?"

"Not a word from any of them." Shandie's dark eyes flashed to Umpily, who shrugged, helpless.

Usually Hub ran a rumor or two about the wardens' doings—a miracle cure here, or a seduction there. Once in a while one of the Four would turn up at a ball or meddle in a political affair. They were secretive, but they were present, like shadows on a wall. Now they just seemed to have vanished, and even Umpily could offer Shandie nothing.

Acopulo thought it was a bad sign. He said it meant they were badly divided and didn't trust one another.

Shandie seemed to have become lost in thought, until

Umpily realized he was gazing at some sort of plaque hang-ing on the far wall. Then, with a sense of shock, he recog-nized what the prince was studying: a shield and sword. He had not known that this was where they were kept! They were battered and ugly. In better times, before this sleeping chamber had become a secretariat, those two bronze antiq-uities must have seemed a strangely discordant element amid the luxury and elegance. Yet they were the most sacred rel-ics of the Impire, for they had belonged to the great Emine II.

Their purpose was to summon the wardens. Was Shandie tempted to try? Had he not yet scraped up the courage, or had he already tried and been refused? Would the Four con-descend to appear for him, when he wasn't imperor yet? Reluctantly Umpily decided his memoirs would not contain the answers to those questions.

He poured himself another cup of coffee, thinking morosely of trilling elves and the dwarf he had seen in the pool . . .

"Where's that signifer scallywag of yours?" the marshal inquired, breaking the quiet. "Thought he ran all this for you?"

Now that was an impudent question, although the rough old soldier would not mean it to be. Apart from the matter of a regency, the imperor was reasonably lucid—unless Ylo was mentioned. Then he raved. To bring Ylo into the room drove the old man into screaming hysterics. Obviously that flagging, clouded mind was still capable of admitting guilt. In a way, that was comforting. It would be one of the major revelations in Umpily's posthumous memoirs and would likely lead to a reevaluation of the Yllipo Conspiracy and Emshandar's handling of it.

"Ylo's taking a day off," Shandie said. "He hasn't had a break since we got back, so the Powers know he's earned it. He's gone riding."

Umpily choked. The prince glared at him and that only made him worse.

What the signifer had said was that he wanted to try out a young filly he had his eye on.

Shandie didn't find the matter amusing. His eyes seemed to turn darker, his voice sharpened. "He's a keen horseman, my lord. He already has two mares in the stable at Oak House. He's got a good eye for horseflesh."

"Oh, quite, sir! I don't deny it." Umpily could feel his face going red now, or perhaps purple. Sourpuss Sir Acopulo was pouting blackly.

Old white-eyebrowed Ithy frowned, knowing he had lost the drift of the conversation.

"Seems a very personable fellow. Remarkable career. The legion voted him a day's pay. That doesn't happen often!" He paused, scowling at Umpily. "Didn't know he was a horseman, too. Good-looking chap. Popular with the ladies, is he?"

Umpily found just enough breath to say, "He's the most eligible stal . . . I mean *bachelor* in the—" and then Acopulo's pompous disapproval made him explode in a fit of giggles, like a silly kid.

The prince smiled thinly. "Ylo has a reputation as a ladies' man, Marshal. The old roué's jealous."

"Don't blame him!" Ithy said. "So am I."

Shandie swung around to Umpily. "Seriously, my Lord, is Ylo getting that sort of a reputation around town?"

Umpily pulled himself together, avoiding Acopulo's eye. "He already has . . . already has gotten . . . that sort of reputation, sir. I know of several mothers who have forbidden their daughters to go near him. Of course that gives him a wonderful air of mystery."

Acopulo sniffed meanly. "You've been keeping count?"

The chief of protocol threw up his plump hands in horror. "That would be a full-time job all by itself!"

The little man laughed and Ithy chortled.

Of course Umpily was keeping count! So far he knew of four, and two probables. Not at all bad for six weeks' work!

Imperially unamused, Shandie bent to fill another coffee

cup, then took it over to the bed to see if he could rouse his grandfather and get a little more work out of him.

Shandie himself might even be a little jealous of Ylo. The signifer could at least take most evenings off, whereas Shandie had had almost no private time to spend with his wife and daughter since his return. Umpily's sources among the Oak House domestics reported that the child still refused to recognize her father. They whispered that Princess Eshiala hated formal affairs so much that she was likely to be physically ill before a major function. They even hinted that she had not been nearly so pleased to see her husband as she had pretended. How odd that a superb motivator of men, which Shandie undoubtedly was, should be so totally blind to women!

This would be a difficult period of adjustment for her, of course. But soon things would be settled . . .

Hopefully.

Soon Shandie should sit on the Opal Throne and the Eshiala girl would be impress.

Hopefully.

Umpily had never been a superstitious man, but now he was almost convinced of the dread prophecies associated with the end of the millennium. What had changed his mind, what nobody but he knew about, was the image he had seen in the preflecting pool. That was a nightmare that had haunted him for six weeks now. They wouldn't believe him if he told them. It was incomprehensible—a dwarf sitting on the Opal Throne? He tried not to think about it.

3

FARTHER NORTH, BUT STILL WITHIN THE CONFINES OF THE palace compound, Princess Eshiala was being entertained by her daughter in the gardens of Oak House. Maya was almost two now and trying to be a problem, although she rarely succeeded for long. Black-eyed and black-haired like her parents, she trotted tirelessly around, clutching a soldier doll not much smaller than herself. When she abandoned it, her mother would pick it up. Then she would demand it back again.

The doll was named Leegie. At times Maya would call her father Leegie, when he was in uniform. Maya had not yet accepted the view that fathers were necessary or even desirable, which was hardly surprising, considering how little time Shandie was able to find for his family.

That was a deprivation Eshiala did not mind very much. They were almost never alone, so their relationship remained purely formal. Indeed, when they did find themselves alone together, they were usually at a loss for something to talk about—he disliked discussing business during leisure hours, naturally. Every second or third night he would come to her bedroom, but they did not talk then. When he had done what he needed, he would usually return to his own room to sleep. She submitted without complaint because it was her duty, but she still could not believe that any woman could actually enjoy it. She was not even certain that Shandie did. They did not discuss it.

As a child, she had dreamed of living in a cottage a little grander than her parents', on the outskirts of a small town like Thumble. She had assumed she would eventually have a husband who left at dawn and returned at dusk. In the evenings they would sit and talk of family, or entertain friends; but no one had friends at court and the entertainment was all formal, balls and dinners. Back in Thumble, she would have had children and a servant, perhaps a horse and chaise if she had been fortunate in her marriage. She would have loved her husband dearly and been loved in return.

Why, why, why had she settled for all this instead?

To make her father a marquis and her sister a duchess?

No. Because the prince imperial had wanted her, and her duty had been to serve. As she did, and would, loyally.

She hated Oak House and its hundreds of servants. She was totally unable to run such an establishment, although nobody cared about that but her. Soon she would be official mistress of the Opal Palace itself, and nobody could run that—it had its own government department and an annual budget that would support three legions. So Prince Emthoro had told her.

Playing in the gardens with Maya was the nearest to bliss she ever came. The goslings had no desire to join her. She could pretend that she was the only woman in the world, that the two of them were the only people. The guards were far away and the gardeners kept out of sight. She knew she was visible to dozens of spying faces behind the dozens of windows, but she could forget about them.

Shandie had been back for six weeks and she thought she was with child again. In a few more days she would know for certain. She prayed that she was, for pregnancy would release her from the looming torture of playing impress at the state funeral and coronation and gala balls. It would also free her from the night thing, too, for a while.

Maya vanished around the end of a hedge into the rose garden; she followed—and stopped. Surprise was quickly followed by annoyance, then panic. There was a man there. He was seated on a bench and had not seen her. He was engrossed in doing something with a large silver bowl.

She moved to snatch up Maya and leave, but Maya had almost reached the intruder before seeing him. She stopped to stare and let Leegie slip to the grass. Eshiala moved forward to recover both.

"Ylo!" Maya said, trotting forward.

So it was, and Maya had done very well to recognize him before her mother did. Eshiala had never seen the signifer out of uniform before. He was wearing a well-tailored riding outfit that might have just come out of the box. If anything, he was even more dashing than usual.

He smiled at Maya with no indication of surprise. "Hello,

there, Princess!" Then he turned his smile on Eshiala. "Your servant, ma'am."

He did not rise. That annoyed her. She did hate the eternal formalities of court life, but he was not to know that. It was mere good manners for a man to stand when greeting a lady. She might be a sham princess, but she had been brought up to appreciate genteel behavior.

"Good morning, Signifer."

"Ylo," Maya confirmed. She clutched the edge of the bowl on his lap and stood on tiptoe to see into it. "What doing, Ylo?"

"Making a surprise. You want to help? Here!" And without even asking permission, the soldier lifted the child up to stand on the bench beside him.

Eshiala was nonplussed. She knew the signifer, for he ate at the prince's table and had his own suite of rooms in Oak House. They saw each other almost every day. He was cool and formal and never addressed her unless she spoke to him first, which was just about never. He was much too good-looking. Shandie had warned her that he was a libertine and asked her to drop a warning to her maids of honor. She had done so with a very embarrassing blush.

"Join us, Gorgeous," he said, smiling.

Not only much too good-looking, he was also extremely impertinent! Before she could frame an adequately crushing reply, he lifted a rose from a pile of roses on the bench beside him and began stripping the petals into the bowl. The bowl was already half full of petals, red, white, yellow, pink.

"What you doing?" Maya demanded again.

"You want to help? Here . . ." Ylo inspected one of the flowers. "No prickles!" He gave the flower to Maya, showing how to pull off a petal and drop it in the bowl. Maya grabbed a fistful of petals and tugged. The signifer gleamed eyes and teeth in another brief smile at Eshiala, then returned to his own rose.

Apparently forgotten, Eshiala stood and . . . and dithered.

She could certainly snatch up her daughter and leave, but Maya would yell the sky down.

She would not go and sit on the bench. She stayed where she was. "Signifer, what exactly are you doing?"

This time the smile went on longer and was more calculated. "That's a secret just at the moment. You mean you've never seen a man doing this?"

"You're making perfume?" A great pile of stripped stalks lay at his feet. He must have been at work for an hour or more.

"No." He shook his head. The sun seemed to dim for his smile. He returned his attention to the bowl and Maya's mangled efforts. "You remind me of Centurion Hardgraa, you know."

Eshiala could imagine no one she less resembled. "In what way?"

"He hates the palace, too."

Her defenses sprang back to their posts at once. "That's absurd!"

"I've watched you," he told the bowl. "Do you know what the domestics call you behind your back? The Ice Impress!"

"What the servants choose to call me is no concern of mine!"

"But servants usually know more of the truth than anyone. They're all spies, of course. The wine steward and the chief coachman report to Umpily. Emthoro's people own a footman and the pastry cook and so on."

This conversation was insane! Shandie had warned her before they were married that her maids of honor would gossip mercilessly, but she had not worried about the servants. "Why in the world should Lord Umpily spy on the prince?"

"This is the court. Everyone spies on everyone."

She did not believe it. "And how do you know about them?"

He shrugged. "Security is Hardgraa's job, of course. I

charmed one of the chambermaids for him and then we traded information. Interesting fellow, Hardgraa. Have you ever had a good heart-to-heart with him?"

She shook her head.

"You should! Son of a quarry worker. He joined the army at sixteen, but his tribune decided he had promise, and his tribune ran an illicit gladiator troop. Hardgraa was killing men to amuse rich folk before he was shaving."

She shuddered. She had heard rumors of such affairs and the vast sums gambled on them. She clasped her elbows tightly.

"Well, that's a bit of an exaggeration," Ylo said, reaching for another flower. "But not much of one. At twenty he blackmailed a legate into . . . well, never mind. Hardgraa fought his way up from the swamp. It's easier for him than you." Still the signifer continued to strip petals from the roses. Maya was beating the remains of her own flower to death on the bench.

"What's easier?" Eshiala felt she was being entangled in a web of words. Every time she tried to move, he stuck her more firmly with some new puzzle. No one else ever talked to her like this.

He glanced up and studied her for a moment, then reached for another rose. "He was born in the valleys. No one expects him to know what wine goes with fish, and he never will. You came up from the foothills and expect to be able to pass on the peaks. You never will, either."

She thought grimly of the hundreds of lessons she had taken in etiquette and dance and elocution and . . . As she drew breath to retort, he added, "Any more than I would have ever made a good legionary."

Shandie had warned her that Ylo was in line for a dukedom. Well, however much that might impress some silly little debutante, it cut no rushes with a future impress. "You are modest, sir."

"True, but no one has ever noticed that before." Ylo inspected another rose, pinched off a few thorns, and tucked it in his hair. Maya broke into yells of laughter and grabbed it out again.

"It was easier for me," he said. "I was born on the mountaintops. I went down, not up. Learning to sharpen stakes with an ax is infinitely easier than mastering the aristocracy's sneaky little games. And you know when you've done it wrong, because you get beaten. Helps to be beaten, because then nobody cares afterward. You learn faster, too. Shandie thinks I'm a genius. Sit down, Princess."

She ought to grab Maya and run. Or at least she should find a couple of her ladies to chaperon her while she talked with this notorious lecher.

Ylo looked up, frowning. "We're certainly being watched from the windows and this little minx is old enough to tell tales if I rape you, but she can't repeat what we say. Who are you scared of, you or me?"

"I am not scared of anyone!"

"Then prove it by sitting down."

"The servants will—"

"You said you didn't care about them. Where was I? Oh, yes. Shandie thinks I'm a genius. That's nonsense. I was a consul's son. I was taught to read and write. Then I became a maggot in the XXth legion. I was taught to work. By the Powers, was I ever taught to work!"

She perched on the end of the bench and he peered around Maya at her. Maya was busy entangling the rose in Ylo's curls.

"Have you any idea of the load a legionary carries? Well, can you imagine marching in the rain all day with a couple of Mayas on your back—and then digging ditches for two or three hours after that? Can you imagine having blisters for months on end because they never get a chance to heal?'

She shook her head, frightened by his bitterness. His changes of mood were throwing her completely off balance.

"And Shandie can't imagine cataloguing reports all day. I learned both worlds. But it was easier for me."

Then he just looked at her under his lashes and her heart missed a beat. If he thought she was a giddy village maid who would fall for a man's good looks, then he had a big disappointment coming. He was far *too* handsome.

"I must go!" she said.

"You just got here. You haven't discovered what I'm doing yet. Princess-brat, why don't you stick that in your mother's ear instead of mine? You've been warned that I'm a terrible womanizer?"

"Yes I have."

"Good. I wouldn't want to sneak up on you." He grinned.

She had returned his smile before she saw the implications.

"You hate the pomp," he said. "No, don't deny it, Eshiala. I know as much about women as any man can. Far, far more than Shandie ever will. Nobody ever taught him to play, I think. How often has he made love to you in a bathtub?"

"*Signifer!*"

"Well?"

"No gentleman would put such a question to a lady!"

He leered at her. "But I'm not a gentleman, I'm a legionary. You're a grocer's daughter. Does he ever just tickle you? Tickle you till you scream? I bet he treats you like a drill squad. *On the count of three . . .* Has he ever recited a naughty poem in bed? Has he ever spread jam on your breasts and licked it off again?"

"What! Are you serious?"

"Of course not! We're talking fun here!"

She sprang to her feet and was about to lift Maya . . .

"I know him much better than you do," Ylo told the silver bowl. "I've studied him carefully for almost two years now. He spoke of you a lot."

She froze. "I will not believe that the prince gossips."

"That's the odd thing! All he ever remarked about you was how beautiful you were and how gracefully you moved. He never mentioned your taste in food, or art, or music.

When he wanted to buy a gift for you, he had no idea what gems you preferred. Maybe he didn't think you would have a preference." The dark eyes turned to her. She tried to hold his gaze, and couldn't. She sat down again, feeling a little shaken at hearing her fears voiced so callously.

"Eshiala, Shandie married you because of your looks—you look like the perfect storybook princess. Beyond that, he doesn't know what he wants in a woman, and he assumes that wealth and power will satisfy you. It isn't only you—he's tongue-tied with women. He doesn't seem to understand them. I know exactly what a woman wants and what I want of her. I am a skilled and ruthless hunter of women. I have six different approaches and I rarely fail."

She gasped. "This is the most disgusting, insulting—"

"I've watched you at mealtimes, talking about forthcoming events, and you can barely swallow. I've watched you preparing to leave for a ball and known your insides were knotted like pinewood. I've watched your husband kiss you when he comes home, and you don't hate him."

His rudeness shocked her speechless.

"But you don't love him."

"How dare you!"

"If you say you love him, you're lying. He's totally besotted with some ideal impress of his imagination, but he can't love a woman as a person in her own right. He should have realized by now. If he has realized, then he doesn't have a clue what to do about it."

"If I tell him what you—"

"Don't. He has enough worries at the moment. I know all about you. You were married at seventeen. Your family twisted your arm until it twanged."

So this was what happened when a notorious womanizer made a pass, was it? She was not very impressed so far. She was more angry than she'd been in years.

"You are being very offensive!"

"But in the end, you married Shandie out of a sense of duty. Do you spread your legs for him out of duty, too?"

Feeling her face flame, Eshiala leaped to her feet and reached for her baby—

"That's what your sister told me."

She said, "Huh?" in a gasp that left her lungs empty, and slumped down on the bench again.

Ylo had a twinkle in his eye now. "I'm having luncheon with the senator today—he has a colt in his stable I'm interested in."

Maya was attempting to fix a rose in her own hair, without success. The senator always had a nap after lunch. *Oh, Ashia, you fool! Fool! Fool! Fool!* No child of Ylo's would look like a baboon.

"A duchess is fair game," Ylo said, coming to the final rose, "but normally I would never be so crazy as to seduce the future impress. I'm sure it's a capital offense and probably involves an especially lingering demise. Red-hot anthills, or something."

"You will not have occasion to find out."

"I certainly hope not. Remember the story of the preflecting pool?" He tossed the last stalk over his shoulder.

"I remember my husband asking us not to discuss . . . Oh, no!"

He leaned back and laid an arm along the back of the bench. "I'm afraid so. With daffodils."

This should be laughable, it was so absurd, but she was too furious to laugh. "Is this Number Six, or are you developing Approach Number Seven? It must be a recent invention. And remember that my husband asked us . . ." She was stopped by Ylo's smile. "It was you who mentioned those prophecies!"

"Would you ever have heard of them otherwise?"

Of course not. Shandie never talked business. "You were planning this even then, right after you got back?"

"I began planning it as soon as I set eyes on you. This is a unique situation. As I said, I am not normally a hero in such matters, nor crazy. I can bull almost any woman I fancy, so why play with the only fire that can hurt me? But it would seem that I have no choice. It is prophesied for daffodil time."

"Daffodil time?" By daffodil time she would be shaped like a bolster, she hoped.

"I saw you in a garden, with daffodils."

"In a state of undress, of course?"

"Stark naked on a blanket."

"What!?"

"And smiling." He rose before she could. Clutching the big silver bowl, he stepped in front of her.

"I swear to you that is the truth," he said sadly, "but I am an utterly unscrupulous liar, so you'd best not believe me. I hope for my sake that the pool was playing tricks, because I have no desire to be hanged, quartered, or drawn, just to add an impress to my score sheet. But I hope for your sake that the prophecy is fulfilled."

This was obscene! "You are too kind, sir."

"There was a girl like you down in Qoble, married too young to a rich man. I showed her what the act of love could be. She told me later that it had helped a lot."

"After three years at court, I thought I knew how arrogant men can be. I see I was mistaken."

"Just inexperienced."

"You imply that I should find adultery with you a wonderfully enjoyable experience?"

Ylo looked exasperated. "Of course you would! Why else do they consent, do you suppose?"

"I have no idea!"

"There's your problem, then. Tonight, take the jam pot to bed and explain to Shandie what he has to do."

She opened her mouth to protest . . . She was smiling. The more she thought about it, the more outrageous the notion seemed. She chuckled unwillingly.

"Why you laughing?" Maya demanded, coming to her along the bench.

She pulled herself together. "Ylo said a funny thing, darling."

"Don't try it on him, though," Ylo added. "It doesn't work the other way."

She looked at his grin, had a vision of Shandie's hairy chest . . .

"Why laughing?" Maya shouted, beating her mother's shoulder with her little fists.

Eshiala caught her breath and wiped tears from her eyes and looked up to see the triumphant glint under those dark lashes.

"How long since you laughed like that, Gorgeous? Try again!" Ylo tipped a blizzard of petals over her. They went in her hair, on her lap and shoulders, all over the bench and the grass at her feet. They were damp and they stuck. Maya could understand that joke. She shrieked with delight.

Eshiala squealed and brushed helplessly at her bodice. "You idiot! Oh, you . . ."

"Idiot." He smiled blissfully. "This is my Number-One Approach—make her laugh. Darling, you are the most beautiful woman I have ever dreamed of, but of course I tell them all that. I did want to hear your laugh, and it's lovely. You can keep the bowl." He handed it to her and walked away across the grass, whistling.

Eshiala stared after him. Even if he had not spoken one true word, he must have spent at least an hour setting up a stupid practical joke! Just to make her laugh?

"Why Mommy crying?" Maya asked.

4

AND SO THE DAYS PASSED. AUTUMN GOLD CREPT DOWN FROM the Isdruthud Mountains and advanced across the plains to

Hub. Three comets hung in the northern sky, a sight never before recorded. Odds of the imperor seeing the year out were being quoted at fifty to one against. Most of the great Winterfest balls had been canceled in anticipation of national mourning.

Suddenly elves became rare as unicorns. The imps chuckled and remarked how Winterfest was normally the most prosperous time of year for elves, and elves were notoriously unable to manage money. All those musicians, singers, couturiers, and so on had undoubtedly squandered their anticipated rewards prematurely and must now flee the capital to escape their creditors.

That failed to explain the departure of the poets, dancers, painters, and sculptors. Then came rumors that elves were hurrying to the skytrees of Ilrane from all over Pandemia.

Funny people, elves.

Considering the famine in parts of Shimlundok and the Ambel earthquake, the Imperial Archivist wanted to declare 2998 the Year of Disasters. Shandie would not hear of it and decreed that it be known as the Year of Three Comets.

Nevertheless . . .

Harvests rotted in southwest Pithmot, due to a shortage of troll agricultural workers. A squadron of the IInd fleet was blown ashore in the Nogid Archipelago and the crews posted as missing, presumed eaten. The caliph's armies rolled the legions back into Ullacarn, recovering everything the djinns had lost at Karthin and Bone Pass. Gnomish partisans ambushed a cohort in Guwush and ripped it to pieces.

Unconfirmed—meaning faunish and therefore nonimpish and hence unreliable—sources claimed that a blaze of three dragons had escaped from Dragon Reach and ravaged Sysanasso for a week, before all three had inexplicably fallen dead from the sky.

And civil war raged in Nordland. It was nice to know that some things, at least, were normal.

• • •

Unbeknownst to anyone else, the good folk of Krasnegar were battling disaster, also. A succession of unseasonable storms took out a section of the causeway at the deepest part of the channel. Without the supplies the wagons brought, the town would starve or freeze before spring. If the herds were lost, it would starve the following winter.

The king organized repairs with wagons and horses and every able-bodied man in the kingdom. The only source of suitable stone was a league away. Furthermore, the blocks could be placed in position only at low tide, and there was no room for traffic to pass on the road out to the damage site. Three times the repairs were begun, only to be ripped out by another storm.

Rap fretted worse than anyone. He wondered if the Gods were testing him, or warning him, or even punishing him. If he had not known before, he knew now that he would never stand by and let the town starve. Yet, as long as there was any hope that the people could solve their problems for themselves, he held back on sorcery. In the end he did not need to use it, but he suffered all the blisters, exhaustion, crushed toes, and strained backs as if they had happened to him.

Meanwhile, the queen had rallied the fishing fleet to ferry the harvest over the bay. That was a wretched business, also, with women wading out into the freezing waves to load the boats. Many a king of Krasnegar had tried building a wharf on the mainland side of the bay, only to see the winter ice wipe it contemptuously away. The little craft could handle foodstuffs, but they were useless for peat or livestock.

Winter came unusually late, so king and queen won their respective battles, but with mere hours to spare. The northern sky was turning to lead as precious cattle and horses stampeded across the finished causeway, laden wagons rolling behind them, and an army of weary foot soldiers tramping in the rear. Krasnegar slammed its door in winter's face and the snow came before the next tide. It was going to be tight, but the king's tallies said the people would live.

Never had so many worked so hard. All through the town, husbands were reunited with wives and parents with children. The wind shrieked in the eaves and rattled casements, while tubs of bathwater steamed and stew pots bubbled. Impromptu singsongs and dances sprang up everywhere. In the saloons, the jotnar began settling long-postponed challenges. Imps began catching up on affairs of all sorts: love, business, and other peoples'.

Similar things were happening in the castle, too. Not in many weeks had Inos been able to gather her family all together. Secure in their private parlor, she and Rap cuddled their children. Holi remembered his father after a little thought. Ten months old now, he was fat and jolly, obviously a royal Krasnegarian misfit, a honey-haired imp with a faun nose. Eva was jotunnish and nine and becoming very protective of her baby brother. Gath and Kadie were soon to be fourteen . . . where did the years go? Tonight Inos had noticed a few gray hairs in Rap's brown thatch, and those were new. She would not think about the windburn her mirror had displayed, nor the rest of its lies.

Sitting in their two big armchairs, smothered in children, king and queen smiled wearily across at each other. *Later*, his eyes said, and *I love you*. She sent back the same signals. The peat glowed on the big hearth, shining brighter once in a while as the wind gusted in the chimney. Candle flames danced on the mantel. Life felt very, very good.

"That was a close-run thing," Rap remarked wearily, from underneath Eva and Kadie. He had said that several times.

"But it will be all right?" Inos cuddled Holi.

"Oh, the food will last. Fuel will be tight, though."

"And we will hold the Harvesthome Dance?" Kadie asked anxiously.

"Absolutely!" Inos said. "This year more than ever. We'll start organizing tomorrow."

"No!" Rap said, and grinned at her surprise. "Tomorrow we'll have a family holiday. You kids can have your parents all to yourselves, for once. What do you want to do?"

Kadie's eyes lit up. "Want you to give me a fencing lesson, Papa dear!"

Rap twisted his head to regard his daughter nose to nose. "All right—but I don't trust that bloodthirsty look in your eye!"

She pouted, not at all displeased. So she thought she could beat her father, did she?

Gath smiled faintly. He was sitting on the hob by himself, because cuddling was beneath a man's dignity.

Eva wanted help with her dolls' house.

"Gath?" Rap said.

Gath's dreamy gray eyes took on a bothered, pensive look. He scratched his spiky golden comb. "You promised to go through the soldier books with me."

"So I did." Rap frowned.

Inos sent him a quizzical look, married code for *Explain!* She sensed something more important than dolls' houses, and Rap's reaction confirmed it.

"Just after Gath and I went over to the—"

"Very first day," Gath said.

"Yes. He saw a vision of a soldier, on the beach."

Gath jumped up and balanced on one foot, with the other behind him and one arm raised. "Like this! Just for a minute. Then he disappeared again."

Inos' contentment dropped a few notches. Why had Rap not told her? Because they had hardly seen each other since, of course. Then why had Gath not told her? But she had hardly seen Gath, even. "Soldiers don't usually go in for ballet dancing. Just that once, or do you see things often?"

"Just that once." Gath resumed his seat, starting to look at her oddly. "An Imperial soldier! Dad says there are old books about the legions somewhere."

"You made out his insignia?"

"Think so. On his breastplate. A star with four points."

"All the imps wear that!" Kadie snorted. "It's Imperial. Expect you were daydreaming."

"And a circle of gold leaves."

"What sort of gold leaves?" Inos said sharply. "Laurel leaves? Fig leaves?"

"You know!" Gath said, excited now, and staring hard at her.

Leaves? She raked over distant memories of Kinvale. "I certainly do not know all the legionary blazons in the Impire!"

"But?" Gath said excitedly. "Yes? Yes?"

But leaves? *Oak* leaves? A circle of . . .

"Oak leaves!" Gath shouted. "Heir apparent! What's oak?"

Yes, of course! But how could he remember her memories before she did? Would she really have blurted that aloud when it came to her?

Rap edged Eva aside and straightened up, scowling from mother to son and back again. "The prince imperial? You're sure?"

She nodded, with a let's-talk-about-it-later frown.

"We'll check it out tomorrow," Rap said. "What's the matter now?"

Gath was looking at him with a very odd expression. "Tomorrow? Er . . . nothing, Dad."

"You can see that far ahead now?"

"No. No, I can't ever see tomorrows. Just . . . Just a feeling. Nothing." He bit his lip uncertainly.

Shadows had fallen over the happy gathering. Why should Inos' son have seen a vision of the next imperor? What was wrong with tomorrow? Evil take it! The world would be a much better place without sorcery.

"Well, I'm famished!" she said firmly. "Ring the bell, someone. I could eat a whale."

"Me, too," Rap said.

Gath smiled sadly. "We don't eat for a long time yet."

Rap frowned. "No? What can you possibly foresee to keep me from eating? A Nordland invasion?"

"The bishop."

There was a tap on the door.

"God of Torment!" Rap exclaimed. "How long have you known about him?"

"Oh . . . Since you went in the bathtub, I suppose."

"I shall speak to you later, young man! Enter!"

Young Pret peered around the door. He was the shortest jotunn in the kingdom, with a heart weakness that kept him from heavy labor. When sober he was a passable footman.

"His Holiness, Sire."

"Show him in," Rap said, glaring at Gath's satisfaction.

Inos sent her husband a warning frown. She knew exactly what he was thinking: *I don't mind the old man getting long in the tooth if he would just stop getting long in the wind.* Rap regarded that as one of his better jokes, but the only person he could tell it to was Inos and she had threatened to have him beheaded if he did so just once more. He wouldn't say it in front of the children, anyway.

Bishop Havermore was elderly, gaunt and stooped. He wore a halo of white curls and he blinked a lot. He offered blessings and accepted a chair.

"We were just about to eat, Holiness," Inos said sweetly. "Won't you join us?"

The bishop said he had eaten, would not stay long—and Kadie rolled her eyes disbelievingly behind his back. He had merely come to suggest a special service of thanks to the Gods for the town's deliverance.

Very good idea, Inos said, smiling more warnings at Rap.

"Thanks, especially," the bishop said, blinking, "to the God of Winter, for staying Their hand so long, and of course to the God of Storms . . ."

Rap caught his wife's eye, bared his teeth, and did *not* point out that the God of Storms had caused all the trouble in the first place.

Once started, Havermore could never stop. He was immune to hints. An hour later he had not run out of Gods and was rehearsing his proposed sermon verbatim, addressing it to the candles. The children were fretting, Inos could hear Rap's stomach rumbling louder than the blizzard outside, and she kept having to unclench her fists.

She saw that Rap had had enough—and Gath had been fighting a grin for some time. Oh, no! Before she could think of a suitable intervention, Rap rose and reached for the bellrope. She eyed him anxiously.

"You have missed someone, your Holiness!" he said.

The aged cleric blinked up at him in dismay. "I have?"

"Four people who made our deliverance possible. Without them, Krasnegar would be facing certain starvation this winter."

Now what? Everyone in the room was staring up at him in puzzled silence—except Gath, of course, who was turning bright red with his efforts not to laugh at whatever was coming. Inos' fists had clenched again.

"I think," the king said, "these gallant helpers should be mentioned by name in your sermon. In fact, I think you should invite them to sit beside you, so that you can present them to the congregation and thank them in person."

"Oh, I agree!" Havermore bleated. "Who are these men?"

The door squeaked as the footman opened it and looked in.

"Two men and their wives," Rap said. "I don't think you have ever met them. Pret, conduct his Holiness downstairs and find the royal rat-catchers for him. The root cellar might be a good place to look first. They were there earlier."

"Rat-catchers?" said bishop and flunky and queen in harmony.

"Rat-catchers!" Rap said firmly. "Most winters we lay away about twice as much food as we have this year. This year is different. What we have will suffice now, but only because the vermin used to eat half our stocks! So you go thank our gnomes on behalf of the people, Holiness. And perhaps you should also thank the God of Hospitality for inspiring me to offer them a home here."

Inos carefully did not look at either Gath or Kadie.

5

THE BISHOP HAD DEPARTED, VERY MUCH ON HIS PATHETIC dignity, the spoiled meal had been eaten, and the children had been put to bed. King and queen were back in their parlor again. This time they were both in the same chair.

Rap was nibbling Inos' ear, but he wasn't very serious about it. She demanded to know more about Gath's vision. Between toothwork he told her, but there was very little more to tell. The figure had been standing in that peculiar position and had seemed to be in darkness, or perhaps moonlight. The incident had happened late in the day, which would have been long after sunset in southern lands, at that time of year. By the time all that was said, he had lost interest in the ear-nibbling business. She gave him a hug. Maybe tomorrow.

"It could have been Shandie, I suppose," she said.

"Are there any pictures of him in Krasnegar?"

"Not that I know of. We could ask around." She pondered uneasily. "Kadie might make up such a tale. Not Gath."

"Never. Not Gath."

Worried silence. The peat hissed softly. It was hard to think of the spindly ten-year-old she had once known being a famous soldier now. Fighting? Killing people?

"The only thing I can suggest," Rap said, glowering at the fireplace, "is that Shandie looked through a magic casement. The illusions work both ways. Remember we saw a vision of a dragon? When that prophecy was fulfilled, I thought I caught a glimmer of something . . . but that was months later! Why would Gath standing on a shingle beach matter to Shandie? It makes no sense."

"You think Gath is the one, don't you?" she said softly. "The one the God mentioned."

Rap set his teeth and said nothing.

She kissed his cheek. "Come to bed, love. You'll think better in the morning." Tired as she was, she thought she had better do some ear-nibbling herself tonight. He needed to unwind.

Rap shook his head. "I've shilly-shallied too long, Inos! I keep pretending it'll all go away, and it won't. I should have told Shandie of the God's warning."

"Nothing you can do tonight. And anyway, this causeway thing . . ."

"I'm going to go upstairs first. I won't be long."

Upstairs probably meant Inisso's chamber. "Tomorrow!" she insisted. How oddly Gath had reacted to that word!

"I won't sleep. It won't take long. Just a quick look."

"I'll come with you," she said.

"No."

"Yes!" Fauns were not the only stubborn people in Pandemia.

The only reason to go all the way up Inisso's Tower would be to escape the occult shield that enclosed the castle. That one topmost room was excluded.

"I have never seen my husband use sorcery," she said whenever the subject became unavoidable, which was rarely. The words were true only so far as they went. She had seen Rap use sorcery, but not since they were married. She had enjoyed miraculously easy births for her children and guessed why. He did not like to discuss the matter, so she never did.

Bearing lanterns and swathed in thick white furs, king and queen made the long climb up the curving stairs within the walls. Their breath smoked. The stones still held some of the summer sun, the killer cold of midwinter had not arrived, and yet the rooms were already chill. The tower was unused now, the first two or three chambers cluttered with things put away until needed and then forgotten. Remembrance crouched in the shadows.

Halfway up, they paused to catch their wind in the Withdrawing Room, which was especially infested with memories. Inos flopped down on a spindly-legged chair, the only one left of Aunt Kade's set. The others Rap had smashed on Darad's head or the jotnar had burned.

"I forgot to ask," she puffed, "just what I was coming up here to do."

Rap had perched on the arm of the sofa. "It was your idea! Just to applaud, is all."

"You're going to send a message to Hub?"

"Gods, no!"

His vehemence surprised her and confirmed her worries. "One real word and three ghost words, you said once. Rap, how much of a sorcerer are you now, anyway?"

"Large sparrow size. Don't worry! I shan't do anything to attract attention."

"Then what?"

He sighed. "I'm going to come out of my mundane shell and take a peek with premonition, that's all. A two-minute sorcery, very unobtrusive."

"Those comets? Do they mean anything?"

"That's one of the things I want to discover. I should have done this months ago. If I'd known about Shandie . . ." He stood up. "You going to sit there and freeze, woman?"

The Chamber of Puissance was stark and bare, a circle of bare floor broken only by the royal treasure chest. Most of the gold Rap had made for it ages ago was still in there. She wondered if he could make gold now.

Three arched windows looked out on the storm, and they

were caked with snow. The fourth opening had once held a magic casement, but long ago a certain faunish sorcerer had converted that into a magic portal, an arcane way out of the kingdom. Kade was dead, Hononin was dead. Only three people knew of this state secret at the top of Inisso's Tower.

"Well, get on with it!" she said.

Rap laid down his lantern. Then he just stood. No lightning, no flames? What a very dull sorcery! Starting to shiver, she moved closer. Just once, very briefly, she had been a sorceress in this chamber, with the town all spread out below her, every room, every cranny. She had spoken with Rap from here, as he rode away out of her life forever . . .

Suddenly he yelled, and his knees buckled. She threw her arms around him to steady him, both of them made clumsy by their enveloping furs.

"No!" he cried, staggering. "No! No! No!"

"What's wrong? Rap! What's wrong?"

Little more than his eyes showed, but those were enough. Even when he had found his footing, she could feel him trembling.

"Bad!" he said. "Terrible! Oh, my love! Danger! Terrible danger." He clung to her. His voice held a note she had never heard in it before. He was frightened. *Rap* was?

"Tell me!"

"I can't . . . can't put it into words! It's too big! Something awful looming. Disaster, everywhere, to everyone!"

"*Rap!* Explain!" What in the Powers' Names could frighten Rap so badly? Anyone else, maybe, but *Rap?*

"Remember this morning? How the sky grew blacker and blacker? It's like that. It's evil, Inos! Pure Evil!"

"*All things include both the Evil and the Good,*" she said automatically.

"Not this! This is just evil." His voice cracked. "It fouls the future like a dungheap!"

"Whose future?"

He shuddered. "Mine. And yours. And Krasnegar's. Oh, Gods! It threatens everything! Inos, I've been a fool, fool, fool!"

"No!"

"Yes! An idiot, hiding inside my safe little shell, playing at being a mundane—I thought I had time. The God said I had time! I thought we had another year left in the millennium."

"You had duties here," she said firmly. "The town needed you when the causeway was washed out. And what can you do anyway? Is it your job to save the world?"

She knew the answer before he said it.

"Yes."

"What?"

"To try. Gods, Inos! It's everyone's duty to fight this— whatever it is. I can't see ahead very far, but . . . Darling, I must go! I must!"

"Go where?"

"To Hub! I must talk with Shandie, maybe Sagorn. Maybe even the wardens."

"Your duty is here!" she shouted. She released him and stepped back so she could see his face in the glimmer of the lanterns. "You have a wife and children and a kingdom . . ." Aghast, she stopped. "No?"

"I think this is bigger than even those, my darling. If the whole world is threatened? I must go!"

With no more explanation than that? Racing off on some harebrained half-baked scheme to save the world? "Rap! You—"

"Stop!" he shouted, suddenly backing away, raising fur-thick arms as if to defend himself from attack. "Don't start throwing orders at me, darling!"

"Rap? What's gotten into you? You—"

"If you start ordering me around, then I can't resist! I put that royal glamor on you when I had a lot more power than I have now."

She hadn't realized. That was almost funny. But it would

not be at all funny if she gave Rap an order and his own magic compelled him to obey her against his will. There would go their marriage.

He spoke more calmly. "I must go. I *do* go, dear. Now, tonight!"

"You promised—" She remembered Gath. "This is what Gath sensed about tomorrow! Do very bad events cast very long shadows, Rap?"

"Could be."

"You're breaking your promise to the children. That's going to seem a very big disaster to them."

Did Gath's premonition make this argument pointless? Arguing with Rap was always pointless.

"Explain to them," he said. "No, don't. Tell them whatever you can, and that I love them. Inos, I'm doing this for them, too! And for you."

"Then you'd better explain to me first. You're exhausted. You haven't slept a full night in weeks. After a thousand years, what can be so urgent that another day or two will hurt?"

Rap closed his eyes and turned around slowly. Then he raised an arm and looked where he pointed. East. "That way!" he said hoarsely.

"Goblins?"

"No . . ."

"Nordland?"

"No, I don't think so. It has a dwarvish feel to it, I think. So Dwanish, rather than Nordland. Not jotnar, but . . . *God of Fools!*" He fell silent.

If evil was indeed brewing in Dwanish, then she knew of one likely suspect. "Zinixo?"

"Maybe. What makes you think so?" His voice was guarded.

"Just a guess. You didn't kill him, did you? And he has reason to hate you." Warlock Zinixo had been the most powerful sorcerer in the world, except for Rap. And also crazy as a drunken bat. "Who else fits as well?"

"No one. That's a good point. No, I didn't kill him. Do you suppose that was the error the God mentioned?"

"No idea. What did you do to him?"

"I thought I made him harmless. I can't believe even Zinixo could represent this much trouble. I don't understand, dear, but for Gods' sakes, stay away from dwarves until I get back!"

"I don't think any dwarf has set foot in Krasnegar in the last hundred years. All right, so you're going to Hub. You'll be back in a day or two, promise?"

"I'll try. That's all I can promise."

She would have been content with that. Would she be happier with a husband who *didn't* do his duty as he saw it?

She watched in dismay as he strode over to the treasure chest. A real sorcerer had no need for gold! How much use was a *large sparrow size* sorcerer? Zinixo was not the only danger waiting out there for King Rap. Any sorcerer might choose to make him a votary, and there were hundreds of sorcerers in Pandemia. Two of the wardens, Lith'rian and Olybino, might still have grudges to settle. Raspnex should be grateful and friendly, but who would ever trust a dwarf, or a sorcerer?

He gave her a hug and a kiss, dry-lipped in the cold.

"Be careful, my darling!" he said. "I swear I'll return as soon as I can."

"You be careful, too. Give Eigaze my love. And the others. All except Andor, of course . . ."

Rap left her the lantern, for sorcerers needed no light. He opened the magic portal, letting warm southern air swirl out like steam. He stepped through and was gone from Krasnegar.

Gather ye rosebuds:
>   *Gather ye rosebuds while ye may,*
>   *Old Time is still a-flying:*
>   *And that fair flower that blooms today,*
>   *Tomorrow will be dying.*
>   —HERRICK, *TO VIRGINS, TO MAKE MUCH OF TIME*

CHAPTER NINE

UNHALLOWED GROUND

1

AQUIALA, THE DUCHESS OF KINVALE, WAS ENTERTAINING A
dozen or so friends to dinner. She remained unaware of the
man who had just stepped out of a wall upstairs, but she
would not have been surprised, for she knew of the magic
portal.

Rap took a minute to catch his breath, then began peeling
off his furs. Kade's private sitting room was dark and musty.
As a tribute to her, it had been left exactly as she knew it—
a well-designed, tastefully furnished lady's parlor, worn a
little shabby. Her last knitting still lay on a table beside her
favorite chair, but she would not have approved of the stuff-
iness, or the dust. She would have thrown open the drapes

and windows and summoned the housekeeper to inspect the twigs in the grate, a sure sign that crows were nesting in the chimney pot.

From time to time Rap and Inos would slip away to Kinvale to attend a dinner party or a ball, although not so much of late, he realized. Was that a sign of age creeping up on them? Kade had acted as the royal purchasing agent, and now Aquiala filled the post. The neighbors knew Inos of old, but none was aware that she had become queen of Krasnegar, or would recall ever hearing of Krasnegar. She was understood to be a princess of some minor frontier kingdom who had married a reclusive local gentleman of faunish descent.

To a Hubban aristocrat, Kinvale would seem quaint, rustic, and old-fashioned, a remote backwater of impire. By local standards it was huge and luxurious. Rap thought it absurdly pretentious or even decadent, but he tolerated it because Inos liked to visit and because he enjoyed Aquiala's good humor and rare common sense. She also threw great parties.

He sensed a fine fall night beyond the walls. The storms of Krasnegar were five hundred leagues away, beyond the mountains and the taiga. The obscene world-size threat still loomed in his premonition, terrifying and impossible to ignore.

What now? A sorcerer could move himself bodily without the need of a magic portal or any other physical contrivance, but such brute-force sorcery was very conspicuous. He would rattle the ambience over half the world. He would draw attention to himself, to Kinvale, and to the magic portal behind him.

He scanned the shadow-plane of the ambience for signs of power at work. He felt nothing, but he was not sure what his range was now. Common sense suggested that he move to a safe distance before using any large-scale sorcery.

The dinner party obviously had some way to go yet. He could summon the duchess with an occult nudge, but he saw no need to disturb her evening. There was writing paper on the bureau. He scribbled a brief note: "Stole a horse. Back in a few days. Inos sends love. Rap." Aquiala would discover the door unlocked and find the message.

He strode to the door and reached for the handle.

Uncertainty prickled his scalp.

The ambience was extraordinarily quiet. He had not visited Kinvale as a sorcerer since his wedding day, and that was seventeen years ago. He did not know how much of Pandemia he could read from here, but surely as far as Shaldokan, which was a good-size city and must contain a few geniuses or adepts, if not a mage or two, or even a sorcerer. They might all be abed, of course.

Or not.

Feeling absurdly self-conscious, as if he were breaking the work rules of some arcane sorcerers' guild, he took up the key that lay on the bookshelf and unlocked the door like a mundane. Then he hurried along the corridor to the servants' staircase. Farsight told him where the inhabitants of the house were—being almost undetectable, farsight was safe to use. He had to hide in an alcove while an elderly cook dragged her aching feet up to bed. He masked himself briefly with an inattention spell as he passed the door of the butler's pantry. When he reached the stables, he used a jab of sorcery to open a locked door.

He required more power to soothe the horses' alarm, but still not much. He enjoyed the feel of their jumpy, inquisitive, juvenile minds, their simple worries and conceits. It was just like old times. He had missed his rapport with horses more than almost anything. He selected a young chestnut gelding that had more spirit than most of the others, and he decided to use bit and bridle, to avoid drawing attention to himself when he arrived at Hub. Horse and rider crossed the yard and out through the gate in misty silence, then broke into a canter.

Long ago, Rap had stolen horses in Krasnegar and set off with Andor on an adventure that had taken them to the ends of the world. He hoped that this little jaunt would be a great deal briefer than that one. He wished he could foresee his return.

The night was dark, so he needed to keep using power on his mount, persuading it that it could see where it was going. He muffled its hooves when he passed by houses. Those sorceries would be more detectable than his farsight, but still minor. Yet he must be conspicuous in this strangely still ambience.

Where was everybody?

Once upon a time, he had driven a carriage from Hub to Kinvale in a few hours. It was a matter of manipulating the ambience, simple enough for a sorcerer to understand, but impossible to describe to a mundane. He might not achieve quite that travel time now, but on horseback he could surely be at the capital within a day or so.

An hour or so away from Kinvale, he could have used sorcery without attracting attention to the magic portal. But he didn't. He had still not picked up one flicker of any other power at work. Until he did, he was not going to swim against the tide.

He reined the gelding back and prepared for a long night's ride.

Every city within reach of the sea had walls around it, although jotnar probably found them more of a compliment than an impediment. An hour after sunrise, Rap's mount trotted through the gates of Shaldokan.

He chose the best-looking livery stable and arranged for his horse to be returned to Kinvale. He wrote a discreet note to Aquiala, asking her to notify his family that he might not be home for Winterfest.

He had still not detected any power at work—none at all. Something was seriously awry with the occult in this corner of the Impire. Unless he was willing to run afoul of whatever was responsible, he would have to stay mundane himself.

By the time he had eaten a hearty breakfast at the inn next door, the markets were open. He outfitted himself in the current style of gentlemen's sportswear and strolled down to the ferry.

On the far side of the river, a milestone outside the posting inn told him he was 693 leagues from Hub.

Fortunately it was a nice day. He hoped the weather would hold up for the next month, but at this time of year that was not exactly probable.

2

THREE WEEKS BEFORE WINTERFEST, AN UNPRECEDENTED snowstorm descended on Hub, ignoring loud complaints from the inhabitants. Snow in even minor quantities was rare in the capital and unheard of so early in the winter.

As Ylo handed her up into the carriage, Eshiala lifted the hem of her cloak with care. It was a full-length miracle of ermine, destined to show every speck of dirt. It already glistened with tiny snowflakes, although she had walked only a few paces down the steps. She settled herself on the scarlet cushions and tucked her hands in her muff so Ylo would not notice their tremor. They trembled almost all the time now.

Ylo sank gracefully onto the seat opposite as the door was closed. He was in uniform, wolfskin cape and shiny breastplate, dazzlingly handsome as ever.

A whip cracked, harness jingled, and the coach lurched forward. She tried to peer out the window so she need not meet his grin, but the flying snow obscured everything.

"The weather should not be so cold so early," she remarked in what she hoped was a steady voice. Her heart raced, and there was a horrible tightness in her throat. She had no idea where she was being taken, or what was going to be demanded of her. Shandie had said to be ready after lunch, that was all.

"Nor you!"

"Nor I what? What does that smart remark mean?" she snapped. He was throwing her off balance already.

"How do you know it's smart if you don't know what it means? I meant that you are too young to be so cold all the time. Ah! I see I have brought some color to your cheeks."

"You are very impertinent," she muttered, knowing that scolding him was useless.

"I can be much worse. Give me one small smile and I'll stop."

She tried to mock him with a simper. It suddenly became a real smile. She found Ylo's cheerful cheekiness very hard to resist, when everyone else was always so formal with her, even . . . Never mind that line of thought! There was no denying that she enjoyed his company now, outrageous though he was. This was their fourth private conversation in two months, and she was ashamed to realize that she was looking forward to it. Ylo always seemed to care what she was thinking. No one else . . . Never mind that, either!

"You have the fairest smile in the Impire, Eshiala." He sighed. "But your gaggle of goslings seemed unusually morose today, I thought. None of them even pinched me."

"They are annoyed that they can't come and don't know where I'm going."

"Good. Give them something to think about." He crossed his arms, grinning again.

It was very hard to ignore that debonair smirk. How wonderful it must be not to feel worried all the time! How wonderful to sleep without nightmares.

"You're not going to have the pleasure of my company for very long this time," he said thoughtfully. "Let's get out the *thali* tiles quickly, and I'll win the crown jewels off you."

"So—where are we going?" she asked.

"You don't know?" He looked startled, and that must

certainly be the first time she had ever managed to startle Ylo.

She shook her head. "I should have asked, I suppose."

"Great Gods! Doesn't he tell you anything at all?"

"Not much," she admitted, feeling disloyal.

"We're going to a rehearsal, that's all." Ylo scowled into silence.

She relaxed slightly. "Rehearsal for what?"

"One of two things. You do know that the imperor's still in a coma?"

She nodded. She also knew that she was not pregnant as she had hoped a month or two ago. State funeral, coronation, all the rest of the horrors—they could not be long delayed now. The terrible prospect hung over her like a headsman's ax, day and night. Shandie seemed almost as worried as she did, although likely for other reasons.

Ylo said, "The Impire can't function without a head. Even Shandie admits that. He's going to wait two more days at the most. Then he'll apply for a regency."

She felt her nerves all tighten up together like a string bag, with her heart inside it. She avoided his gaze, sure he would have noticed.

"On the other hand," he said, "the old man may die first. In that case, Shandie is proclaimed imperor and we have the funeral."

She nodded, wiping the window with her fingers and pretending to look out. They were still within the palace grounds. "And coronation."

"No. The coronation comes after the official mourning, perhaps as long as a year. Coronations take planning, and no one can remember the last one. But there will be the enthronement." He frowned again. "The funeral won't be so bad. You'll be veiled."

"I expect so."

"Masses of black crepe! I'll stand in for you, if you want. No one will notice!"

She tried to look shocked at such macabre humor, but the

absurd idea was reassuring, and a smile escaped before she could stop it.

"The enthronement will be held on the day after the funeral," Ylo said. "In the Rotunda, of course. If Shandie becomes regent, then there's a briefer ceremony, but much the same sort of thing. That's what we're rehearsing. In either case, the wardens must confirm his authority in the Rotunda."

She closed her eyes to mutter a silent prayer. Gawking courtiers were bad enough, but sorcerers . . . !

Ylo sighed. "You honestly have nothing to fear, Eshiala! You always look regal and gorgeous, whatever you may be feeling. Listen, I want to make a suggestion. Do you know Countess Eigaze?"

"I don't think so."

"You probably haven't met her yet. Her husband's been recalled. He's going to be a consul. Ionfeu's a pompous old stick, but trustworthy. One of Shandie's men. His wife is a very pleasant lady."

Were there such women in Hub?

"She was a friend of my mother's," Ylo continued. "She's a friend of almost everyone! You'll have two maids of honor at the ceremonies, of course. I assume your sister will be one?"

"I suppose so." Shandie had not mentioned this.

"Then choose Eigaze as the other. You'll like her. She twitters and she's starting to look her age, I'm afraid, but she's a lot sharper than she pretends."

"And trustworthy?"

He nodded solemnly. "Pour your heart out to her if you want. She doesn't gossip!"

"I don't believe it!"

"Well, of course, you don't tell her about us, but—"

"Don't even joke about it!" she shouted, and at once clapped a hand over her mouth, aghast. *God of Madness!*

She had startled Ylo again, she thought. "You mean you want it to be serious?" he asked quickly, but his easy smirk was a cover for something much deeper. Probably satisfaction.

She stuffed her hands in her muff again to hide their trembling. "That sort of rumor can start very easily!"

"Yes," he said, looking glum. "We don't want rumors, do we?"

"Ylo!" she said. "I do enjoy your company, I admit. I don't have many friends and you cheer me up. But please stop making jokes about . . . about anything more than that!"

He stared at her so intensely that she felt color pour into her face again and had to look away. "I am happy to be your friend for now, Princess," he said softly. "But you are irresistibly beautiful. Come daffodil time, I will be your lover, I swear it."

"You are very unkind!" she muttered.

"I shall be very kind and very gentle."

"If I tell my husband of this—"

"I will not hit the ground this side of the Mosweeps! But I have told you many times what I intend. Why have you not complained to him before now?"

She bit her lip and did not answer.

The carriage was bouncing to a halt. Ylo said, "Emine's Rotunda, your Highness."

3

EMINE'S ROTUNDA WAS THE HEART OF IMPIRE, THE CENTER of the palace, of Hub, of the world. It was so ancient that its exact age was uncertain, but the flagstones in the corridors were hollowed into gutters by the uncountable feet that had walked them in three millennia.

Eshiala had visited the Rotunda once before, when Shandie had taken her on a sightseeing tour of the palace. Then it had been deserted, a huge echoing emptiness. Now there were scores of people bustling around, some standing in groups, others hurrying to and fro, and yet their presence only made the vast place seem even larger. They were as insignificant as ants, the murmurs of voices lost in a frozen timelessness.

Overhead, the high fretted dome wore a dark cap of fresh snow. Around the sides, the glass still admitted light, but it was the gloomy gray light of a winter afternoon, diffuse and sunless, and even those panes had snow heaped on their sills.

Ylo brought her in by the north entrance. Emerging from the entry tunnel behind the White Throne on its one-step dais, they had to walk around that to gain a complete view of the great arena. They stopped to stare around, looking for Shandie.

There was no one at all near the Opal Throne in the center. From the base of its steps the points of the four-colored Imperial star ran out in the mosaic of the floor to the four thrones of the wardens. Outside those, in turn, the bowl of seats rose almost to the base of the dome. They were empty at the moment, but the sight of them reminded her how many eyes would be watching her performance. She shivered, pulling her white cloak tighter.

"No, no, no!" an angry herald proclaimed, striding by with an entourage of harassed-looking footmen. "The temporary seating will come out farther than that." He and his complaints seemed to fade away quickly, as if the fogs of history had swallowed them already. A troop of Praetorians marched in, heading for the center, rapidly becoming trivial also.

Most of the inhabitants were Praetorians, standing in to represent senators, ministers, and many others. The Rotunda was bitterly cold. She thought the air inside was colder than the air outside. The guardsmen had bare arms and legs.

"Aren't you cold?" she asked Ylo.

He glanced down at her without seeming to move his head, amusement gleaming under dark lashes. "I'm not allowed to be cold! The Imperial Army never lets climate interfere with discipline. I wore the same outfit in Zark and was cooked. I expect I would have to wear it in a winter campaign against goblins and lose all sorts of things to frostbite."

"That's not very sensible, is it?"

"An army isn't a very sensible organization. Its purpose is to fight wars, and wars are a form of madness to start with."

"Does Shandie agree with that?"

"I don't know. I'm only his signifer."

The jibe was cruel, but perhaps not undeserved. She took a moment to let the pain subside, then said, "I don't think he's here."

"Will somebody please tell me where the buglers are supposed to stand?" an angry male voice behind her demanded. She heard the slap of many military sandals going past, but she did not look around.

"The last time I was here," she said, "the Opal Throne was facing east."

"They give it a quarter turn every day, so as not to play favorites. Today is a north day. Tomorrow will be east again."

The Opal Throne was a very ugly thing, a massive stone chair of indeterminate color, but mostly green. She remembered it as being more blue. She was in no doubt that it must weigh tons.

"Good exercise for somebody."

"I wonder if they use trolls?" Ylo mused. "Or would that be sacrilege, do you suppose?"

"Or sorcery? They must use sorcery to clean the windows, anyway."

"Trained bats."

She was making idle chatter to keep up her spirits. Ylo was playing along to humor her. Ashia would tell her outright to pull herself together and look happy. Shandie . . . Shandie would not notice.

"There he is," Ylo said. "In the group by the Red Throne."

She saw him then. She should have remembered that he'd gone off in doublet and hose that morning, not uniform. Swathed in a gray cloak and a floppy plumed hat, he was being remarkably anonymous amidst a dozen or so soldiers and civilians. They seemed to be consulting a chart, and there was a heated discussion in progress—as much as anything could be heated in this ice house, she thought.

She was about to walk, when Ylo's hand touched her arm. "He'll send for you if he needs you."

"He may not know I'm here."

"Don't be absurd. You light up the place."

She looked at him for a moment, then said sadly, "Thank you, Ylo."

"Any man knows that a woman needs regular compliments."

"Not any man."

"Most, then. Come, here's someone you must meet. I told you about them, remember?"

He led her over to an elderly couple standing by themselves. The man was tall, but so stooped that he seemed to be permanently half into or out of a bow. He had feathery white eyebrows, and his wrinkled face wore a wry, gentle smile. His companion was short but extensive in other dimensions, wrapped in a voluminous sable coat about the same shape as the sacks of beans that sat on the floor in grocers' stores, but considerably larger, with her smiling plump face centered on the top of it. A diminutive matching sable cap perched improbably on her curly white hair.

Of course these would be Proconsul Ionfeu and his wife. Eshiala braced herself to play her usual fraudulent royal role. As princess, she must lead the conversation—she had been given lessons in how to put people at ease, select suitable topics, make sure nobody got left out . . . and so on. She hated the whole hypocritical procedure. And in this case, something went wrong very quickly.

Ylo had said that Lady Eigaze twittered, and so she did. She also chattered, babbled, and prattled nonstop, but none of her talk held the acid spite so familiar around the court. She decried the unseasonable weather, she made naughty little jokes about the gooseflesh on the Praetorians and the noise their armor made when they shivered. She conjured up improbable images by suggesting that they ought to be allowed to wear long woolly underwear on such a day. She pointed out that she and Eshiala were almost the only women in the whole place, asserting that if there were more of them around, they would certainly speed up the proceedings and let everyone go home. And then she suggested that Shandie ought to make everyone run around the Rotunda three times to warm up.

By that time, Eshiala was laughing. It was she who had been put at ease. She was enjoying herself, a stunningly unfamiliar experience. Had she not been given those lessons, she would never have recognized the skill involved. The consul-elect listened to his wife's performance with a smile of amused resignation.

Eigaze revolved her bulk to face Ylo, smiling tolerantly in the background. Apparently he was an old friend, because she demanded imperiously that he lend the princess his wolfskin. Ylo shot Eshiala a glance full of risqué overtones and offered to exchange garments with her.

"I do so want to meet your daughter!" Eigaze continued. "I adore toddlers! Oh, may I come around one afternoon and be presented to the next princess imperial? All my grandchildren are taller than me now, but I still have a while to wait for the next generation, thank the Gods. Do have a chocolate, my dear."

She offered a large box of expensive candies, although where it had come from was a complete mystery to Eshiala. She accepted, feeling rather bewildered and almost believing that Lady Eigaze was sincere in her desire to meet Maya.

"The only *good* thing about all this nonsense," Eigaze remarked between chocolates, "is that it is keeping me from an *excessively* dull tea party. I know I should have been given fifteen seconds to describe our experiences in Pithmot and then everyone else would have taken an hour apiece to tell me everything that has happened in Hub for the last two years, which I know already. What would you have been doing? Do have another chocolate.''

"I should have been sitting for my portrait," Eshiala admitted.

"How awful! Dressed up in leagues of hot robes and smothered in tons of jewels? Rigid like a statue?''

"Exactly.''

"Dreadful! Who is the artist? Try a round one, they're ginger.''

"About twenty artists. They complain about the light all the time.''

"Elves!" Eigaze commiserated. "Charming people, but they can be tiresome at times. Was there a jotunn there?''

"Jotunn? A jotunn artist?''

"Yes, dear. He's the best of them all. A very short jotunn—I think he must have elvish blood in him. What is his name, Ion?''

"Jalon," her husband said.

"That's right, Jalon! We had him paint all our children when they were small and all our grandchildren, too.''

Jalon? Why did that name seem familiar? "He must be quite elderly, then?" Eshiala said.

"He doesn't look it. That's another reason to suspect he's part elf, I suppose.''

"Beg pardon, ma'am," Ylo said sharply. "Is he by any chance the artist who painted that seascape in the Throne Room?''

Eigaze blinked and popped two more chocolates in her mouth, probably to give herself a moment to think. She eyed him appraisingly. "I haven't been in the Throne Room since we returned, and they change the pictures all the time. But I don't see why not. There couldn't be two artists with jotunnish names, could there?''

Ylo was looking excited. "No, I suppose not. Was he one of the group, Highness?''

"I did not notice any jotnar," Eshiala said. "But I am supposed to keep smiling at a very ugly marble urn, so I can't be sure."

"Something special about this man?" Ionfeu inquired softly.

Ylo nodded. "I need to speak with him."

"Do you recall where he lives, dear?" the old man asked.

Eigaze frowned. "I could look it up. Acacia Street, I think. Number seven, or nine? That's down around the Temple of Prosperity, as I recall." Obviously Eigaze's well-rounded exterior concealed sharp wits.

"Thank you very much!" Ylo beamed at Eshiala as if she ought to understand his obvious excitement.

"Oh, bother!" Eigaze complained. "We've finished the chocolates! Dear, do you suppose we could send someone out to the coach . . . Mmm . . . The prince!" she added hastily. The empty box vanished behind her back and she curtseyed with her mouth full.

Shandie looked harassed. He acknowledged the other's salutations, gave Eshiala a fleeting smile of greeting, then addressed Ylo. "Can you see Sir Acopulo anywhere?"

"Yes, sir."

"Fetch him, will you? Proconsul, Countess . . . I'm sorry this is taking so long."

"We shall be running out of light soon, sir . . ."

Eshiala watched Ylo striding off across the great hall. Now she remembered the significance of the artist Jalon—the picture in the Throne Room was the one that showed Shandie's vision in the preflecting pool. She would much rather have that whole macabre incident forgotten. Especially the daffodils.

Now the rehearsal was about to get underway at last and all her terror of pomp and ceremony came flooding back. An uncomfortable-looking chair had appeared on the dais beside the Opal Throne. That was her place. The banked seats around the Rotunda seemed to fill up with ghostly faces, and imaginary sorcerers occupied the vacant thrones, all staring disdainfully at the grocer's daughter.

An elderly herald came shuffling up to join the group, looking crushed by the weight of his ornate costume. Ylo returned with little Acopulo beside him, beaming his benevolent, retired-priest smile at everyone. Eshiala distrusted him, although she was not sure why. He ignored her most of the time, and when he did speak, it was usually to preach.

"We are ready, your Highness," the herald wheezed painfully.

"One last thing," Shandie said sharply. "Unless the weather improves dramatically, I shall stipulate contemporary court dress."

The old man flinched as if he had heard an obscenity.

"Well?" Shandie demanded. Eshiala had never seen him look fierce before. His eyes blazed. This was Shandie at work, ruling.

"But . . . But formal court dress, your Highness . . . It's traditional!" The herald seemed ready to weep.

Shandie showed his teeth. "I detest it!" he snapped. He spun around to Acopulo. "What do you say? Togas are not too unreasonable, I suppose, however ludicrous they look, but I don't want my wife freezing to death in one of those stupid chitons!"

Eshiala gaped at him and everyone else was looking equally surprised, although perhaps for slightly different reasons.

Acopulo coughed politely. "I agree that the customary garments are impractical for winter, sir, but tradition has its values."

"Such as?"

The little man assumed an expression of weary tolerance. "Such as ostentation. The ceremony will become a Winterfest ball, with everyone outdoing everyone else in sumptuosity. The ladies, bless them, will be much more interested in one another's costumes than in the solemnity of the occasion. Formal court dress keeps everyone more or less equal. It reminds us that we are all equal before the Gods."

Shandie scowled darkly.

"And the current styles!" Acopulo added, undeterred. "No disrespect, sir, but every lady of quality will require three times as much room to sit down. Space is already inadequate."

"I detest togas!"

"Then why not wear your uniform as Commander in Chief, sir? I'm sure the College of Heralds can have no objection to that."

"The College can . . ." Shandie pouted, then shrugged. "Very well. Uniform would be quite appropriate, I suppose. Carry on then, my Lord Herald."

Eshiala wondered what had happened to her death-by-freezing in a chiton. Shandie had apparently forgotten that part of the problem quite quickly.

Ironically, the dress style was the least of her worries. A chiton was a simple thing, not unlike her customary wear. She would be much less discomfited by formal court dress than any other woman in the Rotunda.

4

YLO HAD BEEN GROWING VERY BORED WITH A WASTED AFternoon. He was consoling himself by noting that the rehearsal could last no more than another hour at the most; after that the Rotunda would be completely dark.

The next item on the program involved moving everybody out into the south corridor to Line Up for the Procession. The south corridor was nearly as black as a cellar already, which was no help to the flustered heralds trying to organize things, all of whom seemed to be either experienced and senile or too young and ignorant to be trusted

by the others. As most of the notables who would partici-
pate in the ceremony were being represented at the rehearsal
by Praetorian guardsmen, he was strongly reminded of his
long-ago life in the Praetorian barracks. In any army
Pandemia had ever known, Lesson One had always been
Waiting in Line.

Lesson Two was Advanced Waiting in Line.

Heralds appeared and disappeared in the gloom, struggling to read their lists. They moved Ylo to and fro several
times. Then the babble of confusion crept farther back along
the corridor, and he decided that he was probably in his
correct place.

"May I inquire to whom I have the honor of addressing
the question of whom I have the honor of addressing?" he
asked the two large guardsmen ahead of him.

The larger regarded him with disapproval. "If you were
a man of better character, who attended temple as regularly
as he should, you would have instantly recognized the
saintly demeanor of the Archbishop of Ambel."

"Your Holiness, I am mortified with consternation. Actually, I had always believed that your Holiness was a
woman."

"He is," the other said. "And the same goes for the Sanc-
tified Abbess of the Sisterhood of Purity, namely me, and
what are you doing tonight, Good-Lookin'?"

Tribune Uthursho was out of town again. His wife had
the most incredible breasts. Tonight Ylo was going to renew
their acquaintance.

"I plan to spend the night in worship," he explained
regretfully. "Perhaps some other time, your Profligacy—
preferably not quite so long after you shave your legs."

"Ah! I knew I'd forgotten something this morning."

"I believe we met in some unpleasant surroundings once,
Signifer," the archbishop said.

"Very good for our souls, I expect," Ylo agreed. He had
done time in the brig as a green recruit, which was presumably what the other was referring to. Now that he was a

celebrity, anyone who had known him before was anxious to demonstrate the fact.

"Tell me—" The guardsman lowered his voice. "I understand that Centurion Hithi has returned to normal duties."

"That's correct," Ylo said happily.

"There's an extraordinary rumor going around," the abbess said in even lower tones.

"What rumor is that, your Virginity?"

"It is said—and I stress that I am merely repeating hearsay and put absolutely no credence in such fables—it is said that in order to win his release from temporary assignment to the Bureau of Correspondence, the centurion had to kneel down and lick someone's sandal."

"Not a word of truth in it!" Ylo said. "Flagrant falsehood. You did say *one* sandal?"

"I may be mistaken on the number. Two sandals may have been mentioned. One left foot, one right foot. Would you believe such a story?"

Ylo sighed regretfully. "I am afraid I am most solemnly sworn not to comment on the matter, ladies."

The guardsmen exchanged glances, pursing lips in silent whistles.

Ylo had spread the story widely beforehand, so it really didn't matter whether Hithi had actually groveled to win his release or whether he hadn't. Everyone was going to assume that he had. Hithi hadn't seen that until it was too late.

How sweet it had been!

Shouting up front suggested that the procession would soon begin to move. Ylo turned around and introduced himself to the two men behind him, who were civilians, and apparently exalted members of the aristocracy with the hereditary right to carry Emine's sword and buckler whenever they were brought out for public display, as now.

"You mean those are the real things?" Ylo exclaimed, looking in disgust at the battered bronze relics the noble lords were holding.

The sword bearer bristled and explained how his honor would be sullied were he required to carry a mere replica. That might make sense to some people—elves, perhaps—but it didn't to Ylo.

Then the shouting became louder and the procession straggled into motion. The Rotunda was very dim now. He wondered if a truly heavy snowfall could blanket the dome windows completely. In that case the hall would be unusable, for it was far too large to illuminate artificially. At the entrance the line divided. He was directed to the right. Soon progress stopped while the leaders were led to their stations, and thereafter the columns moved erratically.

He gazed approvingly at Princess Eshiala, leading the far line in her ermine cloak, looking exactly like the Ice Impress of her nickname. She was an incredibly gorgeous girl, still barely twenty years old. He knew how nervous she must be, but he doubted that few others did. If only she realized how well she deceived everyone! Her qualms did not show.

She was far too good for Shandie, who had no inklings about women. If he had any subtlety at all, his wife would not be responding so well to Ylo's blandishments. She was coming along very nicely and he had every confidence that she would be his for the taking, come daffodil time. His flesh quivered with anticipation. He often wondered whether he would have made the effort had the preflecting pool not promised her to him. Probably not—far too dangerous and far too much work. He had never spent so much time on one woman before. By the Gods, though, she was going to be worth it!

Had it not been for the prophecy, he would be duke of Rivermead by now, reveling on his estates—hunting, partying, and wenching to his heart's content. He had postponed that satisfaction, but Eshiala would make it all up to him.

Eventually he found himself at the head of the line, and the heralds went into conference. Apparently Shandie's decision to wear uniform required an amendment to the program. A consensus emerged—his signifer would have to stand by the throne. Ylo wondered what a Commander in Chief's standard looked like. It might be too Evilishly heavy to lift.

He was placed in position like a sapling transplant beside the central dais. Above him, Shandie slouched on the Opal Throne. At his side, in a chair on the upper step, sat Eshiala. She glanced down at Ylo, so he winked. She frowned coldly and looked away.

Lady Eigaze stood behind the throne, being two maids of honor. All this standing must be hard on her feet, Ylo thought. Aunt Eigaze, he had called her when he was a child. Fortunately for her, though, she had been an honorary aunt, not a true relation, or she might have perished in the massacre of the Yllipo Conspiracy.

Gradually the rest of the two processions advanced. Dignitaries or their understudies were directed to their places. The huge space was becoming populated.

The hereditary bearers deposited Emine's sword and shield on a table near the dais, then withdrew. The Rotunda was almost dark.

"My Lord Herald!" Shandie bellowed angrily. "We shall have to adjourn this meeting very shortly!"

The chief herald whimpered and all his underlings began to fluster around like mosquitoes.

Ylo stiffened. Someone was standing beside the White Throne and waving to attract his attention, or possibly Shandie's. He thought it might be Hardgraa. Now what?

Ylo glanced up, and Shandie had not noticed. He was actually chatting to his wife!

The newcomer abandoned his attempt to be noticed and strode forward, straight-arming a herald out of the way. Yes, it was Hardgraa. He must have brought a message. Messages were Ylo's responsibility. Leaving his place, he headed to meet the centurion, ignoring bleats of complaint from the officials. He could think of only one message important enough for this.

They met halfway. Hardgraa's face was rigid.

"It's happened."

The world rocked. "When?"

"About twenty minutes ago."

"I'll tell him." Ylo turned and headed back to the center. The dome had fallen so silent that he could hear the centurion marching away behind him.

Ylo stopped at the foot of the two steps and looked up at Shandie, who was visibly pale, even in the gloom. Eshiala had both hands to her lips.

Softly—"Sire . . . Your grandfather has passed away."

Shandie nodded. He turned and reached out to his wife. Ylo felt an illogical twinge of annoyance.

Eshiala rose from her chair and stepped to her husband's side. Even in that near darkness, Ylo could see the wonder in her face. She bent and kissed the new imperor, who reached up to put an arm around her.

Now what? Ylo turned again and located the chief herald; and beckoned him over impatiently.

Shandie said quietly, "The imperor is dead. My Lord, I fear we must adjourn this."

The old man had been growing more and more incoherent even before this sudden change. Now he just stuttered. "Highness . . . Sire? . . ."

"You will be needed," Shandie said hoarsely, "for the proclamation."

They had all been expecting it for months, but now it had happened their minds could not take it in. Emshandar had ruled the world for fifty-one years. His departure left a hole in all their lives. Hardly anyone could remember the Impire without Emshandar IV. Ylo was picturing the iron-bound chest he called Battle Plan and wondering if there was anything he had forgotten to include. Everything anyone had been able to think of was in there waiting to be dated and sealed—announcements to all proconsuls and praetors and legates, Ionfeu's nomination to the Senate, a million others. There was sure to be something missing, of course.

And all over the hall, everyone else must have guessed the news and be struggling to adjust. From now on the name *Emshandar* would not mean a wily old relic spinning webs but a dynamic young man with fresh ideas and new advisors—a young man who ironically had succeeded while actually sitting on the throne. If he lived to the same age as his grandfather had, he would reign for over sixty years.

Then a sudden light blazed in the Rotunda.

5

THE WHITE THRONE GLOWED WITHIN A NIMBUS OF WHITE fire that made its ivory carvings seem to writhe. A man stood before it, on the low dais. He was very short, grayhaired, and grotesquely thick. He wore shabby workers' garments and heavy boots, and he glowed also.

He bowed.

Shandie was on his feet in an instant, returning the bow. The Rotunda buzzed like a beehive.

"Do it now, Imperor!" the newcomer roared in a voice like grinding millstones. The deep tones reverberated from the dome above. "Hurry! There is not a moment to waste!"

Ylo's scalp prickled—the warlock of the north . . . Rasp-nex.

"Do what?" Shandie mumbled, caught off guard.

"Proclamation and enthronement! Hurry!" The occult light seemed to brighten and take on an urgent reddish tinge.

Ylo looked at the chief herald, who was standing with his toothless mouth open and an expression of complete idiocy on his ancient features.

No soldier he!

Ylo sprang past him and up the two steps to Shandie's

side. Hastily recalling the words on a hundred parchments he had approved, he swung around to face the warlock and the assembled crowd.

"By the Grace of the Gods!" he yelled at the top of his voice, hearing the echoes roll. "Emshandar the Fifth, Rightful Imperor of Pandemia, Lord of the Four Oceans, Fount of Justice, Enhancer of the Good! *Gods Save the Imperor!*" He had omitted about a dozen other titles, but they were unimportant rigmarole.

He leaped to the floor in a single bound, even as the congregation roared in reflexive echo, *"Gods Save the Imperor!"* He grabbed the shield and buckler from the table and raced back up the steps.

Shandie took them, pushed past Eshiala, and turned to face the east. He slammed the ancient sword against the shield. *Clank!* Nothing happened.

Ylo stepped back down to the floor, wondering what he had just written in the history books.

Shandie waited perhaps three heartbeats, then he was around to the back of the throne, facing south.

Clank! went the sword and buckler.

Again nothing.

West . . .

Shandie struck the shield a third time.

Just for an instant, a rosy glow suffused the Red Throne. A dark shape stood before it—huge and hulking, white-haired and pale-skinned. An ancient female troll, she bowed to Shandie.

And was gone into darkness.

Two of the wardens had acknowledged him as imperor. It was enough. The ceremony had been lightning-fast, but legally Shandie had succeeded.

He dropped the sword with a clatter to put an arm around Eshiala. His other arm raised the shield, as if to cover them both. All eyes swung around to the north again, to the dwarf.

"Take your wife and your child and begone, for the city is no longer safe for you." Sepulchral echoes rolled and he boomed even louder, to drown them. *"The Protocol is overthrown and Chaos rules the world!"*

With an ear-splitting crack, the four thrones of the wardens exploded. Colored fire blazed momentarily on the four platforms, brightening the hall, reflecting from the glass and snow of the dome. Men cried out as they were struck by flying fragments, while a rubble of gold and stone and ivory rattled and bounced across the floor. The dwarf had vanished and the Rotunda was pitched into darkness and terror.

Unhallowed ground:
> *Like strangers' voices here they sound,*
> *In lands where not a memory strays,*
> *Nor landmark breathes of other days,*
> *But all is new unhallow'd ground.*
> —TENNYSON, *IN MEMORIAM*, CIV

CHAPTER TEN

WILD BELLS

1

FOR FORTY DAYS THE KING OF KRASNEGAR HAD BEEN RIDING with the west wind at his back. Horse after horse he had ridden to exhaustion, triple-posting, sometimes four-posting, thundering along the great highway, bound for Hub, and yet the foul weather had delayed him. He was thirty-five years old and had lost the uncaring endurance of youth. Numb in his soul and sick to death of riding, of bedbugs and bad food, of rain and cold, he had not dared tarry. Winter fields and gloomy cities rolled past unending. Post followed post. Once in a long while a royal courier would overtake him, but no one else did.

He dreamed of humble, sleepy Krasnegar, of warm firesides, of Inos and his children. He reminded himself sternly that he was doing all this for them also.

Never in his life had he felt a greater urgency, yet he did not know what he feared. Night and day the dark premonition in the east overhung his thoughts, a constant invitation to despair. As he moved over the continent, the source gradually shifted toward the north, confirming that it was rooted in Dwanish, but he still did not understand that evil foreboding.

Stranger even than that, though, was the eerie stillness in the ambience. In his youthful experience as sorcerer and demigod, he had seen that alternative plane of existence alive with flames and flickers of sorcery—or heard it sing, rumble, and moan with sorcery, for the observer could choose his metaphor as he pleased. Now it was dark and silent.

Very rarely he picked up a tremor, usually brief. Only twice had he been close enough to risk a glance of farsight to identify the source. The first had been an elderly rake propositioning a young man in a saloon and the second a portly chef seasoning a sauce. Mere geniuses, both of them, with power so weak that they might well be unaware that their talents had an occult element to them.

Where had everybody gone?

Was he the only sorcerer left in the world? Or were all the others hiding, as he was hiding?

Sorcerers he could understand. Sorcerers and some mages could sense the ambience as he could. Like him, they would have noticed the quietness and sensed the evil portents, and held back their own powers to listen. But the two-word adepts and the one-word geniuses—they could not have felt the danger, so they could not have taken cover of their own volition. They had been silenced. Who could have done such a thing, and for what reason?

The shieldings remained, for the Impire had been home to sorcery as long as anyone could imagine, and occult shields took centuries to decay. They showed up easily to farsight. Some of them had outlasted the buildings they had covered and now guarded only a copse or a vegetable patch. Twice he had taken refuge within such an invisible haven to use power: healing his weariness, mending his clothes, replenishing his purse. He could still make gold—in small amounts—but it took all the effort he could summon. That meant he must rattle the ambience savagely as he did it. It wasn't very good gold, either.

Sleazy inns, spavined horses, sun and rain and wind and cold . . . winter was no time to journey posthaste across Pandemia. On a chilly morning three weeks before Winterfest, Rap rode into the outskirts of the capital's sprawling suburbs as snow began to fall from a morbid sky.

Shivering, he turned in his post horse and purchased an elderly gray mare at the livery stable. She had a forgiving disposition and a comfortable seat and her wind seemed sound. He named her Auntie, patting her neck apologetically when he had tightened the girths.

"I know it is no day to be traveling, old girl," he said, wishing he dared use a little mastery to encourage her.

Auntie flicked her ears resignedly.

Where to? Soon he must decide between three possible destinations, although all of them were many hours' ride away yet, for this was no meager city. He swung shakily up into the saddle.

Once Hub had been a hotbed of sorcery, a constant rumble in the ambience. Now it, too, was silent; or almost so. He knew that there were many occult contrivances in the city—magic doors, phantom watchdogs, bottomless wine bottles, and other such gimcrackery, cobbled together by sorcerers over the years as gifts for their friends, most like. He could still sense many of those gadgets clicking away in the background, but deliberate use of power seemed to have ended even here.

As Auntie trotted out of the yard, he heard a bell tolling in the distance. A few minutes later another joined in. He knew then that there was no use going to the palace today. The palace had never been a promising option anyway.

Waves of sound flowed out from the center until the whole capital reverberated with grief. One by one the other temples entered the sonorous chorus, a measured, mournful clamor that rapidly became a torment. The City of the Gods, the imps called Hub, meaning the City of Temples. Soon it was a madhouse of dolorous metallic clanging on all sides. Dogs howled crazily at the carillon and the very stones seemed to shake.

Rap thought of those ripples spreading across the frozen countryside, from hamlet to hamlet and town to town, outrunning the couriers until they lapped the waters of three oceans. The Impire was paying tribute to Emshandar.

He was surprised at the intensity of the sorrow. As a sorcerer, he could smell grief in the air as clearly as he could see the whirling snow. Imps had a mystical loyalty to their imperor, like bees to a queen. They would mourn any imperor, no matter how brief or unpleasant his reign, and tonight they knew an age was passing. Even the imps of Krasnegar would mourn when the news arrived there, in the summer.

Gradually the streets cleared. Wagons and carriages seemed to disappear first, pedestrians became scarce and then rare. Soon the snow was falling almost undisturbed. Auntie's hooves thumped a muffled note on the deepening blanket, barely detectable through the endless tolling of the bells.

As dusk fell, windows darkened. Obviously the mourning city was going to show no lights, not even the door lamps that the wealthy maintained as a public service to brighten the streets. Rap wondered how footpads and cutthroats viewed their civic duty on such occasions.

His choice was clear now. Sagorn must wait—if he and his gang were even in town. Rap headed for the center, the abodes of the rich and the aristocracy, where the Epoxague mansion was.

2

TAKE YOUR WIFE AND YOUR CHILD AND BEGONE, FOR THE city is no longer safe ... To Eshiala, the words seemed to echo and echo, round and around the dome. Maya was in danger!

Momentarily blinded by the explosions and the sudden darkness after, she groped wildly for the side of the Opal Throne to steady herself. She opened her mouth to speak to Shandie, but Shandie was already barking commands to others.

Maya in danger? The thought was crippling. She was only a baby; her second birthday was just past; but she was a royal baby, second in line to ... *No!* Minutes ago her father had become imperor, making Maya heiress presumptive, the princess imperial, *first* in line.

And she herself was the impress. Gods preserve me!

"Come, my dear!" Shandie swung his cloak up to cover her, also, in a useless gesture. He hugged one arm around her tightly, urging her down the steps to the floor. Then he rushed her toward the door.

"What did ... Who was ..." She struggled to collect her thoughts, for she had so many questions that she did not know what to ask first. The floor was littered with gravel and rubble and she still could barely see. Being entangled in Shandie's cloak and tight embrace didn't help. "What did that dwarf mean about ..." She stumbled.

"Careful, my love!" Shandie said. "Here, I'll carry you ..."

She started to say that if he would stop wrestling her around and perhaps just hold her hand, things would be a lot easier, but he tried to lift her just as he himself stumbled on a pebble, which rolled. He almost fell, pulling her down with him. She broke loose from his grip and now she could see better where they were going, too. She clung to his arm and then they proceeded in a more sensible fashion.

"Why did that dwarf say Maya was in danger?"

"I don't know. Gods, look at that!" On the platform where the Red Throne had stood until two minutes ago, now only a few fragments of rock remained. The rest had been blasted to gravel and spread over the Rotunda. The base itself was cracked. "Can you imagine how old that thing was?"

Did he really think she would care, when Maya was in danger?

They hastened around the remains, plunging into the gloomy tunnel beyond, almost running. She was glad she was wearing sensible shoes, or he really would have to carry her.

"That was the warlock?" she demanded.

"Yes, that was the . . . Well, I suppose it was! Nobody else would dare, would they? Ah! Legate!"

"Sire!" A large man in glittering armor fell into step on Shandie's other side, and all three rushed along together.

Shandie began rattling orders again. "Her Majesty and I are going to the personal quarters. Send a contingent to Oak House—"

"No!" Eshiala shouted. "We are going to Oak House. Or I am at least!"

"Beloved—"

"I want my baby!"

"Oh, very well!" Shandie said, sounding surprised by this sudden rebellion. "We'll go around by Oak House and pick up the child ourselves. My signifer has orders, but he'll need your assistance . . . and of course I want to see you as soon as you have organized this madhouse . . ."

They burst out into daylight and falling snow. Armored men were everywhere, with a coach waiting. Shandie handed her up ahead of him, which was a breach of protocol she supposed, but a welcome gesture. He leaped in himself and the horses were moving even before the door closed.

He settled beside her and peered, as if looking for damage. "Are you all right, my dear?"

"Of course I'm all right! Except that I want my baby and I want to know what the danger is!"

She had never spoken to him like that before.

"You are very brave!" he said.

Brave? Whatever the danger, the two of them were running away—that required no courage. She did not feel brave. She felt worried about Maya and . . . and very relieved that the awful ceremony was over. She was no longer on display. The time for bravery had passed, as far as she was concerned, but she could never expect Shandie to understand that.

Wheels and hooves made strangely muffled sounds in the snow. Even the jingle of harness seemed hushed and the splendid hussars themselves rode without sound.

"I want to know what the danger is!" she said again.

"So do I." Shandie's expression was grim as winter, but it was directed at the front of the carriage, not at her.

"The wardens . . . Why only two?"

He shook his head impatiently, as if he wanted peace to think. "I don't know! They wrangle among themselves all the time, but . . ."

"But?"

"But they would never wreck the Rotunda like that over any normal squabble." He fell silent. She studied him with growing annoyance. Why would he never share his thoughts with her? Why must he shut her out of state business and treat her like a porcelain doll? True, she had no real interest in politics, but a husband and wife must have something in common, apart from the bare-legs-in-the-bed thing. She would gladly listen, if he would only speak!

The carriage pitched and rocked as it rushed down the hill from the Rotunda, through palace grounds already deserted.

Emshandar V, Imperor of Pandemia. Impress Eshiala!

Suddenly he looked around at her, his dark eyes intent. "Oh, my love! I promised you wealth and power and adoration . . . and now I seem to have brought you exile and danger."

If he only knew how little appeal wealth and power and

adoration had for her! Like a brainstorm came realization—
whatever danger the warden had foretold, it meant the
end of public pomp, at least for a while. No state funeral,
coronation, enthronement ceremonies, gala balls . . . A secret, quiet life in hiding? That was a stunningly wonderful
idea!

And perhaps just the three of them? Was it even possible
that the Gods might grant her a space of humble, private
existence with only her husband and child, in some peaceful
corner somewhere? Man and wife together—no affairs of
state to distract him, no court ceremonial to terrify her?
Might she even learn to love this man as a wife should?

"You are smiling!" he said wonderingly.

"Am I? I am sorry!"

"Don't be sorry . . . but why smile?"

"I don't mind losing the wealth and power and whatever
else it was you said. Not if Maya is safe . . . and you are
with me." Not far from the truth—closer to it than usual,
anyway.

"You are wonderful!" he said.

Guilt! Shame! What sort of useless wife was she, to rejoice
that her husband might lose his throne? She felt remorse at
her relief. The Gods had granted prayers she had not dared
speak, and yet she still could not be happy.

Shandie was scowling. "I must not flee the court myself!
I should not be imperor for long if I did that . . . not without
more reason than a dwarf's ravings. You and Maya, yes.
We shall spirit you off to some safe place. Which of your
ladies will you take?"

She turned away. Ladies? She wanted none of them, but
she knew enough of Shandie's thinking—court thinking—
to know that she would never be allowed to travel without
other women in attendance. Ashia, perhaps? Ashia would
not welcome a flight into exile, having achieved semiroyal
status as a duchess.

And there would be males sent along as guards, of course.
Shandie himself would choose those.

She wondered if one of them would be Signifer Ylo. Her heart inexplicably jumped into her throat.

3

EVEN BEFORE THE RACKET OF FALLING DEBRIS HAD STOPPED echoing through the Rotunda, the new imperor was snapping orders: "Ylo, get the group together in the Abnila Chamber and I'll join you there. Tribune, we'll go by the west door. Herald, see that the proclamation is made in proper form. Take this, Ylo." He almost threw Emine's ancient buckler at his signifer, then he was off down the steps with his arm around Eshiala. They disappeared into the gloom and the dust with guards closing in around them.

Which was all very well for him to say, Ylo thought, but how much authority did a mere signifer have in this sort of chaos? The hall was almost dark. He saw everything overlain by a green afterimage of the Red Throne exploding, as he had happened to be watching that one. His ears were still ringing from the blast and something had struck him on the side of the neck hard enough to daze him, although he did not seem to be bleeding. Heralds and civilians—perhaps even a few Praetorians also—were running in circles, tripping over rubble, and having hysterics.

And who exactly did Shandie mean by "the group"?

Ylo stepped up beside the Opal Throne and retrieved Emine's sword from where Shandie had dropped it. So now he held the two most sacred relics of the Impire, and yet they might be totally worthless if the warlock had spoken the truth.

Things could be worse. Shandie's celebrated ability to outrun the lightning had probably carried him and his wife clean out of the Rotunda before anyone else had even started to move. Hardgraa would certainly have had a carriage waiting there.

The racket was fading as if someone had demanded silence at any cost and the Praetorians were establishing it by force. The casualties could not be too numerous, or there would be more screaming.

Afterimages faded. Ylo made out the stooped form of Proconsul Ionfeu, still standing behind the throne. He had an arm around Eigaze. Ionfeu was almost certainly "group" now.

Ylo stepped down to join them. "Aunt, are you all right?"

"A little surprised, Ylo," she said breathlessly. "I had expected more formality."

Ionfeu chuckled. "She needs a cup of hot tea, is all. I presume we may now go home?"

"I think he wants to see you, sir. I was asked to call a meeting in . . . the Throne Room as soon as possible." Ylo was not about to leave a direct trail to Shandie's whereabouts at a time like this—not after the dwarf's warnings. For all he knew, Shandie was already fleeing the city and the Abnila Chamber rendezvous was itself a red herring. "The only problem . . . Ah!"

Light dawned as a torchlight procession came marching in from the east door. The damage was revealed then, and it was shocking. No longer were the entrances concealed behind the thrones. Four shattered platforms lay like islands in a litter of rocks and rubble. Ylo noted sparkling reflections on the floor as the torches went by and he wondered how much of the real stuff the Gold Throne had contained. All the thrones had been encrusted with jewels, too. Someone should worry about that very soon.

The torchbearers divided, a few remaining by the tunnel, others heading for the other exits. One group came straight to Ylo. He registered uneasily that it was led by Legate Ugoatho of the Praetorian Guard.

As a trusted confidant of the imperor, Ylo feared almost no man in the world now, but Ugoatho was a necessary exception. Throughout history, the Praetorian legates had been wild cards in Imperial politics, for they controlled the palace. Several had deposed imperors, and a couple had founded dynasties of their own. When an imperor died, his successor normally confirmed the support of the Praetorian legate even before he spoke to the Senate, or the marshal of the armies, or the wardens.

Ugoatho was a nephew of Marshal Ithy and almost certainly loyal—or rather, Ylo thought, he had been almost certainly loyal before Warlock Raspnex scrambled the board, tore up the Protocol, and predicted revolution. Now anything was possible.

Flanked by guardsmen holding torches, the legate halted and saluted, his face less expressive than an earth berm. Having his hands full, Ylo responded with the imperial regalia. If Ugoatho noticed the humor in that, he concealed his amusement admirably.

"Signifer! His Majesty said you might need assistance."

Holy Balance! Command of the Praetorian Guard? What next?

"Just to collect some persons and transport them to the Throne Room for a council, Legate. Proconsul Ionfeu, here. Sir Acopulo, Lord Umpily . . . Centurion Hardgraa. Marshal Ithy—"

"He is indisposed," his nephew said flatly.

That was not surprising—the old man had been in poor health for months.

"I think yourself, also, Legate. That should do."

"You have forgotten someone, Ylo," said a firm but feminine voice.

Startled, Ylo turned and said, "Who?"

"Me." Lady Eigaze smiled her plump, motherly smile at him. "And I need to talk with you on the way there."

He had never heard Eigaze express any interest in politics before. He could not imagine her snooping out of mere nosiness—that would be completely out of character—but he knew her of old, and the ring of steel in her bell-like tones.

"And Lady Eigaze, of course," he added. "One other thing, sir. Some of the gravel lying around here is pricey stuff. Will you do something to discourage souvenir hunting?"

He was being recklessly presumptuous. Ugoatho gave him a stare that would have blistered paint, then said, "I'll see what we can arrange, Signifer."

Surprisingly, dismal daylight still lingered outside the Rotunda. Feathery snowflakes continued to fall, and the ground was ankle deep in slush. Ylo shivered as it soaked through his sandals.

Embedded in guardsmen, he waited with Ionfeu and Eigaze while their carriage was summoned. Bells were tolling everywhere to proclaim Emshandar's death, but the warlock's dramatic proclamation was being treated as a state secret for now. Ugoatho had sealed off the Rotunda, letting no one out. Among those being held prisoner were the two hereditary bearers of the regalia, one of whom had tried to wrestle Emine's sword away from Ylo. He had been removed by two bullock-size Praetorians.

"What was it you wished to discuss, my Lady?" Ylo asked cautiously.

There was a darkening bruise on Eigaze's cheek. Her plump face was paler than usual. She glanced warily at her husband and he frowned a warning—there were listeners all around. Ylo wondered if the man's permanent stoop was an effect of age, or if he had developed it from hovering over his wife all the time; it put their heads on the same level.

"You expressed interest in a certain painting, Ylo."

"Yes, Aunt."

"A seascape? Ion reminded me of a picture by that particular artist I saw in the Orchid Hall many years ago. It may be the same one."

"You know the place?" Ylo demanded excitedly.

"If it is the one I am thinking of, yes I do. It was pointed out to me by a relative of mine."

"Reliable identification?"

"Yes."

Ylo nodded, satisfied. Somehow that inexplicable vision in the preflecting pool seemed very important now.

Eshiala was impress—or was she? If the Protocol had failed, then the Impire itself was as fragile now as a robin's egg. Shandie had acted as if he took the warlock's warning very seriously indeed. No one had more experience of warlocks' advice than he.

Then the carriage arrived, spraying slush. While the proconsul and his wife were climbing aboard, Ylo's arm was gripped by a shaky hand. He turned to face the rotund form of Lord Umpily, looking terrified.

"Signifer!" he bleated. "What is happening? These guardsmen—" Apparently he thought he was under arrest.

"The imperor wants you to attend a strategy meeting, my Lord."

The chief of protocol relaxed with a loud gasp of relief, but he was obviously badly rattled. "That's good! Very good. Ylo, I have something I must tell him as soon as possible! Very important!"

"Then you'll have the chance as soon—"

"The pool, remember? I lied when—"

"You can tell him yourself, my—"

The fat man failed to sense the warning. He raised his voice over the tolling of the bells. "I saw a dwarf! Not the warlock, another one, but a dwarf—"

"My lord—"

"He was sitting on the Opal Throne!" Umpily wailed.

4

THE DRIVE WAS BRIEF. IN A FEW MINUTES YLO AND UMPILY walked together into a palace eerily hushed and deserted. The darkening corridors bore only a fraction of their normal profusion of candles and lanterns. Already the paintings and statues were draped with black crepe. The Throne Room was almost empty, and dark. Footmen clad in deep mourning had begun lighting candelabra.

Ylo found himself whispering, almost trying to tiptoe. He noticed little Sir Acopulo standing close to the massive form of Centurion Hardgraa and had a brief whimsical image of a bird nesting in a tree. Proconsul Ionfeu and Lady Eigaze were working their way around the room, peering under the crepe hangings to look at the paintings.

They headed for Ylo when he strode over to the east wall. He found the one he wanted at the second try.

"Yes, that's it," Eigaze said. She shot Ylo a worried look. "What is your interest in that place?"

"I am not at liberty to say, ma'am. Will you tell me where it is?"

She bit her plump lip and then shook her head. "I had rather not say. If Sh—If his Majesty needs to know, I will tell him, of course."

Curious! Why should she be concerned with that strange little town and castle?

The imperor might be waiting upstairs, in the imperial bedchamber, or he might be leagues away, fleeing from the city as the warlock had suggested.

Ylo was still carrying Emine's shield and buckler, which were a perfect excuse. "I shall put these back where they belong," he announced, heading for the private stair that led up to the imperor's quarters.

Palace servants in mourning dress lined the corridor, many weeping, all waiting to pay their last respects. The public lying-in-state would start tomorrow. The muffled sobbing and constant clanging of bells grated on Ylo's nerves. He strode to the head of the line, to find the doors closed and guarded.

The officer in charge was Centurion Hithi. He paled and showed his teeth when he saw Ylo. Very likely Hithi's seconds would be calling on Ylo in the near future, although the challenge would have to wait now until the court came out of mourning. Ylo had not decided what to do about that if it happened. Have the man transferred to Pondague or Guwush, probably.

"Their Majesties are in there," Hithi growled.

"Good. I need to see them," Ylo responded blandly.

The centurion gritted his teeth, staring at the regalia. Then he stepped back to let Ylo open the door himself.

He had seen the Abnila Chamber only once, about five months ago, when he had supervised the setting up of tables and desks to make an office. Emshandar had not been present at the time. The room was larger than he remembered, about the size of a twenty-man dormitory in a legionary barracks. It was dim, lit only by tall candelabra at the corners of the great bed, but the opulence of the fittings showed even in the uncertain light. The tables and office clutter had gone. The corpse lay as if asleep, skeletal face shrunken and parchment-tinted. Emshandar was beyond the reach of mortal revenge.

Eshiala sat in a chair by the fireplace with her daughter on her knee. The child looked grumpy and red-eyed. Her mother stared at Ylo without expression, tense with strain. She was wearing a black gown, and black furs lay on another chair beside her.

There was no sign of Shandie.

Ylo saluted the impress stolidly. He inspected the room again. He knew the sword and buckler were kept in here somewhere. Then he saw a doorway that had not been there before, an unframed rectangular opening in the wall. He walked over to it.

The secret room beyond was large and dark, its walls hidden behind shelves and shelves of great books. Shandie was inspecting their spines by the light of a candle. As always when wearing civilian garb, he seemed totally nondescript.

Seeing Ylo, he turned away from his task and came out. As he emerged, the opening disappeared. He showed his teeth in a humorless smile.

"The private Imperial Archives." He pointed with a scroll of vellum he had brought from the room. "Put those down over there. Did you get everybody?"

"They're waiting in the Throne Room, Sire—Proconsul Ionfeu and his wife, Lord Umpily, Sir Acopulo, and Centurion Hardgraa. Marshal Ithy is sick. Legate Ugoatho is on his way."

"Excellent! Why Lady Eigaze?"

"She can identify the town in that painting, Sire, but she wants to tell you personally."

Shandie raised his eyebrows. "Incredible! Yes, that may be very important now. I don't know what I'd do without you, Ylo. Come, then. My dear?" He headed for Eshiala.

She rose with Maya in her arms. When Shandie tried to take the girl, she turned away and clung to her mother. He scowled, then went over to the bed. He studied the corpse for a moment and said quietly, "Thank you, Grandfather."

Ylo thought, *May the Evil have his soul! All of it!*

He hurried to open the door for the impress. He was fairly sure that little Maya would allow her friend Ylo to carry her, but it would not be very tactful at the moment to offer.

The Throne Room seemed eerily empty and haunted, a great darkness with a few puddles of light under the candelabra. The servants had gone. Five men and a woman were waiting by the cryptic Jalon painting, the only one not draped in crepe. As the newcomers approached, the men bowed to the new imperor. Lady Eigaze curtseyed.

Shandie eyed them solemnly.

"You all heard what Warlock Raspnex said?"

"I was told, Sire," Ugoatho rumbled as all the others nodded.

"Then you know that he predicted disorder and trouble. We have no time for formalities. I ask each of you now to accept me as your imperor. I ask you all if you acknowledge me as if you had sworn the customary oath of loyalty. Anyone who has reservations may leave."

The burning black gaze moved slowly around the group. Again the men bowed or saluted and Lady Eigaze curtseyed. No one spoke.

"Thank you," Shandie said. "Thank you all. Now we must decide whether we should take Raspnex's advice. My wife and child, obviously, must be moved to safety. I don't think that is an option for myself at the moment, so soon after my accession. I am disinclined to run from an unknown danger, anyway."

"Highn . . . Your Majesty?" Umpily was looking more upset than anyone. At Shandie's inquiring glance he blurted out what he had told Ylo earlier: "I did see a vision in the pool, Sire! I saw a dwarf sitting on the . . . on your throne! Not the warlock. A man I have never met, but certainly a dwarf."

Fury flickered in Shandie's eyes, but his voice came out very low. "Why didn't you say so sooner?"

"I didn't believe my eyes. Or the pool. I thought it must be malfunctioning!"

"You're a fool!"

Umpily cringed and hung his head.

"The pool is beginning to seem very critical," Shandie said. "I wish I could test its reliability. Ylo, you were shown a beautiful woman. Does she exist? Have you met her yet?"

"I have seen her, Sire. She exists." Ylo met the imperial stare without flinching. He did not look at anyone else—especially not at Umpily, or . . . or the impress. *Gods!*

"That is encouraging," the imperor said stonily. "Acopulo, you saw an image of the celebrated Doctor Sagorn."

The little man frowned like a benevolent priest trying to cope with a dire sin. "I did make some inquiries, Sire, and apparently the sage is still alive, incredible though that seems. I was even told his address, but when I went calling I was refused admission or information."

"When was that?" Shandie barked.

Acopulo flinched. "A week or so after our return to Hub."

"And you have not tried again?"

"No, Sire. Pressure of business put it out of my mind."

"I seem to be surrounded by professional cretins! Who did you speak to?"

"An enormous jotunn, Sire, of forbidding aspect. Surly . . . and very intimidating."

"I can be more intimidating! Lady Eigaze, you know what we are discussing?"

The countess was attempting to make friends with Maya, who was clinging tightly to her mother, burying her face in the black gown and not responding.

Eigaze turned at once to the imperor. "I have no idea, your Majesty, but young . . . your signifer mentioned that you were interested in the town shown in this painting."

"I am. Several of us visited a magic pool and were granted visions. Mine was of that place. *Where is it?*"

"Krasnegar, Sire. A remote little—"

Shandie rarely gestured at all, but now he slapped his forehead with the palm of his hand like a third-rate actor demonstrating inspiration. "*Krasnegar!* Of course! Why didn't I think of that!"

He thumped his thigh with his fist. "Idiot!" he muttered. "I apologize for calling you gentlemen names. I have been moronically stupid myself. And of course you are related to Queen Inos, ma'am?"

"Distantly, Sire, but yes. She saw this painting when she was here and pointed it out to me. Jalon apparently knows the place. He must have put it in this picture for artistic effect. I can't believe the ship had ever been near there."

Shandie shook his head, as if still unable to believe his own stupidity. "I saw a youngster, a jotunn boy. I even thought he reminded me of someone—and of course it was Rap himself! It must be his son, I should think. A jotunn son of a faun? Well, it could be. He's half jotunn himself— I remember him telling me that."

"They do have a fair-haired son, Sire, Gathmor. He must be . . . fourteen, I should think, or thereabouts."

"I would have guessed older," Shandie said, "but jotnar are big, of course."

The men were exchanging uneasy, angry glances, all except Ionfeu, who was frowning darkly.

"May I inquire?" Acopulo asked.

"Rap the sorcerer!" Shandie snapped. "The *faun* sorcerer! You remember . . . twenty years ago? The one who killed Warlock Zinixo and cured my grandfather?"

Ah! Heads nodded in understanding. Ylo had been about four years old at the time, but he had heard the stories often enough.

Countess Eigaze was much too much a lady ever to break into a conversation by coughing. She did so by some sort of social sorcery, perhaps a special way of blinking. Suddenly everyone was looking at her. "Begging your pardon, Sire, but his Majesty did not actually kill the warlock."

"He didn't?"

Her chins wobbled as she shook her head. "The imperor . . . Inos told me that your grandfather had told her that Master . . . er, King . . . Rap had told him that he did not kill the dwarf. But he didn't say what he had done with him. Or to him." Flushing, she fell silent as her audience worked their way through the syntax.

Then everyone looked at Umpily, who had seen a dwarf sitting on the Opal Throne.

"I never met . . . saw . . . Warlock Zinixo," he mumbled. "So I don't know."

"Well!" Shandie said, as if things were becoming a great deal clearer. "Now we know what the pool was trying to tell us, don't we?"

Acopulo scowled as he always did when he could not see an answer. "We do?"

Shandie smiled thinly. "The sorcerer . . . He married Inos, so he is a king now. King Rap was very kind to me. I was only ten or so, and I remember thinking that he was the most

wonderful man I had ever met. I shall always be grateful to
him, for that was the worst time of my life. And he is without
doubt the most powerful sorcerer in the world. Grandsire
told me once that all four wardens together would not dare
a contest with the faun." He laughed aloud. "I suppose I
would have thought of this eventually? Idiot I am! Obviously
the preflecting pool was telling me to seek out his aid again!
Whatever Warlock Raspnex was jabbering about tonight, the
answer is to call on Master . . . King Rap. That does sound
foolish doesn't it—*King* Rap? But Rap's a wonderful man, a
kind and honest one. He will help, I'm sure!"

Legate Ugoatho cleared his throat. "Where is this place?
In Sysanasso?"

"Er, no," Shandie said vaguely. "In the far north, I believe."

"Krasnegar's somewhere up in goblin country," Acopulo
muttered. "Seems to me that Doctor Sagorn once mentioned
having visited it. One of the very few places where imps
live outside the Impire. And jotnar, also?"

"Very far north," Eigaze agreed. "The land road goes
through Pondague, goblin country. It can be reached by sea,
though."

The Praetorian frowned. "With respect, Sire—you are not
considering traveling there yourself?"

"I may have to!" Shandie was still holding the scroll of
vellum. He tapped his other palm with it thoughtfully. "That
may be the preflecting pool's message. Acopulo, I think you
should make another effort to locate your old master. He
may have valuable advice to offer. Where does he live?"

"In Hub, Sire. In the southern districts. At least that was
the address I was given. Near the Temple of Prosperity."

Ylo and Eigaze stared at each other in astonishment, but
it was the Impress Eshiala who said, "Not seven, or nine,
Acacia Street by any chance?"

5

DARK HAD LONG FALLEN WHEN RAP RODE THROUGH THE GATES of the Epoxague estate. Inos still exchanged letters with Eigaze—umpteenth cousins too far removed, they called each other. Eigaze was elderly now, but still hale. Even if she was absent at the moment, there would be a dozen other relatives to choose from. Imps were fanatical about family ties.

Not a light showed, but a sorcerer's farsight could not be deceived by closed drapes. Moreover, a single set of hoofprints in the snow on the driveway implied that someone had come home within the last hour or so.

Rap did not bother to hitch his mount, for poor Auntie was as weary as he was. He left her standing while he plodded up the marble steps.

The tolling bells were a constant torment, like toothache. No wonder the Hubbans were all crazy, if they had to put up with that cacophony very often. One temple was unpleasantly close and its overpowering *Bong!* rolled over all the background noise with an inevitable monotony. He found himself counting seconds, waiting for it.

The ubiquitous magical devices continued to crackle quietly in the ambience, and now an occasional flicker of active sorcery had joined them, as if the imperor's death had released some curse or other. There was still far less occult activity in the capital than normal, but Rap was relieved to detect any at all. At least some of the sorcerers had taken cover; they had not all been killed or abducted.

He risked a glance at his premonition—and slammed down his defenses again instantly. It was closer, much closer, in both time and space. Now Hub itself was infected by that inexplicable, looming evil. He shuddered with a panicky sense of urgency, inner voices urging him to flee.

Down in the servants' quarters, heads had turned as the doorbell jangled among the dozens of bells set high on the kitchen wall. A footman rose resignedly from his dinner and straightened his coat. Rap tugged the rope again angrily, but that foolishness merely made the man slow down, rather than speed up. He strolled leisurely to the stairs, having no idea how near he was to having his powdered wig burst into flames.

Holding a lantern high, he peered out disapprovingly at the bedraggled, unescorted visitor. By that time Rap had established that Eigaze was not home. Ignoring the multitude of servants, he had counted only three people in the whole great mansion, which seemed very strange so close to Winterfest. The residents were all male. The invalid in the bed must be the ancient senator himself, and he was either asleep or unconscious. Last summer Eigaze's letter had reported that he was in his dotage and bedridden, but apparently he still clung to life. A very large man was slouched in an armchair in a library, drinking steadily. A younger man lolled in a bathtub upstairs. Rap recognized neither of them.

"The countess is not at home," the footman reported.

"Then tell whoever's in charge that the king of Krasnegar is here!"

The door closed with a thud.

The temple bell went *Bong!* loudly.

Fortunately a quick stab of mastery was not a very conspicuous use of sorcery—as a general rule, people could be manipulated much more easily than objects.

The footman hauled open the door and bowed low. "If your Majesty would graciously care to enter, I shall inform his Honor immediately!"

Better! A little obsequiousness was just what Rap needed after so long on the road. He stepped inside, pulling off his cloak in a shower of snow. "See that my horse is attended to at once. Who is his Honor, by the way?"

"Lictor Etiphani, Sire!" The footman's face did not reveal his disapproval, but it was obvious to a sorcerer.

Great Gods! Rap watched in disgust as the flunky hurried off to report to the obese lush in the library. Eighteen years ago, Tiffy had been a glamorous, willowy hussar with a notable lack of chin. Now he had a plurality of chins. He peered up blankly at the news of the visitor. Several seconds passed before understanding came and his rubicund face suddenly paled. He had only just struggled out of his chair when Rap was ushered in to drip on the expensive rugs.

"Your Majesty!" The gross man attempted to bow and staggered instead. He was very tall for an imp—taller even than Rap—and he had inherited his mother's tendency to stoutness, or absorbed it from bottles, mayhap. "Yes, by the Gods, it is you, isn't it?"

Rap had not expected to be recognized, as he had been invisible during most of his stay in Hub, but of course Tiffy must have seen him at the imperor's ball, the fateful faun sorcerer who had danced with Queen Inosolan all through one magical night. How very long ago that seemed!

"It is indeed an honor to meet your, er, Honor," Rap said wearily, extending a royal hand to shake. "And of course I extend my condolences on your sad loss today."

Lictor Etiphani was clearly not at his best—sorcerers were rare and unwelcome guests. "Um? Losh? Oh, yes, Emshandar. Evilish pity, of course. Er, do sit down, er, Sire."

"Actually, I really need a hot bath and a change of clothes, Tiffy. Excuse the informality, but Inos always calls you that when she speaks of you."

Tiffy's face seemed to swell and become even redder than before. He cleared his throat several times. *Bong!* went the temple bell, audible even in here. "She still speaks of me?"

"Sometimes."

"Oh! And how is Inosh?"

"She's very well. Home with the children, of course."

"Beautiful woman, er?"

"Just as gorgeous as ever. And your dear mother?"

"Mother?" Tiffy glanced longingly at the near-empty decanter beside his chair. "Can't I at least offer you, er, a drink? Saying farewell to Emshandar, you know, Shire."

"After that bath you promised me," Rap said firmly, "and

please call me Rap." He would be charitable and assume that the drinking had been provoked by the imperor's death. Not being an imp, he couldn't appreciate the scale of the bereavement. "Your mother?"

"Oh, Momshie's fine. Went to the palace for some sort of ritual, you know. Hours ago. Can't think what's keeping her. Terrible business, er, what?"

The looming premonition at the back of Rap's mind seemed to twitch closer.

"What business?"

"Well . . . Actually it's a big secret, you know. Not supposed to . . ." Tiffy hiccuped. "Wouldn't know about it at all, except for Ephie. Praetorian Guard. He wash in the Rotunda when it happened."

Ephie must be the spotty youth in the bathtub upstairs and also the hoofprints on the driveway, a cousin, perhaps, or a nephew.

"Sworn to secrecy, you know," the lictor added. "Warlocks?"

Sodden clothes and all, Rap sank down in an expensive chintz-covered armchair, which tried to engulf him like a soft bog. He risked another jab of power.

Tiffy began talking faster than he had ever spoken in his life. "They were rehearsing the enthronement when the news came of the imperor's death and of course that meant that Shandie I mean Prince Emshandar was imperor right away . . ." He rattled on furiously about Warlock Raspnex and Witch Grunth and exploding thrones, then collapsed back in his chair like a falling tree. He bounced once and stared in bewilderment at his visitor.

Bong!

Rap wiped water from his face while the awful story sank in.

God of Murder!

What in the name of Evil was Raspnex doing? Even with Grunth to help him, he should not be able to overcome

Lith'rian and Olybino. Why had the other two warlocks not intervened? How many dwarves did it take to overthrow the Protocol?

Who was on what side?

And why confirm Shandie as imperor anyway?

Rap could think of no force capable of subverting the occult order of the world, except perhaps the army of votaries Bright Water had assembled during her centuries of rule. They should have been released from enslavement when she died. That was what normally happened. Had she somehow passed on her great array of power to Raspnex? Why on earth would she?

Even that theory seemed farfetched, for Olybino and Lith'rian must wield fair-size factions of their own.

Was Raspnex fronting for his nephew, Zinixo?

Why, by the Powers, had Rap not come to Hub months ago, when he first heard of the dragon attack in Qoble? *God of Fools!*

"Thatsh why you're here, isn't it?" Tiffy muttered. "Shorcerer. More trouble, so you've come back. Should have realized."

"Yes, in a way," Rap agreed sadly. Where was that amiable young man who had wooed Inos so devotedly? Dead, or just lost somewhere inside the blubbery mass in that chair?

"You going to shave Sandie, like you saved his grandshire?" Tiffy asked hopefully.

"Save him from what?" Rap smiled a sorcerer's sinister smile, and that ended the questioning. He wouldn't admit to this buttertub that he did not know who was threatening, or why, or even what. Nor that he was only a shadow of the sorcerer he had once been. Regretfully he said farewell to that vision of hot bathwater and dry clothes. "But I must talk it over with your parents."

"Told you, Momsiesh not here!"

"Her coach is just turning into the driveway. I assume that's your father with her?"

An expression of nausea spread over Tiffy's flabby face. He was not happy in the presence of sorcery.

Bong!

Rap watched with farsight as the count and his wife climbed the steps and were admitted. He saw the footman tell of the visitor, saw the exchange of startled glances. Despite her bulk, Eigaze was capable of a fair turn of speed. With her cloak unfastened but not yet discarded, she raced along the hallway, her husband in pursuit.

She burst into the library. "Rap!"

Rap was on his feet by then. "Lady Eigaze!" He braced himself as she rushed at him and clasped him in a bearhug as if they were old friends. She bussed his cheek. They had never spoken before, but he was family, Inos' husband, and to an imp that was sufficient.

Then she peered up at him, anxiety burning on her motherly, globular face. "A business visit, of course! How is Inos?"

"Fine when I left. And the children. Yes, a business visit. And I fear I have come too late."

Then he had to be introduced to the count, who was also a proconsul now, of course. He was a quiet-spoken, wry-smiling man, with a bad stoop.

Formalities attended to, Eigaze took charge. "Why, you're soaked!" Her eyes took in the decanter and her son's unfocused condition. She bristled. "Tiffy, you idiot, didn't you even have the common courtesy to—"

"I just got here, ma'am," Rap said hurriedly. "Tiffy was telling me about the events in the Rotunda. You were present, I assume?"

"It was ghastly! How did . . . Oh, Ephie, of course! Then you know about Warlock Raspnex and what he told Shandie?"

"I believe so."

She shook her head, dewlaps wobbling. "Well, it's wonderful that you're here. Shandie . . . I must stop calling him that! The imperor had pretty well decided to go to Krasnegar, but now you've come, so he needn't, and that's just wonderful!"

Bong!

An avalanche of weariness crashed over Rap. He flopped back into his chair, staring up at Eigaze, aghast. He thought how astonishingly like old Aunt Kade she was.

"Shandie is going to Krasnegar?"

Eigaze glanced at her husband, then back at Rap. "He expects you to help him, as you did once before."

Rap shook his head. Of course they would all assume that he was a paramount sorcerer still—and he wasn't! Far from it! *God of Horrors!*

"There was a prophecy," Ionfeu said quietly. He had produced another decanter from somewhere and was filling a crystal goblet. "Some months ago his Majesty was guided to a preflecting pool. It showed him a vision he couldn't identify, but now we know that it was Krasnegar."

"Who was in that vision?" Rap shouted.

"A boy, he said. A young jotunn. We think—"

"Gath!"

Eigaze nodded, concern scrolling lines in her face. "We assumed it was Gath. He has jotunn coloring, doesn't he?"

"He is only a child!" Rap said. "He is not a sorcerer! What use can Gath be to Shandie? What possible help?"

Eigaze shook her head, distressed. Her husband handed Rap the goblet.

He took a long draft and then started to cough. It ran through him like molten iron. "He is . . . only . . . only a child!"

But he would not remain a child for long. The War of the Five Warlocks had lasted for thirty years. Rap looked around despairingly. Tiffy was slumped in his chair, too inebriated to follow the conversation. Ionfeu was pouring another glass of the potent liquor, Eigaze rubbing her plump hands in turmoil, with her unfastened cloak hanging loose about her.

Not Gath!

"I will not give up my son!" Rap shouted. *Bong!*

"But . . ." Eigaze seemed to make an effort. She straightened her thick shoulders. "You must talk to his Majesty, er, your Majesty!"

"Yes, I must. Can you take me to him?" Rap fought down his bone-breaking weariness. Shandie had been imperor only a few hours. He would be frantically busy tonight.

She nodded, chins flapping. "I only came home to collect some clothes and things. The warlock said that he—Shandie—must leave the city. He said Hub is not safe. What did he mean, do you know?"

"I have no idea."

"Oh!" She looked to her husband for guidance. He shrugged and offered her the goblet, but she shook her head. "What his Majesty seems to be planning is that the impress and their daughter will go into hiding. He—Shandie—will stay here and fight whatever is threatening. Unless he goes to Krasnegar . . ."

"He can't fight sorcery," Rap said. "If the Protocol has failed, then he is no longer immune to sorcery. In fact, he will be the most likely target."

"The imperor?"

"Of course. A sorcerer who controls the imperor will run the world. The imperor's immunity was the very heart of the Protocol."

Husband and wife exchanged glances of dismay. The bent old proconsul moved to his wife's side and put an arm around her. "I think you must advise him, your Majesty. He will listen to you, I am sure."

Rap nodded. "Can you get me to him?" he asked again.

"Oh, he is not in the palace," Eigaze said. "I told you—I only came home to pick up some clothes. We are going to go and meet him directly."

"Meet him where?"

"At a private house in the southern part of the city."

Rap's premonition jabbed at him like a bony elbow. "Whose house?"

"Doctor Sagorn's."

Rap nodded soberly. It made sense. It had a ring of inevitability about it.

"You have time for a hot bath and a change of clothes, Sire," Eigaze said firmly. "You'll catch your death of cold! I shall get a bag packed. And we can nibble something in the coach . . . If you'll forgive me for saying so. Oh dear! The family is always accusing me of trying to mother people."

"Mother?" Rap smiled gratefully. "It's been a long journey. I could use some mothering right now, my Lady. Mother me all you want! Then we'll go and talk with Shandie."

But he didn't know what good he could do. He had come too late.

Or else the millennium had arrived a little early.

Bong!

Wild bells:
> *Ring out, wild bells, to the wild sky,*
> *The flying cloud, the frosty light:*
> *The year is dying in the night,*
> *Ring out, wild bells and let him die.*
> —TENNYSON, *IN MEMORIAM*

CHAPTER ELEVEN

STRAIT THE GATE

1

WHEN CENTURION HARDGRAA PLANNED AN EXPEDITION, it was well planned. Eight horsemen cantered up Acacia Street and halted at the steps leading to the Sagorn residence. They had brought a packhorse laden with axes and sledges. Hardgraa would gain entry if he had to cause an earthquake.

As had been arranged, only Ylo accompanied Sir Acopulo up the stair, leaving their escort waiting tactfully in the road. The night was white. Snow swirled along the canyon between continuous high buildings, reducing visibility to a few paces. Temple bells fouled the air with their obscene din. No lights showed. Had he come alone, Ylo would have worried for his safety in this shabby, rundown area, but with an escort comprised of Hardgraa and five cedar-size Praetorian Hussars, he was as safe as he could ever be. The doorbell jangled mournfully somewhere in the bowels of the house. The imperor's political advisor huddled beside him in his snowcapped hat and cape, small and miserable, not speaking.

Ylo shivered. Snow melted around his toes and stuck to his eyelashes, yet he felt buoyed up by a bizarre excitement. The imperor is dead, long live the imperor, the Protocol is overthrown, the world is in chaos, and isn't this all thrilling? He floated, as if he had been drinking steadily for hours, but he was totally sober.

Nobody came.

"Once more!" he said cheerfully, tugging again at the rope. Again the bell tinkled, mocking the distant tolling from the temples. A man could learn to hate bells very quickly.

Chains and bolts clattered. A shaft of light flashed out over the snowy step as the door opened a crack. The slender, pale-faced man who peered out was short for a jotunn, no taller than Ylo himself. His torso was encased in a tattered smock liberally smeared with multicolored paint like exotic bird droppings; an incongruous black skullcap perched on hair of silvery-gold.

Ylo saluted. "Have I the honor of addressing Master Jalon, celebrated artist?"

"Er, yes?"

"We wish to speak with Doctor Sagorn.'

"He is not home." The jotunn was staring at Ylo's wolf-head hood with dreamy wonder.

"That's too bad," Ylo said, preparing to throw his shoulder against the door if it began to close, "because we come on behalf of the imperor. My friends are prepared to search the house."

Sudden alarm sparked the little jotunn's attention, his pale eyes meeting Ylo's for the first time. "You can't do that!" His voice rose to a squeak. "You mustn't!"

"We can. We will."

"But I am very busy! I am composing an ode to the emperor's memory and must not be interrupted."

"You can do whatever you like, as soon as you have brought us to the good doctor."

"But . . . You don't understand!" Jalon wailed. He was quite the least assertive jotunn Ylo had ever met. Most would have broken his jaw by now.

"Be quiet, Signifer!" Acopulo snapped. "Master Jalon, I am an old friend of the doctor's, a former student. It is imperative that I speak with him."

The artist opened the door wider and raised his lantern to shed light on the priestly imp.

"Oh, yes! Of course. I remember you."

"I don't believe we have met."

"Well . . . perhaps not." Jalon sighed. "Do come in, then. I shall inform Doctor Sagorn."

"One of our friends will accompany us," Ylo said, beckoning. Hardgraa came trotting up the steps.

They all moved into the entrance hall. Jalon closed the door, but when he reached for bolts and chains, the centurion held out a thick hand to stop him. "My companions will guard your privacy!"

Jalon curled a lip at him nervously, but did not argue. Bearing the lantern, he led the way through what seemed to be a pantry, up a short and narrow staircase with squeaky treads, emerging in the center of an odd-shaped hallway. The house was a ramshackle collection of alterations and renovations, ad hockery gone wild.

The room to which he took them was spacious, but the ceiling cornice showed that it had been carved out of an even larger chamber. The clammy-cold air stank of dust, the unused hearth was piled high with litter. Two candles stuck in bottles on the table shed a meager light over papers, bottles, and dirty plates. Books and more papers lay scattered around on armchairs and all over the floor. A single window in one corner was covered by shutters festooned with cobwebs, obviously not opened in years. Boards showed through the threadbare rug.

"This is the quietest place in the house," Jalon muttered apologetically. "If you will wait here," he added, "I will tell the doctor."

"I'll come with you!" Hardgraa said.

"No! No! You mustn't!"

"Oh yes I must!"

"Wait!" Acopulo peered curiously at the artist, who was becoming more obviously agitated by the minute. "Explain why you do not wish to be accompanied."

"It . . . he . . . I mean, I shall have to explain carefully. He . . . he is old and rather difficult. Give me a moment and I'm sure I can persuade him." However inexplicable, Jalon's distress seemed genuine enough.

The visitors exchanged puzzled glances, then Acopulo said, "Be quick, then, and we shall wait here."

Clutching the lantern, Jalon vanished out the door in haste.

"You'd think a famous artist and a famous scholar could afford at least some sort of servant," Ylo remarked, inspecting the squalor with disgust. His euphoria was fading rapidly.

"Seeing that little sweetie," Hardgraa said, "I can only assume that this is an all-male household."

Acopulo bristled. "Unfounded slurs reflect upon their perpetrators! If you are implying that Doctor Sagorn would stoop to . . . He's far too old, anyway."

"Easy!" Ylo said. "There's something odd going on here."

"You were never more right in your life!" Hardgraa marched out and his footsteps clattered away down the noisy stair. The sound of bells grew louder as he opened the door and shouted to the men waiting outside.

Acopulo wandered over to the table and took up some of the papers littered there, peering at them under the candles. "He was telling the truth about the poetry, anyway. 'He stood a bastion of right, Bulwark of his children's faith and bearer of his fathers' sword . . .' This is strong stuff!"

"Sentimental claptrap!" said a new voice. "Far too many adjectives."

The jotunn standing in the doorway was full size, towering over his visitors. He was still tying the laces on a musty-looking gown of a style that had been fashionable decades ago, while on his white hair he wore a skullcap identical to the artist's. Candlelight emphasized down the deep lines in his face, but a typically massive jaw and an aquiline nose gave it power and authority. Despite his age, he stood straight and steady and unquestionably furious.

"D-doctor Sagorn!" Acopulo quavered.

"You always were a self-righteous pest, Acopulo. I see you haven't changed."

"And neither have you, have you? Not a day!"

"What are you implying?" Sagorn strode into the room, heading for the table.

"That you are remarkably—astonishingly!—well preserved."

"Clean living and a clear conscience! Age has not improved your manners." The sage ostentatiously gathered up papers as if afraid his guests would pry—which they had, of course.

"And youth has not improved your disposition, Sagorn."

The jotunn glared down at his scrawny visitor, then snatched away the sheets he was holding. "Did you drag your juvenile friend from his masquerade party just so you could come here and trade insults, or do you have a significant purpose?"

Ylo stamped to attention and saluted. "Doctor Sagorn, I am personal signifer to his Imperial Majesty, Emshandar the Fifth, who needs your wise counsel on a matter of vast import to the realm." Butter was usually quicker than boiling oil, but it might not lubricate a man who lived in a garbage tip.

The old sage looked startled for a flicker of time, then curled his long upper lip in a sneer. "Tell him to write me a letter." He scowled at the tatty bundle of paper he had collected and heaved it over the back of an armchair, to fall every which way in a corner.

A board overhead creaked.

Acopulo twitched nervously. "Who is that?"

Sagorn snarled. "Your bronzed beasts are ransacking my house!"

"This problem will not wait for a letter," Ylo said patiently.

The jotunn glared at him. "Pah! I would not go out on a night like this at my age were I summoned by the Four themselves."

"The imperor will be here shortly," Ylo said, "and the Four are not summoning anybody anymore."

The pale-blue jotunn eyes seemed to glitter as Sagorn studied him seriously for the first time. "You have brains, Pretty Boy. All right, you have won my attention." He lowered himself carefully into a chair, clasped his hands, and laid the tips of his two forefingers against his lips. "State the problem concisely."

Acopulo took a step forward to upstage Ylo. "First we need settle the question of sorcery before his Majesty arrives. Explain your uncanny longevity."

Sagorn's snowy eyebrows shot up. "The matter is that grave? Very well. I am not a sorcerer. I was befriended by one some years ago and he bestowed perfect health upon me. That is all. I wear well. Now—what ails the Protocol, that you are concerned about sorcery near his Majesty?"

Before Acopulo could reply, Hardgraa came stamping into the room. Two of the Hussars stood out in the corridor holding lanterns.

"Where is the artist, Jalon?" the centurion demanded.

Sagorn smiled with thin old lips. "This house has several exits, Soldier."

Hardgraa's rough-bark face darkened. He moved forward threateningly. "But there are no marks in the snow outside any of them."

"It also abuts many other residences in the block. If you

start tapping every wall, you will irritate a great many people. I don't suppose that will bother you, of course, but you may draw a crowd, and I assume his Majesty intended to keep this meeting secret."

"I want to know where the artist has gone!"

"You won't find out from me. Now be silent in the presence of your betters. Proceed, Sir Acopulo."

"I am going to tear the filthy warren apart plank by plank!"

Hardgraa should have known better than to antagonize a jotunn. A younger one would have thrown him out the window and gone after him, but Sagorn merely clicked his teeth shut. "Then I refuse to cooperate in any way." His big jaw clenched.

"Take your men, Centurion," Ylo said, "and wait outside."

Hardgraa swelled until it seemed his breastplate must rupture.

"Now!" Ylo said.

He really did not think it would work, but it did. Three pairs of sandals stamped off down the squeaky stair. The front door slammed, hushing the mournful knelling.

Acopulo chuckled and gave Ylo a smile of acknowledgment. He removed some dirty dishes from the second armchair, flicked away crumbs and mouse droppings, and sat down to begin the tale. "When the old imperor died," he began, "the prince was sitting on the Opal Throne . . ."

2

ACOPULO HAD FALLEN SILENT AT LAST, THE PROBLEM stated. Lost in thought, Sagorn bowed his head over clasped hands. Ylo was leaning against the fireplace, quietly mourning the neglected breasts of the wife of Tribune Uthursho. Reaction had set in, and he felt the shivery depression that

came after battles, a sensation that life was short and pointless and far too valuable to waste.

The tolling of bells surged louder, warning that the front
door had opened again. The treads began their mournful
creaking, but this time the feet were more numerous.

"There are spare candles in the scuttle, Signifer," Sagorn
remarked, heaving himself stiffly to his feet.

Hardgraa looked in, then backed out. Shandie entered. He
wore an anonymous civilian cloak and a wide hat, which he
did not remove. It had snowflakes on it. Sagorn bowed.
The imperor stepped forward, offering a handshake, which
he changed awkwardly to allow his fingers to be kissed.

Acopulo awoke to his duties and belatedly presented the
scholar. Then Eshiala came in, carrying the babe who was
now the princess imperial. Behind them loomed the indeterminate shape of Lord Umpily, enormous in snow-
speckled fur. He was short of breath, his face haggard. There
were more introductions.

"Pray be seated, Doctor." Shandie steadied his wife as she
settled into a chair with Maya, who appeared to be asleep.
He took the third chair, leaving everyone else standing. The
candles Ylo had set out made the room brighter already.
Hardgraa closed the door from the outside and squeaked off
downstairs.

"We seek your counsel, Doctor Sagorn." Shandie settled
back wearily and rubbed his eyes. "I shall reward as I can,
but you understand that at present my promises may be of
lesser value than I should wish."

A grotesque parody of a smile twisted the jotunn's craggy
features. "Indeed, Sire. I wish I could prove worthy of your
faith in consulting me, but I confess that I am baffled. If you
insist on a brief response, I must advise your Majesty to run
like a hare."

Shandie's face was shadowed by his hat, but his fists
clenched.

"No offense intended, Sire!" the scholar said hastily. "You
can no longer rely on the Protocol to defend you against

occult powers. Mundanes are helpless before sorcery, no matter how exalted their rank."

"I should like an explanation, if you have one, before you tender advice."

"There have been rumors for some time that all was not well with the Protocol. Rumors of dragons? I understand that no one has heard from the wardens since the affair on Nefer Moor."

"Warlock Raspnex attended the Senate when it proffered the usual address of welcome," Shandie said. "His speech was brief. Curt, even."

"And devoid of content, as I recall the popular reports. The preflecting pool is excessively intriguing. It reminds me of a magic casement I once consulted—with disastrous results, I must say. May I ask how you learned of it?"

The imperor frowned, as if reluctant to answer the question. Then he shrugged. "An old woman appeared to me that evening, in a tavern. She knew who I was, and my companions did not detect her presence. Her cloak appeared to be dry, on an exceedingly rainy night."

Ylo glanced in astonishment at Lord Umpily, then at Acopulo, but obviously they were both as surprised as he.

The old scholar had stiffened, pale eyes bright, head tipped with avian alertness. "Describe her, Sire."

"I have never seen her like. She must have been of mixed race. What little I could see of her face under her hood was quite unfamiliar to me, and I have traveled the length and breadth of the Impire. Her eyes were large and slanted, like an elf's, but of a pale hue, not opalescent. Sort of yellow, I thought. Her skin was a brownish shade."

The big jotunn jaw dropped and then clicked shut. Sagorn paled. "A broadish nose, like a faun's?"

"Yes!"

"By the Powers!" the scholar muttered.

Evidently the old jotunn's reputation for wisdom was not without foundation. Ylo caught Acopulo's eye and saw both appreciation and annoyance there.

The imperor smiled faintly. "You will have to be more specific than that, Doctor."

"Some friends of mine once met a group of young men fitting that description, four of them. I was told that they looked like a cross between imps, fauns, and elves."

"And who were these people?" Shandie asked, his tone sharpening.

"They were pixies, Sire."

Acopulo stumbled against the table, knocking over two candles. Ylo went for them and caught one just before it rolled to the floor.

"No one has seen a pixie in a thousand years!" the political advisor bleated.

Sagorn did not look at him. "I just proved you a liar. But that was in Thume, where a pixie might be understood, if not expected. This was on Hub's doorstep. You comprehend, your Majesty, that the incident could have been an occult hoax? Any two-toed sorcerer could project visions on a body of water by moonlight."

"But the visions led us here, to you. And to Master Jalon. I understand he also resides at this address."

"And to Krasnegar," Sagorn murmured, nodding.

"And to Krasnegar. You remember the faun sorcerer who—"

"I am well acquainted with Master Rap, or King Rap as he is now. We traveled widely together. One of my more satisfactory pupils."

The audience exchanged pleased glances. Acopulo bared his teeth in a reluctant smile. Umpily rubbed plump hands together.

"Then we seem to be getting somewhere!" Shandie exclaimed. "It all comes together! All roads lead to Rap. He befriended me when he was here, in Hub. My grandfather considered him the most powerful sorcerer in the world."

"I believe that," the jotunn said wryly. "And probably the only honest one." He did not venture to explain.

"Then you believe that he will agree to help me once more?"

The sage pouted. "I can commit neither kings nor sorcerers, your Majesty, but I do communicate with the faun now and then. I am confident that an appeal from me would carry weight with him. I am sanguine that he would remember certain moral obligations he owes me and would respond favorably, under those circumstances."

"Countess Eigaze has offered to intercede also on our behalf. She is a distant relative of Queen Inosolan and will be joining us here shortly."

Sagorn pulled a face, but restrained his acerbic tongue.

"I propose to send my wife and child to some safe location," Shandie said, "and Lady Eigaze has agreed to escort them." He did not look at Eshiala, whose face was shadowed and unreadable.

Ylo wondered how she felt about the day's shattering turn of events. Exile from the formal life of the court would seem an escape to her, in a way Shandie would not comprehend.

The bells grew louder and voices spoke down by the front door.

"That is probably the proconsul now," Umpily said.

"The invitation would have to be carefully worded," Sagorn mused, still working on the problem. "As a ruling monarch, King Rap has overriding responsibilities toward his own realm, of course."

The door of the room flew open, and Hardgraa marched right in. Ylo stiffened at once, recognizing an untoward glint in that normally obscure countenance.

"But he also has a conscience," the old scholar muttered, not looking up, "unlike most sorcerers."

"His Honor, Proconsul Ionfeu!" Hardgraa proclaimed, "and Countess Eigaze. And his Majesty, King Rap of Krasnegar."

Sagorn sighed. "And he has always had a flair for dramatic entrances."

3

SHANDIE HAD SPRUNG TO HIS FEET, STARING AT THE BIG man who stepped forward. For a moment no one spoke.

Ylo had seen fauns often enough around stables, but never one this size. He was taller than anyone else present, except the jotunn, and the bulk of his heavy cloak made him seem clumsy. No one would ever call his face handsome. A pure-bred faun would have said it was too aggressive and a jotunn that it indicated far too much pure stubbornness. It impressed Ylo with the thought that its owner might be a very difficult opponent, were he on the wrong side. And he was a sorcerer—uncanny foreboding battled with relieved feeling that help had arrived.

"Rap!" the imperor whispered, still staring disbelievingly. "Really Rap?"

A small, wry smile twitched the corners of the faun's wide mouth, changing his appearance dramatically. "My, Shandie, but you've grown! I'll bet you can't wriggle through that transom into the Imperial Library anymore."

"Ah, Rap!" The imperor strode forward; monarch impacted monarch in a mutual embrace.

Lady Eigaze was beaming happily at her husband. Sagorn hauled himself stiffly to his feet. Shandie led the faun over to the chair to meet his wife and sleeping daughter.

Sorcerer? Ylo discovered that he had instinctively eased back against the cracked and peeling plaster of the wall. So had everyone else. The room was crowded now, with eleven people in it, for Hardgraa had remained to watch, but the onlookers were all giving the sorcerer a wide berth.

As he shook hands with Sagorn they eyed each other with what seemed to be mutual respect, but no obvious warmth. Then he moved on to the portly Umpily, waiting for Shandie to make the introductions.

The imperor frowned. "Your Majesty . . . Our Royal Cousin of Krasnegar . . ."

"Ugh! Why not just 'Rap'?"

Shandie nodded brusquely. "Why not? But now that you are here, we can move back to more . . . to the palace?"

The big man was shaking his head gravely. "This is an excellent place for a confidential meeting. The building is shielded against sorcery. It is one of the most private locales in the city, and I vouch for Doctor Sagorn's discretion. No, let us discuss the problem here before we go anywhere else."

Shandie was not accustomed to being overruled. Pique flickered over him like summer lightning, but even imperors did not argue with sorcerers. "Very well. However, we may not need quite so large an audience."

Ylo almost laughed as he watched Umpily's flabby face collapse in dismay. The snoopy chief of protocol would die of chagrin if he was banished from this epochal conference.

The king seemed to sense that, because his wry little smile twitched into view again. He thrust out a hand. "My name's Rap," he said, unnecessarily.

Bristling, Shandie made the introduction, then presented the others also. When Ylo's turn came, he found the experience unnerving. He had never shaken hands with a ruling monarch before, or a sorcerer, and he felt as if the big gray eyes were drilling into his thoughts. Again he decided that he would not want to have this man as an enemy. Then he remembered that sorcerers could read minds . . . couldn't they? He hoped no one was going to ask him about the preflecting pool.

Do not think about the preflecting pool!

The sorcerer shot him a curious glance before moving on to shake hands with Acopulo.

But the courtesies could not last forever, and when the faun had been all the way around the group, the time for business had clearly arrived. Without deferring to the imperor's superior status, he brashly directed Eigaze to the second armchair—the impress, still holding her sleeping child, had not risen. Then he said offhandedly, "You want to sit there, Shandie?" indicating the high-back seat by the table.

"Perhaps not," the imperor replied testily.

"Then Doctor Sagorn can rest his old bones on it." Leaning back against the fireplace, King Rap looked over the company with an expression of unbelievable innocence.

Shandie smiled grimly. "Please do sit, Doctor. I'll be fine here." He perched on the arm beside his wife. Everyone else found a patch of wall, again leaving the sorcerer isolated. The room was unpleasantly stuffy already, the smell of wet clothes now more noticeable than dust or mildew.

It was a very strange setting for an historic conference. Ylo wondered if he would be listed in the history books; if there were to be any more history books. He recalled that he'd had much the same thought on Nefer Moor, just before the dragons came.

"I bring no good tidings," the sorcerer said, suddenly grave. "The only cheerful news I can give you is that I detect no magic on any of you—no loyalty spells or occult glamors or any abominations like that. I can't be quite certain, because a better sorcerer could deceive me."

"You are modest, your Majesty," Sagorn said acidly.

King Rap looked down at him thoughtfully. "No, Doctor. I admit that I had great powers once, but not now. I'm not going to try to explain that at the moment. Perhaps never." He turned back to the imperor. "I shall do what little I can, Shandie, but magically it will be very small. If you are expecting me to solve things, then you will be disappointed."

"I see." The imperor's eyes glittered icily, but when Shandie deliberately tried to be inscrutable he could baffle even Ylo, who had studied him meticulously for the last two years.

The sorcerer shrugged. "I do not even know the name or nature of the enemy. Does anyone?"

No one seemed willing to speak. Finally Shandie said, "Sir Acopulo? You are our advisor in such matters."

The little man pouted. "The problem obviously resides with the wardens. Speculation upon insufficient data is invariably hazardous. As a working hypothesis ... suppose that a serious split developed among the Four, between North and West on one hand, and South and East on the other. The dwarf and the troll support your Majesty's accession. The elf and the imp oppose it, for reasons unknown." He cast a wary glance at Sagorn.

"Continue!" the imperor said, nodding.

"Two being sufficient for confirmation of your accession, Grunth and Raspnex preempted the others by calling on you to perform today's ..." Acopulo dried up, apparently discomfited by the jotunn, who had developed a sneer of fearsome proportions, deepening into bottomless chasms the clefts that always flanked his upper lip.

"And the thrones?" Shandie demanded.

"Lith'rian and Olybino's retaliation, Sire? Or a counterstroke that came too late? Had the four thrones been destroyed sooner, then the ceremony would have been impossible." He hesitated, then blurted, "It fits the facts!"

"It does. Doctor Sagorn?"

The jotunn shook his head pityingly. "It fits a judicious selection of the facts, Sire. As a student, Acopulo was always selective in his use of evidence, and I see he has not changed. The last news we had of the wardens, Lith'rian was hurling his dragons at Olybino's legions. They were at each other's throats! Now we are to regard them as allies?"

Ylo noticed that the sorcerer draped against the mantel was obviously amused. In happier circumstances he also would enjoy watching this battle of brains, this scholarly free-for-all, with its air of sharpened quills, gutters running with ink, massacred hypotheses.

Already Acopulo had lost much of his usual clerical calm. His face was crimson and his white hair stuck up almost as wildly as the faun's did. "That is your only objection?"

"It is the least of them. Granted that the Four often squabble, you have failed to explain why this disagreement is so much more virulent than all others in three thousand years—so dire that it required desecration of the Rotunda.

You did not explain the dwarf's prophecies and warnings. You did not explain why King Rap has come from Krasnegar. And you have most certainly failed to explain why, after a thousand years of extinction, a pixie should reappear now, and to his Majesty." Sagorn leered in satisfaction.

The faun spasmed upright. "Pixie?" He looked to Shandie.

The imperor began to explain about the woman who had told him of the preflecting pool and went on to describe the whole incident.

Evil take that pimping puddle! Ylo's dukedom had receded into the mists now. He should have grabbed it when he had the chance, instead of letting himself be seduced by erotic promises. Eshiala was intent upon her child, who stirred in her sleep. The glow of candlelight on the woman's face would drive a man to distraction. Gorgeous though she was, a few minutes' physical excitement on a lawn was hardly worth a dukedom. She was impress now, but perhaps only in name. Who could say what other changes would come before the daffodils?

Eigaze, in turn, was watching Eshiala. Had the old dear ever managed to stay silent for so long in her life before?

The others were listening to the imperor. Umpily must be in raptures at all the secrets unfolding. Acopulo was probably being driven frantic by his lack of clear understanding. Hardgraa must be fretting about the danger to Shandie. The elderly, stooped Count Ionfeu was . . . was watching Ylo. Ylo looked away quickly.

The story had ended. "So I think I saw your son," the imperor concluded. "I feel that I should apologize, somehow, but of course it was by no choice of mine."

"You did see Gath." The faun glowered. "And he saw you! It may even have been the same night, but it doesn't matter if it was or not. He had a brief vision of a soldier; we didn't realize it was you until about a month ago, or I might have come sooner. I fear I should have come a year ago, for I was warned then that the end of the millennium was brewing trouble."

"Warned by whom?" Sagorn demanded.

"A God," the faun said, with a sudden twinkle of amusement. "I'm not sure which God They were. One doesn't think to shoot questions when Gods appear. I thought that the end of the millennium was awhile off, but I seem to have interpreted the date too literally. A year or two either way . . . When did the War of the Five Warlocks begin?"

"Around 2000." Acopulo frowned, uncertain.

"The Festival of Healing, 2003, was when Ulien'quith fled the capital," Sagorn said snidely. "You are right, your Majesty. A year or two either way does not matter."

"But the millennium itself does!" the faun said. "The pixies disappeared in the War of the Five Warlocks. Now his Majesty has seen a pixie. That seems to fit, somehow, doesn't it? Every sorcerer from the wardens on down seems to have disappeared—I detect almost no occult power in use anywhere. I sense a terrible evil overhanging the world. Warlock Raspnex's warnings of chaos and the fall of the Protocol—those may fit, also, although I am far from ready to trust the dwarf. Any dwarf."

Sagorn and Acopulo frowned, glanced at each other, and then frowned even harder, in reluctant agreement.

"It was the dwarf who arranged his Majesty's formal accession," the jotunn growled.

Acopulo nodded. "Surely if we were to select the warden most likely to be trusted—"

"No!" Rap barked. "Raspnex is the *last* one we should trust. On my way here I could feel . . ." His voice trailed off into silence. He was staring fixedly at Ylo's feet.

The others waited, then began sharing puzzled, frightened glances. Ylo glanced down at his own sandals and could see nothing wrong. They matched. He looked back at the faun, and now his gaze was slowly tracking across the floor.

Had he gone mad? He was pale, tense . . .

Gods preserve us! He was seeing something *through* the floor!

Then he spoke, very softly. "Stand back from the doorway, Centurion. Don't go for your sword. It will do no good."

Hardgraa reached for his sword automatically, then reluctantly took his hand away again. He stepped a pace sideways.

"Cousin!" Shandie said, rising from the chair arm. "Rap? What's wrong?"

"We are about to have a visitor," the sorcerer said hoarsely. "I am not the only one who indulges in dramatic entrances, Sagorn."

There had been no sound from the stair.

The jotunn rose from his chair, tall and silver-haired and grim-faced. "Who?"

"Warlock Raspnex."

The door creaked open.

4

THE WARLOCK HALTED IN THE DOORWAY AND GLARED across the room at the imperor. Even at that distance, he had to tilt his oversize head to do so. He was about half as tall as Sagorn, but twice as wide; Hardgraa would have nothing on him in chest and shoulders. His hair and beard were grizzled. His face had the gray roughness of weathered rock, so that the wrinkles resembled cracks. He was gray and clothed in gray.

"You're a fool, imp!" he growled. Dwarves' voices always sounded like grindstones at work.

Shandie bowed impassively. "You honor us with your presence, your Omnipotence."

"You can forget that rot! No more omnipotences. It's over! No more wardens, no more warlocks, no more witches. Why in the name of Evil didn't you get out of town while you had the chance?" He stumped a few steps forward.

Ylo noticed that there was snow on his heavy boots. His tatty shirt looked wet. Why would a warlock, a preeminent sorcerer, go outdoors on a night like this? Why had he not at least stayed dry, as Lith'rian had stayed dry in the downpour on Nefer Moor?

"Flee, I told you!" the little man boomed. "But oh no! You had to come into this warren, on the one night in centuries when you would leave a trail through Hub that a blind toad could follow! Idiot!"

The imperor flushed darkly in the flickering candlelight.

Another dwarf followed the warlock in, closing the door with a ferocity just short of a slam. He was younger and beardless, although there was a shadow like lichen on his upper lip. His face had a juvenile softness to it—shale instead of slate—but the bovine shoulders were there already and the surly scowl. He wore his hair long, in a style currently favored by the youth of Hub, but its curls were an incongruous silvery-gray. His pants had been repeatedly patched.

Shandie glanced quickly around the company, but found no inspiration. "Tell us why you came, Sorcerer?"

"I'll be buried if I know! Well, I suppose I came to appeal to him." Raspnex pointed to Rap. "But I see now that I wasted my time. I'd hoped he could help, but he can't."

Rap shook his head slightly, making no move to greet the dwarf as he had earlier greeted everyone else. "Who's your companion?" he said.

The warlock did not turn to look at the youth behind him. "Grimrix. He's a votary. Don't laugh at his hairstyle or he may turn you into a woolly caterpillar."

The youngster scowled. A pink-granite glow warmed the sandstone gray of his cheeks. Ylo wondered if dwarves ever smiled.

"Well, imp, you didn't listen to me!" The older dwarf shook his head sadly. "Who outside this room knows where you are?"

"No one except Legate Ugoatho."

"Who's he?"

"Head of the Praetorian Guard."

Raspnex snorted. "They'll have gotten him already, then. One of the first they'd go for. In fact, it's amazing they're not here yet."

"The legate is utterly loyal!" Shandie snapped.

Teeth like quartz pebbles . . . "Not anymore."

"Tell them the problem," Rap said sadly.

"You tell them. I already tried. Seems they don't heed me."

Minutes ago King Rap had denied that he knew what the problem was. Now he just shrugged and looked to Shandie. "I'll have to be quick, though. The problem is Zinixo. I'm sure you remember him."

"Former warlock of the West."

"Right. He tried to destroy me and I won . . ." The faun sighed and glanced at the two dwarf sorcerers. "A year ago the God told me that this mess was all my fault. That must be because I didn't kill Zinixo when I had the chance and the excuse."

"You did worse than that," Raspnex said grimly. "Much worse. But carry on. Can you explain to these dumb mundanes what you did to my nephew?"

Rap scratched his head. "I can try. I wrapped him up in an unbreakable soap bubble that stopped magic. He still had his power then, but he couldn't use it. Er, follow?"

"Like tar on a ship?" Sagorn asked. "Magic-proofing instead of waterproofing?"

Raspnex made a noise reminiscent of a chimney pot falling off a roof; it might have been intended as a chuckle. "You've got it! It was ingenious! Rap's power was greater, so Zinixo couldn't break the spell. No magic in or out. A fitting punishment!"

"So what happened?" the imperor demanded.

"Oh, he went totally insane. He'd always been unstable, even as a kid. He'd always been suspicious and timid. The greater his power grew, the more timorous he became. You believe that, imp?"

Shandie nodded grimly. "I've met people like that. They think the world is out to get them."

All dwarves had the reputation of being cagey, untrusting people. Ylo wondered how bad this Zinixo had become before other dwarves began to notice. Raspnex was Zinixo's uncle, of course; he must have known him for a long time.

"So he can't use his magic," the imperor said, frowning. "Why is he dangerous?"

"Because of Bright Water," Rap said. "She couldn't break my spell, either, but she must have taken pity on him. She gave him a sorcerer."

"*Gave* him?"

Raspnex snorted and snapped his fingers. Young Grimrix stepped forward to stand beside him, scowling as any normal adolescent would at such a summons. "Sir?"

"Tell them how you feel about me, sonny."

The boy looked down at his boots and this time his blush was obvious. "I love you," he muttered.

"There! See? He's a votary. I've laid a loyalty spell on him. He'll do anything to help me." Raspnex glanced at the kid, showing his pebble teeth again. "He'd die for me! Actually his power's greater than mine. It took three of us to hobble him—me and two of my other votaries. Now do you understand?"

Ylo shivered, looking around the circle of shadowed faces, watching the distaste spread as they worked it out. Only Eshiala, with her stoic self-control, was managing to seem unmoved.

The warlock slapped his young companion on the shoulder in a friendly gesture that would have shattered flagstones. "Go and scout. See if anything's happening outside."

The boy nodded—and faded out of existence. Lady Eigaze gasped and put a hand over her mouth. A moment later the bells rang louder briefly as the front door opened.

Why, Ylo thought, why, why, why had he ever turned down that dukedom and gotten himself involved in this?

"Bright Water was mad as a shampooed cat," Rap said sadly. "She gave Zinixo one of her votaries—Kraza, a female dwarf. Kraza wasn't especially powerful, but Zinixo knew the names of a lot of sorcerers. He set Kraza to imprinting them, starting with the weakest, of course. But two or three weak sorcerers can overpower a stronger."

"He's been at it for almost twenty years," Raspnex added in his abrasive rumble. "He's got an army of them now, all loyal to the death. We call it the Covin."

Shandie sat down again on the arm of his wife's chair. His face was taut. "Why did nobody stop him?"

"Because nobody knew!" the dwarf snarled. "Except maybe Bright Water, and she was too crazy to care. I think he was extra careful with her brood, anyway—he made his compulsion secondary to hers, to take effect after she died. So she didn't mind. *Now he's cornered all of the sorcery in Pandemia!*"

The crowded room fell silent as the mundanes struggled to comprehend the disaster. Old Sagorn moaned and sat down on his chair again, shaking his head.

"So although he has no real sorcery of his own," Shandie muttered, "he controls an army of sorcerers? How many?"

"Scores, maybe hundreds. All eager to help. And the little snit may have his own sorcery back too now, if the Covin's been able to break Rap's spell."

"Surely it was the wardens' duty to prevent such an abomination?"

"It was, but they didn't know it was happening until Bright Water died." Raspnex's eyes were hard as agates. "They brought me in as the new North in the hope I could stop him, because I knew him and how he thinks. But it was too late."

The imperor looked to Sir Acopulo, as if inviting him to comment. Nothing happened.

"What does he want?" Shandie asked.

The dwarf snorted. "Everything! I told you—the greater his power, the more fearful he is! He knew he'd become a threat to the Four, so he feared the Four, because they were the only power that could threaten him. That's how he thinks."

"That was why you came to the Rotunda today?"

"Of course it was! Why are you so stupid? We expected him to strike when we answered your summons at the enthronement, so he could swat all four of us at the same time. Probably he'd have blasted us as he blasted Ag-an, years ago. Grunth and I got the jump on him. We made you imperor, sonny, but it isn't going to do you any good."

Shandie's eyes narrowed suspiciously. "And why destroy the thrones? Did Zinixo do that?"

"No! I did!"

"The four thrones were occult," Rap said quietly. "They were portals into the wardens' palaces. He could have forced entry through them."

"I thought you didn't know all this?" the imperor said.

"I didn't, earlier," Rap explained from his place by the mantel. "Partly I'm working it out as I go along, from what Raspnex told me as he came in—you weren't privy to that conversation, is all. He hasn't used sorcery on me yet, although he could. And you'll have to take our word on that. You can't trust anyone now, your Majesty. Once Zinixo's votaries pin a man down, he's theirs. As Raspnex says, Legate Ugoatho would be a logical first choice. He'll serve Zinixo from then on, to the death. They all will."

"To what purpose?" Shandie demanded grimly.

Rap shrugged. "He's mad, he sees danger everywhere. The imperor is powerful, so he must be loyal to Zinixo—everyone must, who has any sort of power at all. He'd make everyone in the world love him, if he could."

"Where are the Four?"

Rap looked to Raspnex.

"Gone," the dwarf said. "Most of their votaries have been stolen from them. Lith'rian panicked first and fled to Ilrane.

Olybino was next. He's just vanished. Can you imagine what Zinixo will do to those two when he gets his hands on them? No, you can't possibly imagine. Even I can't. But it will be long and nasty—that I do know." He pulled a face. "And I'm not on his friendship list, either."

"And Grunth?"

The dwarf shrugged.

Ylo could feel worms of fear crawling around his insides. Umpily was chewing his knuckles, eyes white in the shadows. Eshiala had taken a firmer hold on her child.

The old jotunn was probably the smartest man in the room, and he was the most obviously scared, his face pallid and drawn, his hands clenched on his knees.

"So Zinixo will imprint *me* with a loyalty spell?" Shandie asked.

"Of course. It will be easier than proclaiming himself imperor. The Impire is just too big for him to ensorcel everyone, and a dwarf imperor would not be acceptable—he would always be frightened of revolution, see? But you will reign for his benefit. You will serve him loyally to the end of your days." Raspnex pointed a thick finger at the child asleep on Eshiala's lap. "And so will she and her children after her! You know how long sorcerers live."

"No!" Shandie bellowed. "I won't have it!"

Dwarves did smile, Ylo saw. It was not a pleasant sight.

"And your so-beautiful wife? My nephew is oddly partial to female imps . . . Now don't you wish you'd taken my advice?"

Shandie laid his arm on Eshiala's shoulders, as if that gesture might reassure her. "What is your advice now?"

Again the dwarf shrugged his massive shoulders. "I may be able to get us out of here. *May*, I said. He's so suspicious that he tends to be too cautious. He may not commit his real strength quickly enough to block me."

"If I can escape . . ." Shandie said. "If we can . . . If you can get us out of here, what then?"

"Retire. Hide. You can't hope to win your impire back,

you know. Just go into hiding and maybe, in a couple of centuries, your descendants can come forward to claim their inheritance."

Then the dwarf turned to look up thoughtfully at the king of Krasnegar. Ylo wondered what silent messages they were passing, words mundanes could not hear. He wondered also if the faun was truly his own man anymore, or if the warlock had imprinted him already. Trust no one!

"Zinixo's here, in Hub?" the king asked aloud.

"Maybe. More likely not, not yet. But he's sent his minions. I could smell 'em."

"So could I. And I'm not exactly his best friend, either, am I?"

Raspnex guffawed. Ylo had never heard a dwarf laugh before—and he never wanted to hear that noise again. It sounded like a wall collapsing.

"Not much, you're not! You and your kingdom. Your wife and children. I bet the little turd has dreamed of you every night for twenty years, *your Majesty!*"

Grim-faced, the faun thumped the mantel a couple of times with his fist. "Why did none of you warn me?" he shouted.

"Because we thought you knew! Because we thought you were laying low—and because we thought you could handle the matter when you got around to it!"

The big man paled in shock. "You mean you were all relying on me? Waiting on me to do something? Fools!"

"That's obvious now, but we didn't know that, did we?" the dwarf snarled.

"I'm surprised he hasn't come after me already."

"He didn't know, either! But it won't be long now. And he couldn't try to settle with you earlier without alerting the wardens. Once they're out of the way . . . you're next, I'm sure."

"Suppose he does seize the throne," Sagorn whispered hoarsely, "the Imperial throne, I mean, not Krasnegar— either in his own name or through a puppet—then what?"

Raspnex looked at him with scorn. "He will wipe out any threat, any threat at all. Any hint of disloyalty, any loose talk."

"But it will be his Impire then, won't it? So any threat to the Impire will be a threat to the Living God? The caliph, for example."

The dwarf nodded, with a trace more respect. "Exactly. The caliph is a threat to the Impire, so the caliph will have to go. The goblins are about ready to launch their big attack—Zinixo will smash them. Of course he'll go after Lith'rian and the elves first."

Sagorn snapped his teeth shut with a click. "He will rule the world," he muttered.

"In a year or two, yes."

Ylo shivered. Like all imps, he had always dreamed of a universal Impire, of bringing everybody into the fold and extending to all races the benefits of imperial rule. He knew that the other races had never appreciated those benefits properly. But his mind rejected the idea violently if it was to be all for the benefit of a mad dwarf.

"Is there nothing we can do to prevent this obscenity?" said a quiet voice. Everyone looked around in surprise at Count Ionfeu, who had barely spoken since he arrived. He was elderly and frail and his head stuck forward like a turtle's, but there was a grim determination showing on that wrinkled face.

For a moment no one answered. Then the king of Krasnegar said, "There might be. It's an Evilish long shot, but we could try, if Zinixo hasn't beaten us to it."

Raspnex looked startled. "You'll get yourself eaten if you try that!"

"I'd rather have my flesh eaten than my mind, I think." The faun sighed. "And it *was* all my fault." Now Ylo was certain the two sorcerers had exchanged more words than had been spoken aloud.

"Yes it was," Raspnex said.

The impress spoke next, softly. "Why was it? What did you do, your Majesty?"

"I cut off the supply of magic. I can't tell you all the details now, but I went back to Faerie ..." He winced. "Never mind. I did it and it's done."

"And you can't undo it now, can you?" the dwarf shouted. "Your stupid, blundering good intentions! Where *did* you put the fairies?"

Rap shook his head, his face twisted as if in pain. "I can't even tell you. And no, I can't ever undo it. I used every scrap of power I possessed. It's done now. Forever. Unless the Gods take pity on us."

He turned his back and put his hands on the mantel, staring at the wall. Wife and children and kingdom ... King Rap probably had more to fear from the vengeful Zinixo than anyone, even Shandie.

"I don't understand!" Acopulo bleated.

"He cut off the supply of magic!" Raspnex growled. "The Protocol was set up to prevent exactly this sort of happening! The supply of magic was the prerogative of the warlock of the west. If any one sorcerer ever tried to build a sorcerous army and make himself paramount, West could create an opposing army! As a last resort. That's why it's never been done before, although Ulien' came close in the War of the Five Warlocks."

Sagorn made a choking noise. "A safety net!"

"And your faunish friend cut it down!"

King Rap spun around again, eyes suddenly bright. "Ulien', you said? War of the Five Warlocks? Thume! There's another hope, then!"

Raspnex flinched. "You're crazy!"

"Maybe! But craziness is all we've got left, isn't it!"

The door downstairs opened briefly to admit a sorrowful cry of bells. An instant later a column of air in the center of the room shimmered and solidified into the young dwarf Grimrix. His pebbly eyes gleamed with excitement.

"They're here, sir! Hussars, all around the house. All three streets."

"Any occults?"

"Didn't stay around to look, but if you'll let me go down there again and thump ass, I can find out!" He bared a mouthful of shiny quartz in eagerness.

The half-size stripling was offering to take on a platoon of the finest troops in the impire single-handed. The room fell silent.

Ylo was almost surprised to hear his own voice. "Can't we leave the same way as Master Jalon did?"

The old jotunn snorted. "Quite impossible!"

"You seem very certain of that," Hardgraa said dangerously.

The faun king chuckled. "He's right, though!" What did he know about that incident? "And we'd leave tracks in this snow, wouldn't we? Raspnex, got any ideas?"

"I can try. I'll try to move us all to my palace."

"But the house is shielded."

The warlock scratched his chin noisily. "It won't be in a minute. Grimmy, can you lift this shield by yourself?"

The younger dwarf hesitated, frowning. Then he smiled again. "Easy, sir."

"Don't be too sure—some of these old spells have been renewed a lot of times. Watch out for underlying layers. When I push, lift it. Then slam it back fast! You've got to stay and cover for us."

The kid went suddenly pale, like marble. The joy of battle evaporated. "But if they catch me—"

"Then you'll be just as happy serving him as you are serving me," Raspnex said. "Hold them off as long as you can. Don't try to follow me, understand?"

"Not even—"

"Not at all! You arguing?"

"Of course not!"

"Good . . . Listen!"

Ylo thought he could feel something through his sandals

more than hear it with his ears ... some distance away.
Thumping.

"Axes!" King Rap said. "They're trying the courtyard
door. That one's a poor choice. It's got some occult tricks
to it."

"Nevertheless, the time to go has arrived," the dwarf
growled. "Get up, woman!"

Shandie glared at him, then bent and lifted his daughter.
Eshiala rose to her feet. Eigaze and Sagorn stood also.

In horrified fascination, Ylo watched the youngster,
Grimrix. He was staring at his master with a desolate, heart-
broken expression. Tears trickled down his cheeks. He sniffled from time to time, wiping his nose with the back of his
hand, and yet his obvious determination to follow orders no
matter how much he hated them was a chilling demonstration of sorcerous compulsion.

"This may be rough," the warlock said. "But I've got
some friends standing by to shield us as soon as we arrive—
I hope. If the enemy got there first, then ... well, it's worth
a try."

"Wait!" Shandie said. "What happens after?"

"I told you. You go into hiding and stay there."

"No!" Holding his child in his arms, the imperor yet
seemed to draw himself up in defiance. "Maybe my realm
has been stolen from me, but I will not have my mind stolen
also! I will not give up. I will fight!"

More thumping, closer this time—Ylo decided that the
front door was under attack, too, now. What nonsense was
this about fighting sorcery?

Then Shandie repeated it. "I will never rest until I have
won back my impire!"

"Indeed?" the dwarf sneered. "You and what army?"

The imperor surveyed the room. "These good friends will
do for a start. Maybe there aren't very many of them, just a
handful, but they're loyal and they're good. Are you with me?"

"Gods save the imperor!" Ylo said automatically, as no
other answer came to mind at the moment.

"Gods save the imperor!" the others echoed, some louder than others.

Shandie looked at Rap. "And you?"

The faun smiled grimly. "I have no choice. Zinixo won't rest, either—not until he has my guts in a pot and Krasnegar is gravel. Down with the tyrant!"

"Well said! Victory or death!" Shandie bellowed.

"No!" Astonishingly, the shout came from Eshiala. She lunged at her husband, as if to snatch their daughter away. "You must not!"

"My dear!"

The impress was almost screaming. "You must not risk our baby!" She tried to take the child from Shandie, and Maya awoke with a cry of bewilderment.

"Eshiala! Be silent!"

"She is more important than your precious throne!"

They were both yelling at once and the little princess howled between them.

"Gods of Fools!" the dwarf muttered.

Crash! The house rocked. The bells were suddenly louder.

"Move us, Warlock!" Rap said. "Now!"

Strait the gate:
> *It matters not how strait the gate,*
> *How charged with punishment the scroll;*
> *I am the master of my fate:*
> *I am the captain of my soul.*

— HENLEY, *INVICTUS*